The Ghost of the Mary Celeste

Valerie Martin is one of America's finest contemporary novelists, best known for her Orange Prize-winning *Property* and also the award-winning *Mary Reilly*, filmed by Stephen Frears. She is the daughter of a sea captain but has never been to sea. www.valeriemartinonline.com

Also by Valerie Martin

NOVELS

The Confessions of Edward Day

Trespass

Property

Italian Fever

The Great Divorce

Mary Reilly

A Recent Martyr

Alexandra

Set in Motion

SHORT FICTION

The Unfinished Novel and Other Stories

The Consolation of Nature and Other Stories

Love: Short Stories

NON-FICTION

Salvation: Scenes from the Life of St. Francis

THE GHOST OF THE MARY CELESTE

VALERIE MARTIN

Weidenfeld & Nicolson
LONDON

PP

First published in Great Britain in 2014 by Weidenfeld & Nicolson
An imprint of the Orion Publishing Group Ltd
Orion House, 5 Upper St Martin's Lane
London WC2H 9EA

An Hachette UK Company

978 0 297 87032 6 (cased)
978 0 297 87033 3 (trade paperback)

A CIP catalogue record for this book is
available from the British Library.

Printed by Clays Ltd, St Ives plc

The Orion Publishing Group's policy is to use papers that are natural,
renewable and recyclable products and made from wood grown in
sustainable forests. The logging and manufacturing processes are expected
to conform to the environmental regulations of the country of origin.

www.orionbooks.co.uk

For Adrienne Martin,
who knows how we hope

Why does the sea moan evermore?
Shut out from heaven it makes its moan.
It frets against the boundary shore;
All earth's full rivers cannot fill
The sea, that drinking thirsteth still.

CHRISTINA ROSSETTI

The unknown and the marvelous press upon us from all sides.
They loom above us and around us in undefined and fluctuating
shapes, some dark, some shimmering, but all warning us of the
limitations of what we call matter, and of the need for spirituality
if we are to keep in touch with the true inner facts of life.

ARTHUR CONAN DOYLE

A Disaster at Sea

The Brig Early Dawn
Off the Coast of Cape Fear, 1859

The captain and his wife were asleep in each other's arms. She, new to the watery world, slept lightly; her husband, seasoned and driven to exhaustion the last two days and nights by the perils of a gale that shipped sea after sea over the bow of his heavily loaded vessel, had plunged into a slumber as profound as the now tranquil ocean beneath him. As his wife turned in her sleep, wrapping her arm loosely about his waist and resting her cheek against the warm flesh of his shoulder, in some half-conscious chamber of her dreaming brain she heard the ship's clock strike six bells. The cook would be stirring, the night watch rubbing their eyes and turning their noses toward the forecastle, testing the air for the first scent of their morning coffee.

For four days the captain's wife had hardly seen the sky, not since the chilly morning when their ship, the *Early Dawn*, set sail from Nantasket Roads. Wrapped in her woolen cloak, she had stood on the deck peering up at the men clambering in the rigging, confident as boys at play, though a few among them were not young.

The towboat turned the prow into the wind and the mate called out, "Stand by for a starboard tack." A sailor released the towline, and as the tug pulled away, the ship creaked, heeling over lightly, and the captain's wife steadied herself by bending her knees. Then, with a thrill she had not anticipated, she watched as one by one the enormous sails unfurled, high up, fore and aft. A shout went up among the men, so cheerful it made her smile, and for a moment she almost felt a part of the uproarious bustle. We are under way, she thought—that was what they called setting out. A line from a poem she loved crossed her thoughts, "And I the while, the sole, unbusy thing." Her smile faded. She had left her little son, Natie, with her mother and now she felt, like a blow, his absence. How had she been persuaded to leave him behind?

In the year since their son's birth, the captain's wife had not passed two consecutive months in her husband's company and she was sick of missing him, of writing letters that might never find him, of following his progress on a map. Her mother had urged her to go. Her father, another captain, retired now, home for the dura-tion, avowed that he would have his grandson riding the pony by the time she returned. Her mother offered reassuring stories of her own first trip as the captain's wife, long years ago, and of the won-ders she had seen on the voyage to Callao and the Chincha Islands. "There's nothing like the open deck on a warm, calm night at sea," she said. "The vastness of the heavens, the sense of being truly in God's hands." And her father chimed in with the time-honored chestnut, "There are no atheists at sea."

The captain's wife lowered her hood and turned to gaze at her husband, who stood nearby, his legs apart, his face lifted, his eyes roving the stretched canvas, which talked to him about the wind. He was a young man, but he had been at sea since he was scarcely more than a boy and had about him an older man's gravity. His dark eyes, accustomed to taking in much at a glance, were piercing. He was lean, strong, and steady. His frown could stop a conversation; his laughter lifted the spirits of all who heard him. After his first visit to the rambling house they called Rose Cottage, her father had announced, "Joseph Gibbs is as solid a seaman as I know. He keeps his wits about him."

And now he kept his wife about him. She studied the sailors, absorbed in their labors, each one different from the others, one skittish, one bullying, another diffident, a shirker, a bawler, a rapscallion, and a fool, yet each at his task harkened to the voice of the Master. Doubtless her mother was right—they were all of them in God's hands, but should the Almighty turn away for a moment, every soul on this ship would shift his faith to the person of Captain Joseph Gibbs.

"I'm going below," she said to him, and his eyes lowered and settled upon her. He smiled, nodded, turned to speak to the mate who was striding briskly toward them. Clutching the ladder rails, she backed down into the companionway, where she paused a moment, patting down her hair, before entering the cabin. There was, of course, no one there. For an hour she busied herself with sewing, for another in reading a volume of poems. The ship moved around her, above, beneath, rising and settling, picking up speed. A sensation of nausea, no more than a twinge at first, gradually announced its claim on her attention. She stood up, dropping the book on the couch, anxiously looking about the neat little room. She spied a pot hanging from a hook near the table. As she staggered to it, her stomach turned menacingly, and no sooner had she taken up the vessel than she emptied her breakfast into it. "Oh Lord," she said, pulling out her handkerchief to wipe the perspiration from her brow. She carried the pot through to the cabin and poured the noxious contents into the bucket, then closed the lid and sat down upon it. The sailors, when so afflicted, had the option of vomiting over the side, but it wouldn't do for the captain's wife, who wasn't allowed anywhere near the main deck on her own. She pressed the handkerchief to her lips. Another eruption threatened. Best not stray far from this place, she counseled herself. She wondered how long it would last.

It lasted three days, but during that time her stomach was the least of her problems. When at last the captain descended to find his wife flat on her back in the bunk, fully clothed, with a wet cloth draped across her forehead, it was to tell her that he didn't like the look of the western sky. For another hour she slept fitfully and woke to hear the officers talking in the wardroom. Her husband came in to ask if she wouldn't have a cup of tea, which she declined. The ship was pitching bow to stern and he held on to the bedframe as he bent over to press his cool hand against her cheek. "My poor darling," he said. "You're pea-green. What a way to begin your maiden voyage." At the word "maiden," she smiled; it was a joke between them.

"Don't worry about me," she said.

There was a shout from the deck, a clatter of boots in the companionway. The captain made for the door. "Here it comes," he announced as he went out.

It was a squall out of the northwest, which shifted to the southwest and blew a hard gale for eighteen hours. A jib and a topgallant were carried away, as well as a rooster, last seen wings outspread riding backward on a blast of spray. Gradually the wind abated, though the sea was still high, kneading the ship like bread dough between the waves.

The captain's wife didn't witness the storm. When it seemed the bunk was determined to dump her on the carpet, she turned on her side, gripping the frame. All she could hear was the wind howling, the timbers creaking, and the men shouting. At last it grew calmer; she lifted her head and glanced about the cabin. Her small collection of books had been scattered widely, as if an impatient reader, pacing the carpet in search of some vital information, had thrown down volume after volume. There was a knock at the door and to her query "Who is it?" the nasal voice of the steward Ah-Sam replied, "Mrs. Gibbs. I have tea for you."

She scrambled from the bed, relieved to find, as she sat on the chest next to her empty bookshelf, that her stomach, though decidedly tender, was calm. "Come in," she said.

Cautiously, his head bowed and his legs wide apart to keep himself steady, Ah-Sam came in holding a mug between his hands. "This beef tea," he said. "Good for stomach." She reached out, taking the cup, but before she had time to speak, the man had backed out the door. "Thank you," she said, as the latch clicked behind him. The broth was dark, clear, fragrant, revitalizing. She sipped it, swaying lightly as the ship swayed, and planned her next appearance above deck.

But by the time she had washed and changed her clothes, the wind had turned to the east, the heavens crackled with lightning, the rain came on in torrents, and darkness closed over the ship like an ebony lid. The captain, his face gray with exhaustion and care, descended to invite his wife to the wardroom, where he and his first officer sat down to a hurried meal. Ah-Sam rushed in with the coffeepot and a slab of hard cheese wrapped in a cloth, and then disappeared in his self-effacing fashion. The captain's wife poured out the coffee, declining the mate's offering of tinned meat and soft tack. "Ah-Sam brought me some lovely broth," she told her husband. "Did you tell him to do that?"

"I just told him you were green," he said. "He knows everything there is to know about seasickness."

"Well, he must, for he has cured me," she agreed.

When the men were gone, the captain's wife sat at the table for some time, listening to the fury of the storm and comparing the sensation of being in a ship to that of lying in her bed at home on a tempestuous night. No wonder the sailors were sometimes so contemptuous of landsmen. As the night wore on, she persuaded herself that it was only a matter of time before the storm must abate and she might as well go to bed, as it was impossible to hold a needle, or a pencil, or even a book. She undressed and crawled back into the bunk. After what seemed a long time, but was barely an hour, she slipped into a dreamless sleep.

When she awoke, the room was dark and to her surprise her husband lay by her side, one arm draped across her waist, sleeping soundly. She moved close to him and kissed his cheek. His hand strayed to her thigh, grasped the flesh just above her knee, and pulled her leg over his hip. He whispered her name, nuzzling his mouth against her breasts. The noise of the ship was hushed; the violent pitching and rolling had resolved to a soporific churning that made her think of a child, her child, rocking in his cradle. He was too big for that now. She wandered into sleep again.

Her husband turned over and she did too, so that she faced his back. Now, distantly she heard the clock strike six bells. She opened her eyes to find the room bathed in a shimmering aqueous light. The storm had passed.

She was wide awake, brimming with vitality, but she didn't move, unwilling to disturb her husband, who had slept so little and had only an hour before he must take up his duties again. She pressed her lips against his back; her drifting thoughts settled on breakfast. Brown bread, plum jam—she'd brought seven jars on board herself—and butter. Oat porridge, hot coffee with heavy cream. I'm starving, she thought, amused by that. How good to be safe, warm, hungry, alive. Her husband groaned in his sleep and a shudder ran down his spine. "Are you awake?" he asked softly.

"I am," she said. "You've got another hour. Go back to sleep." She eased her leg from his hip as he turned heavily to face her.

"No," he said. "I'll get up."

They were washed and dressed when the steward arrived with the coffeepot, the porridge, and the bread. The captain went on deck to look at his ship, his crew, the sky, and the sea. When he returned she had the table laid with bread, the leftover cheese, her homemade jam and butter, the pot of coffee, the cream, and the squat ewer of porridge wrapped in a towel. "Is all well?" she asked as she poured his coffee, resting her fingers on his neck before turning to her own cup.

"For the present," he said. "It's squally to the southeast and we're headed for it."

"Can't we stop?" she asked.

He smiled at his wife's naïveté, then, sensing that she spoke in jest, turned and swatted her skirt with the back of his hand. "No, miss. We can't stop. It's not a horse you're riding."

"I want to get out of this cabin," she said. "I'm dying for fresh air."

The captain went up first, while his wife put on her cloak and laced her boots. She passed through the wardroom to the hatch, humming to herself, curious to see how the ship would look now, how the sea would look, as they skimmed across it. As she stepped onto the deck, a blast of frigid air blocked her so forcefully she stumbled back, clinging to the ladder rail. Her husband strode toward the mainmast, in conversation with the mate, who gesticulated at something going on in the bow. A wet, white mist, mingling in the sails, obscured her view. She pulled her hood in close, took a few steps from the hatch, and there it was, the sight she had long imagined—at once she lamented the paucity of her imagination—the sea. Slate-blue peaks studded with white foamy caps, line after line, each wave preceded by another and every one followed by another, as wide as the world was wide, and above it the sky, which was white, flat, and cold, the sun a brighter patch hovering in the distance. There was no visible horizon. She turned to face the bow and there she saw a different sky, the one that worried her husband, a rolling gray above and black below with a band of sickish yellow in between. She couldn't tell how far off it was, but sky and sea appeared all one, moving rapidly, like a wall of lead, toward the ship.

She breathed in the chilly, salt-laden air, gazing up at the sailors who were occupied in shortening sail. When she looked back at the deck, her eyes were drawn to a man crouched behind the main hatch, his hands resting on his thighs, his face turned up to her, his eyes narrowed, as if trying to draw a bead on a target. His beard and hair were all black and wild, as were his eyes. In a sudden grimace, he bared a line of fierce white teeth. The captain's wife stepped back, unnerved, conscious of her accelerating heart rate and a cautionary weakness in her knees. She looked aft, where the helmsman gripped the wheel, his attention fixed on the binnacle. The mist obscured his face. The sea was scarcely visible but made its disposition known; as the hull shifted, the starboard side dropped down and a mass of water rose up, clubbing the side. A tremor of anxiety scuttled up her neck and she felt her upper teeth pressing into her lower lip. There was a new sound, a chugging, pulsing sound, rhythmical and increasing in volume, but she couldn't tell which direction it came from. Was it belowdecks, or in the dark water below that?

She returned to the aft ladder, pausing to look toward the bow in hopes of seeing her husband. Another sea shipped over the deck, washing so forcefully across the planks that no sooner had she turned to see it than she was standing ankle deep in seawater. The helmsman, knocked off his feet, scrambled back to his post without comment.

What was that sound? Surely it was coming from the sea. Or was it the sky?

A man high in the rigging shouted. A sailor on deck was sprinting, as best he could, toward the mate, who was bent over near the mainmast. Another shout went up in the rigging. "Sail-ho," she heard. "Look to your stern."

The mate leaped away from the man who was screaming, and as he too attempted to run along the tilting deck, he called out, "Hard down your wheel." Again she turned to see the helmsman, who whirled the wheel with all his strength. Following his astounded eyes she saw what he saw, and as she gasped at the sight, she heard the helmsman's strangled cry, "She's on top of us."

First it was the bowsprit, parting the mist, carried high on the running sea and aimed directly at the port quarter, and then, far above, the enormous reefed yards that seemed to reach out like arms to gather in everything in their path. Screams from the men rent the air, and the thrumming rose to a fever pitch. The great bow, now visible, dived into the waves between, and the yards came about, angling toward the brig's stern. The captain's wife, frozen on the deck, had a moment in which hope and fear collided and her overtaxed brain, solving at last the mystery of the rhythmical droning, tossed out the useless information that the oncoming vessel was a ship-rigged steamer. Up came the bowsprit again, well above the main deck, the bow rising nearly vertical behind it, so it appeared the steamer intended to leap over this unexpected obstacle, another ship. Then it paused, and for an excruciating moment in which no one spoke and all were suspended in a soundless void, it was as if the universe itself drew in and held a startled breath. In the next, as the sea gathering beneath the steamer's hull reached its peak and commenced its inevitable decline, the bow came surging forward and down, folding the *Early Dawn's* bulwarks like pasteboard, shattering the wardroom skylight, and with a deafening roar, still driving mercilessly forward, rammed the bowsprit up to the stem against the mainmast of the helpless brig.

The captain's wife saw none of this. With the first breach of the bulwarks she was knocked off her feet and hurled facedown onto the deck, where, like a pin before a ball in a ten-pin alley, she was summarily rolled into the scuppers. She landed on her back with her left leg twisted beneath her. Above all the noise, the shouts of the officers, the shriek of steel rending wood, the roar of the steamer's engine, she heard the pop of her ankle as the tendons gave and the small bone cracked. She lifted herself on one elbow but fell back, covering her eyes with her hands, for she saw that the mainmast was tilted and sailors were sliding off the yards into the sea like turkeys in a morning mist. Why did she think of turkeys? She had seen them once, just at dawn, raining from the maple trees on the lawn outside her bedroom window, awkward and calamitous, complaining in their harsh, croaking voices.

The captain, believing his wife to be still in the cabin, made his way to the stern, shouting orders as he went. He clambered across the wreckage of crates, casks, shards of broken glass, lumber, rope. Above him he could hear the panicked sailors on the steamer deck, but he couldn't see them. He pushed his way past what he recognized as a section of the deckhouse and his heart misgave him, but then he spotted something blue flapping in the scuppers. It was his wife's woolen cloak. He called her name and she cried out for his aid. In a moment he was kneeling beside her, pulling her into his arms, pressing her cheek to his breast. "My ankle is broken," she said. "I don't think I can stand on it." The captain rose, drawing her with him. "Lean on me," he said. "We've got to get you in one of the boats."

From the forecastle, men swarmed onto the deck, rushing this way and that in response to orders from the officers. Not many minutes had passed since the call of "Sail-ho," but time stretched now with an arbitrary elasticity—there seemed to be a great deal of it—and it was with a sense of agonized relief that every ear greeted the cessation of the steamer engine's monotonous drone. Again an eerie silence came upon the sea. The steamer had gouged the *Early Dawn's* hull down to the waterline and she was taking on water above and below. As the sea rose and fell, both ships were pushed and pulled deeper and deeper in a fatal embrace from which there was no escape.

Just that moment of silence, harshly punctuated by the mate shouting the order to abandon the ship, and then the men were scurrying, hauling water kegs and sacks of pilot bread to the ship's boats, making harried trips back to the forecastle to grab a pipe, a loved one's picture, a good luck charm. The first boat released from the cradle swung outboard on its davits, as the ship shuddered and the deck shifted. The captain's wife, leaning on her husband's arm and hobbling toward the stern, took heart at the practiced industry around her. The panic of the collision was over and now the business of the sailor tribe, whose god was the sea, was to accept the verdict of their deity and prepare their ship for sacrifice. "There are enough boats for us all," her husband reassured her. "You'll be on the first one."

"I want to stay with you," she protested.

"That's not possible, darling."

Determined to plead her case, she looked up at him and their eyes met. His confidence—in himself, in his command, in his crew, in her—banished her fear and buoyed her up so resolutely that she gave up her suit. "I know," she said.

Two sailors, steadying the boat and handing down oars to two others standing in the bow and stern, hailed their approach. "This way for your missus, sir. All comforts provided," one said boldly, but in a manner so cheerful amid the wreckage of all their hopes, that the captain's wife laughed and her husband smiled. As she made ready to be handed into the boat, she comforted herself with the thought that her darling son, her Natie, was safe at home.

From above, on the steamer deck, the shouts of the men escalated, followed abruptly by the ominous, distinctive sound, low and threatening at first, like a rumble from the earth's core, then rising in pitch: the outraged complaint of a wounded tree tearing itself apart. All eyes turned to the mainmast, which was slowly folding, its yards cracking like sticks on the deck below. The captain's wife turned to her husband, but as she did the sky tilted, the deck rose up beneath her feet, the boat she was poised to enter shifted toward the sea, and a flood of water rushed in upon her, knocking her to her knees. She heard her husband call her name, but she couldn't see him, she couldn't see anything. The cold water lifted her up, up, over the bulwarks and then dashed her down with such force that her cloak was torn from her shoulders and her legs flew up before her as if she had been dropped from a tower.

She struggled, holding her breath and pulling her limbs into her body, but two forces were ranged against her—the ever-downward pressure of gravity and the relentless pull of the deep. As she was carried down she had no conscious thoughts, only her visceral mind fought for life. She opened her eyes, looking for light, but there was only cold and soundless darkness.

The storm advanced upon the shipwreck, first caressing it with a delicate spray, a tentative swell, a distant thunderclap. The sailors in the boat, now suspended at an angle, the bow lower than the stern, clung to the manropes for dear life. The captain had been washed into the sea with his wife, and two sailors on the deck were occupied cutting life rings from the taffrail and throwing them over the lee side. Others readied a second boat, their eyes wildly scanning the water for any sign of their lost commander. "He's there," cried the mate, pointing to the chop beneath the broken mast. And it was true; the captain had surfaced. He turned round in place, desperate to find his wife. "Do you see her?" he shouted to the men gathered above. A well-aimed preserver hit the water just beyond him, but he ignored it. "Save yourself, man," the mate called back. But the captain, a skillful swimmer, continued treading water, turning in place, straining to see through the rain and the rising sea. "She's there," he cried, striking out toward the bow. He made out something there, something darker than the sea.

The mate hung over the rail, thinking, Don't be a fool, but then he too spotted the dark thing floating and the captain approaching it, cutting through the water with powerful strokes. He had reached it, he grasped it, and a cry escaped him as he gathered it into his arms. It was his wife's blue cloak.

Again he treaded, turning in place. She must be near. Another life ring flopped into the sea close to the steamer's hull. In desperation, the captain dived beneath the surface. She must be there, between the two ships. He could see nothing. It was futile, but how was he to give up? He dived again, swimming with froglike strokes beneath the surface.

On the *Early Dawn*, the sailors in the boat had succeeded in cutting through the tackle and one cried out, "She's going!" as the small craft plummeted into the waves. The captain, rising up to take a breath, felt a blow across his shoulders that knocked the remaining air out of his lungs and pushed him cruelly back down. When he tried to rise again, something solid blocked his way. There was no air left in his lungs; he could feel his eyes bulging with the effort not to breathe. He sensed a light behind him and turned toward it. Then, with what terror and sadness he understood that he was looking down, that it was his wife, her pale face raised to his, her hair streaming like spilled ink over her shoulders, her arms opened wide, rising toward him from the depths, coming to meet him, to take him with her, having preceded him, only moments before, entirely out of this life.

The Green Book

❧

This book for my daughter Sarah,
with love from her father
May 12, 1860

$\mathcal{M}$y sister has dreams she thinks are visions. In the dead of night she sees our cousin Maria wandering and wailing outside her bedroom window. Her hair and skirts are dripping seawater, and she cries out, "Help me, help me. I've come home. I'm cold, I'm hungry."

"She wants to come inside," Hannah told me.

"She's with God," I said. "Why would she want to be here?"

"She wants Natie," she replied. "She's come back for her little son."

Little he is and not well. His mother may have him soon enough. He has hardly grown these eight months. His skin is like milk, and his dark eyes set in dark circles, his downturned mouth, his fits of sobbing, as if he knows his parents drowned and he was left among the bereaved; all these trouble our hearts. His grandmother is stalwart. In her view God knows what must be and what must not be and it is ours to bear it with faith in His wisdom. But she must be suffering, for Maria was her only daughter and dear to her. No one could make my aunt laugh like Maria.

Maria was named for my aunt's sister, who died in childbirth and so did the child, leaving my uncle, Captain Nathan, a widower, first to mourn his loss with his sister-in-law and then to marry her. When their daughter was born there was no question that she would be named for the wife and sister whose untimely death had brought them together. Now of their six children they have lost two, both at sea. The first, Nathan, named for his father, was taken by fever on a brig off the coast of Galveston, his body committed to the Gulf of

Mexico; the second, Maria, was swept overboard with her husband, Captain Joseph Gibbs, when their vessel was struck by a steamer as they sailed out from Cape Fear. That was eight months ago.

Our families, the Cobbs and the Briggs, are intimately, even intricately, connected. For a time, when Captain Nathan's shore business failed, my aunt and her children lived in our house while he went back to sea to recover his fortune. My mother was fond of her sister-in-law and it was her idea that we should pull together as a tribe. Those were happy times; with two mothers and so many children in the rectory we slept three to a bed. Briggs children called my mother Mother Cobb and Cobb children called the Briggs mother Mother Briggs. Hannah hardly remembers those days. She was just a toddler when Captain Nathan, having recovered his losses, built their big house, with its piazza and terrace, and the trellises of roses so lush and fragrant all summer long that it came to be called Rose Cottage.

When our mother died, Hannah formed an attachment to Maria Briggs, who returned her affection with great kindness. Since Maria's death, Hannah has devoted herself to the orphaned babe, which activity both my father and Mother Briggs encouraged, as they thought it would be a comfort to Hannah, and so she spends several nights a week at Rose Cottage, helping Mother Briggs and sleeping in the poor orphan's room at night. But Hannah takes the baby's frailty for a judgment against her caregiving. His fretfulness keeps her from both sleep and reason.

My uncle has written to the constables in all the shore towns where the remains of his daughter and her husband might have washed up, but to no avail. They have been swallowed by the sea. If we could lay them to rest, with a service and a stone, Hannah might recover her good sense, but as it is, she's convinced herself their souls are yet adrift.

This morning Hannah had a conversation with Father in his study, which left them both tight-lipped and grim. I was working on the sleeves of a dress when she came into the parlor and threw herself down on the sofa in a huff.

"That didn't go well, I take it," I said.

"He doesn't believe a word I say," she replied.

I ran the needle round the curve of the cuff, raised the pressure foot, and cut the thread. "Well, how could he, dear?" I asked. "He's committed to believing otherwise."

"I don't see why. Jesus raised the dead."

"Oh my. Did you tell Father that?"

"I did."

"What did he say?"

"He said Jesus did it only once and anyway I'm not Jesus."

"Those are good points," I observed.

"No, they're not. What Jesus did just proves the dead can return. He didn't have to do it more than once to make the case. And I'm not trying to raise the dead. That's the furthest thing from my mind."

"Surely you understand why such talk is disturbing to him."

"I can't help that. I can't pretend I don't know what I know or see what I see."

I studied her a moment, considering her argument and her character. She's always had a dreamy side. As a child she talked to trees and made up stories. She wrote sweet poems about the dew being dropped from the drinking cups of fairies, or enchanted woods where elves had tea parties using mushrooms for tables. It was charming, my sister the fabulist, and I encouraged her in her fantasies because she worked them out so prettily and it gave her such pleasure. She struck me as fairylike herself, with her dark hair and light eyes, her slender limbs, the liveliness of her step, as if she could scarce bear to touch the ground. She is of a capricious temperament, and now this loss of our dear cousin has lifted a latch that was never tightly fastened and a dark wind has swept in, carrying all before it.

She sat up on the sofa, resting her elbows on her knees, her forehead on her hands, the picture of despondency. "Do you believe me, Sallie?" she said.

"What does it matter?" I asked.

She lifted her face from her hands and fixed me with a look of puzzlement.

"Supposing it *is* true," I said. "What does it matter who believes you? What can anyone do about it?"

"You mean I should just give Natie up to her?"

This response made me impatient. "You knew Maria, dearest," I said. "Who knew her better? Was she ever cruel? Did she ever hurt anyone?"

"She was lively and clever," Hannah said at once. "And she was fearless. She wasn't afraid of anything."

"Then who is this woman you see weeping and complaining? How can that be Maria?"

As I spoke I had a clear image of Maria in my mind. She was on the lawn at Rose Cottage, whispering some drollery into her young husband's ear, her arm linked through his, leaning into him, raised up on her toes, for he was several inches taller than she was. And then the light in which memory bathed this moment of sweet intimacy went out, and I saw that my sister was sweeping tears from her eyes with her fingertips. I held out my arms to her and she lurched across the floor, collapsing at my feet. "I miss her so," she sobbed, clutching my waist, hiding her face in my skirt. I stroked her hair back from her throbbing temples, muttering soothing words, letting her have what she has sorely needed these long, lonely months: a good cry. "It's all right," I said. But even as I spoke, I felt a stab of fear that nothing would be all right for my poor sister anytime soon.

After Hannah returned to Rose Cottage, Father emerged from his study, his eyes darting about the room nervously, as if in expectation of a swarm of insects.

"She's gone," I said. I'd finished the sleeves and was kneeling over the pattern on the floor, cutting out the bodice.

He approached and took the chair at my sewing machine. "Advise me, Sarah," he said. "I'm at a loss with all this spookism your sister has manufactured." I had pins in my mouth and when I sat up, Father laughed. "What a dangerous enterprise sewing is," he observed. "Aren't you afraid you might swallow one of those?"

I removed the pins solemnly, planting them in the cushion. "I need another hand," I said.

"So you do," he agreed. "But you've looked to yourself and utilized what you do have, which is the mark of a resourceful and industrious nature."

I smiled. Industry is Father's cardinal virtue. His name could be the Reverend Industry Cobb. It would suit him well.

"If only your sister had your temperament," he concluded.

"She's grieving," I said. "She's young. She's only thirteen. And she worshipped Maria."

"You think she'll get over this maudlin fantasy, that time will cure her?"

"I don't know that, but I hope it will."

"She's not steady," Father said.

"She says you don't believe a word she says."

"Nor do I," he confirmed. "Do you?"

"I believe she believes she has seen Maria."

"I could insist that she stay home," he suggested.

"And leave Natie? She would pine for him."

Father clutched his beard, considering my argument. "It's this insalubrious craze for talking to spirits: it's loose in the world. The next thing we know old Abigal Spicer over in Mattapoisett will set herself up as a table-knocker."

"Abigal does talk to people who aren't there," I agreed.

Father gazed at me, bemused by the world and its ways. "So your view is that I should do nothing."

"If Natie thrives, life will bring Hannah back to life."

"And if he perishes?"

"Then she will always believe Maria has taken him, and she will come home."

Father nodded. "Women's counsel is always patience."

"We could wish more men would take it," I said, turning back to my pattern.

Father rose from his chair and went out, his mind more at ease, but mine was less settled. I was thinking about ghosts. Who doesn't whisper a confidence at the grave of the beloved when the wind rustles the trees and lifts the petals of the roses planted there? What draws the bereaved to seek the departed still in this world? Is it hope, I wondered, or is it fear?

A sunny day. I went to Rose Cottage to visit my sister and to my delight, both Olie and Benjamin were at home. Even Hannah's spirits were lifted by the presence of our cousins, who could not be more different from each other, yet there is a strong bond between them. Olie is witty, full of jokes and fun, fond of music and singing, while Benjamin is a serious young man, though not unsmiling, and grown strong and handsome this past year when he has been largely at sea. His light blue eyes are like beacons, and when I feel them seeking mine, I'm as flustered as a chicken before a fox. He has command of the *Forest King* and Olie has the *Wanderer*; both are bound next week in different directions, Benjamin to Sicily and Olie to Peru. They regaled us with sea stories, to which my uncle Nathan added the coda from his own vast experience. Hannah came in with Natie draped over her shoulder. When he began his habitual fussing, Olie coaxed her to let him try his hand at consoling his nephew. To my surprise she passed the boy to him. He paced back and forth the length of the parlor, holding the child across his arm with his legs dangling and kicking. In a few moments the sobbing turned to burbling, and then Natie fell quiet, no doubt awed by the wonder of being transported in such a powerful embrace. I poured a cup of tea for my exhausted sister and handed it to her without comment. She sat taking small sips, her eyes never leaving Olie's progress from one door to the other. Benjamin looked on, his fingertips resting on his lips, from Hannah to Olie and back again. I couldn't tell what he was thinking, but oh, I'd like to know.

. . .

*T*oday again to Rose Cottage. My uncle has been suffering with a spring cold but, now recovered, declared he wants to dine in a crowd, so we were off at his request to supply the numbers. I spent the morning baking rolls, and made two pies, one custard, which is Olie's favorite, and one jam, which is Benjamin's.

Dinah made a potato gallette from a recipe Mrs. Butter brought back from Havre. We packed two baskets, I tucked a few sheets of music into a pasteboard tube, and off we went, feeling we would make ourselves welcome, as indeed we were. Olie met us at the gate with his usual good cheer and at once had my father laughing about a certain lady who described his recent sermon as "a powerful oration," that made her soul "leap up in terror."

"I know the lady," Father said. "She quivers, she grows pale: tears fill her eyes. And all I've said is 'love thy neighbor.'"

"But you recommend it so vehemently," I said, which made us all laugh.

Inside we found my uncle eager to drag Father upstairs for a consultation on the piazza, which Captain Nathan calls the quarterdeck. Olie, having passed our baskets to Dinah, who set off down the stairs to the kitchen, hauled me to the piano, demanding a song. Benjamin was lounging on a chaise near the fire, though it was a fair day. "Ladies love a fire, in my experience," he said. Hannah proved his theory, bundled up in a wool shawl with Natie drowsing in her lap, her gaze fixed on the flames as if she saw an entertainment there.

"We should all be walking," I protested. "It's the finest day imaginable."

"We'll walk after dinner," Olie agreed. "But first a song. Have you anything new?"

I had recourse to my roll. "It's new to me," I said, "and very lovely. It's a duet. We each take a solo verse, then join on the third."

Olie drew up behind me as I placed the sheets on the music rack. "See how beneath the moonbeam's smile," he read. I played the melody while we recited the words, "Yon little billow heaves its breast, and foams and sparkles for a while, then murmuring subsides to rest." Then the refrain, "Thus man, the sport of bliss and care, rises on Time's eventful sea, and having swell'd a moment there, thus melts into eternity."

"It's not very cheerful, is it?" observed Benjamin.

"But the melody is light and charming, that's what makes it interesting," I said. I played the introductory chords and Olie came in, singing confidently. At the duet our voices skirted each other, like waves dancing on the sea.

But our harmonizing didn't suit Olie's petulant nephew, who set up a caterwaul that couldn't be ignored. We finished the refrain and I played a final chord; then all eyes were upon the suffering child. Hannah jollied him, laying him over her shoulder, patting his back, and murmuring sweet reassurances.

"Do let's take him outside," I suggested. "The fresh air will be the best thing for him."

Benjamin raised his long self from the chaise and held out his arms. "Clearly he's not a music lover," Olie said.

"It's your singing he can't stand," Benjamin suggested. He'd taken the baby from Hannah and lifted him high over his head, gazing coolly into his red and apoplectic face. "Isn't that right?" he asked the child.

Natie's eyes grew wide and his crying stopped abruptly, as if in answer to his uncle's question. Hannah got up from her chair, following Natie, who now issued a sound more like a chortle than a cry. "He wants to sing too," she said, and to my surprise and delight, a smile lifted the corners of her mouth and her eyes were soft rather than grim with anxiety. We set off in a troop through the entry and out the door into the golden day, Benjamin and Natie leading the way. I caught up with my sister as we crossed the lawn, slipping my arm around her waist. "Darling," I said. "It does my heart good to see you smile."

She leaned her head upon my shoulder, gazing at our cousins, whose long strides took them quickly out of earshot. "He is so dear," she said.

"Which one?" I asked, thinking she meant Natie.

"Benjamin." She sighed.

. . .

*A*ll night there was rain and thunder and lightning, so that I think no one in this house slept a wink. In the morning, after breakfast, I stepped out to inspect the house for damage. A gutter was loose over the kitchen, otherwise all was intact. The air was fresh-washed, cool and delicious. As I turned back to the walk, I saw my sister coming along the road, her face hidden in the folds of her cloak. In the past weeks Natie's health has improved, and he has managed a few feeble smiles, sleeps more than two hours without a cry, holds down the pabulum Mother Briggs prepares for him, and excretes a substance thicker than water. All agree the credit goes to Hannah, and she appears less absorbed in the gloom of the sickroom.

So I expected better cheer from my sister as I approached the gate to greet her, but when she pressed her chilly hand upon mine and raised her face beneath the hood to apply a cold, dry kiss to my cheek, I sensed a gloom so intense and intractable that my heart sank in my breast.

"Oh, Sallie," she whispered. "I'm so frightened."

I passed my arm about her waist and drew her into the yard, latching the gate with my free hand. "On such a day as this," I chided her, "what is there to fear?"

She sent me an uncomprehending glance, pulling her head back beneath the hood. "Come inside," I urged, guiding her up the walk. "There's a fire in the kitchen. You've taken a chill, that's all. I'll make us a pot of tea and you can tell me what is the matter."

"Where is Father?" she asked, pausing at the sill.

I made no reply. Together we turned in to the kitchen, which was empty, as Dinah had gone out to the market. "Natie is doing well?" I asked, releasing her. She sank down in a chair at the table, pushing back her hood at last. Her hair was loose, and her cheeks flushed. "He wants to stay with me, but Maria won't let him."

My patience was much tried at this remark. "Maria is gone," I said, but not unkindly. "She's in heaven."

"We don't know where she is, do we?" she replied.

I turned away, took up the kettle, and set it on the hob. This was not a conversation I wanted to enter. "You make it hard on us all with this ghoulish fantasy," I said. "Mother Briggs has lost two of her children, yet she doesn't give herself over to useless fancy. She accepts her loss; it is God's will."

"Last night I woke up and she was in the room, standing over the crib."

"You were dreaming," I protested.

The kettle shrieked and she was still, her head bowed, while I filled the pot and set it on the table between us. Then she gave me a long, searching look, so penetrating I couldn't meet it, and busied myself with the cups and spoons. "I woke up," she said, "because I could smell seawater. Her clothes were dripping."

"And did she speak to you?" I inquired, without looking up from the tea streaming into the cup.

"No. But she knew I was watching her. Then she went to the window and disappeared. When I got up, the carpet was wet." She spoke calmly, delivering her final assertion with the confidence of a lawyer charging a jury after an irresistible summation.

I lightened my tea with a splash of milk from the pitcher. "The carpet was wet," I said.

"Yes."

"Did you taste it? Was it salty?"

Her brow furrowed. "I didn't think of that," she said.

*C*heerfully I record the exchange I had with Benjamin this afternoon at Rose Cottage. I'd gone over to have tea with Hannah, but it was too windy to sit outdoors as we planned, so we brought the tray to the parlor. Olie has gone down to his ship in New York and Benjamin will be leaving for his voyage on the weekend. We talked about his vessel, the *Forest King*, which he has commanded for ten months, and the cargo, timber, and brass fittings. He described the crew, in which he is not entirely confident. Natie sat on the floor with some blocks his grandfather made for him. He was sniffling with a cold, but he played in a desultory way, putting one atop the other. He is stronger now, but he tires quickly. When we'd finished our tea and demolished the plate of cakes I'd brought, Benjamin asked me if I would play a song he particularly likes, a sweet nostalgic air called "In the Starlight."

"Gladly," I said, "if you will sing with me."

"That's Olie's line," he said. "He's the nightingale in our family, and I am the crow."

"I think you have a very nice voice," Hannah said.

"You've a fine baritone," I agreed. "You don't sing off-key, so there's no need for this false modesty."

"Well," he said, rising from his chair to follow me to the instrument. "Since you encourage me, I'll essay it." At the piano, I riffled the sheet music until I found the desired piece. I've played it many times, but I've a poor memory and the arrangement is pleasantly complicated. I launched into the opening while Benjamin looked on, waiting for me to start the lyric before chiming in. Though he has a very good ear, he can't read music, which accounts for his shyness in taking part. He can't sing harmony either. We bellowed out the melody, our voices rising at the refrain: "In the starlight, let us wander gay and free." I detected Hannah's thin voice behind me joining in at the last, and I glanced up to see Benjamin with his hands raised, chopping time in the air like a conductor, encouraging her on.

When the song was done, I dropped my hands to my lap. That sweet moment of silence that still carries the notes, though the musician has ceased to play, fell upon us. Hannah said, "That's a lovely tune."

Benjamin turned, smiling at me. "It's a mystery to me how you can just sit down and play like that."

"And it's a mystery to me," I said, "how you can sail a ship to a place you've never seen."

"Well," he said, pondering his answer. "I read the stars."

"And I read the notes," I countered. He leaned over me, examining the sheet music. "They are arranged in patterns," he observed. "Like constellations."

I raised my hand and glided my forefinger along the staff. "These are my stars. They guide me through tempestuous seas of discord."

I looked up at him and for an exhilarating moment our eyes met. "And bring you safely home," he concluded.

What a delightful comparison! That the notes on the staff, arranged in familiar combinations, guide my fingers and my voice to sweet harmonies, just as the stars in the heavens guide my dear cousin through all manner of tempests and gales to distant shores and back again.

I return to this account of my doings after weeks in which little of import has occurred. Our captains have sailed and our circle is thereby diminished. I divide my time between house cares here and visits to Rose Cottage, where my sister and her infant charge occupy a focus of familial interest. Natie hasn't thrived, but he isn't ill, only occasionally fretful. He can walk, though he is not adept. Now and then he sets himself the task of walking across the carpet to the divan, but he usually falls at least twice before reaching his goal. He doesn't give in to anger, but, with patience and fortitude, pulls himself up and tries again. In this way he can pass an hour without complaint.

Hannah is no longer tormented by nocturnal visions, which is a great relief to all who care for her. But yesterday, when we had spread a blanket on the lawn and were lounging there in the warm air with Natie dozing, thumb in mouth, between us, to my dismay she brought up the subject of spirit communication. She has read an article about a Boston lady who is believed to have the power to communicate with what Hannah called "the other side."

"Oh, Lord," I said, scoffing. "The other side of what?"

"Of what we ordinarily see," she replied.

"And where is this place we can't see?"

"It's not another place, I think," she explained seriously. "It's here, right here." And she gestured with open hands, taking in the yard, the little copse of birches, the path to the garden gate. "They come and go, as we do, among us."

"And what are they? Fairies?"

"Not fairies. Spirits. The spirits of the departed."

"All the departed? The other side must be awfully crowded."

She frowned at my levity. "It's unkind of you to mock me," she said.

"I'm not mocking you. I'm only applying practical consideration to the question of whether or not there are ghosts in this world. It's not a new question, as I'm sure you know."

"I don't like that word 'ghosts.'"

"No? Spirits then. Here's my view, darling. If the departed are gone from us in flesh and blood but somehow not gone, somehow still available for consultation . . ."

"And consolation," she added.

This vexed me. "Hannah," I urged her. "If the dead see us and care for us and hang about in the air longing to reach us, how can their eternal homelessness be a consolation to us or to them?"

She raised her eyes to mine with a glittering fixity I found unnerving. "It is if we let them reach us. That's what's been discovered. We shun them, our religion bids us to shun them, but we needn't. If we are open to them, they have much to tell us."

I looked away from her earnest entreaty to the baby, who had rolled onto his side, gurgling in his sleep. Hannah's eyes followed mine and this vision of sleeping innocence softened her aspect. I was thinking that she believed the spirit of his dead mother wanted to steal him away from us. "So, have you talked Maria out of taking him?" I asked.

To my surprise she took my question seriously. "I think she just wanted to know that he's safe. That he's loved."

"So she went away?"

"I think she's still watching over him. Perhaps she always will."

Hannah stretched out her hand to caress Natie's pallid cheek. "I hope so," she concluded.

The boy opened his eyes, wondering at first, but in a moment his mouth puckered and his forehead creased. He drew in a long breath, held it a split second, and released it in an ear-shattering wail.

*H*ow dreadful and sad. I can hardly believe it is true. Last night, when all were sleeping, without so much as a cry, Maria's orphaned son, Natie Gibbs, passed away.

*I*t was Hannah, of course, who found the dead child, no sooner had she waked. In her half-conscious state she couldn't believe what was evident. She took up the little corpse and rushed out to the landing calling for help. My uncle came first. Seeing at once the true state of things, he relieved her of her burden, instructing her to run to Dr. Martin's house, which is a mile down the road. She rushed out in her nightgown and ran the distance without a pause, arriving disheveled, breathless, and babbling. The doctor's wife wrapped her in a blanket and sat with her on the sofa while the doctor saddled his horse and rode off to Rose Cottage. When he arrived, my uncle told him the unhappy truth, that Natie, who had never shown much affection for this world, had gone off in his sleep to the next. Mother Briggs, our stalwart Mother Briggs, was so afflicted by the death of her grandson that the doctor administered some sedative drops and sent her to bed.

My uncle, leaving his wife in the doctor's care, set off to retrieve Hannah. He met her halfway, trudging toward him, head down, wrapped in a light cloak the doctor's wife had insisted she wear, her bare feet brown from the dirt on the road. When he called to her, she raised her eyes, which were red from weeping, and seeing the distress and sympathy in his demeanor, she stretched out her arms, quickened her step, and collapsed in his embrace. "He is gone," she said, and again, "he is gone."

"Yes," my uncle said, relieved that she was so sensible. "I've come to take you home."

I was hanging clothes on the line in the side yard. As I lifted a wadded skirt, I spied my uncle and my sister approaching. He had his arm round her shoulders and she rested her head against his chest, her feet moving without her attention, like an automaton. I didn't guess what had happened, but the vision the two presented, the barefoot girl in her cloak and nightdress guided with a steady and patient hand by the elderly captain, was deeply melancholic. I dropped the skirt into the basket and hustled through the yard to the path. I heard my uncle say, "Look, here's your sister," and Hannah's head came up, but, though I hurried to her, she didn't step away from my uncle; in fact, she turned her face to his shirtfront and closed her eyes.

"What is it?" I asked my uncle.

"Natie has passed away," he said solemnly.

At this Hannah let out a strangled sob, pressing her forehead toward my uncle's armpit, as if she thought to hide there.

"Oh, no!" I gasped. It was a shock and seemed at once so sad and so final that I could scarce take it in. "But he was well, I thought. Wasn't he?"

My sister released my uncle and turned to me with an expression so stricken it hurt me to see it. "Darling," I said, as I folded her into my arms. "I'm so sorry, so sorry."

Uncle stood silent as Hannah allowed herself to be comforted. Over her bowed head we cast each other looks of comprehension and relief. "I must go back to your aunt," he explained. "She is heartbroken."

"Yes," I said. "You should go back." I turned to the house and Hannah loosened her grip, though she kept one arm around my waist.

"Ask your father to come to us when he can," my uncle called from the path.

"I will," I promised. Hannah balked when I turned her toward the house. "Dearest," I said. "Come home now." Her frantic eyes searched my face, then she nodded and yielded to my guidance.

Dinah met us at the door. Behind her, the chorus of Father's Latin students filled the air. *Hiemem sensit Neptunus et imis*, they proclaimed. "Lord," Dinah whispered. "What has happened?"

"Natie has passed away," I said.

"Oh, the poor babe," she cried, then covered her mouth with her palm, as Father forbids raised voices when his study is doubling as a classroom. *Graviter commotus*, droned the scholars.

Hannah was silent as I steered her toward the staircase, Dinah fretting along at my side. "As soon as Father has dismissed his students," I instructed her, "tell him to go at once to my uncle's house."

"Oh, I will," she promised. "I surely will."

We were halfway up the stairs when the door of Father's study was thrown open and we heard the shrieking of his half-savage students racing for the kitchen, where a tray of ginger biscuits was set out for them. I turned to watch over the rail. Strangely, Hannah didn't appear to notice the uproar. When we entered her room, she released me and took a step toward her bed. Then she turned to me, raising her hands to press either side of her skull. "What have they done to him?" she asked.

"He is there," I said. "In his grandmother's house."

"Is he sleeping?"

I wasn't sure how to answer. She appeared so distracted and nonsensical I feared the truth, which surely in some way she knew, must not be repeated. "You should rest now," I said. "Sit on the bed and I'll bring a basin to wash your feet."

She backed onto the edge of the bed and sat looking down at her feet, which were gray with dry, cracked mud. Dinah's steps resounded in the hall; then she appeared in the doorway carrying a tray with a cup, saucer, and two biscuits on a plate. "I've saved these from the scholars," she said pleasantly. "And I've brewed a nice cup of valerian tea. It will settle you." Hannah, who usually resisted Dinah's remedies, took the cup without comment and sipped it obediently. Dinah turned upon me a quizzical look.

"We should wash her feet," I said.

A glance at the feet in question sent Dinah to the washstand.

She removed the basin and filled it with water from the pitcher. Then she dropped the hand towel into it and set it on the floor by the bed. Hannah looked on distantly, unprotesting as Dinah swabbed each foot with the cloth.

"Your father has gone," Dinah said to me. Her tone was cautious. The extreme volatility of our patient was so obvious that the room felt like a tinderbox and one feared to strike a spark.

"Thank you," I said. She wrung the cloth out in the basin and went over Hannah's feet a last time, leaving them clean and damp. "There you are," she said. "Have you finished your tea?"

Hannah took a last swallow, draining the cup and handing it back to Dinah. "It's vile stuff," she said.

"That it is," Dinah agreed. "But it will help you sleep."

Hannah glanced toward the window, where the curtain billowed in the warm breeze. "Why should I sleep?" she asked. "It's daytime."

I crossed the room and pulled the shutter in, splintering the soft morning light into bright strips across the floor. "I'll stay with her," I said to Dinah.

"Very well," she said, taking up the basin. "I've work to do." And she left us in the darkened room.

Hannah drew her legs onto the bed and turned onto her side facing me. Her gaze was so unfocused I could only marvel at the efficacy of valerian. I lifted the coverlet, pulling it up to her waist as she rested her head on the pillow. "I don't understand what Mother was trying to tell me," she said.

I took in a breath to keep from showing my alarm. "When?" I asked.

"Last night," she replied. "I woke up and she was in my room, by the window. Her back was to me, but I knew it was her."

"How did you know?" I said.

"Oh, you know. Just the way she was standing. She was wearing her blue wool morning dress. I remember it so well. And I thought it odd, because it's much too warm for a dress like that."

I knew exactly the dress she was speaking of; it was one of

Mother's favorites. She wore it with a pink scarf about her waist that last Christmas when we went to church.

"I called out to her," Hannah continued. "But she didn't turn round. She said 'Golden dreams,' just the way she used to. It was her voice. Then she was gone, and I went back to sleep. But she must have come to tell me something." Her eyes had closed as she spoke. She added a few words as darkness embraced her. "She wanted me to sleep, just like everybody else."

I stood by the bed looking down at her as her breath grew shallow and her lips parted softly. I brushed back a stray tendril of hair from her cheek. I think I have never been so perfectly miserable.

Hannah was seven when Mother died, and I was thirteen. It was in the spring. Everything on earth was coming back to life, the trees disported themselves in fragrant flowers, buds pushed up sturdy green shoots through the damp soil, but my mother was wasting away. In the cemetery there were daffodils waving their gay heads in the air, and the day was bright. As her coffin was lowered into the grave, which was the only dark place in the world, or so it seemed to me, I hid my face in Father's waistcoat. Hannah stood by my side, holding my hand. She didn't turn away, she didn't cry, as I did. She was too young to understand, and I knew that, but her stolidity irked me. As the brutal raps of the clods being shoveled onto the coffin assaulted the mourners, I turned to look at her. She raised her hand, and in a theatrical little voice with a slight catch of emotion in it, but not a sob, not a tear, she said, "Good night, Mama. Golden dreams."

Father is right, I thought. She's not steady. This world is not enough for my sister, because her mother has gone from it.

*N*atie's funeral was a sad affair. Father arranged everything, including the coffin, which Lon Eadley stayed up late in his shop manufacturing. It was very small, of cherrywood and lined with light blue silk. Mother Briggs dressed her grandson in the embroidered loose blouse and skirt he wore on those occasions when he was well enough for church meeting. We gathered at Rose Cottage in the morning and followed the casket, which rested upon a bed of hay in a cart belonging to our parishioner Mr. Bedford and drawn by his old dray horse. Mother Briggs thought a hearse too big for such a tiny passenger. Mr. Bedford had a black band around his arm and he'd fastened two black bows to the horse's halter, which struck me as both thoughtful and rather silly. Our group was only the family, at Mother Briggs's request: Father, Hannah, the grandparents, Dinah, and myself. The grave was next to the marker that commemorates Natie's drowned parents. Horace Beade, the gravedigger, stood with us, his hat in his hand, as Father read the service.

All of us were anxious about Hannah, who stood at my side in her black dress and black veil, which she had drawn down to cover her face. She was too calm. There was something ominous about her solemn composure. Even at the house, when she had looked down upon the dead child in his coffin, she had shown no emotion. Though I had not known the babe so well, the sight of his pallid innocence swaddled in linen and silk brought tears to my eyes. Mother Briggs stood at the head of the coffin as we each filed by. She was haggard, her lips compressed into a thin line, her eyes sunk deep in their sockets. When we had all bid farewell to the departed child, my uncle laid the lid upon the frame and drove in the nails, each stroke of the hammer resounding in the still air of the parlor. Hannah took my hand and held it, pressing tightly as each nail was driven home.

It was a cool, damp day, overcast and gloomy. As Father led the prayers, a few drops sprinkled over the company. The drizzle increased and he concluded speedily. How much could be said of such a brief life? We turned and walked away stolidly, while Horace took up his shovel to fill the narrow grave. It wouldn't take him long.

At home, Dinah and Mother Briggs disappeared into the kitchen to prepare us a breakfast of biscuits, jam, and coffee. The gentlemen went off for a private confab in Uncle's study, which left Hannah and me alone, sitting on the couch before the fire my uncle had laid in the morning and lit at once on our return from the mournful outing.

I pulled off my gloves and pried my hat loose from the pins that held it in place. Hannah sat perfectly still, her hands folded in her lap.

"You can take your veil off now," I suggested as my hat came free of my hair.

"No," Hannah said softly. "I don't want to."

"Why not, dearest?" I asked. "It's not appropriate in the house." She gave no answer. Dinah came in from the kitchen to call us to breakfast. Seeing Hannah motionless in her heavy veil, she cast me a questioning look, which I answered by lifting my eyebrows. "Will you come to breakfast?" I asked my sister.

"Oh yes," she said, rising from her chair. And so she sat at the kitchen table, pushing bits of bread under the veil and into her mouth while the rest of us pretended we didn't notice.

*T*his morning in the post there was a letter for me from Captain Benjamin Briggs, passed into the mailbag at Messina. Why such excitement beneath my ribs? I carried it home, left the others on the hall table, and hurried up to my room to open it in secret.

A letter, if I may call it that. It is a single page with a simple drawing of the artist standing in the prow of his ship, his face raised to a circlet of stars in the heavens above. At the bottom in an admirably neat hand is written SALLIE'S MUSIC GUIDES ME HOME.

To think of him, in the night, amid the dark, pummeling waves, taking his position from distant stars, recalling our charming comparison, then, perhaps before sleep, pulling a sheet from his drawer, a pen from his holder, and sketching this delightful drawing, this dear message. After that, folding it, addressing the envelope, adding it to the stack destined for the mailbag. How this touches me!

And how I shall treasure it, and also hide it away. Not to be shared.

But how will I reply? I cannot draw.

*W*e passed this day at church and I here testify that Rev. Huntress's sermons could bring sweet slumber to a herd of wild beasts. Hannah and I kept ourselves upright by frequent exchanges of pained glances, which became so intense that we had hard duty to keep from laughter. Father, who was sitting behind the speaker, did not fail to notice our amusement and sent a mighty frown our way. On the walk home we were privileged with a private sermon on the virtue of sobriety. Hannah listened, her lips pursed and her eyes narrowed, as if she were being offered distasteful medicine. She's fine, I tell myself, she's a little petulant sometimes, but she's also affectionate and playful. She's returned to ordinary life and she balks at the change, because it is so . . . ordinary.

Stars, as they make their rounds
Confound the world with stories
Of archers, bears, and hounds,
Of heroes and their glories.

Why won't they sing of homely cares,
Of darning socks and shelling peas,
Of she who sews and watches there
For one who sails upon the seas?

Well, it's not wonderful and there is a false rhyme, but perhaps my cousin will see past my clumsiness to the true sentiment.

And I'll wager I spent more time on it than he did on his drawing.

I made a fair copy of my poem and put it in an envelope, then walked to Rose Cottage to get an address from my aunt. She was in the yard passing linens through the wringer, and her expression when she saw me was not entirely one of delight. Father has told me that she suffers from pains in her joints, so I took that to be the source of the paucity of her greeting. "Is all well at your house?" she asked as I approached.

"Very well," I replied. "May I help you with your washing?"

Her expression softened, but she refused my offer. "That's kind of you," she said. "But I've my own way of doing it and no one can suit me but myself."

An odd answer, I thought, also not a particularly gracious one. And why did she imagine I'd come with bad news?

"And how is your poor sister?" she asked next.

"She's well. She misses Natie, I think."

"Why does she refuse to accept God's will? It bodes ill for her."

"Oh," I said. "I think she'll come round to it soon enough." My aunt is a puzzle to me. One can't deny that she is a devoted, even a fierce, Christian, but her entire apprehension of God's will is that it is inscrutable and must be submitted to without comment or question. Perhaps she's right, but is it wrong for Hannah to miss the orphan she cared for? In what way does her sadness affect the God who has bereaved her? I can't make any sense of it.

"Whom the lord loveth, he chasteneth," my aunt concluded.

"Exactly," I agreed, though I didn't agree at all. "I've come to see if you have an address for a letter to Benjamin. He sent me such a kind note and I'd like to reply before he gets back."

She dropped her fresh-wrung sheet into the basket and brushed her hands together to dry them. Her sharp eyes swept over me so that I straightened my spine, but then she smiled and in a most amiable tone bid me follow her to the house. "He dotes on letters from home," she observed as we entered the house. "I think if you go straight to Dr. Allen's there should be time for it to get to Livorno. That's his last stop before he turns for home." She went to the kitchen cupboard and took out a page of printed addresses, then carefully copied out the one I required. I accepted it gratefully, wondering at her changeability. All her children love her, that I know, and surely that speaks well for her. "I'll go at once," I said, and I did.

On the walk I wondered what she would think of the lines I was sending to her son. And what, after all, did I think of them? Would he have preferred a long, newsy screed about the family doings, the town gossip? I thought I should consign my silly poem to the rubbish; it would only make him think the less of me. But in the end, I arrived at Dr. Allen's office, where he tends to the sick and the mail, copied the address onto the envelope, and consigned it to the whims of the postal service. I consoled myself with the notion that it might reach its destination too late.

𝒯his morning a dreary young man appeared at the door and announced that he had come to see the Reverend Leander Cobb. When I asked if he was expected, he said he should be, but probably was not. His name was Richard Peebles and he had spoken with Father after his sermon in Wareham last Sunday. Father goes over there every few weeks; he and Rev. Huntress exchange congregations so as not, Father says, to become "stale." I informed Mr. P. that I would alert the Reverend to his presence and invited him to wait in the parlor.

With reluctance, I tapped at Father's door. He dislikes being disturbed when he is working on his sermons, but I saw no alternative. "Come in," he barked, and I stepped inside, closing the door behind me.

"What is it, Sallie?" he asked, laying down his pen.

"A Mr. Peebles is here to see you."

"Mr. who?"

"Peebles. He said he spoke to you after service in Wareham."

"Peebles," he repeated, scanning his brain for a recollection.

"Short, stocky, thick yellow beard, dressed all in gray, a very odd hat, like a basin, yellow hair protruding at sides."

Father nodded at each detail, checking it against a mental list. At the hat, he sighed. "Oh merciful heavens," he said. "Mr. Peebles."

"Shall I show him in, or will you join him in the parlor?"

"He knows I'm at home?"

"I'm sorry, Father. I didn't think . . ."

"To lie, Sallie. Well, that's as it should be. And it's base of me to want to avoid Mr. Peebles, but he's one of a company I truly believe to be comprised entirely of charlatans and fools."

"Is he a lawyer?"

Father laughed. "Worse, much worse. He goes about writing on slates and he tells his poor victims the messages are from their dead relatives."

"He's a medium."

"Why did they choose that word? It irritates me."

"What shall I tell him?"

"Hannah's not in the house, is she?"

"She's at the Academy."

"Good. I'll have him out of here before she returns. She has enough nonsense in her head."

"Why does he want to see you?" I asked.

"I foolishly gave a sermon on Ezekiel over there. I didn't know it, but it's one of their sacred texts. Mr. Peebles accosted me afterward and I was polite; I was mollifying. I didn't tell him I think his view is a sacrilege, but now it looks as though he's going to push me to it."

"What can we do?"

"Nothing. I'm trapped. There's no way out of it. Send the fellow to me."

I found Mr. Peebles inspecting the bookshelf, his hands clasped behind his back, his head tilted at an odd angle to take in the title on the spine before him.

"Mr. Peebles," I said softly. He turned upon me with an expression of alarmed inquiry.

"My father will see you in his study."

"Really?" he said. "Not here in this charming room?"

"I'll show you the way," I said, stepping back into the hall. He came toward me with an odd creeping step, as if he didn't want to make a sound, his eyes fixed on his feet. Poor Father, I thought, as I led Mr. Peebles down the hall. He came up close behind me and abruptly pushed out a puff of air from his nostrils, which so startled me, I stopped and looked back. He had brought his hands to cover his face and stood with hunched shoulders, humming through his fingers.

"Mr. Peebles," I said. "Are you unwell?"

"I'm so sorry," he replied, his face still hidden behind his hands. "I'm so sorry for you."

This unnerved me. "I fear it's not a good time for you to visit my father, Sir. You are not well."

The hands came away from his tear-filled eyes. "Forgive me," he said. "I had a premonition concerning you and it overwhelmed me."

"A premonition of what?" I asked.

"Of loss. Of great loss." He dabbed his eyes with a handkerchief drawn from his coat pocket and squared his narrow shoulders, coaxing a sad smile to his narrow lips. "Forgive me," he said again.

Fueled by revulsion, I stepped away from him and rapped sharply on Father's door.

"Yes, come in, Mr. Peebles," Father called. Without a word, I ushered his visitor through the door and closed it upon him.

A premonition of great loss! That sounds a fairly safe prediction in this vale of tears.

*M*r. Peebles's visit has not had a good effect on Father. He has it in his head to preach against the spiritualist doctrine, which has turned the heads of too many good Christians, but as no one in our congregation espouses these views, there's no point in such a sermon here. It might only alert his audience to the possibility of deviance from the straight path, which, Father points out, is not in the mission of the good shepherd. "Point the way!" is Father's abstract of pastoral duty.

After Mr. Peebles left us, Father observed, "Ignoring such people is the best plan. I won't speak to another of that persuasion. If they can't get the sanction they seek from any Christian church, perhaps it will dawn on them that these messages they're receiving are coming from the devil."

"Is that what he wants? Your sanction?"

"He wants me to test his wife. She's a mighty clairvoyant and he wants a confirmed skeptic to sit down with her in one of her unholy séances and attempt to prove she's a fraud."

"Where does she hold these meetings?"

"In their home, in New Bedford. He proposes to send a carriage to take me there and back."

"I wonder why he's chosen you. Surely there are skeptics at closer range."

"It's because he heard my sermon, and because he knows we've lost your mother. They prey on the bereaved. I hold that very strongly against them."

So this Mr. Peebles has promised Father that his wife can put him in touch with my mother. Then he will hear her voice, possibly see her spirit clad in something diaphanous, or at least see her hand scratching out a message to him on a slate. And what might my mother have to say?

I think I know. "Leander, this is disgraceful. Go home at once!"

*O*ur cousins have returned from their sea adventures, one after the other. Olie arrived by train from New York on Wednesday and Benjamin on the omnibus three days later. Mother Briggs sent a message that her plum trees are heavy with fruit and we are invited to harvest tomorrow morning. How fortunate that our captains have returned in time. This yearly harvest is a ritual; we've come together for it since we were children. We harvest one day and spend the next putting up the jam, of which there is always such a surplus that both our houses have a good supply for winter and there are enough small jars to tuck into the church Christmas baskets for the poor. When we were children, we were more numerous. Mother and Maria and Nathan, all passed away now, and my brother William, who is away at school in Philadelphia, as is our young cousin James. As children Benjamin and I always shared a basket and picked side by side, Benjamin scrambling up the tree to get the plums too high to reach. The family teased us, calling us plum sweethearts. Their teasing made me shy, but Benjamin never protested. It's been four years since both brothers have been home for this harvest. So tomorrow I will pick plums with my "plum sweetheart," and he will tell me what he thinks of my silly poem.

*B*enjamin has grown a beard! It makes him look serious, but the smile in his eyes as we approached Rose Cottage gave the lie to that impression. He stood in the open door as we made our way along the path and greeted Father with a warm handshake, Hannah with a soft kiss on the cheek. "Come in, come in," he encouraged us. When my turn came I was surprised at the emotion I felt as he brushed his lips across my cheek and said, "Sallie, at last. Thanks for your message."

"I feared I'd sent it too late."

"No," he said. "It was there at Livorno and it cheered me so much. But it was too late to write a reply. I had plenty of time for that on the trip home. I brought it with me. I'll give it to you later."

Of course I thought of nothing else the entire day. When we all set out to the plum orchard, Benjamin brought me an empty basket and Olie—who is frightfully thin, as his voyage was fraught with difficulty—paired up with Hannah, who looked cheerful for a change.

"Tell me about your voyage?" I said as we walked along.

"It was smooth enough," he said. "There was only one incident of note. One of the mates had been on shore drinking his pay for far too long. He was sober when we sailed and he knew it was a dry ship. About three days out, he went raving mad."

"Good Heavens," I said. "What did he do?"

"He had the idea that he was being eaten by insects. He ran up and down the deck screaming, 'Captain, save me! Captain, save me!' and then, somehow, he got into the rigging, yelling that he was going to jump into the sea. I've never seen anything like it."

"What did you do?"

"I had him hauled down and tied to his bunk. He screamed through the night, all sorts of profanity, and he shook so much his bunk rattled until morning. I had the steward bring him a pot of hot coffee and when I went in to see him, he was blubbering like a baby, begging me not to report him. I told him if he could do his work without trouble to me for the duration, that would be the end of it as far as I was concerned. And so he did, and a very grateful and subdued fellow he was. When I gave him his pay in New York, I said, 'Now you see what drinking can do for a man, and I hope you will never touch another drop.'

"'Nor will I, Captain,' he promised, but of course, as I was leaving, I saw him ducking into the alehouse with his fellows, out to lose their pay and their wits in one bout."

Of the evils of drink, Benjamin is much acquainted. His uncle Daniel has been a dissolute all his life, to the great sadness of his brother, Captain Nathan. Now and then Daniel tries to straighten up, and his brother is ever ready there to encourage him, but it always comes to naught. Though Benjamin is young to be a captain, he has been to sea since he was sixteen, so he has a vast store of experience upon which to draw, and like his father he allows no alcohol on his ship. There are sailors who find this proviso reason enough to stay away.

As he finished his story, we arrived at the orchard with the others and talked no more of travel. The trees were dripping heavy, dark fruit, and the morning passed quickly with the work. We had our lunch of bread, ham, and cheese at the outdoor table under the big maple in the side yard. Mother Briggs urged Olie to eat more, and he spoke of his adventure. His ship sprang a leak a week out and they pumped it for a fortnight, partly in foul weather that came up so fierce and so sudden, and the sailors so occupied with pumping, that the mainsail split before they could get it down. They limped into the Gulf of Mexico and got a tow to New Orleans, where the ship was pulled up for repairs. They spent ten days in port and every one was money lost. There was yellow fever in the city, so they stayed at the port and ate only the food they had in their ship provisions for fear of catching the disease. The rest of the journey was rough, a hurricane nearly capsized them and in the frenzy two sailors were lost overboard. "I always hate to write those letters," Olie said. "One was married just a month before we sailed."

Hannah, who had been listening closely with her eyes lowered, said softly, "And the two sailors were lost on June sixth."

Olie gazed at her—we all did—with surprise; then he calculated dates in his head and replied, "Yes, it was. How did you know?"

Hannah blinked rapidly and touched her brow with her fingertips. "I'm not sure."

"How strange," Father said, "that you should know the day."

"It came to me as you were speaking," Hannah said to Olie.

I glanced at Benjamin, who gazed upon my sister with an expression of profound sympathy.

"I guess it was somewhere in my head and you read it there," Olie said, patting her hand with his fingertips.

Hannah nodded, shy now that she had everyone's attention.

Mother Briggs busied herself pulling in empty plates. "It's a coincidence," she said, and the matter of my clairvoyant sister was thus closed. But I was thinking Hannah's premonition worked in reverse, it was a postmonition; she was mysteriously informed about an event already concluded. It was odd that she would announce the correct date, though perhaps it was not so difficult to figure, as she knew the date Olie sailed, the approximate time to New Orleans, the number of days there, etc., so she could, with a little calculation, arrive at a fairly accurate guess. She may have been counting the days of the trip from the start, mentally assigning dates to the chronology of Olie's story. It probably wasn't clairvoyance, just plain addition. But if this was so, why did she claim to have no idea how she arrived at the correct date?

We rose from the table and set out to the field to finish our labors. Just as Benjamin and I arrived at our overflowing baskets, he slipped his hand into his jacket pocket and produced a much-folded envelope. "Here's my reply," he said. "Read it when you get home. Let me know what you think of it tomorrow."

I took the envelope and unfolded it, my hand trembling with curiosity. He had written SALLIE across the front in his bold script. "I will," I said, depositing it in my apron pocket. Benjamin turned his attention to our baskets. "We'll take this one first," he said. Each of us took a handle and lifted the basket between us; then we began our descent to the house.

Birds at sea sing tunelessly,
But I know one who sings on key.
I long to steal her from the shore,
That she might sing alone for me,
And be my songbird evermore
Sailing on the sparkling sea.

I've read it a hundred times. My cousin wants to take me away! And oh, how willingly I would go.

I woke this morning with a smile on my face, knowing we would soon be off to Rose Cottage for jam making and there I would see my cousin and tell him what I think of his invitation. Well, not exactly an invitation; his plan is to "steal" me.

He wasn't at home when we arrived, but in the afternoon, when the whole house smelled of cooking fruit, he appeared at the kitchen door and looked in at us, highly amused. "Just as I suspected," he said. "Ladies in a jam."

I was putting wax seals on a squadron of jars; Hannah was pitting yet another battalion of plums at the table. Benjamin ducked away to the parlor, where we found him when we were done at last. There was casual talk on the most banal subjects. I did my best not to meet Benjamin's eyes, which I felt steadily upon me, because I knew if I did, I would be too flustered to speak coherently. It was very torture until Dinah came up from the kitchen, brushing down her apron with her palms, and announced that we must set out for home to serve the reverend his dinner. "I'll walk out with you," Benjamin said, and off we went, all four, but we had not gone far before Benjamin, who was walking strangely slow, took my hand and drew me into the shade of a chokeberry tree. Dinah hustled along without pause, but Hannah turned back and cast me a look of perturbation, though she didn't speak.

I couldn't think of her, though I knew I would have to, and soon. Benjamin bent down to pick a few wild phlox, which he then presented to me. "What did you think of my poor poem?" he said.

"Not poor at all. And an interesting proposition." I kept my eyes upon the sweet flowers, turning them between my fingers. They won't last, I thought.

"Would you like to go to sea, Sallie?" he said softly.

"With you?" I asked, ridiculously, and he nodded. "I wish I could," I said. "But how could I?"

In the annals of courting was there ever a more transparently leading question?

"You could if you were my wife."

"I didn't know you were thinking of marrying."

"Nor did I. The idea first came to me that evening, when you played . . ."

" 'In the Starlight,' " we said together.

"Yes, it was then. And it's been with me ever since."

"It was the same for me," I confessed. A pause came between us, as we each considered what had just been revealed.

"Then your answer is yes," he concluded.

I looked up from the flowers into my cousin's inquiring eyes. "It is," I said.

"Lord, how I love that song!" he exclaimed.

I felt my heart literally swelling in my chest, and for some reason our childhood rambles came to mind, and I recalled how we would wander off from the others and make up games or play out Bible stories and pirate adventures. The final line of the song danced in my head: *Let us wander gay and free.* Benjamin had taken my hand

and pressed it to his lips. "Sallie," he said softly. I felt the impress of his lips brightly on my fingers and my face flushed with heat.

"What adventures we will have," he said, leading me now to my father's house. We had walked a little way without speaking when he said, "I'll come and talk to the reverend in the morning. Do you think he'll be pleased?"

Father, I thought. Left with Hannah. "I think he will be," I said.

We walked on to the gate at the street, where Benjamin released my hand and turned to me. For a moment we looked into each other's eyes, both of us smiling. Benjamin brought his fingers to my chin, and lifting it, leaned down to kiss my lips.

Merciful heaven! That kiss. In school, sometimes, boys stole kisses, little pecks, and once a brutish boy I disliked amused himself by forcing a kiss upon me in the church cloakroom after service. But this kiss was something of an entirely different order. Part of the pleasure was knowing it to be the first of many. Benjamin's arm came about my waist, but loosely; he didn't press me in any way, only our lips lingered together so deliciously. I blush to recall it. At last we parted and I stood, my head swimming with delight, a look of stupefaction on my face, I'm sure.

"Well, Sallie," he said. "I guess you'd best go in."

"Yes," I said, sobering myself by lifting the latch on the gate. He stood watching me to the door, where I turned and blew him a kiss. Then he strolled off, humming to himself. "In the Starlight," of course.

I stepped into the hall to find my sister, her back against the table, her face in her raised hands, weeping as if her heart were breaking.

All is well, all is explained, all is forgiven, all is arranged. Hannah's tears, she confessed, were part joy and part sadness. Joy at my happiness and sadness to lose me, both outcomes she had intuited from watching Benjamin draw me aside on the road. In the morning Father conversed with Benjamin for only a few minutes before he called out the door, "Sallie, come here, this is wonderful news." I am betrothed. Not this fall, but the next, I will be a bride, and after that, evermore—Mrs. Sarah Cobb Briggs.

This evening we went to Rose Cottage. Benjamin and I were seated on the settee when my uncle came to us and took our hands in his own. "This is a love match," he observed. "I can see it in your faces."

I blushed and couldn't respond, but Benjamin said, "Like yours with Mother."

"May you be as happy and blessed," Uncle said, releasing our hands.

I was thinking that Uncle's love match was with his first wife, Maria, my aunt's sister, who died, though it can't be denied that he cares the world for Mother Briggs.

"Where will the wedding be held?" asked that lady.

"At home," I said. "As simple as possible."

"She's in luck there," Father observed. "The minister comes with the premises."

$\mathcal{T}$oday the weather was fine and in the evening Benjamin and I took a walk along the harbor. How boldly we walk, hand in hand, as we did sometimes as children, though it is very different now, this hand holding, entirely different. We talk of divers matters, having to do with the wedding and our plan for the honeymoon, which is to sail to the Mediterranean Sea. Some of the ports, says Benjamin, are rough, but beyond them the old Italian towns are bathed in sunlight and lemon trees perfume the air.

We fell silent a few moments, both of us watching a fishing schooner swooping into the harbor, and then, as we turned back, Benjamin said in a frank tone, "Sallie, I feel I must talk to you about Hannah." I thought he might mean her place in the wedding, or perhaps that he knew she admired him and might be jealous of his choice of sisters—though Benjamin and Hannah have never been that close, being twelve years apart in age. "What about Hannah?" I asked.

"My mother told me something in confidence, but it's so serious I fear it shouldn't be kept back, especially from you, so it's agreed between us that I may tell you."

"Your mother is very judgmental of Hannah," I said, without thinking, and regretting it at once.

"Is she? In what way?"

"She was impatient with her when Natie died, because she reacted so emotionally and wasn't consoled by religion."

"I didn't know that," he said. "But this has nothing to do with that. Quite by chance, Mother has learned that Hannah is corresponding with a man in Boston."

"How could that be?" I asked. "I pick up the mail..." And then I thought that I didn't always. Sometimes Hannah stopped at Dr. Allen's on the way back from the Academy. "What's the man's name? Do you know it?"

"Yes, it's Dr. Horace Chandler. Does that name mean anything to you?"

It did not.

"Mother went in the other day and noticed a letter on the stack waiting to be stamped, with the return address of Hannah Cobb. She asked Dr. Allen about it and he told her that there had been two or three letters from that address to Hannah in the last three months."

"What shocking behavior."

"Well, we don't know that yet. Hannah may have a perfectly good reason."

"I don't mean Hannah. I mean your mother and Dr. Allen."

"I'm sure they were thinking of her best interests. She's only thirteen, after all. And she's very vulnerable, I think. Very easily taken in."

"Isn't there a law against reading other people's mail?"

"No one opened the letters," Benjamin protested, making his

voice serious and patient. "They only read the postmarks, which is public information."

I knew he was right, but I felt put out that this secret correspondence, for which there was doubtless some reasonable explanation, should have been discovered by my future mother-in-law, whom I knew to be unsympathetic to my sister.

"You seem agitated by this, Sallie," Benjamin went on. "As well you might. What do you think we'd best do?"

"It's simple enough," I said coldly. "I'll ask her and she'll explain it."

We walked a few more steps in silence, and then Benjamin said, "Yes, I think that would be the best course."

Our charming walk was ruined, though we changed the subject to Olie's health, which is improved. It irked me that our first argument, for I saw it as that, should come over my sister and my aunt. It didn't bode well and I was cast down, but when we arrived at the house Benjamin took my hands and pressed his lips to my cheek, so tenderly that I felt reassured, and he said, "Sallie, in all matters of importance, I will always consult you, and you must speak your mind plainly. Others may have secrets, but let there be none between us."

How my heart lifted at these words. I looked up at him and said, "So let it be, my love."

And this made my darling smile, and with a last, brief kiss we parted friends, as we have always been and will be forever and ever, amen.

*I*nside the house was quiet and I felt descend upon me, after the delight of Benjamin's company, the burden he had put me under. Hannah was at school, Father at a vestry meeting, Dinah, doubtless, napping at the kitchen table as she does these days. Hastily I went up the stairs and stood at my sister's bedroom door. Though I knew she was not in the room, I rapped my knuckles against the wood, hesitating as the expected silence greeted me from the other side. I turned the knob and stepped inside.

How many times had I entered this room without a thought, to borrow a book, or a skein of wool from the basket, or to leave a message on the writing table, advising Hannah of a meeting or an errand to be done? But now I stood in the doorway feeling like a criminal, angry at myself for so willingly taking on the role of spy, a role I'd chosen myself and which I evidently required as preparation for the direct confrontation to come.

The room was orderly, as it always was; the counterpane neatly spread, the washstand clean, the cloth folded over the edge of the bowl. The surface of the writing table was clear, but for the pen in its stand, the inkwell, and the blue leather book with the gold pineapple embossed on the cover—like mine that is green—in which Hannah writes her poems. She has often read to me from this book. The poems are on natural themes, the seasons, the beauty of the woods or the sea. They are odd, which they would be given Hannah's peculiar view of the world. Much circling of death, also great value attached to liberty. There's a dark romantic in my sister. When we read *Jane Eyre* together, she was sick for Rochester and believed that he was a real man. In Jane she had no interest.

Poor Father, I thought. He gave us each these books to write in daily, as he does, an accounting of our spiritual progress. Hannah fills hers with poems and in mine we have this incessant catalog of my doings. How disappointed he would be if he knew what all our scribbling was about.

Father says Hannah reads too many novels and not enough Bible, in which, he maintains, all the best stories are to be found. There on Hannah's bookshelf was her small collection of fiction, the ones she borrowed first and then purchased with her allowance: Mr. Scott, Mr. Dickens, Mrs. Stowe, Mr. Hawthorne, Mrs. Gaskell, the Misses Brontë, and the poems of Mr. Poe, Lord Tennyson, Mrs. Browning, and Miss Rossetti. On the chest of drawers beneath the window was the sewing basket, on the bedside table, a book—*The Moorland Cottage*. Nothing hinted at anything amiss in my sister's small territory.

In search of some evidence of her recent preoccupations, I decided to have a look at the last pages of her poetry book. I opened it from the back. Hannah writes draft after draft, going over them with changes until the lines are nearly indecipherable. Then she writes a final version. I read one titled "Dream Light," much scribbled upon, but the final version was copied out neatly.

> *In the dream of the sun-struck meadow,*
> *From whence flows the warm daylight?*
> *How is it we wake to a moonlit room,*
> *And the meadow lost from sight?*
>
> *If a sun inside lights up the mind*
> *When the dream lit day grows dark,*
> *And we wander in the gloom unkind,*
> *Where dies that spark?*

I turned to the last page and read:

> *Who holds the light that penetrates*
> *The dark above the stair,*
> *Must have the heart to celebrate*
> *The spirit lingering there.*

This made only thin and unpleasant sense to me. The preceding page was covered in a scrawl that unnerved me, as it was unreadable, not English; though some of the letters were Arabic, others were obscure. What could it mean? Then, on an impulse, I held the book by its spine and fanned the pages. A folded page of newsprint fluttered to the desk.

It was a clipping, but from what source wasn't clear. Everything but the section title MESSAGES had been cut away. The heading read "Received by Mercy Dale," and the text was as follows:

Don't believe the advice you've been given, but follow your heart, as it is always in my keeping and will not lead you astray, your loving husband, David.

A second message followed:

I am content here and all is well with me. I see our dear parents every day and they send blessings to you. Have no fear that you are alone in this sad time. We rejoice whene'er we speak of you and think of happy times together at Mill Creek. With you always, your devoted brother.

Why had my sister clipped and kept this article and none other? I truly dreaded our confrontation, but that we must have it was borne in upon me by this scrap of print and the strange writing in her book. I folded the paper and stuck it back into the book carelessly. I wouldn't bring it up if there were a way around it. How much better if I hadn't come snooping among her things. Shamed, anxious, entirely flummoxed, I left her room.

I said nothing to Hannah that evening, only watched her at dinner, careful not to stare, yet on the alert for anything that might hint at her true state. She talked about the songfest the students are planning for the end of the session, which Mrs. Tabor has kindly invited me to join. I attempted to express sufficient enthusiasm for this invitation, and indeed these singing rounds are great fun, but I was distracted and fearful of overdoing my responses. Hannah was natural, but I felt perfectly false.

I had resolved that our conversation should take place outdoors. Today was again bright and cool, pleasant in all its aspects and unlikely to incline any but the most obdurate heart to gloom. Occasionally, if I'm shopping in town, I stop by the school to walk home with Hannah, and it was my plan to meet her in this way. She came out of the schoolhouse in a group, chatting with Amy Wemberly, and she showed no surprise to find me waiting there. Farewells were said to Amy and we set off for home. Hannah, taking a package from my basket to relieve me of the weight, asked, "What's in it?"

"A capon," I said.

"Oh," she said. She settled the package in her arms like a babe. "Poor fellow."

I smiled, amused by her concern for the bird, and I thought that really nothing could be more normal, more companionable, than strolling through the town with my sister. She was looking particularly well, her cheeks lightly flushed, her gray eyes, which can sometimes be so dark, so brooding, now were clear and light. She'd wrestled her wild hair into a single braid but it had loosened and stray tendrils played about her neck and forehead. "How was school?" I asked.

"Mr. Finley lectured us on the subject of his rock collection."

"Oh, yes," I said. "I do recall Mr. Finley's rocks."

We could have gone on like this. I felt no desire to bring her to the subject of her correspondence with Dr. Chandler, though that name was burning in my brain, along with the clear consciousness that when I spoke it, my relations with my sister would be seriously altered, possibly forever. I reminded myself of the articles, the strange writing, and most of all, of Benjamin's conviction that the problem of Hannah was best addressed by me.

And so I addressed it. We were passing the Universalist Church, which Father calls "the Univices," and we both glanced up at the screech of a hawk circling near the tower. "Dearest," I said, as we resumed our walk. "I have to ask you about something."

"It sounds like something serious," she said.

"It is. It's that. Well. It's been noticed that you are corresponding with a Dr. Chandler in Boston."

"Noticed by whom?" she asked calmly.

I hesitated. Was I compelled to keep secret the name of the instigator of this conversation? "Mother Briggs," I said.

Her lips compressed in a smirk; her eyelids lowered, then flashed open wide. "She's lying," she said.

This possibility hadn't occurred to me, and for a moment I turned it this way and that in my mind, but unlikelihood remained its distinctive feature. "Why would she do that?" I asked.

"She dislikes me. She blames me for Natie's death."

"Surely not," I protested.

"She made it up to hurt me. Have you told anyone else? Please tell me you haven't told Father this libel."

"No, I haven't. I came straight to you. But evidently Dr. Allen has seen the letters as well. I don't think he would lie about the mails."

She pressed her upper teeth into her lip, her head bowed, the picture of guilt in search of an escape.

"Hannah?" I said.

"Everyone in this town is so small-minded and mean. I'm suffocating here. I can't breathe."

"That's not true," I countered. "Your family cares for you very much."

"As long as I'm docile, as long as I sit through Father's sermons without protest."

"Why should you protest?"

She was silent. At the turn toward the house we both stopped, still without speaking. "Let's walk to the harbor," I suggested.

She nodded and we went on. "It seems to me you've something burdening your mind," I said. "You must know that you'll find no more sympathetic listener than me."

Again she nodded. We walked out Harbor Lane, where the workers have wrapped the hotel in scaffolding, adding a third floor. The breeze off the water was fresh and brisk enough to make me wish I'd brought my shawl. Then my sister sent an icy dart to my heart.

"Mother talks to me," she said.

"In dreams," I suggested hopefully.

"In spirit," she said. "I see her."

"Oh," I said.

"And others."

"Others?"

"People who are with her. William and Harvey are there."

William and Harvey were our brothers who died before we were born. "Where do you see them?" I asked.

"In the spirit world. They speak to me too."

"Often?"

"Not so often. I have to concentrate very hard to hear them."

"I see," I said.

"But Mother is with me often."

I looked out at the sun, still high enough to wash a pinkish light over a fishing schooner just setting out, its triangular sails churning up the masts. A charge of pity and fear ran through me and I was unable to speak. What could I say that might restore my sister, whom I loved with my whole heart, to sweet reason? She was of a fanciful nature, but she wasn't a liar, at least not a good one; her effort to discredit Mother Briggs had folded almost at once. What tack should I take to relieve her of these delusions, which had evidently taken her over almost entirely? Sensing my hesitation, she spoke.

"I have a gift," she said. "It's like a gift for music or painting. I can't just ignore it. I can't make it go away because other people don't like it."

"Is that what Dr. Chandler says?" I asked, feigning an interest I hardly felt.

She gave me a quick, hard look. So Dr. Chandler could be admitted to without a fight. "He does say that. But I didn't need him to tell me."

"How did you come to be in touch with him?"

Here the glance was furtive. "I read an advertisement in the New Bedford paper. He prints a journal; it's called *Spiritual Condolence*, and I was curious about it, so I wrote to him. Well, his name wasn't in the advertisement. I wrote to the journal."

"To offer your mediumistic services," I suggested. "Is that the right word?"

"No, I didn't do that. Not at first. I just inquired about the journal, about how it came to be."

"And Dr. Chandler wrote back at once."

She nodded. Something stronger than anger was closing my throat, not at my sister, but at this charlatan in Boston.

"Oh, Sallie." Hannah sighed. "It's such a relief to tell you. I send in messages that I receive, that I don't always understand, because they're not really for me, and he puts them in the journal."

So my sister was Mercy Dale.

I took her arm in mine. We'd come to the end of the promontory and stood gazing out at the outer harbor. "I know everyone here thinks there's something wrong with me," she said. "And Father is so adamant against those who believe . . . who believe as I do. He wants us to keep our minds and efforts always directed upon the living, and there's nothing wrong with that, but why should we turn our backs on those we have known, those we have loved, who are only waiting for us to listen to be heard?"

"What sorts of things does Mother tell you?" I asked, to show my goodwill.

"She's pleased about your engagement."

"That's a blessing," I said.

"She's sad that she can't reach Father."

It's difficult to describe my feelings at these tender messages, which might as well have been nursery rhymes, for all the import of them. So the dead were as banal as the living, I thought.

"She is happy in the place where they are," Hannah concluded. Still holding her by the arm, I turned away from the harbor, and she came along without comment. As we entered Allen Street, she said sadly, "Even you don't believe me."

"I believe you miss our mother very much and wish she was still with us. And I share that wish."

"So you think my seeing her is just wishful thinking."

"If you like."

"Well," she said lightly. "It doesn't matter, Sallie. There are people who do believe me. Quite a few of them in fact."

"Not just Dr. Chandler," I said.

"Many of them are ladies of excellent reputation and good society in Boston. No one makes a fuss there and my gift may provide great solace to many."

Again I was at a loss for words.

"Are you going to tell Father?" she asked.

We had come to our house and I lifted the latch of the gate. "I don't know, darling," I said. "I don't know what to do. I'm vexed past reason at you for being so credulous."

She stepped back, as if struck. "I'm not credulous. I just can't pretend I don't see what I see. It's cruel to try to stop me. If you tell Father, Sallie, I don't know what he'll do."

"How can I keep such goings-on a secret, these letters to a man you know nothing about, these publications! Does he know your age? No, I thought not. How can I keep this from Father, who is responsible for you to God and man alike?"

"If I promise to give up writing to Dr. Chandler, will you not tell him?"

I felt I had been reduced to accepting a scurrilous deal in order to protect my sister from herself, and from Dr. Chandler, whoever he was. "That would be a start," I said. "Yes. If you promise to cease this correspondence, I won't tell Father what you have told me."

"I may as well, then," she said wearily. "If you do tell him, he'll make me stop. He'll snatch the letters from the box and lock me in my room, so I may as well give in."

And with that agreement, unsatisfactory as it was, we went into the house.

There was such a fierce storm last evening, it seemed the heavens were in a rage. The thunder rolled, the lightning flashed in jagged bolts, and the rain poured down all at once as if a tub had been turned over. The west wind drove it in horizontal sheets. Father, Hannah, and I sat in the parlor, he reading, we pretending to embroider, and at each boom of thunder my sister raised her eyes and lifted her needle with a faint smile.

In the morning, Benjamin came calling, and we walked out to the graveyard to refresh the flowers on the markers of the Briggs and Cobb families. Of course he wanted to know what I'd learned from Hannah, but, perhaps for shame, I felt unwilling to say more than that she had agreed to cease all correspondence with the gentleman from Boston. "Well, what manner of correspondence was it?" he asked frankly.

"I'm not at liberty to say," I replied. "Her promise that it would stop was very clear and final. I think we need worry no more about the subject."

"Sallie," he said, laying his hand on my arm as we arrived at the grave. "You're so serious. Of course I won't press you."

I smiled. "I appreciate that," I said. "I just can't say more, not yet."

Benjamin took up the old bouquets much pummeled by the storm. The stone vases were full of rainwater, so we had only to replace the flowers and we were done. At Mother's marker, I pulled a few weeds that had cropped up among the columbine I planted there some years ago, which has done well there, being shade tolerant. The blooms are fading now, but the plants are healthy. Then Benjamin and I stepped back and gazed at the grave that contains the remains of my mother and the two boys I never knew. I couldn't help thinking of Hannah's remark, that Mother was pleased about my engagement. Well, she would have been, had she lived. Benjamin remembers her well; he was eighteen when she died and she was fond of him. He had his heart set on following the sea and she teasingly called him "shipmate," and "sailor boy." As if he read my thoughts, Benjamin said, "Your mother was light at heart. She always brightened a room when she came in."

"She did," I agreed. "When she could no longer leave her bed, she claimed her illness was a grand opportunity to read frivolous novels." Whereas, I thought, Mother Briggs will still be chewing over the Bible at death's door.

"Well," he said, "I wish she was with us now."

And oh, I did too. I need my dear mother to tell me what to do about my sister.

"By their fruits, ye shall know them." That was a favorite saying of Mother's, especially when her children were idle. She took her religion to be a practice, not a test, and she was an active, not a submissive, Christian. She wanted her children to be alive to the possibilities of life, to show in our actions our moral engagement with our fellows. And, of course, we were her fruits and by us she would be known; I do think that was implied in her remark. I've been thinking of her so much today, though, unlike my sister, I haven't seen her lurking about the house. Does she watch over us here? Does Father believe that? After her death he said, "She will always be with us." Presumably he meant in our memories and in our hearts.

I confess that there is a shred of jealousy in my conflict with my sister. Why wouldn't Mother show herself to me, if she could? That is a thought not worth pursuing.

But what I've been thinking about Mother is how she would feel, and what she would say, if she were here to guide Hannah past this crisis in her young life. She never gave orders or forbade actions, unless we were rude in public, which merited a frank rebuke. She had a way of looking at you with sympathy and understanding and hope and then asking the exact question that placed the matter in a clear moral light. The answer came of its own accord, and one cheerfully mended one's ways.

Have I done this with Hannah? Have I asked her the right question, the one that will bring her back to me?

I have not.

Last night I woke from a frightening dream. Benjamin and I were running through a forest, running away from something, an animal or a man. We held hands, but the ground was uneven and I tripped, losing his grip. When I got to my feet, I found he had gone ahead without me. I followed, but the space between us grew wider and wider and I could hear the pursuer, whatever he/it was, coming closer. There was a harsh sound, very close to my ear, a snarl of rage, and then I woke.

I lay still in the bed, waiting for my heart to slow, and wondering, in a dreamy sort of way, why Benjamin hadn't waited for me. Gradually I became aware of an odd sound in the real world, a kind of scratching, like nails against wood. It was soft, barely audible, but insistent. I thought it might be a mouse nibbling inside the wall. I closed my eyes, waiting for the embrace of Morpheus, but the scratching distracted me. I listened and listened; was it in the hall? At last I decided to get up and investigate. I lit the candle, crossed to the door, and looked into the hall. A thin, milky light spilled across the floor from beneath Hannah's door. She was still awake.

The sound paused, then resumed, paused again. I was barefoot and the floorboards were chilly under my feet. I stepped along quickly to her door. The scratching took up again. What was she doing? "Hannah," I said softly, laying my palm against the door panel. The latch was up and the door drifted open before me, revealing bit by bit a nightmare far worse than the one I'd just escaped. Would that it had been a dream.

Hannah was seated at her writing table, where the lamp burned brightly, with a pen in her hand and a page before her. Strangely, her body leaned away from the table, supported by her right arm propped rigidly against the seat of her chair. Her head was thrown back as if she had been struck, her loosened hair tumbled past her shoulders, her mouth was agape, and her eyes, unnaturally wide, fixed on a corner of the ceiling. The muscles of her face were so strained and tense she was hardly recognizable. Her left hand, holding the pen, scribbled hurriedly, moving from right to left on the page, seemingly without her knowledge or her will.

I had the sense that I was entering the equivalent of a gale at sea. Nothing moved, save that demonic hand. My skin tingled the way it does when the barometer drops suddenly and those with old injuries claim to feel them anew. "Hannah," I said again, firmly this time, but she gave no evidence of hearing me. I approached—what else could I do?—and though I stood looking down at the writing spiraling from the pen, I couldn't read it. It was that same cryptic language I'd seen in her journal. I looked at her face, which was turned away from the light, as if to keep as far away as possible from the writing hand. Her eyes were utterly vacant, flat, and unmoving as the false eyes in a china doll.

I brought my palm down hard upon the writing hand. There was no resistance, her fingers sprawled. Hannah screamed, rose from the chair, and collapsed in my arms. I heard Father's feet hit the floor in his bedroom, and then his hurried steps coming toward us in the hall.

Documents

Concerning the Recovery of the Brig *Mary Celeste*,
Found Derelict East of the Azores on December 4, 1872

Cable: Gibraltar, December 13, 1872
To: Board of Underwriters, New York
> BRIG MARY CELESTE HERE DERELICT IMPORTANT SEND
> POWER ATTORNEY TO CLAIM HER FROM ADMIRALTY
> COURT
> HORATIO J. SPRAGUE

Cable: New York, December 13, 1872
To: Horatio J. Sprague, United States Consul at Gibraltar
> PROTECT BRIG MARY CELESTE WANT VOYAGE
> PERFORMED
> OGDEN

Cable: Gibraltar, December 14, 1872
To: Parker, New York
> FOUND FOURTH AND BROUGHT HERE MARY CELESTE
> ABANDONED SEAWORTHY ADMIRALTY IMPOST NOTIFY
> ALL PARTIES TELEGRAPH OFFER OF SALVAGE
> MOREHOUSE

New York Times—Dateline Gibraltar
December 14, 1872

The brig *Mary Celeste* is in the possession of the Admiralty Court.

New Bedford Evening Standard—Marine Intelligence
December 21, 1872

Brig *Mary Celeste*, from New York Nov. 17 for Genoa, is reported by cable as having been picked up derelict and towed into Gibraltar 16th inst. She was commanded by Capt. Benjamin Briggs, of Marion, who had his wife and child with him, and much anxiety is felt for their safety.

The Boston Post
February 24, 1873

It is now believed that the fine brig *Mary Celeste*, of about 236 tons, commanded by Capt. Benjamin Briggs of Marion, Mass., was seized by pirates in the latter part of November, and that, after murdering the Captain, his wife, child, and the officers, the vessel was abandoned near the western Islands, where the miscreants are supposed to have landed. The brig left New York on the 17th of November for Genoa, with a cargo of alcohol, and is said to have had a crew consisting mostly of foreigners. The theory now is that some of the men probably obtained access to the cargo, and were thus stimulated to the desperate deed.

The *Mary Celeste* was fallen in with by the British brig *Dei Gratia*, Capt. Morehouse, who left New York about the middle of November. The hull of the *Celeste* was found in good condition, and safely towed into Gibraltar, where she has since remained. The confusion in which many things were found on board (including ladies' apparel, &c.,) led, with other circumstances, to suspicion of wrong and outrage, which has by no means died out. One of the latest letters from Gibraltar received in Boston says: The Vice Admiralty Court sat yesterday and will sit again to-morrow. The cargo of the brig has been claimed, and to-morrow the vessel will be claimed.

The general opinion is that there has been foul play on board, as spots of blood on the blade of a sword, in the cabin, and on the rails, with a sharp cut on the wood, indicate force or violence having been used, but how or by whom is the question. Soon after the vessel was picked up, it was considered possible that a collision might have taken place. Had this been the case, and the brig's officers and crew saved, they would have been landed long ere this. We trust that if any of New-England's shipmasters can give any information or hint of strange boats or seamen landing at any of the islands during the past ninety days, that they will see the importance thereof.

The Boston Journal
March 15, 1873

The brig *Mary Celeste*, found deserted at sea and taken into Gibraltar, as before mentioned, has been libeled and a suit commenced in the United States District Court in this city, the libel alleging that the vessel had obtained American registry by fraud. It has recently been stated that there are strong suspicions that her desertion at sea was done to defraud the insurance companies. Nothing is known as to the fate of her crew. And the whole affair is involved in mystery.

Letter: April 4, 1873

To: Department of State, Washington, D.C.

I beg to enclose a copy of a communication which I have this day received from Prussia, asking for information regarding some of the missing crew of the derelict *Mary Celeste*. It is somewhat gratifying to learn three out of the five men composing the crew of the *Mary Celeste* were known to the writer of that communication as being peaceable and first-class sailors, as it further diminishes the probability that any violence was committed on board of this vessel by her crew.

Horatio J. Sprague, United States Consul at Gibraltar

Letter Enclosure

March 21, 1873

INVENTORY of the contents of a desk found on board the American Brig *Mary Celeste* of New York, by the Marshal of the Vice Admiralty Court of Gibraltar, and delivered to me this day, by the said Marshal; the said desk is supposed to belong to Captain B. S. Briggs, the missing Master.

A desk containing: Twenty one letters; an account book; a pocket-book; a ruler; two pieces of sealing wax; four United States postal stamps; a pencil; a paper cover containing sundry papers, envelopes and accounts; wafers; a case of leads; three receipts signed by J. H. Winchester & Co., New York, viz: for $1,500 dated 3rd October 1872, for $500 dated 16th October 1872; for $1,600 dated 22nd October 1872

Consulate of the United States of America,
Gibraltar March 21, 1873

(Signed) *Horatio J. Sprague, U. S. C*

An African Adventure

S.S. Mayumba, *1881*

A SUMMONS

One wondered whether the colonies were really worth the price we had to pay.

ARTHUR CONAN DOYLE

A loud rap at the house door startled the young doctor, who was carefully embellishing architectural curlicues in the margins of a page half-filled with his own neat cursive script. As there was no one but himself to answer, he crossed the small parlor in three steps and pulled the door open wide. There he found a thin, bedraggled boy, dressed in a dark-green woolen jacket bearing some resemblance to a uniform and some to a jockey's coat, stovepipe pants that ended well above his bare, scrawny ankles, and dusty brown boots with the nail heads exposed around the soles. In his gloved left hand he held out a yellow envelope. "Dr. Doyle, innit?" he inquired.

"So it is, my boy," said the doctor, taking the envelope. It was a telegram. The doctor produced a penny from his coat pocket and pressed it on the boy, who, taking the coin without a word, dashed off down the street.

A telegram. Was it the longed-for hospital appointment? Was it evil news concerning his poor father? The doctor carried the envelope back to his writing desk, where the half-finished page rebuked him. Ignoring it, he tore open the flap and drew out the brief message.

Here was news. The African Steam Navigation Company was cordially responding to his now ancient and nearly forgotten query with orders for Dr. Conan Doyle to proceed at once to Liverpool and there take medical charge of the steamer *Mayumba*, bound for Madeira and the West Coast of Africa.

Africa. He glanced down at the page he had yet to finish, a tale of the American West, a place he had visited only in his imagination, or, more correctly, in the imagination of Bret Harte, whose adventure stories had brightened many a gloomy hour of his youth. Africa meant Stanley and Livingstone, Victoria Falls, jungles screaming with monkeys, villages populated by naked cannibals, so black they could not be seen in the dark and the whites of their eyes disembodied in the humid night air accosted the unwary. As ship's surgeon, he was unlikely to see much beyond the coast; the interior of the continent would be closed to him. The experience would be geographically speaking the opposite of his previous post on the Arctic whaler *Hope*, during which he had clubbed seals and gone out with the harpooner in the boat, holding fast to the rope beneath the mountainous side of a right whale. The blue sky, the white gleam of the drift ice, the endless daylight, the intoxicating air—for seven months every moment had been filled with wonders, and the work so constant and challenging that in none of those moments had he been idle or bored.

The steamer *Mayumba* would be an adventure of a different order, his function an official one, doubtless requiring a coat of blue serge, gilt buttons, white duck trousers, and shoes that would slip on the decks and take on water when the ship did. The captain wouldn't encourage him to participate in the business of the voyage, which was purely the transport of goods and passengers to Africa, discharging them, taking on new goods and passengers, and turning the prow for home. His work would be among and at the behest of these passengers, and he was unlikely to visit the forecastle unless a man was dying there. Instead of shifting ice and sparkling skies, there would be beaches, rivers, and tropical jungles. The doctor's brain buzzed pleasantly over the contrast between his seagoing excursions, the first to the white world, where men pursued and slaughtered beasts as big as houses, the next to the dark continent, on a mission to administer quinine and morphine to various valiant servants and civilizers of the Empire.

In a week he was in Liverpool, lining up his books on the narrow shelf in his berth. Compared to the cramped and heavily populated whaler, the *Mayumba* was enormous, with space for twenty passengers and two saloons; the passengers' saloon was as ponderously furnished as a hotel lobby. But unlike the *Hope*, she was dirty. Rust had a grip on her rails and spars, the skylights were streaked, and the upholstery faded and dingy.

The passengers would equally have benefited by a sprucing up. Among them were a parson named Fairfax, his wife, and two cadaverous boys of eight and ten, bound for Lagos; a pretty brunette, Miss Fox, not in her first youth, possessed of an educated air and an oversize bonnet, going out to meet her father in Sierra Leone; a Scottish crone, forever nameless, with bad lungs and a face like an ailing horse; two Negro tradesmen, dressed showily in the worst possible taste and escorted to the gangway by a phalanx of evil-smelling prostitutes; a British Negress with the manners of a she-wolf, who was betrothed to a missionary in the interior; and finally an Englishwoman, Mrs. Rowbotham, lively, cheerful, neatly dressed, and immediately flirtatious upon meeting the doctor as she was passing out of the saloon.

The captain, Duncan Henderson Wallace, a small man, bald on top with a flowing, well-tended white beard that thrust out from his face suggesting the prominent chin beneath, promised to be good company. He moved gracefully, without fuss, inside a force field of authority. He greeted the doctor with a firm handshake and a bright eye that ran over his new colleague appreciatively, as if he'd seldom seen such a fine figure of a man, and indeed, the doctor was several inches taller and stones heavier than his commander. "Come and have a brandy in my office," said Captain Wallace. "First time to Africa, is it?"

"It is," said the doctor, following the captain into his private quarters, which were cleaner than the rest of the ship, and neatly appointed. In the conversation that followed, Doyle learned Mrs. Rowbotham was en route to her husband in Sierra Leone, and the querulous Negress was some madman's idea of a desirable wife.

"I've had Parson Fairfax and his family before," Wallace continued. "They go out once a year for six weeks, then back at the missionary work. It's killing the wife, but she doesn't complain."

"The boys don't look fit for much either," the doctor observed.

"It's the beastly climate. If they left those boys in Edinburgh, or better yet, Dundee, they'd fatten up in no time. But you'll see, as we go on."

"And we sail?"

"At dawn. It may be rough going this time of year."

In the morning the weather was fine, but it deteriorated as the *Mayumba* made her way down the Mersey. At Holyhead there was such a gale blowing they had to put in for the night. The next day, in rough weather, they made for the Irish Sea, pitching and rolling, plowing through a fog thick as cream. The lighthouse beam was only a dull sheeny patch in the white sheet off the starboard bow. The crew labored earnestly, each wrapped in a white shroud that kept him from seeing his mates. Nor did conditions improve on the open water.

All the passengers were seasick. The doctor ran from one cabin to the next, dispensing blue bowls, and when the bowls ran out, buckets, to grateful ladies and gentlemen whose complexions, as they clung to their bedsteads or bent over their bowls, were distinctly green, except for the Negroes, who were gray. The steward arranged for the orderly rotation of bowls and buckets, which it was the doctor's business to supervise. The waves tossed the ship up and then pounded her down and the seas swirled across the decks. The sailors were forever hurtling fore and aft, the captain and his mate washed in and out through the companionway, relieving each other on the deck. As the second day passed exactly as the first, Dr. Doyle recalled the captain's weather prediction. The fog cleared off, and they could see the waves crashing over the prow.

The third day was worse. The aft cabin flooded and the only sound belowdecks was the moaning of the passengers. Occasionally retching could be heard, though most had emptied their stomachs completely by then. The doctor could do little to be of help, so he sat at his desk reading Macaulay, those beautiful sentences, his bare feet ankle deep in the briny water on the floor. The fourth day was like the third.

"But are we making any progress?" cried Parson Fairfax when the doctor looked in on him and his family. The boys were flat on their backs like two skeletons, their mouths agape, and the wife sat clinging to the bedstead, her hair loose over her shoulders, emitting a sharp groan with each lurch of the ship.

"Of course we are," the doctor assured him. "This is a steamer. We make progress no matter the weather. Make sure those boys take some limewater, whether they ask for it or not," he advised, going out the door.

In the officers' mess he found the mate, a taciturn man, but pleasant to his fellow officers. He was drinking coffee, his eyelids heavy as he gazed into the cup he held between his hands. There was no putting it down on the table, where it would be swiftly transported to the opposite side when the ship rolled. He glanced at the doctor, weaving in at the door. "Join me, Doyle," he said. "There's some gin, if you care for it."

"Just coffee," the doctor said, pouring it out from the pot, which was lodged in a tray screwed down to the counter. He had put on his shoes to visit the passengers and his feet squished as he took a seat at the table.

"And how are your ladies and gentlemen bearing up?"

"As best they can," Doyle affirmed, "under the circumstances. The parson fears we are making no progress."

"Does he?" said the mate.

"I think he's only frightened."

"Well, it's foul going, that's sure. But we're going all the same."

"Yes, of course." The doctor smiled at the foolishness of the parson.

"It's lucky for them you've a seagoing stomach. Our last doctor was worse off than his patients in bad weather."

"It's not my first time at sea."

"Is it not?"

"I was ship's surgeon on the whaler *Hope*, under Captain John Gray."

"A whaler," said the mate. "Now there's sailing. You've no retching passengers on a whaler."

"I liked the life," the doctor said simply. He would have told how Captain Gray had offered his doughty medical officer double duty as surgeon and harpooner on his next voyage, but the mate drained his cup and pushed back his chair. "I'm up, sir," he said. "I believe we are in for a wild run for our money tonight, but by morning, if we don't founder, we may find smooth sailing. The Bay of Biscay is a hellion, but by God she moves you, she moves you."

The mate's prediction proved true. In the night, it was as if they had entered a mountain range made of water. The doctor, aghast at what he saw through his porthole, made up his mind to go on deck. The ship lurched and trembled like a living thing and he held tightly to the handgrips as he came up. There he saw a sight that made him gasp for breath. In every direction great walls of black water, heavily veined with white, loomed so high they blocked the sky. The ship, which had seemed large, was here revealed to be a child's toy. There was a continual rush of phosphorescent sea across the decks, hip-deep liquid green flames, which cast upon the pale faces of the sailors manning the pumps an eerie, otherworldly pallor.

From somewhere a voice came to him like something from the

Bible, clear, firm, distinct, a voice from the fire. "Go in, you fool," it commanded. "Go in." The doctor looked about and saw that it was the captain, waving one hand at him from the quarterdeck, holding on to the rail for dear life with the other.

Doyle ducked back into the companion and sloshed off to his cabin. He was as soaked as if he'd actually dived into the sea. He stripped off his clothes, draped them around his furnishings, and then, strangely exhausted by what he had seen, he fell into the bed and was instantly asleep.

How changeable is life at sea. When next the doctor opened his eyes, a warm beam of sunlight gleamed across his outstretched hand. Nothing in the room was moving up, down, or sideways, and there was a hum, as of a man gently snoring, coming from belowdecks. When he rose from his bed, the water he stepped into barely covered his foot. Outside his cabin door, he heard cheerful voices, then the slap and slop of a mop, and the roll of the bucket moving down the passageway. He found a dry shirt and trousers. He had no choice but to put on the sodden jacket, as he owned no other. He opened his door to find the steward grinning at him. "As you're up, sir, I'll just pass in with the mop."

"And welcome you are, wherever you show yourself this morning, sir, I don't doubt," said the doctor.

"It's true. I've found none to complain at the sight of me, would it were ever so."

The doctor passed out, anxious to be on deck, to see that great roaring bull that had bellowed and threatened in the night transformed into a willing beast of burden.

All hands were in good cheer; full steam was ahead. "Good morning, sir," called the captain from his post on the quarterdeck. "Will you come up?"

The air was delicious, charged after the storm with a luminous glamour that made even the old *Mayumba* sparkle. The decks were marvelously, miraculously dry. "I will tell you, Doctor," Wallace said, as the two men surveyed the scene below them, "there were moments last night when I thought we would not meet again."

"It was a furious sea."

Wallace gave his medical expert a close look, pulling down the corners of his mouth, as if something provoked or displeased him. "I expect our passengers are a chastened lot, and a hungry one," he observed.

"Yes, I heard a great hubbub in their saloon."

The sound of four bells was accompanied by the appearance of the mate, smiling up at them from the foot of the ladder. "I've an appetite myself," said Wallace. "Have you breakfasted?"

"I have not."

And so the two men went down to the officers' mess, where, for the first time since leaving land, a hot breakfast was laid out for them.

A CONVERSATION WITH THE CAPTAIN

One ship which I call to mind now had the reputation of killing somebody every voyage she made.

JOSEPH CONRAD

Like mushrooms after a rain, the passengers commenced popping up everywhere. They paraded on the saloon deck, converged in the saloon and in their dining room. Passing one another on their shipboard excursions, they chattered volubly in the passageway. In the afternoon, cards were broken out and the doctor joined his charges for a game of whist. All the hatches were open, the air was fresh, and one could sit at the table with a glass of wine or a brandy with no need to hold tightly to the stem. The day passed pleasantly and in the evening Dr. Doyle took his dinner with the officers. Over brandy, Captain Wallace entertained him with stories of the sights afforded the tourist on the Dark Continent. He told of native tribes who offered human sacrifice to alligators, which devilish creatures swarmed the shore when they knew their tribute was due. One could hear, he said chillingly, the screams of the victims for miles down the river. On another occasion, the captain had seen a human skull protruding from a giant anthill, a fate, he learned, reserved by one tribe for its enemies in another. White men couldn't survive for long in Africa, he opined. Its malignancy infected their souls, no matter how much liquor they took, and they took a lot.

Doyle, startled by these horrors, spoke of the more wholesome oddities of the Arctic, of a captain who, seeing it was light for twenty-four hours a day, decided to change day for night, and of the massive white bears, stretched out full length on their stomachs, wrapping their great paws around an ice hole, waiting patiently for a seal to come up for a breath of air, and when it did—whack, lunch was served.

"Clever creatures," chuckled Wallace, amused by this image.

At length the two men, in companionable spirits, agreed to take a turn on the quarterdeck, where passengers were strictly forbidden to roam. Wallace swept a sharp eye over his vessel, to the bow, the waist, the strolling passengers on the saloon deck, and at last, to the horizon, which was shrouded in a damp mist. The fresh air of the morning had given way to an oppressive humidity and the doctor would have shed his coat had he not thought it an impropriety to do so. As they contemplated the lazily lapping waves, the dog watch went down and the first watch came on, saluting their fellows as they passed with mild humor. "Wasn't Mither right?" said one cheerily. "Sell the farm and go to sea."

"They'll sleep tonight," Wallace observed. "And dry for a change."

"Was the fo'c'sle flooded?" asked the doctor.

"Was it, indeed? Their beds were awash and the cook got up the stove, so it was a veritable steam bath, I'm told, and they could hardly find their way about their slops."

"They are stalwart fellows," Doyle opined.

Again, Wallace fixed upon his medical officer a stern look. Then he turned away and positioned himself at the rail, gazing out over the water as it streamed away behind them. Dr. Doyle, unflustered, joined him there.

"I say, what's that?" said the captain, pointing to the air off the starboard bow.

The doctor followed the line indicated by the captain's raised arm. "I don't see anything," he said.

"Don't you?" Wallace replied. "Look again."

Obediently, the doctor surveyed the sea. It was dark, and the heavy mist confused him, but he thought he did see something, a triangle of brighter white than the mist. He saw it, then it was gone, then he saw it again. "What is it?" he asked.

"It's a ship," Wallace replied.

"Is it? Is it coming our way?"

The captain had his binoculars out and for several moments he stood at the rail peering through the glasses. The doctor could only try to see, unassisted, what his commander saw, but he made nothing out, if he ever had. A feeling of helplessness and lethargy—it was really so much warmer than one might expect an open deck could be—came upon him and he coughed, trying to clear his head. The evening cocktail ritual might prove a mistake.

"No," Wallace spoke at last. "No, she's gone on. She's on an odd course." He pulled the glasses down, and grinned at his companion. "She must be the ghost of the *Mary Celeste*."

Doyle recognized the name, as who would not? He was a boy at school when he read about it. It must be ten years, he thought, since that ship was hauled into Gibraltar for a salvage hearing that quickly became international front-page news. A ghost ship she'd been, but was she still? The doctor felt the fine hairs at the nape of his neck stir infinitesimally. "The *Mary Celeste*," he repeated.

"She was picked up in these waters, and it was this time of year."

"And you think the ship itself is a ghost?"

The captain grinned again, shaking his head slowly from side to side. "No, Doyle, I don't, man. But you're such an impressionable lad, I thought I'd try it out on you."

The doctor was unabashed. "I haven't thought of that story in years," he said. "I recall it was a great mystery at the time. Was it pirates took the crew? I can't remember."

"There haven't been pirates in these waters in fifty years," said Wallace. "And there were no signs of violence and nothing taken."

"Yes," Doyle agreed. "That's right. The ship was in good condition, but not a soul on board."

Wallace nodded, his brow thoughtfully knit. "I knew the captain a little," he said. "A Yankee gentleman, upright, family man. Name of Biggs, or Tibbs, something like that. I happened to be in port with him at Marseille; it must be twenty years now. He was a young man then, and a handsome one. He had his wife along, and she was much relieved to find English speakers. She had no French and they'd been loading a week. Very dark-eyed, pert creature, confident in that American way, always slyly mocking anything foreign. I invited them on board for dinner and we had a pleasant enough time. He was teetotal, but he didn't fuss if others took spirits. I liked him for that. There was nothing puritanical about him; he was a cordial man. I remember one thing especially about that night. We got to singing round the table, more polite songs than usual because the lady was present, and his wife took a turn. She had a lovely voice, almost a professional voice, and she sang a song I didn't know, an American song, I presumed. I'd never heard it before or since, but I recall the refrain. It was 'All things love thee, all things love thee, so do I.'" Wallace tilted his head to one side, as if listening to the remembered voice, while the doctor studied him with a questioning eye. "She stood up to sing, and when she got to that refrain, she turned to her husband, and he, with a smile of the purest satisfaction, looked back at her. They looked into each other's eyes, you see, while she told him she loved him, and it was as if there were no other people in the world but those two. The look on her face! I've never thought to bring my missus along on a voyage, but I think if she ever looked at me like that for one moment in my life, well, I might consider it. I can tell you there was not a man there that didn't feel envious of Captain Tibbs at that moment. We were all going off to our bunks with a last tot of brandy for a bedmate, and he was going back to his cabin with a woman who adored him." Here Wallace paused, having concluded his story.

"And the wife and child were aboard, when they abandoned ship."

"Yes. They were never seen again."

"Wasn't there something odd about the cargo? Do you know?"

"Well, that's an interesting detail. The captain kept a dry ship. There was not a drop of spirits allowed above deck, but he had loaded a thousand barrels of alcohol at New York. That fool proctor at the Admiralty hearing tried to make something of that. He was convinced the crew had gotten at the barrels and killed the officers and the family in a drunken fury. Then they put down the yawl and sailed away."

Doyle considered this scenario. "One of them would have had to be able to navigate," he suggested. "It's possible, I suppose."

"It would be if the alcohol was brandy. But it was distilling spirits. If you could make yourself swallow it, it would kill you."

Doyle frowned at this thought. "So it wasn't mutiny and it wasn't pirates."

"No. I mean yes, it was neither of those."

"Do you have a theory?"

"I do not. It appeared that she was abandoned in a hurry. That, I believe, is a fact. But she had too much sail set to tie up to her with a painter, as the salvagers claimed must have happened. Any sailor would have more sense than to try that. Ten people in a yawl on the open sea, tying up to a ship rigged to run dead downwind; it would be suicide."

"So, in your view, leaving the ship as they did was an irrational act."

Wallace expelled a huff of exasperation. "You may say so, sir."

Doyle pressed his fingertips over his lips, disarranging his mustache. His eyes scanned the horizon, which was dimly visible now, as the mist had cleared and the moon was half full. "Then there must have been foul play."

"Or they were mightily frighted of something."

"Out of their senses with fear. Yes. But if the captain was, as you say, a steady man, of some experience . . ."

"That's what has always puzzled me about the incident. I can't think the man I met in Marseille would abandon a seaworthy ship in a panic."

The doctor smoothed his mustache ruminatively, and the captain moved his head from side to side, pondering the unsolved mystery.

"Perhaps," concluded the doctor, "they didn't all leave at once."

A COLORED GENTLEMAN

In his own time, a man is very modern.

Joseph Conrad

At Madeira, the *Mayumba* disgorged seven of her passengers and took on only one, a heavyset one-legged American as black as his coat, with snowy side chops descending past his strong jaw and wadded gray knots receding from his wide brow. He hobbled on his crutches directly to his berth. The night proved a rough one and the ship plunged through the turbulent water, sails trimmed, engine sputtering, her prow monotonously slapping down into the trough of every wave. By morning all was calm and the passengers gathered, bleary eyed, for their breakfast, but the American didn't appear. It was not until afternoon that the doctor found him ensconced in the saloon sipping weak tea, genially charming the generally reticent Miss Fox. Though Doyle had half a mind to turn away, Miss Fox caught his eye and waved him into the conversation, announcing to her companion, "Here is our good Dr. Doyle." Henry Garnet, for that was the American's name, raised himself slightly in his chair, holding out a manicured hand, his lips parted suddenly in a smile too broad and too ready. A brief exchange followed in which it was revealed that he was the freshly appointed American consul to Liberia on his way to take up his post. To the doctor's commiserating remark about the rough weather of the night before, Mr. Garnet offered the astonishing reply that he had hardly noticed, being distracted by his reading of Prescott's *Conquest of Mexico*. Was the doctor perhaps acquainted with this excellent volume?

Doyle pulled up a chair and settled into it with a sense of being snared by a complex web of previously unimaginable stickiness. He did indeed admire Prescott's work. The consul enlarged upon the subject of recent histories, revealing his thorough familiarity with Motley's *Rise of the Dutch Republic*. The conversation strayed to philosophical authors. The Negro confessed that in spite of certain reservations a strong favorite of his was Waldo Emerson. "One admires him for the felicity of his style, if not for the depth of his vision," he concluded.

Had Mr. Garnet encountered the works of Oliver Wendell Holmes? Doyle earnestly inquired.

"Indeed," was the reply. Mr. Holmes's essay collection *The Autocrat of the Breakfast Table* had delighted him when he was a young man. He had followed them in *The Atlantic* with the greatest pleasure and benefit.

Doyle fairly rubbed his eyes in wonder. Surely this man had been born into slavery or was the son of a slave. How was it possible that he should have acquainted himself with Prescott and Motley; at what sort of table exactly had he enjoyed the "benefit" of Holmes's table talk? Miss Fox interjected a remark Doyle didn't follow, so deeply had he fallen into puzzlement. When he came to himself and sought to reenter the conversation, he found the black man's black eyes twinkling with such evident amusement it was as if he had read his thoughts. Miss Fox shot Doyle a chilly, incomprehensible glance; had he spoken without his own knowledge? His wonder dissolved into something sour and defensive, and still the confounded Negro glittered at him, his mouth lifted at the corners, a faint chuckle issuing from the thick throat pressed tightly against his white cravat. He withdrew a folded handkerchief from his breast pocket, swabbed it over his gleaming forehead, and, folding it once, patted his moist upper lip. Miss Fox excused herself; she was off to her cabin to dress for dinner. As she swept past, Doyle caught again a cold, disapproving cast of her eye.

"A delightful woman," Mr. Garnet observed.

"Indeed," the doctor agreed, looking after her. He was stymied. Ladies were fond of him; that was the rule.

"Between us, I think she was a trifle bored by our conversation about books."

Doyle turned his attention to the man, whose sonorous, cultured voice, the voice of a professional lecturer, was so at odds with his moist black amplitude. Beads of perspiration formed as mysteriously as dewdrops across his forehead. This time he applied the handkerchief in quick dabs. "When we left New York, it was snowing," he observed. "And God willing, it was the last snow I shall see in this life."

"Then you don't intend to return to your home," Doyle concluded.

"I am going to my home, dear Doctor, though I have never been there before," was the consul's enigmatic reply.

Two days out of Las Palmas, the *Mayumba* lost the trades and, all sails set, staggered through the tepid seas into a furnace. The sun, red with fury, hurled itself up, setting the very heavens ablaze. The sailors stumbled from the forecastle, stripped to their breeches, shoeless, their hair tied back in rags. The passengers had not the luxury of dishabille and their only recourse, once they had accomplished the arduous task of dressing, was to sit very still beneath the dull whir of the fan blades that paddled the torpid air in the saloon.

Doyle sat in a stupor before a cup of tepid tea, his eyes resting on the bright cubes of sugar in the silver bowl. The pristine whiteness, the sharp architectural edges, put him in mind of the great ice floes that had hemmed in the *Hope* during his Arctic adventure. How their looming purity had fascinated him on those days without nights, when he strode the deck bristling with energy, alert to the tireless pumping of his own blood in his veins. Once the mate invited him to take the wheel and he felt the whole quivering, breathing enterprise of the ship through the chilled flesh of his hand. Such light, such clarity; a world without shadow in which to take a breath was to experience an influx of health.

A dull whine near his ear materialized as a fly lazily circled the sugar cubes before landing on the edge of the bowl. After a moment of anthropoidal dithering, the creature set out upon the white landscape, manically working its spindly legs and rotating its compound eyes. A visceral revulsion caused the doctor to stretch his upper lip down and draw his head back on its stem, as if he'd encountered putrefaction. Absently his thumb and index finger smoothed the surface of his mustache. It was damp. His eyebrows held back a line of perspiration; he could feel it gathering there. Though he made no decision to do so, his hand sought out his breast pocket and pulled forth the folded handkerchief, unfurling it like a flag, and mopping his brow. A trickle of sweat escaped from the nape of his neck, rushed down his back, cooling him as the limp linen of his shirt absorbed it. The fly had gotten itself so jammed between two white cubes that it had actually managed to dislodge one from the other.

"Sadly, I report that it is no cooler on deck," a voice informed him. "I thought there might be a breeze."

The doctor lifted his eyes to the frankly sweating visage of the American consul. It interested him that the black man's perspiration held together in round globules, which sparkled over the pores from which they issued. Did Negro skin perspire differently, or was it only the dark background that made the droplets appear to stand out so? "Hello, Garnet," he said.

The American lowered himself into a chair, easing down from his crutches with practiced skill. "I don't think tea is the proper prescription for this climate," he observed, nodding at the half-empty cup.

"No? What do you recommend? Coffee? That surely heats the blood."

"I recommend water," Garnet said. "Though I believe the preferred spirit of the British colonialist is gin." He grinned his toothy grin, like a bridge of yellowish stones connecting the white clouds of his sideburns, and raised his hand to the waiter who was unloading a tray of this very remedy at the next table. Although summoned by the black man, the waiter addressed his attention to the white. "Let us have a pitcher of tonic, a bottle of gin, and two glasses," Doyle commanded. As the waiter drifted away, his tray lifted above his shoulder in a show of youthful confidence, Doyle addressed his companion gloomily. "I take it you don't approve of the Colonial enterprise."

Garnet chuckled, raising his eyebrows and bugging out his eyes, evidently delighted by this opening salvo. There was no offending the man, Doyle observed, nor was he capable of giving offense. He oiled his way through the world with a jovial brand of ironic courtesy. "I'm not against exploration," he began. "Who can speak against discovering the grand variety of the wide world? No, if the adventure is undertaken as a tourist, I approve that human impulse. I would be an explorer of foreign parts myself, if my health would bear it."

"But when it's not so wonderfully various or grand," Doyle countered, "and one has the means to improve the lives of those who suffer needlessly—"

"Oh yes," Garnet interrupted. "You are speaking as a doctor and a healer. As such you are welcome everywhere you go. But it isn't troops of doctors we see trekking through the underbrush with rifles and bayonets."

Doyle smiled at the idea of troops of doctors. It didn't strike him as absurd.

"Doctors," Garnet continued, "and tourists. These will improve the lives of the impoverished and the suffering in this great continent. But missionaries and soldiers, we can do without."

Doyle noted the pronoun. "So you see yourself as an African."

Here the drinks arrived and were set down between them while the consul indulged in a disturbing hoot of laughter. "Doctor," he said, when he had recovered his breath. "Look at me."

Doyle tipped a splash of gin into the glass and filled it with tonic. He was uncomfortable, and not just from the heat, though that was, he noted again, astounding. Why should he have known that an emissary of the American government thought himself adequate to speak for all Africans, to say *we* need this and *we* do not do that? He glowered at the liquid in his glass—there was a dab of quinine in the tonic, but not enough to ward off malaria, if indeed quinine was actually prophylactic even in large doses. Garnet took up the tonic pitcher and filled his glass to the brim. "Yes, dear Doctor," he continued. "Even an African can be edified by the table talk of Mr. Holmes."

Though there had clearly been an edge of hostility in this remark, when Doyle lifted his eyes he found the self-proclaimed African gazing at the sleepily rotating fan blades with an expression of rueful melancholy. "I've traveled widely," he said, addressing the fan. "I've been to your country."

"Have you?"

Garnet smiled and turned his attention to the doctor. "I'm a Presbyterian minister," he said. "The church in Scotland offered me its gracious hospitality some years ago. When I was a boy I sailed to Cuba and Jamaica. I've traveled in England as well. But it has been the dream of my life to put my foot on the land of my ancestors. My father was a slave in Maryland, but his father was a Mandinka prince."

So it was pride of descent. Pride of descent Doyle could understand; the sense of having come down, which he had imbibed at his own mother's breast. We are come down, that was the message. From the Plantagenets, from the Packs and the Percys, from the D'Oyleys, a lineage to be proud of, a family descended from the highest families, with crests and seals, variously connected, even to royalty, albeit his own family of eight lived in three furnished rooms and his father was confined to an asylum. And here was Henry Garnet, looking beyond his own parents' tumultuous fall, come down all the way to slavery, clinging to the cherished family legend of an African prince, who, though he may have worn rings in his nose and danced with his subjects around a fire, served no man and was held in esteem by many. This was what made all the wit and good cheer possible. Garnet was a man among men, a rightful heir to an estate that he would, in time, regain and rebuild.

"You must be eager to arrive and begin your work," Doyle observed.

Garnet was frowning at his glass. "My work," he repeated, as if the word had a certain novelty for him.

The fly, having pawed over every millimeter of the sugar cubes, hoisted itself onto the rim of the bowl. Both men watched as it teetered drunkenly over the table, disappearing with a sudden cessation of its infernal buzzing engine, into the pure white folds of the doctor's napkin.

Doyle didn't speak to the American consul again. Henry Garnet stayed in his berth, doubtless reading *The Conquest of Mexico*, and when the ship docked in Monrovia, he was whisked ashore by a pompous delegation dressed in garish nightshirts waiting on the wharf. It was not until the *Mayumba* was steaming determinedly toward Grand Bassam that Miss Fox, finding the doctor listlessly thumbing a back number of *Punch* in the passenger lounge, enlightened him on Mr. Garnet's true mission in Africa. "He's a dying man," she said. "He won't live a month. He wanted to die on African soil, so his friends got together and secured him the consul post, but it's all a sham. It's just to pay the passage and have a place for him to rest when he arrives."

"But how do you know this?"

"He told me. Of course I knew who he was at once. He was a tireless abolitionist in New York before the war and some say Liberia is his creation. Really, he's quite a famous man." Miss Fox drew herself up so that she could gaze down her nose upon the spectacle of the young doctor's colossal ignorance.

A famous man. A dying man. But how was it possible? He had betrayed no sign of illness. His breathing wasn't labored, his mind was clear. His appetite was good. The sclera of his eyes was perhaps tinged with yellow, but Doyle had taken that to be a feature of his race. And as to his fame as an abolitionist—he had shown more interest in Motley than in the struggles of the emancipated American Negro. His chaffing about tourism and imperialism had been more speculative than heartfelt. Or so it had seemed to Dr. Doyle, who had surely not made the trip to Africa to be condescended to by the likes of the self-appointed know-all Miss Fox.

"I really must go and have a look in at the Fairfax boy," he said, pushing up from his chair and away from the line of Miss Fox's long nose. "He has a cough and I don't like the sound of it. I fear his lungs may be affected."

OBSERVATIONS OF AFRICA

The deathlike impression of Africa grew upon me.

Arthur Conan Doyle

Onward chugged the *Mayumba*, courting the shore breezes, though these were rare, and so hot they were more like the exhalations of hell. Doyle marveled at the sameness of the view, the breakers, the shore, the bush, and at night the fires, which the captain informed him were set by natives intent on "burning the grass," to what end he didn't know and couldn't imagine. Miss Fox alighted at Grand Bassam, a miserable hole where her father, a stooped, wizened figure dressed all in white with a pith helmet cocked back on his head, eyes the color of water, and the complexion of a Morocco leather chair, awaited her on the flimsy dock. Doyle watched from the deck as she approached her progenitor. He was curious to witness the manner of their greeting. It was a handshake, brief, courteous, the elbows pressed into the sides, and then they turned away from the shore and the intellectual lady followed her father into the jungle.

To live how? To do what? Doyle mopped his brow with his sodden handkerchief. Near an open-air shed perched with its back to the bush, an anthill of half-naked natives suddenly dispersed, marching in a loose formation toward the stern of the *Mayumba* to receive the cargo already being dropped down by the sailors. Captain Wallace, restless and cantankerous, joined the doctor at the rail. "Fancy doctoring that lot, eh Doyle?" he said, indicating the porters at their work.

Doyle, having looked over but not at the men, who were making a noisy fuss about unloading a pallet of heavy burlap bags, concentrated his attention on a pair of tall, muscular fellows engaged in posturing and angrily baring their teeth. "They look healthy enough," he observed. "They certainly have white teeth."

"It's veterinary work, sir," the captain crudely attested. "They're animals and no more. They don't even know they're sick until they drop. And they contract all manner of evil from the ground, because they sit on it and sleep on it and even eat it. Every kind of worm and parasite known to man and some as none has heard of is out there. I've seen yaws open the flesh of a leg to the bone. And elephantiasis. I don't suppose you've seen what that does to a man. Scrota the size of melons."

A burst of wild glee broke out from the natives. The two men, who had seemed about to come to blows, leaned into each other, laughing so heartily they plopped down on a pallet, while their coworkers shouted the joke to each other.

"Do you understand them?" Doyle asked the captain, meaning their language.

"There's nought to understand," Wallace replied. "Poor, stupid brutes. What in thunder are they laughing about?" And with that he left the doctor and called out to one of the sailors as he approached the loading platform, "Latimer, what are they up to? We'll never get out of here at this rate."

Doyle watched the men a while longer, thinking about parasites. He had a treatise on tropical medicine in his berth. He had read in it an article about tiny worms that burrowed into a man, depositing their eggs deep beneath the epidermis. When the eggs hatched, the larvae gnawed their way out. Unthinkable.

His gaze wandered listlessly over the scene. There was a dog lying in the shade of the shed, some mad bird shrieking from the impenetrable bush beyond. Nature here was virulent, producing all manner of venom, not to mention large, carnivorous beasts and people as black as coal. The heat alone, he thought. The poleaxing heat.

A prickling sensation called his attention to his wrist, where he discovered a large mosquito tilted back on its rear legs the better to gorge itself on exotic blood. Case in point, he thought, as he squashed the life out of the insect. He might stroll out to the shed and back, just to have solid ground under his shoes. But between the dock and the shed was only a stretch of unwelcoming, baked, shadeless, dun-colored dirt.

The heat alone, he thought.

"Beware, beware, the Bight of Benin, for few come out, though many go in."

The first officer delivered this cheerful advice as the *Mayumba* swung listlessly on her anchor chain in the oily brown water off the coast of Lagos.

"And why do few come out?" asked Doyle.

The mate drew closer, lowering his beard toward the doctor's ear with a confidential air. "Why," he said. "Presumably." A pause, a deeper register. "Because they die there."

The doctor grinned; gazing out at the long swells rolling into the inevitable strip of sand. Another port not fit for human habitation, another infernal pit of hell where black demons fed the flames with bits carved from unwary travelers. A buzzing near his ear provoked him to clap his hand against his head. Was it worth it, he asked himself, this place? Men didn't last long and women not as long as that. And all to extract palm oil and rubber.

And of course to extend a sorely needed civilizing influence, which might, in a hundred years, beam a few rays of light into this universal moral darkness. The mate wandered away in pursuit of his duty. The doctor patted his pockets, in search of his pipe.

At dinner the remaining passengers were preoccupied with their packing arrangements, as all but two were departing at Lagos. Doyle noted the downcast expression on the habitually resolute face of Mrs. Fairfax, who must surely look upon her destination as a death sentence. Her sickly boys picked at their plates, the younger one taking up his napkin at frequent intervals to cover his mouth while he coughed. His father studied him distantly. The man of God, and his good woman, Doyle thought. What poor luck to be born that man's son.

Though at least the Reverend Fairfax did, in a manner of speaking, provide for his family. At least he did that.

After the passengers had departed and the blasting sun had set, the ship was quiet and still as the inside of a sleeping whale. In his narrow cabin the doctor sat down at his table to begin an overdue letter to his mother. *Dearest,* he wrote, and put down the pen. What to tell her? That he detested Africa, its heat, its smells, its people, and longed for a breath of cool, fresh air? He gazed at his porthole. It made no difference if it was opened or closed; it was suffocating inside and out. He drew in a slow breath and released it. Hotter going in than out, or so it seemed. An insect's dizzy buzzing came closer, drifted away, came close again. He picked up his pen. *Here is my carcass stewing like a fowl. Never was there such a pesthole of a place as this, good for nothing but swearing at. I shall not. . . .* The buzzing came close, sounding oddly fierce, as if the creature had turned up its own volume, but he determined to ignore it. He felt the infinitesimal thud on the nape of his neck, the tentative tickling like loose threads unraveled from a collar, and then the sharp sting. His moist hand had smeared the ink on the page. He set down the pen, slapped his palm across his neck, dragged it free, and glowered at the smashed insect, a black smudge in a streak of bright blood.

The image of the Fairfax boy pushing his fork through the mush he'd made of his dinner, languishing beneath the indifferent eye of his righteous father, recurred in the doctor's imagination, striking a moody, somber chord, definitely in a minor key. He couldn't escape the conclusion that the boy was trapped and perhaps doomed by the single-minded zealotry of a parent who cared more for the souls of benighted savages than the health of his own family. If the boy survived he would certainly have some tales to tell, though he might prefer to close them away, to condemn his childhood as a prisoner to a prison.

Unbidden another image rose. The tall gentleman, rolling over on his side in the gutter, howling gibberish at the jeering boys who pelted him with pebbles, and the lady, fabricating an excuse about the urgent necessity of a conversation with the draper, gently steering her son into a byway; the son who knew his mother had seen the gentleman, and also knew she would never admit it.

And another, the lady again, one hand pressed against the kitchen table, the other covering her mouth, keeping in what she might say, what she must be thinking. Before her, uncapped, cast aside by the desperate, trembling fingers of the gentleman, the empty bottle of furniture varnish. The boy was there, in the doorway, but he didn't speak, and the lady didn't know he was there, not then, not to this day. She didn't know the boy watched her as she buried the bottle in the trash bin, and she couldn't know that later, when she went out to her ladies' educational meeting, the boy had fished the bottle out and sat for some moments puzzling over the meaning of it. Until he grasped the meaning of it.

The voice of the captain in conversation with the mate drifted in from the passageway. Doyle crumpled the smeary page, used it to wipe away the mess in his palm, and went out to join his fellow officers in the saloon.

There the drink was gin; the atmosphere was masculine, smoky, and amiable. The talk was all sea tales, some as tall as the mainmast, of survival against impossible odds, dereliction of duty, cannibalism in extremity and as accepted practice, madness on board and on shore, ships cursed, ships derelict, ships on which the crew was found all dead, or all dead save one man, raving at the helm, collisions on dark stormy nights and in strange ports, ships sailed purposely into reefs or shoals in order to defraud insurance companies, ships rammed by enraged whales. At the close of the whale story,

Doyle would have offered his adventure on the ice, in which he had fallen through a hole and saved himself by clinging to the flipper of the seal he'd just clubbed to death, but the occasion didn't present itself. As the evening wore on, his brain fogged over and he could no longer follow the conversations. A queasy rumor stirred in his gut. He stopped drinking the captain's gin and switched to tonic water. Something was definitely amiss in the waist, he thought, amusing himself with his pun. He wasn't feeling entirely seaworthy.

He excused himself from his companions, pleading fatigue, and went out onto the deck for a breath of fetid air. The night was black. The ship rocked gently at anchor in the black water. Even the stars appeared to have been dimmed. Looking up hurt his eyes. His head was throbbing, his throat dry and constricted. No, he was not well. His legs had gone rubbery, and from somewhere in his core a chill commenced, washing up to his face and down his limbs, so fierce and abrupt that his teeth chattered. How curious to be cold in the broiling African night.

He knew what must come next and steadied himself at the rail, then, with decision, pushed off and made his staggering way, clutching the boom, careening into the housing, down the hatch to his berth. He drank water from the pitcher, pulling the sheet off the thin mattress, feeling about the storage space in the bunk for the heavy socks and woolen muffler he'd worn on the trip from Edinburgh to Liverpool; when was that? A world ago. With trembling fingers he pulled on the socks, wrapped the plaid round his neck, crossing the ends over his chest, folded the sheet, pulled it tight across his shoulders, and sat there on his bunk, shivering like a man in a blizzard. His thoughts were disordered, darting from hypothetical diagnosis of his condition, malarial fever being the most likely, to anxiety about the state of his intestinal tract, which had a seismic feel to it, to regret that he hadn't told the seal story, interspersed with the repeated observation that it was passing strange to be shivering in a broiling cabin, and a vague premonition, distant now but beckoning, like that tall, wan gentleman standing in the corner there, insistently wagging a bony index finger, that he was entering an entirely different order of consciousness, one that would preclude attendance upon his medical duties. He wasn't afraid—he was never afraid—but he was helpless. The cadaverous gentleman closed his fingers in a fist, narrowing his watery eyes in a theatrical glare. Something familiar about the fellow, though he clearly wasn't really there. Doyle rubbed his fists into his eyes, clamped his jaw against the appalling clatter of his teeth. Damn this gentleman, in his woolen vest and frock coat; absurd attire for a specter. He lowered his fists and blinked his eyes at the man, who had the temerity to bare his rotting teeth in a fiendish grin.

"The hell you say," Doyle cried, lurching from the bunk, shoulders hunched, fists drawn in close to his chest, legs buckling. He made two steps and toppled headlong into the empty corner. Determined to fight, he rolled onto his side, raising himself on one arm, but someone slipped a warm, wet, black bag over his head and he went down again without a struggle.

He awoke, fully clothed in his bunk, which was on fire. Or so it seemed, until amid a mighty but unsuccessful effort to rise and flee, he realized the flames were inside him. It wasn't surprising; one didn't need a medical certificate to know the bone-rattling chill of the night before must be succeeded by a fever. But how had he gotten back to his bed, and what was to be done about the unbearable, suffocating weight of his clothes, which he was too weak to remove? His fingers, unbidden, pushed away the muffler, fumbled at the buttons of his shirt; his feet flailed together, working the horrid socks down to his ankles. Why was he wearing woolen socks?

The chill. The wan gentleman. He attempted a groan, but what issued from his dry lips was a croak. If only he had the strength to reach the water pitcher. He could see it in the bowl on the stand. The pinkish light glinting from the lip informed him that it was early morning. Again a furious effort to rise, resulting in a sudden gush of water from every pore, a fog descending from somewhere, thick as porridge. If only. Water.

. . .

When next he opened his eyes and took in the ordinary aspect of things—the afternoon light playing over the compact furnishings of the room, the deep, sonorous pulsing of the ship's engines, the sound of cheerful voices exchanging courtesies outside his door—a convalescent gratitude swelled in his chest. He was soaked in sweat; the pillow was a sodden rag but when summoned his limbs obeyed the call. No, more than that, they gathered force in a valiant, glorious effort, and in the next moment he was sitting with his feet on the floor, swaying but upright, weak, stunned, ravenous. His tongue, dry and heavy in his mouth, felt like a desiccated toad.

The doctor's appearance in the officers' saloon was greeted with a round of applause and the alarming news that three days had passed since the evening he had staggered forth, having failed to relate the seal story. The next morning the steward had discovered him in his bed, unconscious and burning with fever. As the doctor was himself the patient, there was no one to attend him, and he had been left to recover or not. Or not had been the case of a luckless sailor who had come down with the same malady on the same evening and whose earthly remains had been solemnly committed to the Bight of Benin that very dawn. It was more information than the invalid could comprehend, and he sank beneath it into an armchair, mumbling apologies. "Still a bit unsteady." The captain spoke to the steward, who bustled off to his galley to prepare a tray.

"It's well we have so few passengers," the captain observed. "When the doctor himself is ill, it makes them anxious."

Doyle raised his eyes. Was the man implying that he had failed in his duty by succumbing to a near fatal illness? But no, Wallace's regard was moist with an indulgent sympathy. "You have had a close call, sir," he said. "I feared we might lose you, and that would have been a woeful conclusion to your African adventure."

Doyle nodded. The telegram sent to his mother, what would it say? *Your son, Arthur Conan, dead of fever, buried at sea, yours truly.* No one for her to turn to, no help but her damnable lodger, Dr. Waller, who would take over, as was his damnable way. His poor sisters,

Lottie, Connie, and Annette, condemned to drudgery as governesses for the rest of their lives. Unbearable.

"I'll be fine," he assured the captain. "I'll be up and about in no time."

He took a light meal, for his stomach was tender, and drank a great quantity of water. His fellow officers urged him to return to his bunk, and as he was too weak to be of use to anyone, he agreed. Lifting his water glass was a heroic effort. He made his way out to the deck and stood at the rail, looking at the sea.

While he was spooning in his soup, Captain Wallace had told him about the dead sailor, an elderly fellow named Wentworth. Wentworth hailed from Liverpool and had been at sea since he was a lad. He had a wife and children; the officers couldn't agree on how many. He would be missed in the fo'c'sle, as he was something of a practical joker. Once he'd caught a water snake and put it in the empty kettle. With much snoring and muttering, all hands had feigned sleep, waiting for the riotous moment when the cook opened the kettle lid in the morning.

Wentworth's illness had run the same course as the doctor's, but he hadn't the strength to withstand the fever. Presumably his heart gave out under the assault of the microbe.

Doyle leaned over the rail, feeling queasy, but it passed. The sea before him was deceptively calm, and the morning sun, already brutal, smeared it with a gelatinous glow. Wentworth was down there, wrapped in his canvas shroud, carried ever downward by the weight attached to his feet, plucked at, nosed about, shaken, devoured by creatures of that other world. Wentworth, the joker, and thousands like him. How many thousands?

The sailors referred to the end of time as that day when the sea gives up its dead. It was a cliché, but Doyle vexed his brain to imagine that day. It might, after all, be tomorrow. Would the waters withdraw and the souls of the dead rise up through the wreckage of the ships littering the ocean floor? Or would the dead be disgorged onto the coasts of every landmass, clinging to rocks, floundering in the shallows, pushing forward in waves like the sea itself, waves of the dead, with their pale flesh and hollow eyes?

It was absurd. The sea would not give up her dead. To be committed to the sea, as Wentworth had been, and as he might himself have been—he had seen that in Captain Wallace's eyes—was to be lost forever in an immensity beyond comprehension. If every living soul on earth were dropped into the deep, would it even raise the level of the oceans? Would a great tidal wave be engendered that would sweep across the sea and flatten everything, including islands and coastal cities that stood in its path? And even if that did happen, it would make no difference. The oceans of the world could absorb mankind entire and still the tides would roll in and out, the sun would rise and set, the moon wax and wane, pulling the waves to the shore.

He could not look at it, this vast and temperamental creature that was the sea. And he would not, as he had once thought he might, spend some formative part of his life upon it. It was too lonely and cruel, it didn't pay well, and it made men melancholy, fatalistic, and mad.

As he made his way back to his bunk, his thoughts turned to home. Or not to home, which had, until recently, been a series of increasingly smaller and more crowded rented rooms, but to the spacious, sunny, stylish flat at George Square that his mother and his three sisters now shared with her lodger, Dr. Waller. A lodger who paid the entire rent; in what sense was such a man characterized as a lodger?

A lodger who was young enough to be her son, who had conspired with her to send her husband to the "sanatorium." A lodger who was the godfather of her baby girl, named for him. An aristocratic lodger, with an estate and a coat of arms quartered with the royal family of France; a pompous and demanding lodger who had refused to fight. It was clear now; Waller had been on his mother's hands and in her confidence for years. He could not be dis-lodged.

A usurping lodger, like a cuckoo, soiling the nest and driving out the chicks, the rightful heirs of the poor pale gentleman who cowered in his room by day, and wandered the streets by night, trying to sell his own clothes in exchange for a drink. Did the pale gentleman set fire to the nest? That was the charge against him, among others. The dry-eyed mother had appealed to her son. "We'll need your signature," she said, while the lodger gazed out the tall, handsomely corniced window at the park opposite the square. "Here, and here."

And of course, he could deny her nothing. He picked up the pen and signed.

Now, in his berth, he took out his diary, opened to the last entry, November 18, 1881, and reread his own description of the fires on the African shore at night and his recollection that in Hanno's account of his voyage along the same coast two thousand years ago, he had spoken of a world on fire, of active volcanoes sputtering red lava rivers that poured into the sea, the steam rising in blasts of white smoke that clouded the night. Now these volcanoes were shiny black peaks, rising cold and indifferent above the florid green of the coast.

He left three blank pages to account for the days he had lost. *November 22*, he wrote on the next. But the pen was mysteriously heavy, and his fingers hadn't the strength to hold it upright. He laid it across the page and collapsed onto his bed, where a deep, restorative sleep swallowed him up completely, as if he were a fish and sleep a great, black whale.

THE VOYAGE OF A STORY

Three Years Later

Habakuk is going to make a sensation. I have had several letters in praise of it. Yesterday came one from James Payn asking me "How much foundation there was for my striking story."

ARTHUR CONAN DOYLE, LETTER TO MARY DOYLE

In the January 1884 issue of the British magazine *Cornhill*, a prestigious publication originally edited by William Thackeray and now under the able editorship of James Payn, there appeared an article titled "J. Habakuk Jephson's Statement," which purported to solve the mystery surrounding the crew of the American brigantine *Mary Celeste*. As it was the policy of the *Cornhill* to publish its contributions without attribution, the innocent reader was invited to believe that the eponymous Dr. Jephson was in fact the author of the tale, and that his account offered an accurate record of the final days of the crew and a definitive answer to the question that had so perplexed the public: Why had an experienced captain abandoned a perfectly seaworthy vessel?

Dr. Jephson begins his "statement" with a recounting of the known facts of the case:

> In the month of December in the year 1873, the British ship Dei Gratia steered into Gibraltar, having in tow the derelict brigantine Marie Celeste, which had been picked up in latitude 30° 40′, longitude 17° 15′ W. There were several circumstances in connection with the condition and appearance of this abandoned vessel which excited considerable comment at the time and aroused a curiosity which has never been satisfied.

Dr. Jephson then quotes at length from an article in the *Gibraltar Gazette*, as well as a telegram from Boston, "which went the round of the English papers," detailing those curious circumstances: the sighting of the derelict *Marie Celeste* drifting on a calm sea by the captain of the *Dei Gratia* and the subsequent boarding of that vessel by two sailors, the discovery of the log, which was "imperfectly kept, and affords little information," the absence of any signs of violence or damage from bad weather, the dresses and sewing machine found in the cabin, suggesting the presence of the captain's wife, the boats intact, the rigging and sails in good order, the inevitable conclusion that there was "absolutely nothing to account for the disappearance of the crew."

Having thus summarized the mystery, Jephson reveals that he has "now taken up my pen with the intention of telling all that I know of the ill-fated voyage."

Why has the doctor waited eleven years to enlighten a mystified public? He confesses that the story is so fantastic no one will believe him, as he learned when he told it to the police and even to his own brother-in-law, "who listened to my statement with an indulgent smile as if humouring the delusion of a monomaniac." However, as "symptoms which I am familiar with in others lead me to believe that before many months my tongue and hand may be alike incapable of conveying information," he feels it incumbent upon himself to record the truth for posterity. "J. Habakuk Jephson's Statement" is, therefore, a tale told by a survivor, and one who will not live long past the telling of it.

Dr. Jephson, a vain, pompous, observant, credulous personage, sociable and self-important, introduces himself as a prominent Boston lung specialist and noted abolitionist. He twice reminds the reader of his influential pamphlet "Who Is Thy Brother?" carefully including the name of the publisher and year—Swarburgh, Lister & Co., 1859—for the perspicacious reader who may wish to look out for this noteworthy though now moot argument for the abolition of slavery, which attracted "considerable attention" at the time of its publication. After a lengthy aside about an odd encounter during the Civil War, in which a dying slave woman entrusted him with a curiously carved black stone, Jephson turns to the year 1873. At that time overwork in both his professional and social capacities had taken a severe toll on his health and, having received a diagnosis of "consolidation" in his left lung, he was advised to take an ocean voyage.

His wife is eager to accompany her husband, but "she has always been a very poor sailor and there were strong family reasons against her exposing herself to any risk at the time, so we determined that she should remain at home." A meeting with a young acquaintance who is the heir to a shipping company results in Jephson's booking passage on the *Marie Celeste*. "She is a snug little ship," his friend assures Jephson, "And Tibbs, the captain, is an excellent fellow. There is nothing like a sailing ship for an invalid."

Thence follows the complex account of Dr. Jephson's voyage aboard the *Marie Celeste*, a bizarre tale that includes the African talisman and a mysterious fellow passenger, one Septimus Goring, a mulatto from New Orleans, unpleasant to look upon but well educated and evidently wealthy, who has made up his mind to murder as many members of the white race as he possibly can.

"J. Habakuk Jephson's Statement," like the abolitionist pamphlet touted by its narrator, attracted considerable attention at the time of its publication. The *New York Times* reviewer derided the absurdity of its plot and pronounced it a story that "would make Thackeray turn in his grave," but *The Illustrated London News* praised it as "an exceedingly powerful story," which might have come from the pen of Robert Louis Stevenson, though the American theme and the elements of mystery and madness suggested, at least as inspiration, *The Narrative of Arthur Gordon Pym of Nantucket* by Edgar Allan Poe.

Though most of its critics recognized Jephson's "Statement" as fiction and placed it in the long and honorable tradition of elaborate flights of imagination inspired by real events, there were, there always are, readers who believed the article to be a true account.

Immediately upon publication, five copies of the *Cornhill* left London bound for Gibraltar, where two important gentlemen took immediate and vocal offense. One of these was Horatio James Sprague, the American consul, who had been instrumental in freeing the *Mary Celeste* from the clutches of the other, Frederick Solly Flood, the queen's proctor at Gibraltar. Flood had impounded the derelict vessel and waylaid the captain and crew of the *Dei Gratia* for a salvage hearing that more resembled a criminal trial. Within two weeks of the journal's publication, Consul Sprague redirected a copy of the *Cornhill* to the attention of the Honorable John Davis, assistant secretary of state in Washington, D.C., referring to the "full particulars" of the salvage hearing that had, eleven years earlier, been "duly transmitted to the department."

It having ever since remained a mystery, regarding the fate of the master and crew of the Mary Celeste, *or even the cause that induced or forced them to abandon their vessel which, with her cargo, were found when met by the* Dei Gratia *to be in perfect order, I ask to myself, what motives can have prompted the writer of the article in question to refer to this mysterious affair after the lapse of eleven years; especially as the statement given, is not only replete with inaccuracies as regards the date, voyage and destination of the vessel, names of the parties constituting her crew, and the fact of her having no passengers on board beyond the master's wife and child, but seems to me to be replete with romance of a very unlikely or exaggerated nature.*

Frederick Solly Flood, equally appalled by the inaccuracies of the article, issued a public statement, which appeared in the British press, denouncing "J. Habakuk Jephson's Statement" as "a complete fraud from start to finish." It was still his conviction, he reminded the public, that the officers had been murdered by the crew, who had then abandoned the vessel in the ship's boat and were probably still alive. The *Cornhill* article, in his considered view, might well have been concocted by one of the survivors to throw off the investigation, which had never been closed in the mind of the queen's proctor these eleven years.

On January 8, fifty copies of the *Cornhill* set sail from Liverpool in the deep hold of the brig *Claudius*, which after a smooth crossing encountered severe weather off the Nantucket coast and limped into Boston harbor partially dismasted, the rigging in a tangle, and the crew bedraggled from lack of sleep and double shifts at the pumps. Once unloaded, the copies were quickly dispersed along the Eastern seaboard.

On February 3, Prosper Hayes, an aspiring poet and literary critic for the *Boston Herald*, was pleased to find the familiar journal in the stack of transatlantic mail on his desk. He had been closely following a serial, *The Giant's Robe*, and was eager to read the next installment, which promised an important revelation. There was always something of interest in the *Cornhill*, unlike *Blackwood's*, which had, in his opinion, rather fallen down in recent times. James Payn at the *Cornhill* was ambitious for his journal and ever on the watch for the coming men of letters, though it was hard to tell, sometimes, exactly who was coming, as the stories and articles were all unsigned. Prosper opened the cover to the contents page. Here was a writer who had found a way around this problem of attribution; he'd put his name in the title of his piece, and what an almighty biblical moniker it was: J. Habakuk Jephson. When Hayes turned to Jephson's contribution, he found that it commenced with a description of the famous ghost ship, the *Marie Celeste*, being towed into Gibraltar harbor.

Prosper Hayes raised his eyes from the page and gazed out the window alongside his desk, which gave onto the chilly confusion and noise of Beacon Street. He noticed little about the scene, as his thoughts strayed to the unsolved mystery of the abandoned ship, a tale he had not thought of in many years. He'd been at Harvard College when the goings-on at Gibraltar were first reported in the press. Early versions suggested that the crew had murdered the officers in a drunken fury, then, when sobriety set in, thrown the bodies overboard and escaped on the ship's boat. As the captain hailed from Marion, that lovely but cantankerous village on Buzzards Bay run entirely by retired sea captains, the fate of the ship had been of considerable local interest. Hayes had a classmate from Marion who knew the family. The captain of the ghost ship was survived by his mother, who didn't believe the mutiny story. It was rumored that she was convinced her son and his family, for he had his wife and daughter aboard, had been picked up by a passing vessel and would, in due course, arrive at some destination where they might announce their survival to the world.

But they never had. The trial had ended unsatisfactorily, with only a small award to the salvagers, because the judge believed they might have had a hand in the murder of the captain. Others maintained that the captain of the salvage ship and the captain of the derelict ship were friends, and that the whole abandonment and recovery of the vessel was some species of insurance fraud. Whatever happened, it was a sad and strange business, and one that Prosper Hayes had followed for a bit and then forgotten. Was the family still waiting for some word from their lost ones after all these years? And what might this new article by Dr. Jephson add to the sum of available knowledge about the case?

A rattle and fizz from the stove jolted the reviewer from his reverie. He laid the journal on the desk, scooped up a shovel of coal from the scuttle, opened the grate, and dumped in the fuel. As he settled into his reading chair, pulling his blanket around his shoulders, he noticed the first flakes of snow drifting past the window.

A sea yarn on a snowy day, safe in his cozy office—what better employment could a young man find?

The mysterious passenger, Septimus Goring, was bending over the dead captain Tibbs, who held in his rigid hand the pistol with which he had taken his own life, when Hayes looked up from the page and observed that the snow was falling thickly, clotting in the hollows of the maple stripling across the road and forming neat white caps on the light posts. He returned to his reading. At long last, here was the truth about the infamous ghost ship, the crew of which had suffered a fate more diabolical than anyone could have guessed.

Those light flakes gathering silently upon the throbbing metropolis of Boston constituted the western edge of a blizzard that would pack the East Coast from Maine to New York City in ten feet of heavy, wet snow, leaving the streets impassable and travelers trapped far from home. By morning the beach at Truro would be littered with rubble from the clipper *Miltonia*. Thanks to the sure command of Captain Reginald Berry, the crew and passengers, six-teen in number, took to the small boats from which, after ten hours in storm-tossed waters, they were picked up by the passing steamer *Endor*. All landed safely at Philadelphia the following morning, with much praise for the courage and courtesy of the rescuing vessel's captain and crew.

When the streets were cleared of snow, five copies of the *Cornhill* left Boston in a mailbag on the ferry *Bernadette*, bound for New Bed-ford. The following morning one copy was delivered to Mr. David Hamley, the librarian at the New Bedford Public Library, which had a subscription to the journal. A week later, in the drafty read-ing room of this stately edifice, Dr. Samuel Moody of Marion took up the journal, and settled himself in a comfortable chair near the tall west-facing window, content to pass a few hours in perusal of the current literary scene in Britain. He had not been long absorbed in his reading before a soft huff of surprise escaped his lips. He had come to a description of an event with which he was well acquainted.

For the next hour, punctuated by the occasional grunt, and a general increase in the intensity of his interest, Dr. Moody read what was, he assumed, a fantastical tale. Though the author had changed many of the names, presumably to protect himself from accusations of libel, there was too much resemblance to the facts of the famous incident for any reader to doubt his true intention, which was to raise the specter of the long unsolved mystery of the derelict brigantine the *Mary Celeste*.

At length Dr. Moody returned the *Cornhill* to the shelf and strode out into the freezing afternoon, directing his steps toward the home of his friend James Briggs, the youngest brother of the ill-fated Briggs family of Marion, who had lost seven of his closest family members to the sea. Three of that number—his brother Benjamin, his sister-in-law Sarah, and an infant niece Sophia Matilda—had disappeared from the *Mary Celeste*. James lived with his wife, two daughters, and widowed mother in a new section of town, a mile's walk from the center. The house was of solid construction, spacious, yet cozy. There was a kitchen garden on one side, and an arbor over the walk that led to the front door.

At the specific request of its owner the house was so situated that, unlike its neighbors, it offered no view of the sea.

A second copy of the *Cornhill* was delivered to the Italianate mansion of the widowed New Bedford socialite Mrs. Amanda McClinton Pink, who was not at home to receive it. The January editions of *Blackwood's* and *Longman's Magazine* arrived in the same mail. Mrs. Pink was an anglophile—how she regretted the revolution. She traced her own descent to a British viscount and a Scottish bard. There was an Irish strain as well, indistinguishable in her name as well as in her conversation, yet evident in her temper and her psychology. Like her Irish ancestors, Mrs. Pink possessed the "sight" and communicated with spirits of all kinds on a regular basis.

The housemaid arranged the journals on the hall table, alongside the tray laden with letters and cards from tradesmen. When Mrs. Pink returned from her round of social calls, she snatched the

British magazines and carried them to her own bedroom. It was her habit to lie abed in the mornings, drinking her tea and reading. She placed the *Cornhill* atop the stack on the rosewood table next to her bed. She was following *The Giant's Robe* and looked forward to the next installment.

That night, before she turned out her light, Mrs. Pink couldn't resist having a look at *The Giant's Robe* to reassure herself that the new installment concerned the difficulties of the somewhat dubious character named Mark. As she opened the journal, her eyes fell upon the title of an article by someone named J. Habakuk Jephson, but neither the style nor the subject appealed to her, and she flipped through the pages until she found what she was looking for. To her delight, Mark was mentioned in the first sentence and he was clearly in interesting difficulties.

The perils of Mark kept Mrs. Pink up to a late hour. In the morning when the maid arrived with her tea, she found her mistress in a petulant mood. She'd devoured the treat she'd meant to save for morning and now, like a child who has gorged herself on a box of chocolates and wakes to find the empty papers scattered about her bed, she had the unpleasant sense of having done something shameful. When the maid went out, Mrs. Pink pushed the *Cornhill* from the stack and muttered to herself as it slipped off the table edge to the carpet. Nothing for it but *Blackwood's*, she thought, without enthusiasm. But a glance at *Blackwood's* table of contents lifted her spirits to a giddy height; here was a new work by Mrs. Oliphant, who never failed to please.

Two hours later a jubilant reader closed the journal decisively. The story was so exactly to her taste it had caused her to pause in her reading, savoring the details of the characters and the plot. It concerned a wealthy widow, like herself, who, unlike Mrs. Pink, has failed to make a will and dies intestate. But how beautifully she dies, passing from her bedroom to another place where, for some time, though time means nothing there, she can't comprehend that she is no longer alive. When she does, against the advice of her new and old friends, she determines that she must go back among the living and right the wrong done to her goddaughter, the rightful heir to her grand estate. And—this was the exciting part—she is allowed to return to her house. Children, in their innocence, can see her, but no one else does, no one else can, or perhaps it's that no one else will.

Mrs. Pink rose from her downy pillows and luxurious bed linens in a state of exaltation. She would go straight to her friend Mrs. Drover, and bring her the welcome news that the divine Oliphant was clearly in sympathy with their own enlightened Spiritualist company.

The *Cornhill* lay facedown on the carpet until the afternoon, when the maid set it back on the nightstand. Mrs. Pink didn't open it again; other matters claimed her attention. Mrs. Drover had invited her to a séance with a distinguished medium from England, and she had no doubt that her beloved Captain Pink would have some message for her. It had been ten years since his ship had gone down in a hurricane off the coast of Mauritius with all hands lost, but she had never lost faith, as she had never lost it when he was alive, that he would find a way to return to her.

The next day the *Cornhill* joined the July through December issues on the shelf in the drawing room. Months passed. Spring came, brutal and tender by turns. The walls of snow that lined every human passageway turned to slush, the tips of the tree branches swelled, the sap rose in their trunks, and every maple in town sprouted a spigot and a bucket.

At last it was full summer and the preparatory bustle of the annual migration to Lake Pleasant enlivened the atmosphere at the house of Pink. Twelve volumes each of the *Cornhill*, *Blackwood's*, and *Longman's* were packed into boxes and carried away in a cart, along with three trunks of clothing, a selection of pots and pans carefully chosen by the cook, four carpets of various sizes, another trunk of linens, a medicine cabinet, a box of expensive British tea, a full tea service, a china and flatware service for six packed in a specially designed crate, and a hamper of smoked meats and hard cheese.

In the opinion of Mrs. Pink, it was a pity and a disgrace that so many of her fellow Spiritualists, who kept up well enough with politics and were acquainted with the reputations, if not the actual persons, of the most excellent mediums from Chicago to the Russian court, could not tell you the name of a single contemporary British poet or novelist. On her arrival at her simple cottage on the lakeshore, carefully timed so that the maid and the cook should have a full day to arrange everything to their mistress's taste, Mrs. Pink sent to the hotel for a boy with a handcart to collect the boxes of British journals. On the next day she supervised the placement of the year's editions in the glass-fronted bookcase she had herself purchased expressly to provide guests who might seek to entertain themselves in the lounge with matter of more substance than *Godey's* or the *Woman's Home Companion* might provide.

And so it was that on a rainy July morning in 1884, Phoebe Grant, a journalist employed by the *Philadelphia Sun*, having settled herself in an armchair in the lounge of the Lake Pleasant Hotel, opened a copy of *Cornhill* magazine and began reading an article with the ungainly title "J. Habakuk Jephson's Statement." Unbeknownst to her, another lady entered at the door and with elaborate stealth came up behind her chair. At first, this lady contemplated the shoulders and bowed head of the absorbed reader with an amused expression, as if she intended to play some girlish prank. But after a moment her eyes drifted to the page held aloft before her and a frown of interest lightly pursed her lips.

"I know you're there," said the journalist calmly.

But her friend made no reply, continuing her silent inspection of the opening lines of the article. After a moment, in a tone suggesting righteous offense, she observed, "That isn't correct. It was 1872. And the ship wasn't in tow. They sailed her to Gibraltar."

From: PERSONAL RECOLLECTIONS:
MY LIFE IN JOURNALISM
BY PHOEBE GRANT, EDITED BY LUCY DIAL

ON SPIRITUALISM

In October 1888, on assignment for the *Philadelphia Sun*, I was in the audience when Margaret Fox, the founding mother of the Spiritualist movement, stood before a packed hall at the Academy of Music in New York and confessed that she had been "instrumental in perpetrating the fraud of Spiritualism upon a too-confiding public." A year later she recanted that recantation, bringing the whole filthy business full circle. One had the sense that it could never have been otherwise, that by discrediting herself as a reliable witness to her own actions, Margaret had achieved what had always been her objective. All she would own to was her invincible capriciousness. The press called her confession "the Death Blow to Spiritualism." But the Spiritualists ignored Margaret's call to disarm, and ultimately the founder was abandoned by the religion she created.

Violet Petra never publicly admitted to fraud. There are those who still believe she was the genuine article—a clairvoyant of extraordinary powers. However, near the end, there was a confession of sorts, wrung from her in a paroxysm of sobbing before a solitary auditor in the lounge of a shabby Philadelphia hotel, on a chilly afternoon in November 1894.

I was that auditor.

Fraud has long been one of my interests. Doubtless it began in childhood when, like most children, I experimented with pushing the casual fib to the outright lie. I said I'd drunk my milk when I'd actually poured it down the drain; I pretended to be ill when I was perfectly well; I blamed a little friend for breaking a toy I'd broken myself. I remember these three episodes because my falsity was quickly detected and the consequences were harsh. The devil, my mother adjured me, is a successful liar and his reward is a permanent residence in hell.

In my childish imagination this made perfect sense. For the duration of my effort to carry off the thing-not-true, I had felt I was living in a furnace. I gave up lying and became, in fact and in practice, a seeker after truth, such as I find it. And when I do find it, it is my business to record it for the public benefit. I am that risible hobgoblin of the contemporary male novelist's imagination: the female journalist.

In the course of my investigations, I've closely observed some talented and professional frauds—they abound in our times as in all others—and have even been caught up in the havoc they inevitably wreak upon those weak-minded enough to trust them. Truly accomplished frauds are rare, but there exists a superfluity of ordinary and presumably intelligent people who are eager to court and to credit them.

The perversity of the liar is that he does not, as I did, dread the thought of being caught in the lie. In fact, the likelihood of exposure is for him no more bothersome than a buzzing insect, and his triumph is most complete when the contempt he has always on reserve for those who catch him out can be fully brought to bear.

A constant alternation between contempt and belligerence is essential to the *amour-propre* of the confirmed liar. He may be said to be driven from the pillar of one to the post of the other, a hectic gauntlet that constitutes for him a simulacrum of identity. As wind fills a sail, the flagrant dispersal of that which he knows to be false inflates his sense of self. His need for an audience is great, for a podium even greater, and it matters not if his auditors be only his family taken hostage at the dining table or a mob of strangers gathered on a street corner; his lies must be broadcast on the first available soil, they must be watered and cultivated and encouraged to bloom into misshapen flowers—not of evil—but of banality and inutility.

FIRST ENCOUNTER WITH
THE CHARISMATIC SPEAKER AND CLAIRVOYANT
MEDIUM VIOLET PETRA

I first saw Violet Petra in 1874 at a private gathering in the home of her patron, a banker named Jacob Wilbur, at his well-appointed town house near Washington Square in New York. She was very young, scarcely more than a girl, and her performance, while affecting, only hinted at what was to come. There was a rage for female trance speaking at that time and men of substance were combing the provinces for attractive young women to grace their parlors with prodigies of clairvoyance. Often these sessions began with a display of the speaker's better than average knowledge of a subject; say, astronomy or Roman history, chosen at random by the assembled guests. It was understood that the speaker's eloquence was attributable to the intercession of "spirit guides," deceased know-alls who spoke through her, without her will or even her consciousness. Some of these were historical figures—Ben Franklin was a popular resource, which struck me as appropriate, given his reputation for meddling in the affairs of others and his preference for the company of pretty women. Once the fad for guides got under way, American Indians were much in evidence, presumably chosen for their spiritual purity. These guides served as conduits to the immense, sunny, happy land where the spirits of the dead wandered aimlessly waiting for a summons from the loved ones they had left behind.

Violet Petra didn't have a spirit guide at that first gathering in New York. She spoke for fifteen minutes on the subject of magnetic attraction and took a few questions written on scraps of paper and tossed into a hat. I remember one, an inquiry about the health of the questioner's relative who had recently decamped for California. This traveler, described only as "my niece," had insisted on making the trip to join her husband, though she knew herself to be in a delicate condition. Violet read out the question to the group in her soft, clear voice, keeping her gaze upon the paper. Her eyes closed, her lips parted, and she dropped her chin upon her breastbone, which caused her dark, waving hair to fall forward, curtaining her features. A long moment passed, long enough for the gentleman next to me to finger his pocket watch and the air to grow thick with anticipation. Then she lifted her face, brushing her hair back with one hand, and I saw the trademark oddity of her left eye, which bulged in its socket, the iris wandering off to one side.

This peculiarity of Violet Petra's eye was to become part of her myth. According to the brief autobiographical account sometimes appended to her speaking programs, it was the result of her first contact with the spirit world, which occurred when she was nine years old in a meadow near her bucolic childhood home in upstate New York. It was a warm summer's day, and she was busily gathering clover to weave into a crown. Her older sister, propped against a maple tree with her writing desk in her lap, was composing a letter. Little Violet could hear the *crop-crop* of her pony grazing near the fence of his pasture. The sun brushed the world with a liquid light outlining each flower in gold, or so it seemed to her. She felt a kiss of cool air against her cheek, once, twice. Startled, she brought her hand to touch the spot. A voice close to her ear whispered her name, a voice she recognized as belonging to her grandmother, which was odd, as she knew her grandmother was far away, at her home in Philadelphia. But here she was, gently summoning her granddaughter by her pet name, which was Viva. The delighted child raised her eyes and for a moment looked into her beloved granny's sweetly smiling face. In the next moment, with the speed and *thwack* of an arrow striking a target, a bolt of light sliced into her left eyeball. She was knocked backward by the blow, and sprawled unconscious upon the clover with her bouquet still clutched in her hand.

Some hours later she woke up in her own bed. Her mother rose from her chair nearby, laying her knitting on the side table as, with tremulous lips and moistened eye, she approached her daughter. "Where's Granny?" lisped the winsome child. "I know she's here. She called me."

Late that night a telegram arrived from Philadelphia with the woeful news that Violet's grandmother, a sprightly widow of independent means and spirit who until that day enjoyed excellent health, had collapsed on the sidewalk outside her town house. Before a doctor could be summoned to her aid, she passed from this life, expiring, speechless, in the arms of a stranger.

I've never been able to determine whether this story had some basis in the original trauma that resulted in the peculiarity of Violet's eye, or was entirely fabricated to take advantage of a condition predating her first experience of spirit communication. Apart from the autobiographical sketch and another carefully documented article that has to do with her accurate prediction of a shipwreck during the war, Violet Petra's history is a carefully guarded secret. She appeared in Boston, like Venus, full blown from some westerly town she refuses to name. She was, she claims, eighteen at that time, but she may have been younger. Like many of her coreligionists, she has a thorough knowledge of the Bible, which book she holds in contempt. She has a strong background and a keen interest in geology, suggesting to me that Petra is not her real name.

I knew nothing about her that evening in Mr. Wilbur's lavishly furnished drawing room. When she raised her face to her attentive audience, the alteration in her features—for it wasn't just the eye; her complexion was deathly pale and her lips dark and tumid—was so striking that I joined in the general intake of breath. She coughed, bringing two fingers to her sternum, as if opening a path from her heart to her throat. When she spoke her voice was deeper than her ordinary speaking voice. It wasn't an entirely different voice; it wasn't, as is sometimes the case with female mediums, a masculine voice, but it had a sonorous, humorless gravity, an irresistible authority that held her listeners in her sway.

"Bridget and her baby son have come over," she said. "They are happy, they send love to Aunt Jane." She paused while Aunt Jane, who had revealed neither her own name nor that of her niece, burst into tears. "I hear another name," Violet continued. "It's Jack. No, it's Zachary, Bridget is watching over him. All will be well."

Zachary, the sobbing Aunt Jane testified, was Bridget's younger brother, a boy of ten who was very ill; in fact, it was feared, near death's door, and under the doctor's watchful care.

Violet closed her eyes, her head tilted to one side in an attitude of listening. The room grew silent, but for the subdued weeping of the questioner, as all attempted to hear what the medium was evidently no longer hearing. Perhaps thirty seconds passed before she fell back in her chair and opened her eyes, a smile of pure serenity lingering about her lips. "Have I been helpful?" she asked pleasantly, hopefully. Mr. Wilbur's enchanted guests burst into wild applause.

How wild a guess was it that a pregnant girl on her way to California wouldn't survive the trip? Or that a child sick with fever would recover? The odds are even, and an educated surmise tips the scale this way or that. In the case of the sick child, his death could be passed off as the result of his dead sister's calling him home to her. Either way, Violet Petra's prediction was pretty safe.

Of course, diligent journalist that I am, I spent the following morning tracking down the ailing Zachary, which wasn't difficult, as the family was eager to give out the glad news that the boy's fever had broken during the night, that he was cheerful, hungry, eager to be out of bed, and that his full recovery was confidently anticipated by all who loved him.

After that first trance-lecture in Mr. Wilbur's lavish New York flat, I didn't see or hear of Violet Petra, nor did my thoughts linger upon her, for ten years. During that time the Spiritualist movement flourished until its adherents were so numerous that a confession of orthodoxy was called for and briefly embraced. As Mr. William James has observed, "When a religion becomes an orthodoxy, its day of inwardness is over; the spring is dry," and so it was for the quarrelsome Spiritualists. In 1872, failing to achieve unanimity at their national convention, they splintered into diverse camps. And by camps, I don't mean associations of coreligionists with conflicting views, but actual meeting places, complete with grounds, tents, and cottages, materializing like ectoplasm at a séance on the shores of sparkling New England lakes, and serviced by railroads, restaurants, furniture movers, cleaners, farmers, farriers, florists, resident musicians, photographers, and butchers. No one knew where the spirits of the dead spent the winters, but once the last trace of frost had retreated from the hinterlands, they gathered at Silver Lake and Lake Pleasant in anticipation of their devotees among the living. These camp meetings were so popular that they came to the attention of the press, and so one hot afternoon in August, having boarded the train at Fitchburg, I alighted at Lake Pleasant clutching my valise, and followed the wooden walkway through a shady grove of white pine, past the open-air dance pavilion, and down the sturdy staircase to the wide and welcoming veranda of the gleaming new Lake Pleasant Hotel.

Inside was a bustle of people and a few barking dogs, all evidently acquainted with and enthusiastic about the prospect of long summer days and nights passed in one another's company. As I approached the desk, the strain of a violin rose above the chatter, weaving a cheerful, countrified ribbon of sound through the general uproar. The mustached clerk greeted me with extreme affability; my reservation was in order and my key at the ready. He regretted that I had requested only four nights; or rather he maintained that

I would regret it. "Once our guests arrive, they generally don't want to leave. You won't find better company or a more beautiful setting in the state."

"It is a lovely spot," I agreed.

"And no end of entertainments," he continued, folding a printed sheet and pressing it upon me. "Here's the daily program, and the list of speakers for the week. There's a band concert at the shell twice a day, and the orchestra in the evening at the dance pavilion. Everyone enjoys the dancing, young and old."

I opened the sheet and glanced at the headings: "Instrumental Music," "Vocal Music," "Illuminations," "Public and Test Mediums," "Entertainments," "Boating," "Board and Lodging."

"I had no idea it was so festive," I observed.

"Well, Miss Grant," replied the sharp-witted clerk. "You're not among the Methodists here."

I smiled knowingly. The Methodist and Spiritualist brethren were notoriously antipathetic, though they have at times shared the same campgrounds. Some years ago their summer meetings overlapped at Lake Pleasant and the results were, especially on the Methodist side, rancorous. "They have given themselves over to Satan," the Methodist preacher complained to the local newspaper in a letter printed beneath the caustic heading "The Devil Takes Lake Pleasant." The editor responded that most townspeople preferred the Spiritualist meetings, as "all are welcome at the dances and musical events." After that, the Methodists retreated, and the Spiritualists virtually owned Lake Pleasant.

Considering the increased level of eccentricity facilitated by residence among the like-minded, I climbed the stairs and turned the key to my small but comfortably furnished room. If one person in a crowd of skeptics falls on the floor and declares that the spirit of Black Feather has a message for Mrs. Green, he may be presumed mad and carted off to an asylum. But if all the bystanders agree that Black Feather is as reliable as the newspapers, then the message will be duly delivered to Mrs. Green, and it won't be long before someone else receives a message from Black Feather, or

White Arrow, or Pocahontas, and the circle will begin to close out anyone who doesn't find recourse to dead Indians a perfectly legitimate practice. There I was, unpacking my blouses in a sunny room in an efficiently run hotel booked solid with pleasure seekers who, on a summer day dedicated to the salubrious pastimes of boating, singing, dining, whist playing, and dancing, would find time for a séance or a session with the spirit photographer. I gazed from my window at two women seated on a wooden bench shaded by towering pines: a white-haired dowager with hooded eyes and a hawkish nose, engaged in feverish conversation with a plumpish matron in a billowing white lawn dress, the bodice trimmed in pink satin, languorously fanning her face, which was partially obscured by the wide brim of her straw hat. Farther down the dirt-packed lane, an elderly man with a flowing white beard, his plain farmer's flannels covered by a long striped linen apron, pulled a wagon laden with colorful vegetables toward a cluster of bright summer cottages fronting on the lake. It didn't look like an asylum, nor did it resemble a religious community, but it was, in my view, surely a little of both.

When I had unpacked my valise and hung my apparel in the wardrobe, I took a seat at the writing table and perused the program, which I noted was professionally printed on good-quality paper. There was a long list of speakers' names and a short one of "Public and Test Mediums," most of whom were men. Some qualified their listing with their specialties. There was Mr. Cyrus Walker, *Slate Writing Medium*, and Mrs. J. J. Spence, *Clairvoyant Physician*, and Dr. Charles Hodges, *Magnetic Healer*. I'd done a little research in preparation for my assignment, and some of the names were familiar to me.

My editor would be satisfied with a lively description of the scene, but my curiosity was aroused, and I had in mind a longer, investigative piece, something I might offer freelance to a journal—I knew of a likely one—devoted to debunking all things unscientific.

But how, exactly, might I best carry out my investigations? Should I fake an illness and seek the services of the "clairvoyant physician," or simply appear at a test séance as what I was, a skeptic requiring persuasion? How close was the community, how incestuous the chatter among the practitioners? Upward of five thousand visitors were expected through the season; should I seek anonymity in the crowd or declare my intention to herald the glories of the Spiritualist movement to the world at large?

At length, noting in the column headed "Board and Lodging" the possibility of dining at the Lakeside Café, I made up my mind to do nothing more investigative than seeking out my supper. It was too warm in my room and lakeside dining might include a breeze.

This dining establishment consisted of a tent with low wooden sides and a wide, planked floor. The canvas on the lakeside, raised to form an awning, gave the diners a view of the various boating parties gliding on the smooth water. The tables were set with clean linens and vases of wildflowers, and the ceiling strung with Japanese paper lanterns that were not yet lit, as the sun was still low in the western sky. Though several groups were already seated, the room was by no means full. A young woman in a starched apron showed me to a table near the water. I ordered my food—there was no menu, only a few choices, fish or roast beef, two soups, potatoes or green beans—and settled myself, glancing about at my fellow diners. A breeze, as I had hoped, rustled among the lanterns, but it was stale and damp, like a human breath. I could feel my hair frizzing along my forehead and at the nape of my neck. At the table nearest me, an elderly couple earnestly spooned up soup as if engaged in a competition to empty their bowls. Beyond them, his back to me, a gentleman with wavy silver hair and wide shoulders stretching the seams of a striped linen jacket laughed abruptly. I leaned out past the soup-eaters to take in his entertaining companion, a young woman I could see only in profile. She was small and willowy, dressed in an odd, vaguely Grecian gown of white crepe, her heavy dark hair bound in a topknot and pierced by two large white feathers. She gazed at the man, who was dabbing his napkin to his lips in an attempt to stifle his laughter. Her own lips were slightly parted, her eyebrows lifted, her expression hesitant, as if she had not expected to provoke hilarity.

"I beg your pardon," he said, spreading the napkin in his lap with feigned solemnity.

"I don't see what's funny about it," she protested, but amiably, willing, with his assistance, to discover the lighter side of her own discourse.

"It's just that you are so charming, my dear," he said.

"Ah," she replied.

Their waitress arrived with two plates of meat swimming in pale gravy. "Here's your dinner," the man said.

A crush of guests gathered at the opening of the tent filtered into the room, joyful and cacophonous, swooping down upon the tables like an invasion of crows on a calm summer evening. The waitresses went among them, taking orders, filling water pitchers and glasses, lighting the lanterns with long tapers, and in a few moments the scene was transformed and what had seemed a triste, tacked-together affair became a lively, glittering hall. My fish arrived, its flat dead eye gazing solemnly up at me. The flesh looked a little dry, I thought, though the waitress assured me it had been pulled from the lake only hours earlier. As I consumed my former fellow lake resident, I allowed myself the pleasure of anonymity in a place where strangers are few. I guessed at the relationships between various couples, wondering as I watched them which were the mediums and which their patrons. Or were they called clients? Sitters, perhaps, as séances involved sitting. Or seekers. It would be useful to know the agreed upon euphemisms of the Spiritualist trade.

I could no longer hear the conversation between the couple nearest my table, but my wandering eye returned to the fetching young woman, who had finished her dinner and was now tucking into a large slice of pie. As her jaws worked, the feathers in her hair shifted lightly from side to side. I couldn't see the face of her companion, whose hands moved among the tea service, pouring out a cup for each of them, pinching sugar cubes from the bowl with the silver tongs—two for her, I noted. I thought he must be amused to see the relish with which his companion—was she his daughter?— devoured her dessert. She scraped the fork across the plate, gathering up the last crumbs, her free hand moving out to pull in the cup of tea.

There was something familiar about her, but I couldn't place her. She was an intriguing combination of a child and an adult. Her back was perfectly straight and strong; there was nothing gangly about the long pale neck that rose above the artfully arranged folds of her gown, or in the muscular forearms visible beneath the gauzy sleeves. The top-heavy mass of luxuriant hair gleamed with health. She looked strong enough to climb a tree, yet she was so slender, her movements so graceful, her hands small, manicured, the fingers tapered; all this gave the impression of delicacy and fragility. With her jaunty top feathers, she was like a hummingbird that hovers over the lily, whirring gently, its feathers smooth and sleek, its bony chest quivering over a heart the size of a grain of rice, giving no sign of the power and tenacity that allow it to fly the length of a continent. Her napkin slipped from her lap, and as she leaned down to retrieve it she felt my eyes upon her and glanced up at me. She smiled affably, as one safely smiles at a stranger in a sociable setting. I felt my own lips compressing at the corners, returning the courtesy. Still, her wide gray eyes lingered a moment beyond the smile, and I was conscious of a change in every detail of her expression, an alarming, speaking change, best described as a shift from "Have we met?" to "Save me." Then she fished up the napkin and, straightening effortlessly, returned her attention to her table companion.

And that was when it came to me who she was: Violet Petra. That simple girl I'd seen in a rich man's parlor so many years ago. She was much altered, thinner, paler, lovelier, a woman with a style all her own, and evidently a new patron, for Mr. Wilbur had been a round, balding man who by no feat of nature could have transformed himself into the impressive and well-coiffed individual who rose from his seat, extending his arm, and his protection, to the youthful Miss Petra. As they passed through the summer dining room, heads came up; greetings and hand flutterings were exchanged. And then the handsome couple passed out into the firefly-lit night.

On my return to the hotel, I learned that Miss Petra neither lectured nor advertised as a "test medium." "She's a reclusive lady, and much sought after. She only does private sittings," my loquacious clerk informed me. "Folks make their appointments months ahead of time. She's that much in demand."

"And why is that?"

"Well, they say it's because she is such a powerful clairvoyant and there's no showmanship about her. She just asks you a few questions and then she knows all about you and your loved ones."

"Dead and alive?" I said.

"Mostly the former, I'd say. You can find out about your living relatives fast enough with the telegraph these days."

"That's true," I agreed, taking up my heavy room key. "We live in marvelous times."

A MESSAGE UNDER THE DOOR

Dear Miss Grant,

As we are neighbors (I'm across the hall in 204), I thought you might not mind if I took the liberty of inviting you to join me for hot chocolate and some excellent doughnuts in my sitting room tomorrow morning. I generally rise at seven and the restaurant sends up the breakfast at eight. Please forgive the drama of a note beneath the door, but I didn't want to disturb you by knocking—yet I am eager to make your acquaintance and to welcome you to our blessed idyllic community. The weather promises fair and the room opens to a charming balcony.

And the doughnuts really are delicious.

Can I tempt you?

Yours truly,

Violet Petra

This is the text of the remarkable document that appeared with scarcely a whisper on the bare wooden floor inside my door. I was standing in my chemise at the washstand, patting my neck and shoulders with the hand towel, and I was momentarily startled by the manifestation of the envelope. My first thought was that it must be a message from the management. I listened for the sound of departing footsteps, but there was nothing save the rustle of the curtains in the evening breeze, carrying the muted voices of a few late-night guests returning from the lake. I hung up my towel, and, crossing the room, took up the envelope. The note was written on hotel stationery in an open, leftward-slanting script. I read it over twice, noting that the word "blessed" had been struck out and replaced by the word "idyllic." A telling revision, though what it told, I couldn't say. Taking the curious page to the writing table, I seated myself and read it over a third time. I thought it playful and daring, yet studied and designed to disarm. The careful dissembling of the author's true intentions in the formulas of acquaintance-making and welcome, the puerile enthusiasm for sweets, the consciousness of possessing an element of drama and urgency in the manner of delivery, the final titillating, seductive wink ("Can I tempt you?" said the serpent, proffering the . . . doughnut), and the schoolgirlish closing, all fascinated me. No expectation of a negative reply was alluded to, no precise time was set, though presumably, I had best arrive in time for the doughnuts. Chocolate and doughnuts, I thought, a child's breakfast. I wondered if the gentleman of the night before would be in attendance.

And I wondered who was paying for the suite with the charming balcony.

And why the "powerful clairvoyant" so seriously in demand was eager to make my acquaintance. What did she know about me?

I put the missive aside and climbed into my narrow bed, where I slept tolerably well, rising at six, as is my habit. Once dressed, I found I had time for a stroll to the lake. Wanting to be alert for my meeting with the clairvoyant, I stopped in at the dining tent for a cup of coffee, which I drank at my ease, gazing out at the amusing miniature steamboat drifting on its anchor chain above its rippled reflection in the calm water.

At a quarter past eight, I presented myself at the door of Room 204. Before I could raise my hand, the door flew open, and Violet Petra, dressed in a filmy white muslin gown heavily embroidered with tiny violets and embellished by a gold satin sash at the waist and a froth of old lace at the sleeves, her masses of dark hair loose and curling over her shoulders, her full lips rouged and parted, her clear gray eyes fixing tightly on my face, greeted me with the breathless affirmation of her own psychic powers. "I knew you would come," she declared.

"How did you know?" I asked.

She ignored my question, her eyes flickering over my plain blouse and dirndl skirt, as she stepped back into the room, inviting me to follow with a wave of her hand.

Near the open doors to the balcony, a round table with a good linen cloth was laid for two. Between the plates an ornate china pot crouched above a plate of doughnuts covered by a screen cage. On a side table, next to a beige silk upholstered chaise longue, I noticed a copy of *Godey's* and the daily camp news bulletin. The Boston paper, much rummaged, was scattered across the carpet. So our clairvoyant kept up with fashions and current events. Violet pulled a chair from the table and bid me take it. "We have much to talk about, I think," she said.

I let her stand a moment as I appraised her offer with a purposefully mystified eye. I wasn't willing to play the game of instant intimacy, which she evidently had in mind. As she apprehended my reluctance, for she was an adept at reading the subtlest changes of mood in her audience, her brows drew together thoughtfully. "You must think me very forward," she said.

I advanced to the chair, maintaining my puzzled air as she took her seat across from me. "I admit," I said, "I wonder how you came to know my name."

She fussed over the pot, which had a candle beneath it to keep the contents warm, and poured the fragrant beverage into the cups. "Oh," she said lightly, as if my naïveté was amusing, "everyone knows your name. Or everyone who reads the register, and many do. We're a close community here, you'll find, and you are a newcomer. There's a great curiosity about you."

"I see," I said, lifting the cup and sipping the chocolate while she served us each a doughnut. She smiled at me so candidly that, as I set the cup back in its saucer, I decided to drop my defensive manner. "It's very good," I said, nodding at the chocolate.

"It is," she agreed. "I never drink it at home, but when we're here, I want it every morning."

I remarked the plural pronoun, presumably not the royal "We." "Are you here with your family?"

She lowered her eyes to the plate and said, with just the right vibration of regret, "I have no family. They've all passed away, some years ago now."

"Then the gentleman you were dining with last night was not your relative."

"Mr. Babin is my sponsor."

"Which means?"

"He arranges things for me, introductions, appointments, things of that sort. Sometimes I have speaking engagements, but only for small invited groups. He sees to all that."

"He's your manager."

Her spine stiffened; she fixed me in an icy glare. "I'm not an actress, Miss Grant."

Her hauteur made me smile.

She looked down, picked at her skirt, failing to entirely suppress an answering smile flickering at the corners of her mouth. "Really," she said. "You are a most exasperating person." Then she helped herself to an unladylike big bite of her doughnut.

"I haven't had chocolate since I was a girl," I said.

She managed to smile through her zesty chewing, then swallowed hard. "Of course," she said. "You drink coffee, and lots of it."

"Why do you say so?"

"Don't all journalists drink lots of coffee?"

"What makes you think I'm a journalist?"

"I don't think you are a journalist. I know you are."

"Really?" I felt rattled to have been unmasked so early in my investigations. "And how do you know that?"

She dropped the uneaten fragment of her doughnut onto the

plate and patted her lips with a napkin, her eyes mischievous, almost gleeful at my discomfiture. Carefully she opened the square of cloth and laid it across her skirt, lowering her eyes to her preoccupied hands. "Oh, I know things," she said. "Haven't you heard?"

"What? People's professions? Is that clairvoyance?"

As she lifted her cup, her eyes still lowered, the martial strains of a band striking up near the lake jauntified the quiet atmosphere of the room, but when Violet looked up again, her expression was mirthless, even sullen. "No," she said. "It didn't require clairvoyance to know who you are. I read the Philadelphia papers, and I've a good memory for names."

"I see," I said, which was true. I did see quite a long way, but not far enough, as it turned out. I saw only what she wanted me to see: that she was a very pretty, frank, ambitious little woman. Nothing she said or did would be of any importance to me personally; she would not, she could not make a difference to me, yet I believed there was more to her than met the eye. Above all, I believed she was a charlatan, and as such, no matter how she might admire me, no matter that she might actually feel affection for me, someday she would be driven to deceive me and then to despise me for having failed her, for having been deceived by her. I determined to interest myself in her because I wanted to expose her. To do that I would have to catch her off her guard, and what I most clearly observed at this first interview was that her guard was very high, remote, and impressively fortified. She was innately cautious, perversely non-committal. She presented what she knew was presentable. What was not, she kept to herself.

I also observed that she wasn't suspicious of me. Her desire to know me was entirely a product of her self-interest. She thought I might be in a position to advance what she would have called her "cause."

Her defensive mood had veered abruptly back to gaiety. "Are you disappointed?" she teased. "Is it just too ordinary of me to take note of a byline?"

"Not ordinary at all, in my experience," I replied. "Most people don't notice the names of journalists, unless they happen to be famous, which I decidedly am not."

"Not yet," she agreed. "But you might be. I thought your articles about that murder trial in Uniontown were first rate."

I sipped my chocolate, raising my eyebrows over the rim of my cup, stupidly flattered and knowing I was stupid, but unable to help myself. I was particularly proud of the series she named.

The accused in the Uniontown trial was a young, handsome, charming, and promising lawyer named Nicholas L. Dukes, who was engaged to marry a wealthy young woman named Lizzie Nutt. For reasons no one could explain, including Dukes himself, shortly before the wedding day the future husband sent several outraged letters to his fiancée's father, Captain A. C. Nutt, alleging that Lizzie was known to have been "criminally intimate" with a number of men and that he must therefore withdraw his proposal of marriage. Captain Nutt, mystified and incensed at the offense to his daughter's honor, arranged a meeting with her accuser. During that confrontation, Dukes produced a pistol, and shot his future father-in-law to death. Dukes claimed to have acted in self-defense, as the older gentleman had threatened to strike him with his walking stick.

Captain Nutt was a prominent citizen and the community was much agitated by the trial, which was a long one. At last the fatherless Lizzie appeared to testify against her suitor. There was a hush when she entered the courtroom, for Lizzie was a woman of great beauty, poise, and distinction. She expressed her bemusement at her fiancé's bizarre letters to her father. "If he didn't want to marry me," she explained calmly to the prosecutor, "he had only to say so. Why send slanderous messages to my father? I don't understand it."

I couldn't understand it either. Surely this elegant, lovely, and wealthy young woman would have no difficulty finding another suitor, and it was equally clear that she was unlikely to be showering her favors upon the butcher or the postman. But Dukes was not on trial for slander, and in the end, to the fury of the mob in the street outside the court, he was acquitted of all charges.

Violet leaned back in her chair, pressing her fingertips to her lips, her eyes searching my face intently with an unwavering solicitude that unnerved me. "You drew those characters so clearly," she said. "You must see all manner of cruelty and violence in your work."

What was she imagining? That I followed murderers down dark alleys? That I frequented squalid tenements? "Not really," I said. "I tend to see the consequences of cruelty and violence."

"Those articles were so well written; it was like reading a story."

"Thank you," I said, taking up a doughnut. In the hopes of closing the subject of my profession I asked, "Do you live in Philadelphia? When you're not here?"

"When I'm in Philadelphia, I stay with Mr. and Mrs. Babin," she said.

"And where is your home?"

"I don't, strictly speaking, have a home," she said mysteriously. Outside the band, audibly on the move in the direction of the hotel, broke into the refrain of "Oh, My Darling Clementine." Violet smiled, gazing at the balcony. "You are lost and gone forever," she sang in a clear, high voice. "I like that song." Turning back to me, she said, "Do you?"

I nodded. The marchers had paused beneath our window, and the music was so loud I didn't attempt to speak over it. The voices of two men standing on the wide side balcony broke out raucously, "In a cavern, in a canyon . . ." while Violet and I sat smiling blandly at each other. I finished the doughnut, a heavy, sweet, chewy wad covered in fine sugar, which cascaded over my dark skirt. I dusted the powder away with my napkin while the band played on. At last, with applause above and shouts below, the marchers turned away, taking Clementine back to the lake where they had found her.

"They do that every morning," Violet informed me.

"Surely not the same song?"

"No," she said. "They have a repertoire."

"How entertaining."

She leaned forward, her elbows on the table, her chin in her palms, studying me closely as if trying to determine what sort of animal I was. "Have you come among us as a skeptic or as a seeker?" she asked.

"Neither," I assured her. "I try to maintain a professional objectivity at all times. Though I can't deny I'm curious about what goes on here."

She nodded, pursing her lips thoughtfully. Then her eyes brightened and she stretched her hand toward me, tapping her fingers conspiratorially on my arm. "Are you 'on assignment'?"

I laughed at her eagerness. "I'll be doing a short piece about the attractions of Lake Pleasant," I said. "The charm of the setting, the comforts of the hotel, that sort of thing." This wasn't entirely a lie. I had a longer piece in mind, but my editor's charge had simply been: "See what's going on over there," and he was giving me only four days of room and board in which to carry out that quest.

Violet was downcast. "It's not just a resort, you know," she said.

"I know that," I replied. "But what I find odd is how much it does *feel* like a resort. Everyone seems so determined to have a good time."

"Why shouldn't we enjoy ourselves?" she replied. "The spirits of our loved ones are among us."

"Yes," I said. "Of course."

"Of course, what?" she asked gently, as if she suspected that my mind had wandered.

"The spirits," I said, wagging my fingers at the air, where, presumably, they hovered.

"Which you don't believe in."

"No," I said. "I don't."

"Have you never had an experience of . . ." She paused, searching for the word that wouldn't offend me. "Communication?" She paused again. "With someone you know is not . . ." Another pause.

"Alive?" I concluded for her. "No. I must say, I have not."

She closed her eyes, touching two fingers to the bridge of her nose. It was the briefest of gestures and appeared to be entirely involuntary, so much so that I congratulated myself for having noticed it. In the next moment she rested her chin back on her hand. As her eyes, calm and solicitous, recommenced searching my face, she asked, "Not even on that night, in that cold, dark little room, when your mother died?"

ON GHOSTS

When asked, most people will tell you they don't believe in ghosts. I know this, I've asked. I also know that with a little pressing it emerges that everyone has a ghost story. In an otherwise ordinary life of toil and struggle there intruded in this house, in that room, on that night, something extraordinary, inexplicable, something not of this world. One heard something: footsteps on a stair, a child crying, whispering voices in the hall; another saw something: a curtain rustling in a closed room, the impress of a head upon a pillow, a locked window standing open, a shadow stretching across a floor and up a wall. There was an oppressive atmosphere of sadness or malevolence, sometimes associated with a crime or a tragedy that one sensed upon entering the scene. Even the most thoroughgoing materialist has some little anecdotal evidence, some moment of doubting all, now easily recalled, and eagerly dismissed.

Ghosts. Great Caesar's. Hamlet's father. Christmas Past.

Violet was right. My mother died in a cold, dark little room in a scarcely respectable boardinghouse not far from the old Philadelphia station. We could hear the engines, like tired cart animals, wheezing and coughing at the end of their runs. We had once had better lodgings, but as the money ran out and her illness wasted the flesh from her bones, our options had dwindled. I wrote pleading letters to distant relatives, but as we kept changing addresses, I could never be sure there had been no reply, so I wrote again, reminding them of the new address.

In exchange for our miserable room and two meals a day, I did the washing up, assisted the laundress, cleaned the downstairs parlor, and ran errands for the proprietor, a blowsy, furious Irishwoman who could never be satisfied. That night I came in, exhausted from a run halfway across town in the bitter cold with only my cloth coat to protect me from the chill. I lit the lamp and carried it to the bed stand. Mother lay on her side, her breathing labored, her eyes wide and staring at the open door of the wardrobe. I stroked her forehead, which was damp and cool, arranged her blanket, and spoke reassuringly of the bread and cheese I'd saved from my dinner, though I knew she'd lost interest in food and was unlikely to be tempted. She seemed not to hear me or even to be aware of me. I turned away to pour some water from the pitcher into the glass, and when I looked back she was moving her legs under the blanket, flailing her arms as if she intended to rise from the bed, which I knew she hadn't the strength to do. My effort to capture her hands was stymied when she suddenly gripped both my wrists hard, pulling me closer. I tried to break away; I was truly frightened by the power and fierce animation that had come over her. She raised herself from the pillow, moving her dry lips, her eyes burning with the urgency of her message. "I want to stay here," she said. "I don't want to leave. I want to stay here. I must stay here." The effort to say this much—she had scarcely spoken for several days—exhausted her and she fell back, releasing my wrists. She lay panting while I looked down at her in the gloom, trying to think what I should do. Water, I stupidly thought, and turned away again. I heard a long intake of breath, followed by a quick plosive puff of air, like a child making a wish as she blows the fuzz from a dandelion. When I looked back her sunken eyes were closed, her mouth ajar, and I knew at once that she was gone.

She who had wanted, in spite of our poverty and friendlessness, to stay here.

I went to the door, stood there, but couldn't open it. Something heavy and adamant stayed my hand. I approached the bed again, noting with a shudder that Mother's eyes were now open, lightless and sightless. I crossed to the wardrobe—why, I asked myself, had it been left open? I could hear my own heartbeat, but otherwise the stillness in the room was confounding.

I stretched out my hand, laying my palm flat on the smooth wood of the panel. "Phoebe," Mother said, in the exhausted, petulant voice I knew so well. "Don't close the door."

With a shout, I darted to the hall door, threw it open, and rushed out onto the landing. Mr. Widener, a fellow boarder, stood on the stair gazing wonderingly up at me.

"Sir," I cried. "Please help me. My mother has passed away."

I was fifteen years old.

ENTER THE PATRON

How did I respond to Violet's unsolicited display of her clairvoyant powers that first morning at Lake Pleasant? I don't now perfectly remember, but I got past it somehow, probably by employing the journalist's strategy of failing to acknowledge that anything exceptional has happened. I must have changed the subject, because we were talking about the origins of the Scalpers marching band when there was a sharp rap at the door and Mr. Jeremiah Babin, evidently expected by my hostess, appeared, having come on purpose to make my acquaintance. I recognized him at once as the distinguished gentleman from the café the night before. He regretted that he hadn't been informed of my presence, as he would certainly have invited me to join their table if he had. It was agreed that I should do just that for the rest of my visit, unless, of course, I had other engagements. Mr. Babin was respectful of my profession and approving of my mission. "I am at your disposal," he declared. "You must ask me any questions that come to your mind. I am something of an authority on our residents here."

"He's something of a legal counsel to half of them," Violet observed wryly. "But he won't tell you their secrets."

Mr. Babin chuckled at her witticism. "Confidentiality is incumbent upon me."

"I understand perfectly," I said. "Journalists have ethical obligations as well." They both nodded knowingly at this assertion.

In the afternoons, Violet had appointments with "visitors" who craved messages from the next world or advice in this one, as it was known that her intuitions were acute in both venues. While she was thus employed, I made my investigations of the camp. I attended a lecture entitled "Summerland Eternal" by Dr. Albert Weevil at the speakers' "grove," enjoyed an excellent concert of Strauss waltzes at the Dance Pavilion, visited the bookstore where I bought the local papers—the camp was served by a surprising number of these, with names like *The Wildwood Messenger* and the *Lake Pleasant Siftings*—climbed up to the "highlands" for an ice cream at Gussie's Tea Room, worked on my notes in the hotel reading room, or passed a pleasant hour catching up on the latest New York and British literary journals with which this bizarre outpost was impressively supplied.

On two occasions Mr. Jeremiah Babin joined me for a stroll around the lake, during which he divulged, at length and in detail, the dramatic story of how he had come to be so importantly connected to the clairvoyant Miss Petra, and how privileged he considered himself to be in that connection.

"I understand she lives in your house," I commented.

"She does," he admitted. "And I hope she may never leave us."

"Then your wife feels as you do."

"Oh, yes. I think it's not an exaggeration to say that Miss Petra has rescued my dear wife from a despondency that threatened her very life."

"How wonderful," I said.

"Yes." He nodded, gazing out across the lake at the neat façade of the hotel wherein Violet Petra was perhaps at that very moment rescuing another sufferer. "To have such power," he mused, "and yet to wear it so lightly."

I agreed. Violet was a study in contrasts: a lighthearted, silly-headed, fashion-conscious child-woman whose influence was coveted by a bevy of large, prosperous, educated, self-confident men and women, all of whom willingly entrusted to her—in my view—their sanity.

"Do you think she knows," I asked her patron, "how much power she has?"

He paused on the path, turning upon me a thoughtful, serious look. After a moment he blinked a few times, as if to disperse an unproductive line of thought. When he spoke, his tone was rueful. "My dear Miss Grant," he said. "Let us hope not."

A TRAGEDY RECOUNTED

Jeremiah Babin occupied himself chiefly in the administration of his family's business and real estate interests. The fortune had its origins in the distant past when an enterprising relation cornered the Canadian fur trade, but it was solidified by lucrative investments in the railroad, the manufacture of steam engines, and the acquisition of vast tracts of real estate in the now burgeoning middle of the country. Jeremiah's wife, Virginia, née Millbury, though of an old and respectable Boston family, had so many beautiful and charming sisters that her dowry was not sufficient to attract any but the most sincere suitors. Given that among these sisters, Virginia was neither the most beautiful nor the most charming—though all agreed she possessed that most winning of female virtues, a sweet disposition—her marriage was widely considered something of a coup. That she adored her tall, handsome, rich husband was a given. The marriage was blessed with two children, a boy, Victor, and a girl, Melody.

Like so many in their set, the Babins moved among their houses from season to season; spring in New York, summers in Maine or Newport, fall at the family's manse in Philadelphia, and winter in Florida, though Jeremiah was sometimes forced by his business affairs to remain in Philadelphia through the early snows. It was in December during one such delay in the family's migrations that tragedy struck a devastating blow.

All that morning, as a light snow drifted down from the pristine white sheet of the sky, the children had pleaded with Miss Jekyll, their governess, to be allowed a sledding expedition in the park. Diligently they worked at their lessons in hopes of the adventure, and at lunch they were rewarded when their mother, smiling at their eagerness, granted their teacher's request. They had not far to go; the spacious plains of the park began just across the road from the Babins' big stone house on Chestnut Street. When Victor and Melody were sufficiently wrapped in fleecy hats, scarves, gloves, woolen stockings, and fur-lined boots, and their sleds extracted from beneath the stair landing, they ventured out into the chilly air while their mother looked on indulgently from an upstairs window. The trio stood at the curb, each child holding a sled cord with one hand and Miss Jekyll's kid-gloved fingers with the other. The traffic was light. A carriage passed on one side; a gentleman on horseback trotted by on the other. When the way was clear, they hurried into the cobbled street. Halfway across, Miss Jekyll's boot skidded on an icy patch, and as Virginia watched from above, the governess came down awkwardly upon her side. The children dropped their sleds, rushing to her aid; Victor manfully bent over her shoulder to offer his assistance. Melody, standing behind him, looked back at the house, spotted her mother's anxious face at the window, and waved. Miss Jekyll sat up in the street, adjusting her hat.

From out of nowhere, or so it seemed, though it was actually from around the corner, a cab hurtled into view. The horses were galloping full out, their muscular necks stretched to the limit, their heavy lips folded back over the bits, green with foam. Steam rose from their wet nostrils, their great chests heaved, and the furiously grinding hooves struck and struck the cobbles with the indifference of machine pistons. The driver had braced his boots against the ridge at the front of his box and wrapped the reins around his forearms. He was pulling with such force that his back was nearly horizontal to his seat. His hat was gone, his face crimson with fury and terror, his mouth open wide, teeth bared. His eyes looked down his face, focused on the surging heads of his horses. He couldn't see the helpless woman, the attendant children, huddled in the street.

Virginia screamed and threw herself against the window, tearing at the sash, though it was certainly too late. By the time she had pulled it free and the cold air rushed in, carrying the din of the approaching annihilation, Miss Jekyll had risen to her knees and was attempting to push the children out of danger. Melody took one tentative step toward the house; Victor clung to his governess, determined to help her to her feet. The shriek of the wheels against the stone, the pounding of the horses' hooves like rifle fire in a battlefield, the driver's shouts, and Miss Jekyll's anguished cry combined in a deafening, unearthly roar. In the last moment before the hooves struck, knocking the woman flat on her back, tossing the boy beyond her to be trampled before he could rise, Virginia saw her daughter look up, her expression confused but not frightened, and mouth the word "Mama." Then the carriage wheel struck her from behind and she sprawled facedown before it.

A RESCUE

How does a mother recover from such a loss, how pass one night without revisiting, awake or asleep, some detail of that gruesome scene and its aftermath—the crushed, mangled bodies, the bloodied stones, the shards of Melody's sled found wedged between the rails of the park fence, Miss Jekyll's kid glove clutched in Victor's death-frozen hand?

Virginia retired from the world. The window through which she had witnessed the destruction of all her joy was covered by a black drape. She couldn't bear to leave the house where her children had been happy, yet every room reproached her with reminders of what was not there. She was silent, broken, a specter wandering through empty days in search of a door that would lead her out of her suffering. But there was no door.

"Inconsolable" was her husband's diagnosis. He shared her grief, he felt it; his children had been infinitely dear to him, but he couldn't stop living because they were gone. He grieved for the children and for his wife as well. He couldn't reach her. She, who had been so generous, so loving, so admiring, now regarded him as if he were a stranger who couldn't be entirely trusted. He longed to comfort her, but she shuddered at his touch.

Three years passed and Virginia showed only small signs of improvement. She went so far as to send brief messages to various well-wishers, but she would neither leave the house nor receive visitors. She wasn't unkind and she encouraged her husband to take up his ordinary life; she had no wish to enclose him in her personal version of hell. Jeremiah, a lively, impressionable man, thrived on society as a plant thrives on watering, and was much in demand. Once a suitable period of mourning had passed he began to appear, with his wife's permission, at small social events around the town.

One evening in early spring, when the trees were swollen with buds and the ground squishy underfoot, an old family friend invited Jeremiah to a gathering at which a "remarkable clairvoyant" would be presented to the gathered company. The host, Mr. Harold Bakersmith, dabbled in Spiritualism, hypnotism, and telepathy, and fancied himself something of an investigator into psychic phenomena. "There's a lot of fraud out there," he confided to Jeremiah, "but that doesn't mean there's nothing in it." He had visited the clairvoyant at a "sitting"—she didn't like the word "séance"—and all present agreed the results had been simply staggering. "She's as close to the real thing as can be found anywhere, in my opinion, and I am not easily persuaded."

The company gathered, a group of fourteen, made up of lawyers, doctors, several fashionable ladies, and a few unfashionable dowagers, all lightly acquainted, agreeable and cultured personages. Mr. and Mrs. Bakersmith offered their guests refreshments and directed the servants in the arrangement of chairs so that everyone might have a comfortable view of their guest of honor. At length, Mrs. Bertha Bakersmith wandered to the makeshift stage, a small table and armchair facing the room, where, holding aloft a crystal glass and tapping it with her spoon, she urged her friends to take their seats, as Miss Petra was prepared to speak to them.

Violet came in at a side door, dressed all in white, her dark hair subdued in a thick braid wrapped over the crown of her head. Impractical golden slippers flashed beneath the loose pleats of her skirt as she crossed the carpet to the stage. She perched upon the armchair, sitting well forward so that her feet, in their golden slippers, could reach the floor. She adjusted her position, arranged her skirts, keeping her eyes down so that her audience could take in this pale, lovely, ephemeral presence, and only when every eye had settled firmly upon her did she look up. Her lips were lifted at the corners, her gaze as still and pellucid as a spring-fed pool. Mrs. Bakersmith approached, turned to the company, and, resting her palm on the wing of the chair, announced, "We are so pleased to have Miss Violet Petra with us this evening, and to introduce her to our dear friends in our own home. Many of you have heard tell, I doubt not, of her extraordinary gifts. If you have not, prepare to be astounded and comforted, for she bears tidings of peace and joy for us all." Then, touching her fingertips to her breastbone to indicate the tumult within, the proud hostess took her seat, leaving the stage, such as it was, to the medium.

Violet remained perfectly still, her eyes moving candidly from face to face, like a schoolteacher taking in a class of restless children, seeking out the eyes that met her own as well as those that looked askance. But they were not children, as she knew very well. They were grown men and women, prosperous, powerful, and educated— what could they want from this frail creature with her golden slippers and her penetrating gaze? She was so small, so friendless, in that room that her courage alone commended her to them. The sight of her animated maternal feeling in even the gloomiest dowager's heart and aroused in the gentlemen their most chivalrous and indulgent sympathies. The air in the room was still, yet charged with beneficent energy.

"I sense great loss, deep sadness," Violet observed. Her voice was low, but it carried to the farthest corners of the room. "Fear, disappointment." She paused, leaned back, then smiling, added, "but there is cause for joy as well. A new baby, a girl—her name is Dora—will be with us by morning."

A startled "Oh" escaped the lips of a stout matron near the stage. "My grandchild is expected this week," she said. "If a girl, she will be named for me, Dora Louise."

Violet nodded. "She is well. Mother and child will be well."

A light rustle of silk moved like a whisper through the audience as the ladies leaned toward one another. The gentlemen straightened up in their chairs to catch the eyes of their fellows. They perused each other, gauging the level of receptivity or skepticism in the open faces of their neighbors. For a few moments no one looked at Miss Petra and she took in her fill of them all. In twos and threes they returned their attention to her. When she again held them in her sway, she perplexed them by closing her eyes. Again the attentive, breathing silence freighted the atmosphere of the room. Violet raised her hands just above the armrests of her chair, her eyes still closed. When she spoke, her clear, soft voice had the intonation of one reciting a creed. "Our suffering ends at death's door," she said. "Our loved ones are among us."

A furtive movement of eyes greeted this curious announcement; some glanced up behind the medium's slightly bowed head, others looked from side to side, lifting their chins, tilting their heads, as if to listen more closely to a barely audible sound. A few cast their eyes down, lips compressed, like children who hope to escape attention.

Violet kept her eyes closed, her hands raised, palms forward, her eyebrows lifted, lips slightly parted, breathing softly through her mouth. A few long moments passed before she spoke again. "Is there a spirit present who will speak to us?"

Another silence, during which a gentleman near the front cleared his throat.

"No? Are you timid? Oh, I see." She dropped her hands, opened her eyes, gazing at the audience with an expression of affectionate amusement. "It seems there is a skeptic among us," she said. "Perhaps more than one?" Leaning to one side of her chair, she met the chilly eyes of a mustached gentleman, who, bristling at her cheerful scrutiny, looked down at his waistcoat, where he found some bit of infuriating lint to brush away. Violet's gaze moved to a frail dowager sunk in an armchair near the door, so deeply ensconced and muffled in shawls and veils that it was impossible to see her face. Having identified the sources of incredulity in the room, Violet resumed her posture, hands raised, eyes closed, in an attitude of intense listening.

"But it doesn't matter," she said. "There are many here who long for some message, some comfort." She paused; nodding her head to some proposal only she could hear. "Of course. Yes. I will tell Abigail that you are content. This is a young man, very blond with such blue eyes. He is content. You are not to concern yourself with the will. The lawyer can be trusted."

All attended the snuffle and gasp of a young lady, who murmured, "Oh, my darling," as she applied her handkerchief to her eyes.

"This is a venerable gentleman," Violet continued, "with a snow-white beard. He wishes to say that he was never happy on this side; that he was sometimes cruel and thoughtless to his son, whose name is Fredrick—no—Hendrick? Henry, yes. He regrets his cruelty, he is happy now, he watches you with love and affection. He approves. Well . . ." She paused, frowning. "He's becoming teary, I'm afraid. He says, 'Forgive me.'"

A middle-aged gentleman, known to all present as a prominent physician, leaned forward in his chair and covered his mouth with his hand.

"And here are two children. They are laughing, holding hands. Are they brother and sister? The boy has dark hair, the little girl is a pretty child, with such straight flaxen hair; she looks like a little Dutch girl. Tell Mama it is so lovely here. Tell her we miss her. We miss Papa too; the boy says that. Tell him there are many children here."

Abruptly Violet dropped her hands and sank back in her chair.

"They've gone," she said, evidently speaking to herself. She raised her head, but kept her unfocused eyes lowered. After a moment she pressed her left fingertips over her left eye and sighed. "They've gone," she said again. "I'm very tired."

Mrs. Bakersmith rose from her chair, facing the audience as she advanced upon Violet, who appeared incapable of movement. "She's exhausted herself," she explained to the curious onlookers. "These sittings are so taxing to her faculty." She bent over the clairvoyant, helping her to stand and to lean upon her arm. Then the hostess led her guest to a smaller parlor off the hall, where she eased her into a comfortable chaise, crooning sweet compliments and solicitous advice. "Let me bring you a glass of port to fortify you."

"Port would be lovely," Violet agreed.

Jeremiah Babin waited in the hall for twenty minutes before he was allowed into the parlor for his first interview with the woman he hoped might deliver his wife from the darkness of never-ending despair.

For two weeks Virginia Babin resisted her husband's entreaties to allow Violet Petra into her presence. Perhaps, as is sometimes the case with the bereaved, she had discovered in the intensity of her suffering a kind of strength. The loss of her children had alienated her from God, and she had no wish to be reconciled to anything resembling a faith.

Jeremiah pointed out that Miss Petra required neither a profession of belief nor excessive ritual. In his conversation with her after the Bakersmith demonstration, he had found her to be without artifice or guile. She didn't know how she was able to do what she did, but she was willing to assist anyone who believed she might be of use. "She told me she could try," Jeremiah explained, "but it wasn't so unlikely that she would fail."

"No," said Virginia. "I refuse to sit in the dark while some strange person goes into a trance at my dining table."

"But the room isn't dark and there's no table," Jeremiah protested. "There's no tapping or writing on slates and she doesn't speak in any voice but her own. She doesn't accept money, she doesn't go about to halls or put on shows, she gets no advantage from it. Honestly, my love, I do believe this young woman is genuinely gifted."

"No," replied Virginia. "Please don't ask me again. I can't bear it."

In the end Virginia agreed that she would bear it, and Violet Petra was invited to tea. "And nothing but tea," Virginia insisted. In this introductory meeting it was her intention to judge for herself the level of the clairvoyant's guilelessness and artificiality.

Violet was delivered to the house by Mr. Bakersmith, who handed her off to Jeremiah with the hushed enthusiasm of an art dealer presenting a truly exceptional little picture to a possible buyer. "I'll be back for her at four thirty," he promised, doffing his hat to Virginia, who stood at the parlor door, obscured by the impenetrable gloom that seeped from the dark carpets and walls of the still and joyless house. Violet, dressed in a cream cashmere tea gown with a pleated lettuce-green silk underskirt, her hair braided tightly across her forehead and looped up at the back, resembled a slender column of light beamed into the foyer from some mysterious chink in the edifice. She had noticed Virginia on entering the hall and leaned out past Jeremiah to keep her in sight, as distracted and tense as a child who must endure formalities before opening a present. Murmuring the appropriate pleasantries, she offered her hand to Jeremiah, but her eyes remained on her hostess.

This eagerness of manner alarmed Virginia, and she took a step back from the door, feeling much put upon by the two wealthy and powerful men who had obviously been taken in by the fragile beauty of this clever, brazen impostor. She wanted to bolt up the stairs and hide in her room, but in the next moment Violet advanced upon her, confidently outstretching her gloved hand. "Dear Mrs. Babin," she began. "Bertha sends you her warmest regards and she has asked me specifically to say that she is in great hopes that you will come to visit her in the nearest possible future."

Virginia took the hand, ignoring the busy scrutiny of the unabashed eyes. "I don't go out, Miss Petra," she said. "As Bertha well knows. Will you sit down?"

Jeremiah followed, filling the doorway with his impressive bulk. His wife cast him a reproachful glance as he stepped inside and occupied himself by examining the tea service. It had been so long out of use that it was badly tarnished, and the maid, enthusiastically embracing the challenge, had polished it to mirror brightness. The pink iced cakes artfully arranged on a tray next to it were reflected in its round belly.

"I believe," Violet replied as she took the chair her hostess indicated near the comforting warmth of the fire, "that Bertha hopes your kind invitation to me might be an . . ." She paused, searching for the word. Both Virginia and Jeremiah unconsciously lifted their chins in anticipation. "An indication," she continued, "of your willingness to rejoin the many friends who so sorely miss the pleasure of your company."

"Is that what Bertha hopes?" Virginia replied. Her tone betrayed little interest in any response to this rhetorical question. She seated herself before the tray, turning her attention to the duty of pouring out.

Jeremiah took up a glass plate and helped himself to the cakes. "Three years is a long time to stay indoors," he remarked.

The cup in Virginia's raised hand rattled lightly against the saucer. As she righted it, setting it on the table next to the pot, Violet studied her. The pressure of her guest's close inspection disturbed in Virginia a myriad of conflicting emotions, the strongest of which was a determination to suppress any expression of genuine feeling. She expected Violet to echo her husband's callous observation: Oh, yes, three years was too long. It was time to return to the larger world of her eager and sympathetic friends. Three years was an eternity. She steeled herself for some such effrontery, but when after a thoughtful pause Violet spoke, she said exactly what Virginia wanted to say. "Oh, I don't think three years is such a very long time at all."

Virginia allowed her hand to rest on the handle of the pot, raising her eyes to meet the penetrating gaze of this pert young woman whose intrusion into her solitude she had so dreaded. Violet sat stiffly, her eyebrows lifted, her lips compressed, her hands folded in her lap. Her expression was neither sympathetic nor solicitous, but rather disinterested and uncomplicated. No one had looked at Virginia without some internal shrinking from the magnitude of her loss since that day, three years, three months, and seventeen days ago. It was as if someone had thrown open a window and a gush of fresh, warm air had rushed in, dispersing the chilly, stale atmosphere of the long-closed room. Virginia took a long breath, experiencing as she did a pleasant release at the inner corners of her eyes, across her forehead, and in her jaw.

Jeremiah, munching one of the cakes and wondering why Miss Petra had contradicted his effort to bring Virginia into a more receptive frame of mind, considered the best method of encouraging his wife to speak of what he believed was always nearest her heart. Virginia poured out, added a dash of cream, and offered the filled teacup to her guest, who rose lightly from her chair to receive it. As Violet settled back, she looked up at him and he thought she would speak, but she didn't. Instead Virginia, who had her back to him, addressed him. It gave him the odd sensation that Miss Petra was somehow speaking through his wife. But her voice was her own, calm, agreeable, and firm: the voice, he recalled, she had used when advising the children's governess. "I wonder, my dear," she said, "if you would be so very kind as to leave Miss Petra alone with me for half an hour."

Jeremiah swallowed his cake. After all, this was exactly what he wanted. That his wife should actually express a desire to talk to someone, really anyone, was a much longed for event. Yet as he looked down upon Virginia's unmoving head, a tinge of resentment at this cool dismissal pulled the corners of his mouth down—an unconscious reflex Violet was quick to notice. In the next moment he recovered his good humor, wiped his fingers against a napkin, and replied cheerfully, "Of course, of course. I'll be off. You ladies have much to discuss."

Turning hard on his heel, he crossed the carpet and let himself out at the hall door, closing it with exaggerated care behind him. Then he stood there, gazing mournfully up at the staircase. What was he to do for half an hour? He hadn't even gotten his tea.

Virginia Babin and Miss Petra both knew why they had been brought together, but for several minutes neither of them alluded to it. The time-honored niceties of tea occupied them. Violet admired the painting of a dour ancestor over the mantel, correctly guessing the artist's name, a name that had been fashionable during his life, but had languished in obscurity since his death, some half-century ago. Virginia asked a few polite questions about Bertha Bakersmith and her family. Neither woman mentioned what both knew: that Bertha's oldest daughter, Margaret, had died from complications attendant on childbirth scarcely a year earlier. They spoke instead of Bertha's son, who was studying at Harvard Divinity School, having turned his back, to his father's chagrin and his mother's delight, on the Law School.

Violet appeared so content to gossip that Virginia began to wonder if her guest might not be relieved to have no immediate demand for an exhibition of her celebrated powers. She chattered pleasantly, she was respectful but slyly amusing. She observed that Bertha wrote long and frequent letters to her son and received short and infrequent responses, whereas the epistolary exchange between Mr. Bakersmith and said son was exactly the reverse; the son wrote at length and often to his father, but received only brief and scarce replies. "It may seem odd that I know this," Violet concluded, "but I am much entrusted with the mails at the Bakersmiths'. It's a small service to offer when they have been so generous to me."

"I'm sure having you there is a great comfort to Bertha," Virginia said only to say something. She wasn't sure of anything about Miss Petra, and she was out of practice at conversation. The young woman appealed to her, but there was something disturbing about her presence.

"I believe she has formed an attachment to me," Violet confessed. She sipped her tea; her eyes, engaging Virginia over the edge of the cup, were as affable as a dog's. Guileless, Jeremiah had said. Was it possible? When Violet had drained the cup and set it down on the side table, she dabbed her napkin against her lips. Was she preparing some polite formula for parting?

"May I pour you more tea?" Virginia asked, turning her attention to the pot.

"No, thank you," Violet replied. She pressed her palms against the edge of her chair, lifting herself slightly and shifting forward on the cushion. "Perhaps a little later."

Virginia took up the glass plate. "You haven't tried these cakes. I believe they are excellent."

But her guest made no answer, so she eased the plate back onto the table. When she looked back, Violet was leaning toward her, her back straight, her hands resting on her knees; her head, lifted on the slender, pale stalk of her neck, rotated oddly from right to left. She took no notice of Virginia. Her eyes were lowered, almost closed, her lips slightly parted. She was listening. A log fracturing in the fire gave a sharp pop, which startled Virginia, but Violet, who had now reversed her head's trajectory from left to right, only fluttered her eyelids.

Virginia could feel her own brows knitting together and her mouth went dry. *Oh, no!* she thought, but she could not have said what she meant by this mental exclamation, only that she was suddenly swarming with fear. Violet completed her circuit and came to attention, resting her wide, calm eyes, like caressing fingers, upon the furrowed brow of her hostess.

"Miss Petra," Virginia began. She felt a headache coming on rather fiercely—that would be the import of her remark. But she never got to deliver this bit of personal information. Violet lifted her hands, opening them before her, as if she were lightly pressing on an obstruction. A door. Or a window, Virginia thought. A wave of nausea rose so insistently at this image, which had triggered an intolerable recollection—a woman pressing at a window—that she laid her palm across her waist and sank back in her chair, conscious only of the need to escape. Yet she was also certain that she wouldn't escape, that she was captured there, every nerve in her body arrested and strained, fixed and fascinated by the silent woman leaning toward her.

When Violet spoke, her voice was low and intimate, as if she were sharing a naughty secret with a trusted confidante. "There is no death," she said. "Our loved ones are among us."

A moment passed, than another. "Are there . . . ?" she said, then, with a laugh, "Oh, I see. I'm not going to have to ask. This room is crowded with spirits. I wonder how you sleep in this house. Here is that gentleman in the painting. It's a fine likeness, I see."

The clairvoyant's eyes were closed and Virginia had the opportunity to recover a little of her habitual skepticism. Her terror abated, but she had the eerie sensation that the room was, as Violet suggested, crowded, that the air had taken on substance.

"Here is a young woman," Violet continued. "Very attractive. She says she regrets, that she tried, that she hopes you forgive her."

What young woman? Virginia thought. Was she expected to believe this was Miss Jekyll?

"Ah, there they are. I knew they would come when I came in the front door. What pretty children. The little girl says, Tell Mama we are happy here, and the boy, he's a serious boy, he says, There are many children here. They all long to send messages to their parents. He says that he is well, he misses Papa very much, and Mama very much . . ." She paused, appearing to listen to something she didn't quite understand.

Virginia was coming to herself. Everyone knew how her children had died. There was nothing in these silly messages that distinguished these "spirits" from any other children, of which there were, evidently, so many. She drew herself up, recomposing and resisting the pull of what she now recognized as a frantic and irrational desire to believe that her children might somehow be restored to her. She frowned upon Miss Petra. Guileless, indeed, she thought.

"The little girl is anxious about someone," Violet continued. "Is it a friend? No. Oh, bunny. Yes, it must be a pet. She wants you to be sure to take care of Bunny. No. She's frowning. She's not a pet. And her name is *not* Bunny." She paused, stretching her chin forward, turning her ear as if to identify a sound at the limit of her hearing range. "Not bunny," she repeated. "It's Bunchie."

Virginia came out of her chair with such force that her hips, colliding with the tea table, sent the cakes and cups flying onto the carpet. In three steps she had crossed the room and flung open the door. Jeremiah, slumped in an uncomfortable armchair in the hall, looked toward her with the dim hope that he might now have his tea. But when he rose to meet his wife, that expectation was dashed. Virginia rushed upon him, one hand outstretched, the other clapped across her mouth, her eyes overflowing with tears, her breath coming in tortured gasps, like a fish suffocating upon air. He opened his arms to her and she collapsed against him, her chilly hands encircling his neck, clinging to him. She was trying to speak; he was trying to understand. She brought her lips close to his ear. "My God," she croaked in a voice he didn't recognize. "They are here." Then her knees gave out and Jeremiah bent over her, clasping her waist as he eased her unconscious body to the floor.

Bunchie, Jeremiah Babin informed me during a long walk around the placid lake, was his daughter's doll, which she had so named for her own childish and mysterious reasons. "No one who didn't know Melody could have known that," he said. "It was prodigious."

I couldn't deny the prodigiousness of this incident. But what, I wondered, had Violet herself had to say about it?

"She remembers nothing," he explained. "When she's in contact with the spirits she is entirely a medium. They speak through her, without her knowledge."

"So she didn't know what she had told your wife."

"Not a word," he said. "It was . . ." He chuckled, pausing in the path to call up his sensation at the time. "Well, it was almost comical. Virginia came out of her swoon in such a state that I rang for the maid and we got her up to her bed, where I administered a sedative. I completely forgot that Violet was still in the parlor. When my wife was calm, I went downstairs and found her sitting by the fire. The dishes were all over the floor, but she'd poured herself another cup of tea and was eating one of the cakes, perfectly composed, as if she were at home. I went in, quite agitated, as you can imagine, and she looked up with that odd little smile she has, and she said, "Have I been helpful? I do hope so."

THE ENNUI OF THE PSYCHIC

On my last day at Lake Pleasant, having largely completed my researches into the ways and means of the Spiritualists, I found myself with the opportunity to while away an hour or two before dinner in reading an issue of the British magazine *Cornhill*. This was a welcome distraction. The weather was stormy, which quite literally dampened the spirits of the Spiritualists, who believe the dead dislike bad weather and seldom materialize when it is raining. It never rains in Summerland where they abide, though miraculously the air is fragrant with flowers.

I was alone in the reading room. When I heard someone come in at the door, I knew by the stealth of her step that it was Violet. She took a childish pleasure in all manner of pranks and had nearly sent Mr. Babin backward down the stairs the evening before by jumping out from the linen closet in the hall as he came up to escort us to dinner. I pretended I didn't hear her as she crept up behind my chair and stood silently looking down at me. "I know you're there," I said. She made no reply, but leaned forward, scrutinizing the paragraph under the title. "That isn't correct," she said. "It was 1872. And the ship wasn't in tow. They sailed her to Gibraltar."

I looked up, holding the journal open with my palm. "Have you read this account?"

"No," she replied. "The name is wrong too. It wasn't the *Marie Celeste*. It was the *Mary Celeste*."

"You seem to know a great deal about it," I observed.

She straightened, but she kept her eyes fixed gloomily on the offending text. "I knew the family," she replied.

Then she crossed the room and she threw herself down on a settee near the bookcase, taking up one magazine after another, and paging through them distractedly until I had finished reading the article, which I found preposterous, though suspenseful and engaging. Before I could say a word, she snatched up the journal and disappeared to her room.

I took out my notebook and ensconced myself at the writing desk, elaborating my notes on Lake Pleasant. The gallery of the hotel was so wide that tables could be set up without fear of damp, and these were soon filled with whist players, chatting and drinking tea. Snippets of their conversations wove their way into my observations. "Hattie has derived great benefit from Dr. Skilling's magnetic treatment. She says she hasn't felt so invigorated in years." "Mr. Leary's corn is obviously the best, but the price!" "Mr. Whitaker's son Harvey has come through again. Such a loving boy." At length I capped my pen, closed my book, and went up to my room. Inside I found a folded sheet of paper wedged against the carpet. Writ large with more than necessary pressure on the page were three words: *COME TO ME*.

I crossed the hall and tapped on Violet's door. "Come in," she called out. She was collapsed upon the chaise, one hand over her eyes, the other brushing the floor where her shoes were lined up neatly next to the splayed copy of the *Cornhill*. As I took the chair opposite, she lifted her hand and scowled at me. "Who is this person?" she inquired. "This Dr. Jephson. Have you ever heard of him?"

"He says he's from Boston," I observed.

"It's an outrage," she said. "Poor Arthur. I'm sure he's seen it already."

"Who is Arthur?"

She pulled herself up, dropping her feet to the carpet, poking the journal with her toes. "I thought you journalists had standards. This account is replete with factual errors."

"I don't think Dr. Jephson is, strictly speaking, a journalist."

"Well, he's a doctor. Surely doctors have standards. Surely they're not allowed to broadcast bald-faced lies in print."

"I had the sense that the account was actually intended to be read as a fictional piece."

"That's not what it says," she snapped. "It says . . ." She picked up the volume and turned its pages impatiently. "'J. Habakuk Jephson's Statement.' It doesn't say story. It doesn't say anything about it being fictional."

"I think that may be the point."

"The point of what!"

"Well, the author isn't Jephson, but someone pretending to be Jephson. It's not an entirely new thing. But the *Cornhill* doesn't print the names of its contributors, so there's no way of knowing."

"But they know, don't they? The people who published it must know if it's meant to be a story or a true account. And they know people will read this—whatever it is—and think it's true and that the ship actually went to Africa and this lunatic passenger—there were no passengers, by the way—killed everybody on the ship one by one, and that the crew was made up of Negroes, when they were only four Germans . . ." Here she threw the *Cornhill* at the breakfast table. "It's just lies," she concluded. "How is it possible, after all this time?"

"Who is Arthur?" I asked again.

She stood up and began pacing about the room, stopping when she reached an obstacle and turning back again. "He's Sarah's orphaned son," she said. "He must be, let me think, he's nineteen now. And Benjamin's mother, Mother Briggs, she's still alive, poor woman, though everyone she loved is dead. I'm sure she's read this travesty."

"Who is Sarah?" I persisted.

"Sarah Briggs," she said, exasperated at my slowness. "Mrs. Benjamin Briggs. The captain's wife. She was on the *Mary Celeste* and so was their daughter, Sophia Matilda; she was just two years old."

"Jephson says the captain's name was Tibbs."

"He didn't even get that right. Are there laws?" she exclaimed, stopping before me with her hands spread wide at her sides. "Can this Jephson person be sued? Or the *Cornhill*? Can the *Cornhill* be sued?"

"I don't think so," I said. "Not if the author changed the names."

Tears filled her eyes and she balled up her hands into fists, which made her look like the child she must have been not so very long ago. She stalked back to the chaise, sat down upon it. Resting her elbows on her knees, her chin in her hands, she muttered at the floor. "It just brings that whole awful time back," she said miserably.

"Were you close to the family?" I asked.

A few tears, funneled by her hands, slipped down alongside her nose. "Sarah was my best friend in this world," she said. Then, sniffing, she sat up straight, wiping her tears away with the backs of her hands. "I shall speak to Mr. Babin," she said. "He will give me the benefit of his legal counsel."

I was less interested in the legal recourse recommended by Mr. Babin than in Violet's strong reaction to Dr. Jephson's account, or story, or whatever it was, and whoever Dr. Jephson was. Her exclamation that Sarah Briggs had been her friend was the closest thing to a past she had owned to. I had been under the impression that her home was in upstate New York, but it was unlikely that a seafaring family would live that far inland. So, I concluded, Violet was from the East Coast, possibly Boston. I'd noted that she read the Boston papers assiduously.

Though all manner of spirits were welcome in Lake Pleasant, the alcoholic variety was forbidden. As the evenings wore on, it was clear that some of the band members and the wild young men who had a clubhouse and dressed up as Indians, terrifying old ladies who thought they were native spirits returning from the dead to scalp them, were clearly under the influence of something stronger than the ubiquitous lemonade. Jeremiah Babin, being a man of sophistication and culture, had provided himself with a bottle of excellent port, which he offered to share with us as a digestive aid after our dinner at the Lakeside Café. No sooner had we taken our seats in Violet's sitting room and he had poured out three glasses of the ruby potion than she brought the issue of the *Cornhill* to his attention, expressing her conviction that the lead article constituted an actionable offense. "It's full of errors and lies," she avowed. "He doesn't even get the captain's name right."

Jeremiah, recognizing at once the ship's name, recalled what he knew of its melancholy fate. "At first they thought it was pirates. Is that right?" he asked. "But then, it was the crew. A mutiny? Was that it?"

Violet sipped her port, giving him a steady look that betrayed no feelings in the matter. "It was not a mutiny," she said calmly. "That has been ascertained. But this account says that it was."

Jeremiah nodded. "Yes, well. I would have to look into it. But I can tell you that if the names are changed, there's probably nothing to be done about it, by way of legal action I mean."

Violet turned upon me an inclusive smile. "Is there another kind of action?" she asked.

Jeremiah, seeing my puzzled expression, said, "She's thinking of investigative journalism."

"He has read my mind," Violet said.

I considered the matter. "It might be difficult to interest the public in the factual basis of a story that appears in a literary journal, especially as it concerns an incident that happened so long ago."

"You call it an incident," Violet said glumly, reaching for her glass.

"Whatever it was," Jeremiah said, rising from his chair. "It was a famous story at the time, and evidently this fellow is using it to put himself forward. I'll leave you ladies to discuss your scheme of retribution. I have an early appointment with Dr. Plunkett. His magnetic treatment has cured my bad knee. I wonder if I can persuade him to set up in Philadelphia."

When we had said our good nights to Violet's benefactor, she and I sat for a few moments in silence.

I had enjoyed our dinner on the lakeshore. It was a mild, clear evening, the paper lanterns glowed charmingly, the food, though plain, was good, and the conversation wide-ranging and thought-provoking. Jeremiah Babin was a quirky gentleman, full of enthusiasms, an opera lover, a reader of contemporary poetry, well-traveled and informed about world affairs. There was no talk of spirits or second sight, though the ghost of Sir Walter Scott might have enjoyed the enthusiasm we three discovered we shared for his romances. Jeremiah was a great fan of Robert Louis Stevenson and spoke so highly of his *Kidnapped*, which I confessed I had not read, that I vowed to take it up at the next opportunity. Violet and I encouraged him to give Mrs. Gaskell his attention.

The meal ended on a lively note as a sudden breeze whipped in off the lake and set the lamps flickering. Our fellow diners smiled and laughed to one another, saying the spirits were off to bed, and so should we be. Violet had not mentioned her pique about the fallacious article and I assumed she'd forgotten it, but now I understood that she had been waiting to bring it up in a more private setting. Jeremiah's dismissal irked her; I could feel that as we sat there without speaking, sipping the wine he had considerately left for us. This suited me, as it was my intention to draw her out on the subject, which so conveniently opened a door upon her past. I took up the journal, which Jeremiah hadn't bothered to examine. "Are you still in touch with the Briggs family?" I asked.

She gave me a mildly startled look, a clear signal to me that her guard was down. "Not at all," she said. "There's not much left of them."

"Were they numerous?"

"They were," she replied. "Mother Briggs had six children. They all died at sea except for James, who had the good sense to go into business. And two of her grandchildren died as well. Well, one died, Maria's boy, Natie, and then Sophy, Sarah's little girl. She was on the *Mary Celeste*."

"And Mother Briggs was Sarah's mother?"

"Her mother-in-law. Also her aunt. Sarah and Benjamin were first cousins."

"How devastating for her, to lose so many children."

Violet looked away toward the open balcony, where two night birds were twittering in an overhanging branch of a pine. "Oh," she said, watching their fluttering movements indifferently. "She had the comfort of her religion."

"She was a pious woman?"

Violet smiled to herself, lifting her glass to her lips, taking, I noted, a healthy swallow. Then she turned to me with an eagerness I recognized—she had decided to reveal something she ordinarily would not. She'd regret it later, I thought. Perhaps we both knew that.

"People said that family was cursed," she confided. "Mother Briggs's husband, Captain Nathan, was an amusing old fellow, something of the town crank. He was killed by a lightning bolt that struck him in the hall of his own house."

"Good heavens," I said. "Was this before Benjamin and Sarah died?"

"Disappeared," she corrected. "It was a couple of years earlier. Sarah's father, Leander, the Reverend Leander Cobb"—she pronounced the title Reverend with mock solemnity—"he died scarcely two months before Sarah sailed on the *Mary Celeste*."

"So he never knew."

She frowned. "I was . . ." The pause was slight, occasioned, I suspected, by some subtle alteration of the actual sequence of events. "I visited Mother Briggs just after the first telegram came. I wanted to send Sarah a letter and I went to ask her for the proper address. She was calm as a clam. She told me the ship had been found derelict, so there was no point in sending a letter. Then James came in with Arthur, Sarah's son. He was a grim little boy, nervous and timid, and of course, they'd told him nothing. James believed, we all did, that another ship might have picked up the crew and we'd hear from them as soon as they got to a port."

She glanced up at me to see how I was responding to her story. Wanting to give the thin edge of agitation in her voice room to expand, I said nothing.

"It was so dreadful," she continued. "Benjamin's brother Oliver— he was a charming man, full of gaiety—he had sailed from New York a week later than Benjamin and Sarah. They all had plans to meet in Messina. Oliver had even told his mother what songs he planned to sing at their reunion—she told me that later. He had a fine voice. He and Sarah loved to sing together. What we didn't know then, when they got that first telegram . . ." Again she paused, this time to raise her glass for another bracing draft of wine. "What we didn't know was that Oliver's ship—it was the *Julia A. Hallock*—went down in a storm in the Bay of Biscay. He and the first mate clung to some pieces of the deckhouse for four days before Oliver gave up and let go. The mate was rescued not two hours later." Tears gathered in her eyes and she extracted a handkerchief from her sleeve.

When a heartfelt account moves the teller to tears, the natural response of anyone with ordinary human feeling is to offer kind words of sympathy and consolation, but my profession precludes such natural expressions, and the sight of tears tends to stir in me nothing so much as a sense of predatory anticipation. I watched Violet without comment. She dried her tears, sniffed mightily, coughed. Her eyes fell upon the journal, which was resting on my lap. "How could that person, that Dr. Jephson, how could he make such a mockery of other people's suffering? People he didn't even know."

"Did the Briggs family live in New York?" I asked.

She gave me a look of consternation. She was having a difficult time getting anyone to share her outrage at the scurrilous Dr. Jephson. "They lived in Massachusetts. Why would you think they lived in New York?"

"I thought you grew up in New York. I seem to remember reading that. Upstate somewhere. Isn't that correct?"

"Gloversville," she said, too quickly. "We lived there until I was twelve. Then we moved to Marion."

"I see," I said. "And that's where you met Sarah Briggs."

"We went to the Academy together."

"Do you still have relatives there?"

Her eyes narrowed slightly and she lifted her chin, contemplating me for a moment before speaking. "I have an aunt," she said. "But she disapproves of me, so we're not in contact."

"She lives in Marion?"

"I don't know where she lives now," she replied. "Nor do I care."

I smiled, thinking of my mother's sister Claire, who had refused to help us when we were destitute because mother had married, in her view, beneath her.

"Have I said something funny?" Violet asked, looking pouty.

"I have such an aunt," I said.

A snort of glee escaped her. "Do you?" she said. I nodded wisely. "Bad luck to them both." She was now relaxed and warmed to me. We were two of a kind—orphans with heartless relations. I wondered if she had any money of her own.

"May I ask you a personal question?" I said.

"I think I know what it is," she replied.

"What do you think it is?"

"You want to know if I have an income."

It surprised me that she should have guessed my thought. "Yes," I said. "I understand you don't charge for the services you render, so I wondered . . ."

"I have a little money from my grandmother," she replied. "Not enough to live on. But I can't charge for what you call my services because if I did the people who really matter wouldn't seek me out. They would assume I was a fraud, that I was in it for the money."

"I notice at these séances advertised here, the psychics all charge admission."

"Exactly. Twenty-five cents. How many of those would one have to do to make up the price of a pair of shoes?"

"Yes. I had that same thought."

"Those people are hobbyists, and many of them are just ludicrous, obvious frauds. They make disembodied hands appear, or instruments play themselves. It's entertainment."

"I see," I said. And I did, though I didn't understand why people found being roundly duped an activity worth paying even twenty-five cents to enjoy.

Violet cast me a look tinged with desperation. "Oh, I wish I could be like you and earn my living by my pen!" she exclaimed.

"I fear you'd find it dull and tiring."

"You're out in the world, editors send you off to find out things and write up what you find, doors open to you, people respect you. No one patronizes you. Jeremiah said he thought you a brave sort of person. Level-headed and sound."

"Did he?"

"Yes. He admires you." She plucked at her skirt peevishly. "You may be sure no one ever thinks of *me* as level-headed."

"Do you want to be level-headed?"

She raised her eyebrows as if the question bore consideration, then sighed, dropping back in her chair. "They tire of me," she said. "At first it's very exciting and I'm in a trance half the time, keeping them in touch with their loved ones. But after a while . . ." She raised her hand to her hair, patting a straying curl back into place absentmindedly. "Often the gentlemen develop little crushes on me. At the Bakersmiths' it was the son. You should see some of the letters I've received! Then the wives begin to think of how much good I could do for their friends, a soiree is arranged, and I know I'm about to pack my bags."

"They pass you on."

"Exactly," she said.

"How long have you been living like this?"

She sent me the frank look of appeal I'd seen that first evening, when she bent over to pick up her napkin. "Ten long years," she said.

"Good heavens."

"I'm just a pet. I'm the in-house clairvoyant." She chuckled sourly. "Sometimes I play the tyrant, just to keep from dying of boredom."

I pictured Violet in a tyrannical mood, doubtless a fearsome sight.

"What do you do?"

"Oh, I make them wait, or I get headaches and have my meals in bed. I actually do suffer from blinding headaches, so no acting is required. Sometimes I flirt with the husbands until they get so carried away they fear I'll tell their wives. But I never do. I used to hope one of them might marry me, but now I know, if there's one thing they dread, it's scandal. And marrying a psychic would be a scandal, especially if a divorce was involved."

"Tell me about the trances," I asked. "Can you make them happen?"

"Oh, why is everyone so interested in that? Is that what you want to write about?"

"Not necessarily. I'm just interested," I said. "Like everyone."

"I have no memory of anything that happens in a trance," she said firmly.

"Yes, Jeremiah told me that. It must be like hypnotism."

"I don't know about hypnotism. At first it happened when I was alone, working on my poetry. There would be this lapse of time and when I came back, I'd written several pages I had no memory of writing. And they were messages, but not to me."

"You write poetry?"

This question pleased her. "I do. I always have. I have notebooks full of it. Would you like to see some? I never show them to anyone because I'm afraid they may be very bad."

"Why would you show them to me?"

"That's a good question," she said, leaning over her knees to make some adjustment to her skirt. "Perhaps I won't."

I ignored this display of coquettishness, though I could see how well it might work on an interested gentleman. "Do you still receive messages while writing?"

She sat up straight, folded her hands in her lap, and presented me with the prim expression of an innocent bystander who has just been sworn in to the witness box. "Not much. It's easier to just repeat what I'm hearing. Evidently the spirits prefer to use me in that way."

Everything about this last statement irritated me. "Do they?" I said. "I wonder why."

"That's not something I could know."

"It's so convenient, that part, where you don't remember what you've said."

She frowned. "I don't get to choose whether or not to hear what I hear and see what I see. Do you?"

"No. But I wonder, why you ... I mean, why did these spirits choose you and not someone else?"

"I suppose because I'm open to them."

"Could you close yourself to them? Could you make them go away?"

"You're making fun of me."

"No, I'm serious."

"You don't believe a word I say."

"Let's just say I believe you're being used, but not by spirits."

She was silent. Her gaze was so free of resentment that I was intrigued to hear her next words. "You think I make it all up, just to please people who will help me."

I nodded.

"Do you imagine that possibility has never occurred to me?" she said.

"Has it?"

Abruptly she stood up and took a few steps toward the balcony, leaving me with a view of her profile. She took a deep breath, then another, evidently in the grip of a strong emotion. Her long, slender hands clenched into fists at her sides. More tears, I thought, more earnest protestations.

So I was surprised when she turned to me with dry eyes and an expression of powerful resolution. "I want to stop," she said. "I want another life. Will you help me?"

· · ·

I didn't tell Violet I was unwilling to help her, but I did point out the unlikelihood that I could. My employment, which she persisted in envying, was a hand-to-mouth affair, and as she had no commercial skills beyond the one that currently provided a comfortable, albeit restricted, existence, there was no definite track that I could set her upon. She had the childish notion that if only her efforts were brought to the attention of the public, she would make her way as a poet. I recommended a course in typing, as it was a skill always in demand. When I asked if she had told Jeremiah Babin, who was in the most likely position to assist her and appeared to have a keen interest in her welfare, of her ambition to find gainful employment, she laughed. "No," she said. "And don't you tell him. He would *not* be pleased to hear it."

Our conversation, as I recall it, was amiable, but I could see that she was disappointed, that she had imagined I would be her deliverer. By morning, when she woke with a headache from the port, she would be ashamed of her declaration at the window and resentful of my part in the dissolution of her fantasies.

When we said good night, I promised to consider her situation and perhaps recommend a course, beyond typing—which clearly had no appeal to her whatsoever—that she might take toward self-sufficiency. As I crossed the hall and let myself in at the door of my room, I reflected that my own situation, which sometimes struck me as arduous, lonely, dull, and pointless, was actually far preferable to the lot of the various citizens whose doings I was, as Violet put it, "on assignment" to investigate. All that day my article about the Spiritualists had been taking shape in my mind, and I had that pleasant, ticklish sensation of mental busyness, as well as a burgeoning confidence that must result, very soon—I could feel it—in my taking up my pen and my notebook and setting out on the journey into print. In my room I paused, admiring the moonlight, like spilled milk, on the desk. The apple I kept at the ready for midnight munching floated in a dark blue pool of its own shadow. I crossed to the balcony and stepped out into the still, warm, pine-scented evening.

The Spiritualists believe their spirit friends are fond of flowers. Summerland, their dwelling on the other side, is a garden that needs no tending, and they fill their airy rooms with all manner of blooms. As wildflowers are abundant in the woods and fields bordering Lake Pleasant, the guests are in the habit of gathering bouquets and setting them out in vases, pitchers, baskets, or even buckets, at odd places around the camp.

These portable arrangements were constantly falling over, or they were picked up, refreshed, rearranged, and moved about by passing campers; it was a harmless, charming game they played, one of their more sympathetic practices. I noticed that a new collection of colorful pitchers had magically converged at the end of the bench just across from my balcony. If only they would confine themselves to flowers, I thought. In a dreamy state of mind I turned back to my bedroom, pondering the bizarre revelation that Violet Petra imagined herself a poet.

I drew the curtain, leaving the door ajar to have the benefit of fresh air. My toilette was a simple washup at the basin, a few strokes of the hairbrush, and a quick change into my dowdy cotton gown. As I slipped beneath the stiff, starched sheets, I imagined Violet, just across the hall. Her gown was doubtless embroidered satin with lace insets across the bodice. She had expensive tastes and habits. At dinner she had pointed out that what I took to be amethysts sparkling on the broad bust of a psychic competitor were in fact "cheap garnets." She was right to be worried about her future, as she couldn't afford to live in the style required by the company she kept. For the time being the Babins provided her with a clothing allowance. "Even with that," she had confided, "I have to have my shoes resoled."

In this manner, puzzling over the question of what would become of the fascinating, though often aggravating, object of my investigations, I drifted into sleep.

I awoke in the oppressive and humid darkness of a deep wood on a cloudy moonless night. For a few moments I lay still, my eyelids heavy from sleep, listening to a repetitive clicking that had summoned me back to consciousness. At length I determined it was coming from the wardrobe. What was it? I also became aware of a hushed whisper, like leaves rustling in a mini-whirlwind, such as one observes of an autumn day. It was the pages of my notebook, I speculated, being riffled by a breeze.

When I turned my face toward this sound, a current of air brushed lightly across my cheek, like warm caressing fingers, tentative and tender, grazing my brow, lifting a strand of hair loose at my temple. Why was my room so dark? The curtain at the door was a summery voile, and the moon, though not full, had shone brightly when I stood on the balcony, but now my eyes couldn't penetrate what felt more and more like a swirling current of blackness. It was as if I were in a whirlpool.

I sat up in the bed, pushing my pillow to one side. The clicking sound must be the wardrobe door, which, unlatched, was knocking again and again against the frame. The whispering intensified and had an impatience about it that made me think of old women defaming some young beauty in a church—I don't know why this image came to me, but it did. A storm had whipped up, I concluded, and I must feel my way to the open balcony door and close it tightly. I swung my legs over the side, stood up, one hand resting on the bedpost, and waited for my eyes to adjust to the dark. My movement animated the quarreling currents of air and a kind of pandemonium broke loose in my room. The wardrobe door slammed hard, the hinges complaining at the force. The cyclonic air ripped the curtain, which I could dimly make out fluttering grayly before the door, free of its rod, and sent it rushing toward me, as if to wrap me in its embrace. I heard small objects—my cologne, my hairbrush, my fountain pen, my ink bottle—scattering in all directions from the dresser and the desk.

I took a step, confident that I would reach the door, which I could dimly see, and close this maelstrom out. Another step. Abruptly something cold and hard struck me on the forehead, as if it had been thrown with pent-up malice by an assailant with excellent aim. I staggered and sat down on the floor. My notebook hurled itself from the desk and slapped me cruelly on the collarbone. I touched my forehead, which felt sore from the vengeful missile. Determinedly I crawled toward the door while a fresh gust lifted the pitcher from the washstand and smashed it against the floor. One of my shoes flew up and slapped me on the hip. I pushed on.

When at last—though it was not half a minute—I was near the door and could grasp the handle, I found to my astonishment that it was closed. At the moment when my fingers pushed against the panel, determining that the door was tightly seated in its frame, the fury in my room entirely ceased.

I was so confused that I sat there, my back against the glass panes, staring into the darkness. What world was I in? The room began to lighten, and I made out the apple resting against the leg of the dresser. Of course, I thought. The apple was the missile that had struck my forehead. Carefully I got to my feet and returned to the bed, my mental state still much confounded. As the dawn light gradually flushed up the walls, I sat on the edge of the mattress and surveyed the wreckage of my room. The curtain lay in a twisted skein near the door; my meager possessions were scattered across the floor. It looked as if some barroom brawler with a raging tooth-ache had taken the place apart.

But he was gone now; the room was quiet and still, the air cool, charged as it is often after a storm. But what puzzled me was that there was no sound of wind or rain outside. The branches of the pine trees shading the balcony were unmoving, not even their nee-dles trembled, as they did in the faintest breeze. I crossed to the door and stepped out onto the balcony.

It was a soft, fragrant summer morning of infinite sweetness, and the only sound was the soft cooing of a dove, and distantly the sharp rap of a woodpecker investigating a tree trunk. I stepped out to the rail. Surely the ground would be strewn with fresh needles and the flimsy vases toppled, the flowers strewn across the path. I looked down at the bench.

And there they were, undisturbed, four clay pitchers top-heavy with wildflowers, cheerfully greeting the day, announcing to passersby that the spirits of the dead were welcome in this place, that they might come and stay and do just as they pleased.

How was it possible?

All I wanted was to quit my room. I dressed quickly, stepped into the hall, locking the door behind me, and walked purposefully away from the hotel. I wanted to walk to Philadelphia and never see Lake Pleasant again, but I was soon standing on the shore, looking out at the still, calm surface of the eponymous body of water. The chortling ripples playing in the grasses near the edge mocked me. A ghostly mist lay across the water and in the hollows of the forest beyond. It was early; the waitresses were just setting up in the tent and only myself and an aged crone who sat muttering on a bench under a tree were about. To recover my composure, I decided to walk along the path to the highlands.

The natural world is rife with anomalies, but I believed everything in it could be explained by a thorough understanding of its properties and laws. Water, for example, which seeks the lowest ground, could be forced to run uphill, as it did in the aqueducts the Romans designed to refresh their citizens' thirst from sources far away. Fire, with its ravenous appetite for fuel, could be cajoled into accepting a steady diet of candlewick or cotton strips soaked in kerosene. Wind, well, one couldn't say wind was actually harnessed, though sailors liked to think so, and they had made such a study of its various temperaments that they contrived to use it to accomplish a marvelous feat; by adjusting sheets of canvas, they could move large ships across entire oceans. Wind in my view was the most capricious element, but there was one thing it couldn't do and that was whip up a tempest in a closed box. Therefore, it was clear that the wind had entered my room from the outside. The door had been open and slammed shut just as I reached it. As for the vases of flowers, they might have been protected by the bench and the low shrubbery near the path.

So I reconciled myself to a practical view, and exercised by my climb, I arrived at Gussie's Tea Room in a rational state of mind. As I drew closer, to my surprise, the screen door flew open and Jeremiah Babin barged out, walking briskly toward me, his head lowered and giving off an air of agitation, which struck me as odd because his nature, as I had observed it, was expansive, sociable, and not prone to vexation. When he glanced up to see who stood in his path, he appeared at first startled and then annoyed. "Good morning," I said. "You're up early."

He stopped, scowling at me so intently that I took a step back. "I've been up since dawn," he said coldly.

I felt nothing but relief at this news. "Was it the storm?" I asked. "It got me up too, but not before it wrecked my room."

"I don't know what you're talking about," he said. "I've been up since dawn attending on our dear Miss Petra, who is in quite a state, thanks to you."

"Now it's I who am mystified," I said. "She wasn't the least excited last night."

"Really?" he said, meaning he didn't believe me. "She says you accused her of being a fraud, and she says you tried to get her to admit it, and she's sure you have every intention of writing horrible lies about her in your newspaper and she's back there"—he flung out his arm in the direction of the hotel—"packing madly because she wants to leave at once, though she has an important sitting this afternoon with Mrs. Grover Greenwich who has come all the way from Ohio on purpose to see her."

"But that's not true," I protested. "I said nothing of the kind."

"Well, you must have said something, Miss Grant. And I think it very small of you, as we've been nothing but welcoming and generous and willing to answer all your nosy questions since you came among us."

My conscience stung me, but not because of my conversation with Violet. It was because I had allowed Jeremiah to pay for my dinner the night before. I shouldn't have, and he knew it as well as

I did. "I'm very sorry to hear that something I said upset Violet," I said. "But I assure you, I made no accusations or any kind, nor do I intend to write anything critical of her."

"What *did* you say?"

"I hardly said anything at all. I just asked what you call 'nosy' questions. Perhaps she regrets her answers, but not because I suggested she should."

This appeal tempered his anger, but he was still uncharacteristically sullen. "I shouldn't have left her alone with you," he said. "Now I don't know who to believe."

We had been walking in a leisurely way as we talked and had arrived at a bench set in the shade of three birch trees that hovered over it, as if to eavesdrop on any conversation that might take place in their domain. "Let's stop here," Jeremiah suggested, and I agreed. When we were seated, he repeated his dilemma. "I don't know who to believe."

"What motive could I have for dissembling?" I asked.

He considered this question, and its corollary—what motive might Violet have for not telling the truth—and for several moments neither of us spoke. I was thinking over anything I might have said to Violet that would make her desperate. "I hope you won't be offended," I said, to break the silence. "But I think it isn't a good idea to give her wine."

His heavy brows drew together and he cocked his head to have a closer look at me, as if I were a cat who had unexpectedly offered advice. "That's what Virginia says," he admitted. "But Violet says it helps her sleep. She can be very insistent."

"I believe that," I said.

"That wine helps her sleep?" he asked.

"That she has trouble sleeping."

He studied me with unnecessary intensity. "And why do you think that is? Why can't Violet sleep?"

"Because," I said measuredly, "Violet is a deeply unhappy woman."

"Is she?" The thought appeared entirely novel to him. "But why should she be?"

I shrugged. *How could he not know?* was what I thought.

"Insomnia is a common female complaint, isn't it? Many women suffer from it; men seldom do. Virginia takes a sedative most nights. She can't do without it. Women have very complex nervous systems. They are too highly strung."

"I've heard that view expressed by medical men," I agreed.

"Yes," he said. "It's widely understood." He stroked his hair back from his temple, as if to assist his brain in its pursuit of the solution to a puzzle. "Do you have difficulty sleeping?"

"Not as a rule," I replied. The sleepless night I'd just passed nagged at me, and I realized it had left me shaken and dispirited.

"But you're an unusual woman. I've observed that. I don't think many women could live by their wits as you do. I certainly don't think Violet could, nor should she. Her gift is too important; it must be protected."

"You think she's too sensitive to take care of herself."

"I know she is."

"Perhaps that's what makes her unhappy."

"Why should it?" he said sharply. "People come from miles around to consult her. She's welcomed everywhere she goes. She's had a great success." He shook his head in profound perplexity.

Violet, I thought, had spent the morning "playing the tyrant" with her protector, and she had managed to vex and even to frighten him. My sympathies were not unengaged by his dilemma; he was an intelligent, open-minded, amiable, unimaginative man who wanted life to go smoothly and pleasantly. But where Violet was concerned, he was paddling about in a pond that was deeper and darker than he could possibly know. To such a man, Violet Petra must be well nigh unfathomable. Nothing in his nature could account for what was in hers. Now he regarded me with pleading eyes, eager for some useful feminine clarification, blissfully unaware that the obstinacy of his befuddlement had begun to wear on my patience. "No," he concluded, "I can't believe she's unhappy. She has a fascinating life."

I recalled Violet's weary reply the night before—*Ten long years.*

"Is it such a life as you would want for your own daughter?" I asked my insistent companion.

The slow intake of breath, the drawing away that followed this question, didn't surprise me. I lowered my eyes, waiting for his momentary confusion to be replaced by resentment or hostility. A gnat had struck at him, after all. But Jeremiah had better defenses in his arsenal. After a proper, nearly ceremonial silence, he said softly, without agitation, "I see."

I met his eyes, which buried me in an avalanche of contempt. "I see," he said again, calm and distant. All his courtesy and interest and earnest entreaty of my opinion had evaporated like the mist the sun had burned away while we had been talking.

"What is it that you see?" I asked, deflecting his iciness with a chill of my own.

He smiled joylessly. "What you do," he said. "And why I found Violet hysterical this morning."

Abrupt reversals in the terms of a professional relationship are not uncommon in my experience. A previously willing party to an investigation decides all at once to become an obstacle. My questions have touched some nerve, my intentions, which—I really think because of my sex—are presupposed to be honorable, are revealed to be ignoble. The story I'm after is not the one my subject wishes to be told. I may well take the liberty of printing "horrid lies." I made no reply, as I had nothing to say, and I expected Jeremiah to fire some dismissive parting shot and walk away, but he sat there glowering at me in what could best be described as a huff.

Our fellow campers began to appear, sauntering in small groups toward the lake or up the path to the waterfall, eager to take in the delights of the new day. Two pretty children in white dresses and light summer shoes skipped on the path, their straight black hair cut in identical bobs, their heads inclined together, deep in conversation. They didn't notice us as they passed, but I watched Jeremiah notice them, and some sliver of sympathy awakened in me—he must think of his own lost darlings whenever he saw living children,

children who would grow up, children who would have more to say than "we are happy here." His eyes rested upon them as they passed, but his expression didn't soften.

A young man stepped out of the teahouse and, seeing the girls, called out to them. "It's Mr. Talbot," one gasped to the other, and they took off at a run to greet him. Mr. Talbot was the proprietor of the spirit photography shop; I'd seen samples of his work in the window. One sat for him and the resulting photograph invariably included a misty spirit hovering over the chair, or funneling in from the ceiling like a cloudburst. If these innocent girls had a dollar to spend between them, they might pass a titillating half an hour inside the tent, while Mr. Talbot, a handsome young impostor who always wore a boater hat and a floppy black tie, posed them and teased them and swore he could see the veiled face of a spirit rising up behind them, but they must not turn to look or the picture would be spoiled. I watched the girls, holding hands and laughing at some witticism from the droll photographer. An old couple, the man thin, the woman portly, appeared at the edge of the forest path, their eyes strangely glittering in the morning light.

A powerful sensation of revulsion rose up in me. Who were these bizarre, complacent people, these obstinate monomaniacs fixated on the patently absurd? Amid all this natural beauty, what most enlivened them was their conviction that death was not momentous, that life, as they put it, was continuous. The spirits they peddled had no mystery; they were ghosts stripped of their otherness. In their cosmography, the dead were just like us and they were everywhere, waiting to give us yet more unsolicited advice. That and the news that they were happy being dead, that life as they now lived it was better than it had been when they walked the green earth disporting themselves in flesh and blood.

The tumultuous events of the night, the condition of my hotel room, my anxiety to get away from it, the rush to the lake, the beauty and serenity of the scene, the timely intrusion of Jeremiah Babin with his provocative innocence and his sham interest, it all struck me as of a vicious piece, but a piece of what I couldn't tell.

Jeremiah, emanating superiority and indifference, leaned forward beside me and dangled his hands between his knees. Did he really believe it? I wondered. Did this powerful, wealthy, educated man believe in the continuity of life? Or was he more interested in the continuity of his own comfort?

As if he felt my question, he turned to me. "I'd like to assure Violet that you won't write anything against her," he said.

"You may assure her," I said. "I will tell you that when I met her, it was my intention to expose her as a fraud. And she may well be, for all I know. But I find I haven't the heart to do her any harm. My article won't mention her name."

He was faintly disappointed, but I could see that his wish to return Violet to a state he thought of as normal was gratified by the idea that I would cause no further disturbance to her sensitive nervous apparatus. He stood up and looked down at me. "I'll carry your message, Miss Grant," he said. "And I trust you'll make no further attempt to contact her."

This amused me. "I never attempted to contact her to begin with," I said. "She summoned me."

"Did she?" he said, though of course he knew this, had been in on it. "Well, I don't think she will again. Good day to you."

"And to you, sir," I said. Without looking back, he strode briskly down the path to the hotel. I watched his strong back, his well-coiffed hair, until he turned off at the lake and left my line of sight. I sat for a few moments more, mulling over my best course. At length I stood up and made my way down to the Lakeside Café, where the waitresses were serving coffee. I decided to drink a cup to brace myself for the tiresome business of putting my room back together and packing up my belongings.

An hour later, as I checked out, I asked the ever-cheerful desk clerk if he had been disturbed by a sudden storm in the night, which, I regretted, had resulted in my water pitcher being now in three pieces inside the basin. "No," he said. "I sleep like the dead." He winked at his own cleverness. "But things do go bump in the night here, don't you know," he continued. "We call them polterguests.

There won't be no charge for the pitcher." I thanked him, paid my bill, and set out along the wooden walkway, past the dance pavilion and down the steps to the station platform. A soft breeze rustled in the white pines, a woodpecker was up and drilling, and I could hear the band running through scales in preparation for their morning parade. I plopped down on the platform bench, grateful to spend my last fifteen minutes at Lake Pleasant communing with nothing more spiritual than my valise. I made out the train, like a drop of ink spreading on a page, far down the track.

I had been waiting for perhaps ten minutes when I glanced up the hill and noticed a woman walking swiftly on the path from the hotel. As she reached the board walkway, she paused, bent over her ankles, and unbuckled her shoes. Then she sprinted, her skirt billowing, her dark hair loosening from the pins that restrained it, her stockinged feet flying across the wooden planks. At the stair landing she paused, gazing in the direction of the oncoming train, then at me, before she came pattering down the steps to join me on the platform. It was Violet, of course, flushed, wide-eyed, laughing at her own impetuosity. I stood up as she rushed to me, holding out her hands. "I couldn't let you leave without saying good-bye," she said, her breath coming in gasps. She took my hand in her own, shaking it gently as if we were just meeting. "Jeremiah said he told you I was angry at you, which is just ridiculous, I hope you know. I was angry at him!"

"I'm glad to hear it," I said, and I meant it. "But—"

"I couldn't sleep after you left," she continued. "I just paced the room until I couldn't stand it anymore and I knocked on Jeremiah's door and made him get up and listen to me. I tried to tell him how excited I was, and how I wanted to change everything, but he is so dense. I got frustrated and wound up in tears."

The approaching train wailed as if in sympathy to her plight. Violet raised her voice over the racket. "But I was never angry at you. I had to tell you that."

"I'm glad to hear it," I said again. "But I fear you've torn your stockings."

She raised one foot and we both laughed at the shredded silk. "I haven't run in years," she said. "Why do we never run?"

Now the engine was grinding and huffing and the brakes squealed as it lumbered to the platform. I picked up my valise and turned toward it. As I did, Violet caught my hand to stop me, and I turned to her. She released me at once, drawing back as if abashed by her own impulsiveness. "You have completely shaken me up, Phoebe Grant," she said.

"I didn't mean to," I replied. The two carriages glided in before us; there was a wheeze and a cloud of white steam rose from below. The attendant yanked the heavy door open from inside. "Good luck to you," I said, handing in my valise and following it.

When I looked back, Violet was smiling. "And to you," she said. She had gripped her skirt in one hand, pulling it up and back so that the hem was lifted above her ankles. Another belch of steam issued from the train, washing over her torn stockings, her lifted skirt, up to the hand clutching the cloth at her hip. It alarmed me; I felt she was being swallowed up, and though I was perfectly aware that this was not the case, I had a strong premonition of something dark, something like doom gathering around this small, pert, eager woman who had made a most unladylike spectacle of herself in her anxiety to bid me farewell.

"Don't forget me," she called out, as the door slid shut and the train, with another wail of the whistle and screech of metal against metal, pulled away from Lake Pleasant.

On Tour in America

Philadelphia, November 1894

The Anglo-Saxon race will own the world.

Arthur Conan Doyle

When the last guest was gone, Dr. Doyle bid his host good night and climbed the deeply carpeted stairs of the mansion to his luxurious bedroom. Two consecutive nights in the same bed felt like a novelty. He had been traveling nonstop for a month. Hotel rooms, no matter how dreary and overheated, were welcome enough, since most nights he and his brother got what rest they could in the narrow bunks of the Pullman cars. Each day they were greeted at another small, overheated railway station by representatives of the reading circle or lecture hall or booking agency sent out on purpose to gather them in. Unfailingly polite, enthusiastic, obsequious, and curious, these Americans never failed to inquire, first, what he thought of America and second, whether he would bring the famous detective back to life. They took him to dinner in rooms festooned in ribbons and flags, where the tables were decorated with unsubtle references to his characters. Large groups of strangers sat

{ 171 }

down with him. His glass and his plate were constantly replenished, toasts went round and round; he proposed a few himself, and even his brother joined in.

He had wanted to see America since he was a boy. He had imagined it intensely, particularly the great western territory, and he was familiar with American scenes sketched by the American writers he admired. But none of these writers had bothered to mention a perplexing and ubiquitous detail of American life: America was overheated. In the hotel lobbies, hotel rooms, lecture halls, train stations, restaurants, and eating clubs the temperature was consistently more suited to orchids than to human beings. Even the dining room in the stately residence of tonight's host, the charming, urbane Craige Lippincott, rivaled the *caldarium* in the Baths of Diocletian.

His bedroom was mercifully temperate. Once the door was closed and the window thrown open and he was stripped down to his woolen combinations, his pores dried out and he could feel the flush draining from his cheeks. He was pleasantly befuddled from the excellent wine and full from the dinner, which had gone on for many courses, and many hours, served by silent waiters dressed like haberdashers—so democratic, these Americans.

The bed was enormous and piled with comforters, but these could be pushed aside and the sheets against his skin were deliciously cool and silky—what were they made of? He stretched out full length and gazed up at the baronial vaulted ceiling. "Yoove come a lang way, laddie," he said softly. "An' nee jist athwart th' wild wide brine."

He was thirty-five years old. With scarcely a hint of what he might achieve, but driven by a furnace of ambition to strive in every field that opened before him, he had made himself up. To all he met now, he was a success, a man to be reckoned with. The wealthy American gentlemen, doctors, writers, editors, all were eager to dine with him because he was someone they felt they ought to know. After so many tasteless, insipid meals among the crowds of dull-witted strangers, this at-home dinner with ten cultured and powerful men who knew one another and took a lively interest in everything, but particularly in literature and medicine, had soothed his *amour-propre* like a plunge into a river of balm. Not once had the name Sherlock Holmes crossed the lips of his fellow diners. Not once had he been asked what he thought of America.

In fact he recalled, but distantly, there had been a noticeable lack of enthusiasm for his prediction that the English-speaking races must one day, perhaps not so far in the future, unite under one flag. Mr. Owen Wister, who blinked at this suggestion repeatedly as if before a blast of grit that affected his nearsighted eyes, pursed up his full lips—there was something effeminate about the man—and sputtered, "Whatever for?" Very well, he hadn't urged the point. He hadn't gone on about it ad nauseam as the Bok fellow had about the suffragist cause.

How agitated they all were by the woman question! Bok edited a ladies' magazine and Mitchell tended a clientele made up exclusively of wealthy neurasthenics, but even Wister, who did have some fine stories to tell about his western travels, expressed his solidarity with the cause of female enfranchisement. They were voting already in the West, he announced, and all agreed that the West was where the future of the great republic lay.

As he turned onto his side, pulling in a pillow the size of a ewe, he congratulated himself on having kept his views on the subject to himself. And then it had changed, the subject, but to what? He rolled onto his back and stretched his arms out wide on either side—what luxury after too many nights in the Pullman cars. Innes always took the top bunk because, he said, he was younger and could sleep anywhere. The thought of his good-natured brother sent a smile flickering over the doctor's lips, as sleep came, closing his eyes, silencing his thoughts. The bed was not moving anytime soon, and neither was he.

In the night he woke to hear someone calling his name. The voice was familiar; he'd heard it infrequently over the course of many years, calling him from sleep in just this way. It wasn't urgent, but there was an element of entreaty to it. "Arthur." He took it to be the vapor of a dream.

As he gazed into the darkness of the spacious room, his senses alert to the domed weight of air overarching the bed, there stirred in him a feeling of alarm. This voice had not wakened him for over a year, and he had reason to believe it never would again, for in that time the speaker, having moved over many years from one closed and distant room to another, had arrived at his final residence, a very small room indeed in the cemetery at Dumfries.

Yet here he was, still calling. Doyle lay still, listening to his heart pulsing doggedly in his ear. Nothing had changed. Neither death nor an ocean was a barrier.

"Papa," he said tentatively into the enormous silence. "I'm here."

Of course, no answer. Just the sadness and shame always associated with turning away, as he did now, closing his eyes and wishing he didn't know what he knew, namely that his father had died alone in a madhouse, where, for thirteen years, he had devoted his heavy accumulation of free time to painting pictures of sprites and fairies and the angel of death.

In the morning, on waking, Doyle recalled his anxiety and the voice calling him in the night. Sleep was a treacherous business. He could have dreamed he'd dreamed a dream of waking, for all he knew. Pulling himself up, swinging his legs over the side of the bed, he consciously thrust his dead father firmly out of his mind.

Now, as he trimmed the block of black bristles over his upper lip before the dressing mirror, the conversation round the dinner table played again in his thoughts. The subject had rambled from the treatment of hysteria to the question of psychic transference and the efficacy of mesmerism and hypnotism as medical procedures. It was a topic that interested Doyle, and he had offered the company a summary of his forthcoming tale—it would appear in the next issue of *Harper's Weekly*—which he believed might entertain them. The story concerned a promising young doctor, very much a materialist, who is invited by his charming and beautiful fiancée to witness

{ 174 }

a demonstration of hypnotism by a visiting lady adept. This lady proves to be unlovely, over forty, not well dressed or appealing in any part—she's even a cripple and uses a crutch to walk—but of course she does have intense and searching eyes. She makes bold claims for her dark art, and vows she can require a subject to do her bidding even if she is nowhere near him. To prove his superiority, the doctor submits himself to a course of hypnotic treatments. He is scarcely a challenge to the hypnotist's powers and very soon finds himself completely under her spell. When he makes up his mind to resist and free himself from her influence, she vows to take vengeance upon him, and it evolves that she has such complete control of his thoughts and compulsions that, during black-out spells of which he has no memory, he wantonly, and even in the case of the fiancée violently, destroys all his prospects for future happiness.

The assembled gentlemen, attending closely to this plot summary between the fish and the meat course, found it worthy of comment. Dr. Weir Mitchell opined that this scenario was, in his view, not entirely outside the realm of possibility. Some of his patients were so highly suggestible it was as if they had no minds to lose. Owen Wister put in that the story reminded him of the clairvoyant his friend Henry James's brother William was so keen on investigating in Boston. He'd begun seeing her in the hopes of discrediting her, but his failure to do so had resulted in his allowing her a too central position in his life. "Of course," he added, "Mrs. Piper is a most charismatic creature. Even Mrs. James has great faith in her authenticity."

Dr. Mitchell had heard of this case and observed that William James called Mrs. Piper his "white crow."

"And why is that?" Doyle asked.

"He says to disprove the statement that all crows are black you needn't look at all crows; you need only produce one white one."

Doyle nodded with the others, hiding his mystification behind a thoughtful brow. He was gratified when Wister persisted. "What have white crows to do with psychics?"

Lippincott chuckled. "He means that to disprove the statement 'All psychics are frauds,' you need only produce one who is not."

Bok, who had heard of Mrs. Piper, said, "There's no doubt, she's an impressive candidate. But I believe Mrs. Piper is no match for our own Violet Petra, though I haven't seen or heard of her for several years now."

"Oh, Violet Petra is still very much among us," said Dr. Mitchell. "She has agreed to be tested by my colleagues Bishop and Bradley, who are both charter members of the Society for Psychical Research. Bishop told me he's kept her secluded for weeks on end, but there has been no diminution in her powers. He's quite the believer in Miss Petra."

The talk then turned to the useful work of the SPR, created to debunk and expose the glut of fraudulent mediums and séance mongers who were a plague upon the reason of ordinary folk. So it was with some pride that Doyle confessed he'd recently become a member of the sister organization in London, founded by Myers and now headed by Arthur Balfour.

"Then," said Mitchell, "as you are a psychic investigator, you really should have a look at Miss Petra. I'd be curious to hear the impression of a foreign observer. And I'm sure she'd find time to transmit any messages from the spirits who are hovering over the creator of Mr. Sherlock Holmes."

Yes, that was right. Mitchell had made the only mention of the great detective in the entire evening. Now Doyle patted the hand towel against his damp mustache, recalling with satisfaction his response to this patronizing jibe from the distinguished windbag, Weir Mitchell. "Perhaps I should," he'd said. "Perhaps she'll have a message from Holmes himself. He's dead, you know."

At breakfast the doctor and his brother laid their plans for the day. Dr. Doyle was bound for Newark, but Innes would be at his leisure in the town. Their host suggested a tour of the state buildings, or a visit to the picture gallery. As they spoke, a servant appeared and presented a salver scattered with cards, which Lippincott examined one by one, separating them into two stacks. "Your fans have detected your whereabouts," he said, sliding a stack of half a dozen across the tablecloth to his guest.

"There never was such a pack of superior sleuths as there is among his readers," observed Innes.

Four of the cards were from ladies who hoped the author could find half an hour in his busy schedule to come and talk to a splendid literary club, meeting, tea, or luncheon. One, addressed to Sherlock Holmes, offered the services of an excellent hat maker. The last was from Dr. Mitchell. Doyle squinted at the nearly illegible scrawl on the back.

"Why do doctors always have such crabbed handwriting?" asked his host.

"It's professional vanity," Doyle replied. "And contempt for the pharmacist." He cracked the mystery of Mitchell's different versions of the letter R and the message came clear. "*As you've an interest*," he read out, "*I've contacted Dr. Bishop, who would be pleased to introduce you to Miss Violet Petra anytime tomorrow afternoon, at his home, 742 Walnut. I think you will find it worth your trouble. Please reply appointing time, yours sincerely, Silas Weir Mitchell, M.D. P.S. Bishop is a great admirer of your new medical stories, as are we all!*"

Craige Lippincott, who sipped his coffee while listening to the message, smiled at the postscript and set his cup in the saucer. "That's so like Weir, that last bit."

"The book has hardly been out a week," said Doyle.

"Still, you may believe him. He's a great reader and keeps up with everything new."

"And this Dr. Bishop?"

"Oh, Bishop is a fine old gentleman. He's Colonel Bishop as well. He saw some hard service during the war. He and Mitchell were at Turner's Lane Hospital, where they sent the nerve injury cases. Of course, those injuries often included a lot more than the nerves."

Doyle turned the card over, rubbing his finger against the embossed name on the front. "I suppose I could go tomorrow. Is it far from here?"

"A ten-minute walk. If that sort of thing interests you, you might go. You'll enjoy Bishop. He's a brilliant fellow, in his way, and a great sportsman. He was quite a boxer in his youth."

"Was he?" Doyle raised his eyebrows at his brother, who drew down the corners of his mouth and shrugged.

"Very well," said Doyle. "I'll go along and see these gentlemen and their psychic wonder."

All morning long a sullen mass of slate-blue clouds brooded over the rooftops of Philadelphia. As Dr. Doyle set off from the Lippincott mansion for his appointment at Dr. Bishop's, the first patter of drops struck his hat. He'd just passed an hour with an enthusiastic journalist from the *Philadelphia Times* who asked him for his impression of America and urged him to bring Sherlock Holmes back from the dead. "So you believe the dead can return," Doyle replied cheerfully.

"Well, no. I mean, not really," the young man demurred. "But he might not really be dead, you know."

"I think it's safe to say he may never really have been alive," suggested the author.

"Of course," the flustered reporter agreed. "I know that."

It was tiresome, the daily interview, and he did his best to liven it up, but the newspapers wanted pap for the masses, and he dutifully supplied it. So steadfastly did he decline to speak ill of America that his refusal had been noted in the press. He was the rare British writer who admired America, who had always wanted to visit, who vowed to return.

He had scarcely walked a block when a low, distant rumble announced the imminence of the storm. In the second block, as if some frayed seam in the clouds had split, a great sheet of water swept down from above. Doyle was not much given to regarding the weather—one went out in it, no matter what—and his pace was naturally brisk. As the puddles quickly gathered underfoot, he charged along the pavement, oblivious to the weight his woolen tweeds were taking on and the sodden condition of his stockings. In fact, this thorough soaking suited him, as it constituted a change, something unexpected in the tedium of his schedule. The American rain, at least, wouldn't ask him how he felt about American rain.

He was also enlivened and pleasurably engaged by the nature of the coming interview, the only one in over a month in which he was not the subject. The role of psychic investigator appealed strongly to his sense of himself as both a scientist and an adventurer in the realms of psychological possibility, of thorny questions, which, in his view, might yield solid, empirical answers. He was a good judge of character and not easily duped. Many of these mediums and clairvoyants were doubtless frauds, so his mission was a complex one—to be circumspect and alert, yet open, to outfox foxes, to separate the true gold from the dross. He had a limited experience in the field, some thought transference exercises, which had persuaded him that such phenomena were indeed possible, a séance or two, unrewarding but not entirely discouraging, and an investigation of a haunted house he had undertaken with Major Podmore, which had proved no more haunted than any house in which an unhappy young woman resides with her repressive family.

As he approached the stern gray stone façade of Dr. Bishop's town house, he had, he assured himself, no expectation that anything extraordinary would happen within its precincts. This was the correct attitude to take. Americans were a credulous race; they wrote letters to fictional characters, they coined religions as if there were a shortage on the market. He vaulted up the few steps and turned the bell.

Dr. Bishop himself greeted Doyle at the door, relieved him of his coat and waterlogged hat, and ushered him into an overheated parlor where a tall, sallow-faced young woman seated near the requisite blazing fire jumped up from her chair and stood stiffly, nervously blinking her eyes like a daydreaming student who has been called upon in class. Was this dreary personage the renowned clairvoyant?

She was not. Dr. Bishop acknowledged that it was his pleasure to introduce his distinguished guest to Miss Constance Whitaker, who would be the registrar for the sitting this afternoon. Miss Whitaker held out her hand in the automatic fashion of Americans, and Doyle pressed it briefly in his own. "I'm so thrilled to meet you, sir," she said, blushing urgently.

As Miss Petra was not in evidence, the three stood talking about the weather; it had been a wet fall in Philadelphia and an unseasonably cold one. Dr. Bishop praised Miss Whitaker's abilities at transcribing the sittings of their subjects. Today's report would be the seventeenth they had carried out with Miss Petra, and some excerpts were to be published in the Boston Society's proceedings in the coming months.

Doyle hid his astonishment at being kept waiting beneath the set smile and amiably quizzical manner he had perfected for all such uncomfortable moments. He asked Dr. Bishop questions about his boxing enthusiasm and found him to be, as advertised, quirky and intelligent. He was also hard of hearing. Doyle found himself raising his voice and speaking with exaggerated care. At last the bell sounded and his host rushed off to the door, leaving him to contemplate Miss Whitaker's awed and awkward silence.

"Have you been assisting Dr. Bishop very long?" he asked kindly.

She started, as if pinched. "Oh," she said. "I'm not sure."

They both heard the rustle of movement and exchange of voices in the hall, and then Miss Petra appeared in the doorway, where she paused a moment, as if offering herself for viewing. Dr. Doyle, the investigator, took her in closely. She was a very small, slight creature, not in her first youth. Not at all what he had expected. She was dressed neatly, though oddly, in muted colors, a pale lavender silk blouse beneath a tight-fitting mauve velvet jacket of a stylish cut. Her gray silk skirt, rucked up at the back and sadly out of date, was too short, so that an inch or two of her black stockings showed over the tops of her neat black boots. Her hair was artfully arranged and pinned tightly at the back. The loose curls at the front, he noted, were shot with silver. Her eyes, large, of a translucent gray that seemed to give off light, frankly studied him. He noted a slight protrusion of the soft tissue in the left eye, possibly an orbital pseudotumor—no treatment for it, and none necessary for the most part, but it could be painful. She had good posture, her long neck was extended, her chin lifted to hide the weakness in the jawline. She'd applied a touch of rouge to suggest the blush of youth on her cheekbones, but it didn't succeed in hiding from Dr. Doyle the likelihood that Miss Petra was over forty.

Dr. Bishop came up behind her as she advanced into the room, her hand outstretched; her smile, parting her lips over straight, even teeth, was charming. "Dr. Doyle," she said. "What a pleasure to meet you here. Your wonderful books have given me so much pleasure."

He took her hand, holding it a moment and fixing her with his twinkling ready-to-be-delighted expression, which reliably disarmed the ladies. "I'm pleased to hear it."

"*The White Company,*" she continued, "I believe that one is my favorite. It so put me in mind of Walter Scott—I love his novels too. But yours was different, just as noble but somehow more relevant, less obscured in the mists of time. I'm not sure how you did it, but I found it tremendously moving and powerful."

This comparison to his own favorite author, as well as praise for his favorite among his own books, filled Doyle's senses like a perfume. And there was an actual perfume working on him as well—Miss Petra must be wearing it—a scent he associated with his childhood, the white heather of Scotland, which, a schoolmate had once told him, only grows over the graves of fairies.

Having entirely disarmed Dr. Doyle, Miss Petra turned the force of her presence upon Miss Whitaker. "Constance," she said. "Here you are with your notebook. How is your mother faring?"

"She's better." Miss Whitaker stepped cautiously closer to the medium, as if to warm herself by a fire. Doyle exchanged a look of medical superiority and confidence with Dr. Bishop as he came into the room. "I'm sure you know Dr. Doyle's reputation as an author," he said to Miss Petra, "but you may not know that he is a member of the British Society for Psychical Research."

"Indeed," Violet replied, looking from the resident doctor to the visiting doctor, while Miss Whitaker sank into a chair and opened her leather-bound notebook. "And you are enjoying your first visit to America, Dr. Doyle."

"I am," he replied. "I've been gratified by the hospitality of Americans. They make one feel so welcome."

She nodded, as at common knowledge. "You've experienced no anti-British sentiment."

Doyle chuckled, as a recollection surfaced. "There was an excitable gentleman speechifying at a dinner in Detroit. It was after many rounds of toasts."

Dr. Bishop frowned so that his beard moved down his chest. "He spoke against Britain?"

"He spoke against the Empire," Doyle replied.

"In Detroit?"

Doyle glanced at Miss Petra, who appeared interested in his reply. "The wine flows very freely in Detroit," he said.

"Your schedule has been hectic, I believe," Miss Petra observed.

"I've spent many a night sleeping in your excellent Pullman cars."

"You prefer our trains to those on the Continent."

He nodded. It struck him as odd that Miss Petra seemed incapable of asking him a question. She made pronouncements with which he was invited to agree. It was like being fed one's lines by a fellow actor. "The Pullman car is more commodious and more private than any I've seen there."

"I should think privacy would be welcome on such a tour. You are much in the public eye."

"Well, I don't mind that. I came to see America. My lectures are the price I pay, and it's not a steep one."

"As Americans are so hospitable," she finished for him.

"Shall we sit down?" their host suggested, taking for himself the armchair nearest Miss Whitaker. Miss Petra settled in the chair facing Miss Whitaker, leaving to Doyle the hulking Pembroke nearest the fire. When his legs were pressed against the smooth leather of the seat, he realized his trousers were soaked from the thighs down. The heat from the flames made him feel like a sheep in a steam bath.

Miss Petra observed him shifting his weight from one hip to the other. "I confess that I was surprised you should find time in your schedule to come and see me," she said.

Doyle crossed his feet at the ankle, then uncrossed them. "Dr. Mitchell assured me I shouldn't miss the opportunity."

"Ah yes, Dr. Mitchell," Miss Petra said softly.

"He speaks highly of your gift."

"Does he?" She appeared surprised. "I haven't seen him in years."

"Weir Mitchell keeps up with everything," Dr. Bishop put in. "He's not a member of our society yet, but I know he reads the proceedings."

This reminder of his official capacity as a psychic investigator and the duties attendant upon it distracted Doyle from his skirmish with the chair. "I hope you won't be offended if I take the liberty of examining certain particulars of this room." He turned to Miss Petra, as if she needed reassuring. "It's purely a formality."

"Of course," said the doctor. "That would be proper."

"By all means," said Miss Petra.

Doyle stood up and strode about the room, peering under tables and behind the chairs. The Pembroke was open beneath, so a glance assured him of its uselessness as a place of concealment. He glanced overhead at the chandelier and down at the plush, expensive carpet.

"I believe Mr. Sherlock Holmes often finds useful clues behind the curtains," Miss Petra observed drily.

Doyle gave her a chilly look. She was too flippant for his taste. He liked a woman with spirit, but there was something confrontational about this one that repelled him. "I'll forgo the curtains," he said. "As no crime has been committed here."

"Not yet," she said cheerfully.

"What did you say, my dear?" asked Dr. Bishop.

She leaned toward him, speaking clearly. "I said no crime has been committed here yet," she replied.

Doyle wandered back to his chair, sitting down disconsolately.

"Crime," exclaimed Dr. Bishop. "I should hope not."

"Poor Constance," Miss Petra said. "She is taking down all this idle chatter."

The gentlemen turned their attention to the young scribe, who raised her pen, but not her eyes, which were firmly fastened to the open page of her notebook.

"That's true," said Dr. Bishop. "Perhaps we should begin."

"Do we sit at the table?" asked Doyle.

"No," said Miss Petra. "But you should be comfortable and I'm sure *you* are not. Dr. Bishop, would you be so good as to change chairs with Dr. Doyle. He is burning up next to that fire and you are always chilly. *Frileux*—I believe that's the French word for your temperament."

Doyle rose at once, looming over his host, who took a moment to grasp the suggestion. "Change chairs," he said. "What. Does that suit you, sir?"

"It does," said Doyle.

As the large men followed her instructions, Miss Petra pursued her observations of their physical types. "You are of an igneous constitution, Dr. Doyle. The Arctic must have suited you perfectly."

Dr. Bishop, subsiding into the depths of the oversized chair, crossed his legs toward the fire. "Have you been in the Arctic, Doyle?"

"I was ship's doctor on a whaler, fresh from my medical studies," Doyle announced to the doctor. To Miss Petra he added softly, "You've done your research."

"I would be remiss if I didn't," she replied. "I make no secret of it. You understand that I may be of little or no use to you today. I expect your reputation has preceded you right out of this world, and the spirits may be intimidated."

"Do you think so?" asked Dr. Bishop. "Is that possible?"

Doyle detected the edge of irony in Miss Petra's tone, and it struck him that she was enjoying herself at the gentlemen's expense. "Miss Petra is joking, I believe," he said.

"Yes," she agreed. "That's my poor idea of a little joke. Are you comfortable now, Dr. Doyle?"

"I am," he said.

She leaned forward in her chair and for a moment he thought she might reach out to take his hand, as he understood some mediums did. But instead she flattened her hands over her thighs and allowed her gaze to travel the length and breadth of the room, pausing here and there as if taking note of important details. "We stand at the gate," she said softly, opening her hands and closing her eyes. "The spirits of our loved ones are among us."

In the pause that followed, the two men exchanged a nervous glance. As Dr. Bishop had experienced whatever it was Miss Petra had on offer many times—seventeen was it?—the trepidation in the older man's expression puzzled Doyle. Was a cold hand about to grasp him by the throat? He studied Miss Petra, who, as far as he could tell, had not moved a muscle. As he watched, she brought the fingertips of her left hand to her left eye, massaging it gently beneath the lid. "Is there someone who will speak to me?" she inquired.

But there was, evidently, no one.

After a moment she said, "Oh, dear, it's as silent as the tomb." Then, with a chuckle she added, "That should rile them up."

As he watched her, Doyle allowed the antipathy he felt for her to expand unchecked, so that his senses seemed to swell with it. If she were at all sensitive, she would feel the pressure of his hostility bearing down upon her. Growling at her, he thought, and though he didn't growl, the idea amused him and he smiled his inward smile that no one could read.

"No one?" she asked the air, with her eyes still closed. "Wait. Yes. Dr. Bishop is here."

Dr. Bishop uncrossed his legs—it was odd for a man to sit like that, huddled at the fire like an old woman—and leaned over his chair arm, turning his good ear toward the medium.

"This is a young woman, very dignified and serious. She says would I please say that you've nothing to reproach yourself for. Yes. I've told him. She insists I say it again. You have nothing . . . Oh,

Dr. Bishop, here is your uncle again. He is still anxious about that investment in the railway."

Dr. Bishop nodded gloomily. "As well he might be," he said. "I've lost a bundle."

"Well," said Miss Petra. "He warned you. Perhaps you'll think twice about future investments. He recommends the gas. He thinks the gas would be an excellent investment."

"I don't see it," said Dr. Bishop. "The electric is the thing. Everyone agrees on that."

"He repeats that he recommends the gas."

"Does he?"

Doyle looked from one to the other. It was absurd, he thought. Too banal for words.

"Here is another person, a tall gentleman with a long beard. He has such gentle eyes. He is timid, I think. He is anxious. Yes. Dr. Arthur Doyle is here. I can certainly give him a message."

"Who is he?" asked Doyle.

"He says he has been having a delightful picnic with the most charming fairy. She lives beneath a Chinese primrose and she is no bigger than his thumb. Her wings are gossamer and her hair is a golden cloud. She was frightened by a rude crow; it was after their sandwiches."

Doyle felt a tightening in the skin at his temples and a chill in his chest. He couldn't look at the dreadful woman, and so he allowed his eyes to settle on the still moist tweed sticking to his thighs. Dr. Bishop, listening with all his energy, said, "He is seeking Dr. Doyle?"

"Oh, yes," Miss Petra replied. "He has a message. But it isn't for Dr. Doyle. No. He entreats Dr. Doyle to carry the message to this person. It is a doctor. Dr. Rud. Dr. Rudder. No."

Doyle's eyes flickered up, bright in the pale skin of his blood-drained face. "Dr. Rutherford," he said, looking back at his knees.

"Is that it?" asked Miss Petra. "Is it Rutherford? Yes. Yes. He wants to be sure the doctor has been paid for his services. He wants you to remind him—something about gold."

"The gold dust," Doyle said gloomily.

"Yes. That's it. The gold dust." Miss Petra paused, and the only sound was Miss Whitaker's scratching away. "He's tired now," continued Miss Petra. "He says it's very tiring to send messages. He hasn't done it before and hopes he won't have to again. But he's thinking of Dr. Rutherford, who was so kind. Now he's going." She paused. "He's gone," she said. "Is there no one else? No?" Again she paused; Dr. Bishop coughed. "No, they're gone."

Miss Petra fell silent, but Doyle didn't look up to see her open her eyes and fold her hands in her lap. He sat with his head bowed over his chest, and as Dr. Bishop mumbled some appreciative remark, he raised one hand, spread it across his forehead, and rubbed his temples. His mother had shown him the letter from Rutherford describing his father's last days. The patient, he said, was uncomfortable, suffered from cold hands and feet, and wanted, as always, to be home with his family. Very near the end he'd seemed to improve and had brought the doctor a piece of folded white paper in which, he explained, he'd gathered gold dust left by the sunlight on his bed. He offered it in payment for the doctor's services to him.

Why here? Why in America?

He closed his eyes, blinking back an unwonted gathering of tears. Miss Petra was speaking, her voice gentle, full of tenderness. When he looked up, she was standing before him, her hands clasped loosely at her waist, a small spectral figure, and her unearthly eyes bathed him in a warm, maternal sympathy that required nothing in return. "Are you well, sir?" she said.

He gave his travel-weary head a little shake, raising and lowering his shoulders, resuming his clear-headed, strong-minded, medically trained, observant and indulgent identity, braced and bracing, a man who offered support, but never required it. "I'm well," he said, not meeting her eyes. She was, he understood, as observant as he was, possibly more so. As she stepped back, remarking to Dr. Bishop that she found his drawing room a particularly conducive environment, the fierce antipathy Doyle had felt for her subsided like a tide going out, and what came in on the next wave was a solid and committed devotion. He would, he vowed, go to the wall for this woman. He would wire Lodge and Myers as soon as possible and arrange to have her brought over. Violet Petra, he would tell them, was the one they had been searching for. She was the white crow.

From: PERSONAL RECOLLECTIONS:
MY LIFE IN JOURNALISM
BY PHOEBE GRANT, EDITED BY LUCY DIAL

A PSYCHIC'S CONFESSION

My last interview with Violet Petra took place in the lounge of a small, barely respectable Philadelphia hotel in November 1894. She had sent me a message at my newspaper office asking if I would be willing to see her, as she had something to discuss with me, which she could only do in person. My curiosity was aroused, as it always was by Violet, and I replied that I would meet her the following afternoon.

The desk clerk, a pallid, lifeless individual, repeated my name as if it were a puzzle he hadn't the energy to solve. He then ordered a gloomy-looking boy of twelve or so to run up the dim, thinly carpeted stairs to advise Miss Petra of my presence in the hotel. I wandered into the lounge, where I assumed our interview would take place.

After half an hour of waiting, and having examined the meager collection of books on the shelf over the writing table, I accosted the boy, who had returned to lurk sullenly near the front desk, and ordered tea. He informed me that tea had to be transported from the shop two doors down and I must expect an extra charge for the delivery. "Very well," I said. "I'd like a pot and two cups, milk, and if there's brown bread to be had—"

"There isn't," interrupted the boy.

"Well, milk and sugar at least."

"You're wanting a full service," he proclaimed, which brought up the head of the somnolent desk clerk, who slid from behind the counter literally wringing his hands. "Be assured, madam," he cajoled me. "We can provide anything you'd like, including . . ."— here he rapped the boy sharply on the shoulder—"brown bread, with, I may add, an excellent comfiture of wild strawberries."

"That sounds very fine," I said. "I'll expect it in the lounge." Which refuge I reclaimed, leaving them to muddle out a scheme for the provision of an "excellent comfiture."

The newspaper I discovered on the sideboard was a scurrilous rag no person of decency would be caught reading, with the additional noninducement of being two days old. I heard the boy banging out the front door, the desk clerk retreated to his domain behind the counter, and a gloomy stillness fell upon the scene. I pulled a small table in place between a pair of threadbare chairs, took my seat, removed my gloves, and resigned myself to waiting for Violet to make her appearance. We were close in age, both in our fifth decade, and I hadn't seen her in ten years. *But she hasn't changed*, I thought. She still made everyone wait.

I'd had my tea, read the competition, and been stared at secretively for several minutes by a shabbily dressed former gentleman who came in and dashed off a letter at the writing desk. I amused myself with imagining who might be the recipient of his urgent message: a potential employer, a disillusioned wife, a wealthy relative, a friend who cared for him before his fall from grace? He went out and I finished off my bread. At last I heard a step on the stair, and in the next moment Violet stood leaning against the doorsill, holding a small brown parcel against her skirt. "I knew you'd come," she said.

I hadn't seen her in ten years, but this echo of her first words to me on that long-ago morning when she opened her hotel room door and welcomed me so confidently into her mad little world made me smile. I had no idea how she'd passed the intervening decade, but my own life had not been unrewarding. I'd carved my little niche in the profession I love; I worked with men and women who admired me and whom I admired. I still lived in a rooming house, but it was a well-kept, bright, and airy house in a respectable street, and my comfortable sitting room was adequately heated in winter and in summer the long windows looked out on a flower garden that perfumed the air.

Violet took a step into the lounge and paused, resting her hand on the edge of a table. The step was unsteady, but she gathered herself with a stiff, determined smile and made the rest of the journey to the chair facing mine without incident. I glanced at the clock over the mantel—it was three fifteen and she was evidently either very late from bed or early to the bottle. "I'm afraid the tea has gone cold," I said. "Shall I send for a fresh pot?"

"Tea?" she said, sliding into the confines of the chair and cradling the package in her lap. "I didn't think they served it here."

"They send out for it," I said.

Her eyes, after trailing over the china service, the crumb-strewn plate, and the open jam pot, settled on me. "You're such a resourceful person, Phoebe," she observed. "I'd forgotten that."

I ignored this empty flattery. "You're looking well," I said.

Which was true. In spite of her muddled entrance, she was still a lovely woman. She'd changed her style from flowing to fitted and it suited her; her figure was lithe, her back straight. Her elegant long neck was exposed at the nape by an upsweep of her black hair, which cascaded in gay ringlets over her forehead. She didn't, as I knew I did, look her age.

"You haven't changed," she said.

She meant my style, I thought. My everlasting skirt and blouse. "I'm still the same," I said. "But how are you? How long have you been staying here?"

"Can you believe it?" she said, casting a horrified eye over the furnishings of the room. "It's even more dismal upstairs."

"It's not so bad," I lied.

"I've been here a month, but thank God, I'm leaving on Friday. That's why I asked you to come."

"You're leaving Philadelphia?"

"I'm being investigated," she announced, as if the prospect delighted her.

"Investigated?" I said.

"They try to figure out exactly how I do what I do. They bring in different people and invite me to different rooms. They took me to a graveyard one night; that was horrific. There's a secretary who copies down every word I say and she types it all up and they send it around to their colleagues."

"Who are they?"

"They call themselves the Society for Psychical Research. They're mostly doctors." She paused, gauging my response to this sudden outpouring.

"Did Mr. Babin tell them about you?"

"Oh no. Jeremiah and I parted company several years ago, just after the Fox sisters' fiasco. I think that business killed poor Virginia, or at least it drove her to stronger medication and that killed her. Jeremiah remarried a young woman, quite an heiress too. They have a little son now. But he didn't desert me. He was kind enough to introduce me to Mrs. Bitters, very aptly named as it turned out, whose daughter had died in childbirth. After that there were several others—I won't bore you—and then Dr. Bishop got wind of me and persuaded me to be a subject for the Society. They're very keen on me."

"And have they figured you out?"

"Oh, they've given up on that," she said. "Now I think they're just trying to kill me." She made this surprising statement with an air of amused indulgence; wasn't it silly what she had to put up with. Her eyes sought mine, then darted away. There was something hectic about her, something false. I said nothing, which forced her to lurch on. "You'll never guess who's taken an interest, a very great interest, I must say."

"Someone I know?"

"Someone you've heard of," she said gaily. "Someone everyone's heard of."

"Who could that be? The president?" I asked.

"It's Dr. Arthur Conan Doyle."

I stared at her. It occurred to me that she'd been shut up in the dismal hotel so long she'd lost touch with reality. "The author?" I said. Even as I spoke, I recalled that this gentleman had passed through our city in the last week—the papers were full of his American tour, and of his audiences' insistence that he bring back his famous detective, Sherlock Holmes, from the grave. "You've seen him?" I asked gently.

"He's one of them," she said. "One of their Society in England. He's a charming man. Very large and talkative, not particularly observant, which is surprising, and full of enthusiasms. He thinks America and Britain should reunite under one flag."

"I've read that," I said. "The press is having fun with it."

"You should interview him," she suggested.

"Authors aren't really in my line," I said. She gave me a blank, uncomprehending look. "You do know Conan Doyle wrote that story you were so upset about at Lake Pleasant."

"What story?"

"The one about the ship. The *Mary Celeste*."

Her eyes widened. She didn't know.

"It was in a collection of his. I read it a few years ago. I thought of you when I found it."

"I didn't see it," she said. "I've read some of his Holmes stories; they pass the time. And I looked over *The White Company* when I learned I would be meeting him." She paused, looking vexed. "So he wrote that story?"

"Too bad you didn't know. You could have upbraided him."

"All that seems so long ago," she said. "I'd forgotten about it."

"Then you forgive him."

"I'll have to," she said. "He's sending me to London."

"London!" I said.

"He believes his friends at the Society there should have a look at me."

"Do you want to go?"

She pushed out her lower lip, looking peevish. "I may as well go," she said. "I've pretty much exhausted the possibilities here." I studied her without speaking. Her mood had changed, the light-hearted bravado dropping away like a mask. "I don't want to go," she continued. "But I don't have a choice."

"Surely you can decline the invitation."

"And do what?" she replied sharply. "Learn to type? I'm forty-five years old."

This was an irrefutable assertion. She stood up, laying her package on a side table, and paced the length of the room. She was steady on her feet; consternation had sobered her. At the door she stopped, looking out at the desk clerk, who was occupied in sorting a stack of mail. "They're killing me," she repeated.

"You exaggerate," I said.

"It's not just them," she said. "It's that I find . . ." She sighed, touched her fingers to her forehead, and wandered back to her chair, searching for what "it" was. "It's getting more and more difficult for me to . . ." Again she paused, frowning at me, recalling to whom she was speaking. "Make contact," she concluded.

"The spirits have abandoned you."

She nodded gravely. "That's a good way of putting it. That's how it feels."

"You may find a whole new cast of them in Britain," I suggested facetiously. "It's full of ghosts, I hear."

She considered this absurd proposition. "That could be," she said. "But I don't think it's them. I think it's me."

"Perhaps you've only come to your senses at last," I said.

She smiled. "I wish it were that simple."

"I don't see why it can't be simple."

She bristled. "Could *you* just give up what you do, what you've done for so long now, what you know you do as well or better than most? What people want and need you to do?"

"It's different," I said. "I'm paid for a service. I'm not a captive of my audience. My mission is to search out and report the truth."

She shrugged. "Really? Have you had much luck with that?"

I laughed. I'd forgotten her aptitude for puncturing hot-air balloons. "Well, I try," I said.

"I know you do," she replied. "That's why I admire you. Because most people, you know, don't even try. They just make it up."

"And are you most people?"

This question appealed to her. "I didn't think I was," she said. "I believed what people told me, that I was specially placed, that I have a gift. And I've always had these—I don't know what they are—these lapses, when I feel I'm both here and not here, that there's a presence. The sense of a presence." She paused, and her eyes rested on the teapot. "Is there any left in that?"

"There is," I said. "But it's gone cold."

"I don't care," she said, taking up a cup and filling it with the lukewarm brew. She sipped it, savoring it as if it were a rare vintage. "It's very good," she said.

I cleaved to our subject. "And do you no longer have these lapses?"

"I think it's these awful investigators," she said. "You should see how they look at me. They're supposed to be skeptical, but they practically drool over me. And that wretched girl with her big teeth copying everything down."

"It sounds intimidating."

"Well," she said, tempering her anger. "I suppose it's no more than I deserve."

"Why do you say that?"

But Violet ignored the matter of her just deserts. "I don't know why they call it a gift," she said. "It's more of a curse. Everyone I meet knows one thing about me, and that's all they want to know."

"That you can talk to ghosts."

She drained the cup and set it roughly back in the saucer. "I wish you wouldn't use that word!"

"What difference does it make what you call people who aren't there?"

"That's just it. I don't know if they're there or not anymore."

"You don't hear them."

She drew her head back, covering her mouth with her fingers and moving her chin slowly from side to side, struggling against the tears that moistened her eyes.

"Did you ever hear them?"

She continued her struggle, slowly shaking her head in the negative, while the tears overflowed. I extracted my handkerchief from my skirt pocket and passed it to her. "Thank you," she blurted, and pressed the linen over her eyes, succumbing to a wave of racking sobs.

For a few minutes Violet wept while I watched. I confess I've seldom experienced such a profound sense of companionship. I didn't try to comfort her, nor did she seek reassurance; she just wanted to cry. I had the unexpected realization that I liked her. We were two middle-aged women with not much in common, but we had arrived, through our several conversations, which didn't total more than a few hours over ten years, at a surprisingly resilient bond. She had drifted into her present life, or been herded into it, whereas I had manufactured mine by a concentrated effort of the will, wresting a career from those who would have been equally content to see me fail as succeed. She envied me my freedom, and I didn't blame her for that, she was right to envy it. But I knew I had succeeded only because I had found myself at an early age in the position she was in now, when she had neither the youth nor the energy to change it. I'd become what I was because I had had no choice.

An enormous patience settled over me. I could have sat there forever, waiting for Violet to stop weeping and get back to our talk. I even fancied having a drink with her—I knew her to be amusingly caustic when her tongue was loosened by alcohol—and I didn't doubt there was a bottle of something in her room. I glanced up to see the desk clerk craning his neck over the counter, his face cramped with anxiety. He could see me sitting there peacefully, and he could hear Violet's disconsolate sobbing, but he couldn't see her. I smiled at him and he popped back into his cubicle lest I make some impetuous demand.

We were safe there for the time being, I thought, in that seedy lounge with the empty cups and plates, the stained carpet and rachitic furniture; no one would bother us. I had no sense of triumph over Violet, though surely she had just made a damning confession. Instead I felt protective and kindly toward her. That she'd been used, and been willing to be used, by insane gentlemen in frock coats and top hats and wealthy ladies as well—they'd joined the circus with a good will—didn't excuse her, but it mitigated her guilt. For my part, I absolved her in my heart, and this cheered me considerably. I took up the spoon and served myself a glistening lump of the sweet jam. As the tears were abating, Violet lowered the handkerchief and watched me eat the jam with the expression of a convalescent who has discovered that life is proceeding without her participation. She swabbed her eyes one last time, blew her nose as discreetly as possible, folded the handkerchief, then balled it in her hand. "I'll wash this and return it to you," she said.

"Keep it," I said.

She folded the cloth again and slipped it into her sleeve. "I will," she said. "I'd like to have something of yours."

This struck me as enormously sad, and I wished I had more to offer her. The thought of Violet going out, unsure and alone, to confront the British investigators with no more protection than a handkerchief might afford her unsettled me. I was no clairvoyant, but I foresaw more tears in her future. "Did you tell Dr. Doyle about these troubles you're having?"

"We hardly spoke." She batted the air with the back of her hand as if to shoo away an insect. "And now he's gone. He's in Rochester or Buffalo, or someplace up there. He just stopped in long enough to change my life. *They* made the arrangements, Dr. Bishop and the

London fellow; Myers is his name. I don't think anyone ever asked me if I wanted to go."

"How presumptuous," I said.

The slow smile she sent me was dry with irony; she was herself again. "You don't see it as a grand opportunity?"

"I do not."

"I'm wondering what will become of me when they tire of me."

"They can't just dump you out on the street," I assured her, though I knew nothing about what they could do. "You're an American citizen."

"That's true," she agreed.

"When do you sail?"

"On Sunday. I go up to New York on Friday, then spend two nights with a Spiritualist family who live in Brooklyn."

"So, you're packing."

"Well, that doesn't take long." She tapped the parcel she'd left on the table. "But it's the reason I wrote to you. I have something I don't want to take with me, something not mine, really, and I want to return it to the rightful owner."

"Did you steal it?"

"Not exactly."

"What is it?"

"It's just a book," she said. "I have a compunction about taking it with me. It's not valuable in itself, though there is someone for whom it has great value. If anything happened to me, I fear it would be thrown away."

"You want me to deliver it to that person."

"I do. The problem is, I don't know where he is."

"I see," I said. "You want me to play at being a detective."

"I thought you'd be rather good at that. You're always investigating things."

The idea amused me. "I have occasionally entertained the idea that if I couldn't make my living as a journalist, I might offer my services to Pinkerton's."

"That's perfect. I believe you could do it. You should do it. Phoebe Grant, Pinkerton Detective. You'd be a great success."

"Detectives are actually a pretty unpleasant lot," I said. "And they mostly follow rich men's wives about in the rain."

"You always take such a dim view of everything," she complained.

"I'm a realist," I said. "But I'm willing to carry out your mission, if I can. Who is the missing owner?"

Again she fingered the package, looking embarrassed, perhaps by the notion that she was sending me on a "mission." "I could pay you a little for your trouble," she said.

"Does Mr. Sherlock Holmes take payment for the opportunity to solve an interesting case?" I protested. "Never. Nor shall I."

"Thank you," she said, lifting the package and passing it to me. I read the name—Arthur Briggs—printed across the top in large square letters. "And who is Arthur Briggs?" I asked.

"He's Sarah Briggs's son," she said. "He was a boy when his parents disappeared."

The name surfaced in my memory. "From the *Mary Celeste*."

"That's right. I've had this book all these years. It was his mother's, so by rights, it should be his."

"Does he know of its existence?"

"He doesn't."

"And you know nothing of his present whereabouts."

"I know the Briggs family—what was left of it—moved from Marion some years ago. I suspect they didn't go far."

"So, I'll begin in Marion. That's in Massachusetts, isn't it?"

"Yes," she said. "But there's no hurry; there's nothing of an urgent nature in the book. I know you're very busy."

"Not at all," I said. "I'm thoroughly on the case. I'll begin by contacting the postal authorities."

"You're so professional," she said.

"Naturally," I assured her, closely scrutinizing the parcel in my hands. "I think I know where this paper was manufactured. It's a factory near Latham, New York; they get their stock from Alabama. I observe that this knot was not tied by anyone in the nautical line. Now for the string. The string, Miss Petra, the string is fascinating."

"How funny," Violet laughed. "Do you like those stories?"

"Of course. They're clever and amusing. Don't you like them?"

"I think there's something mean about them."

"Really? And did you detect something mean about the author?"

"Not at all. He's young and very full of himself—well, why shouldn't he be. There's something sad about him though. His manner is hearty and he likes to laugh. He's all beefy and overheated, excitable, like a big child. He's putting on a good show, but there's something wounded about him. He's nothing at all like his famous detective."

"Will you meet him again when you get to London?"

Her jaw clenched and she touched two fingers to her forehead, as if warding off some pulse of pain. "*If* I get to London."

"Now who's taking a dim view?"

Her mood had darkened again and she ignored my chiding. "I have a terror of the sea," she said. "It has taken everyone I loved."

"You mean the Briggs family."

"I think of them so often now. I was too young to know what a paradise we were in. I felt no one understood me; that I was trapped and must escape. And then they were all gone, just gone. They sailed away . . ." She lifted her hand, looking up as if she saw a ship in the air. The impression was so strong that I seemed to hear the sound of the oceanic whisper that mysteriously calls from the convoluted depths of seashells, and an image of a ship's sharp prow slicing through dark water and of enormous wind-filled sails developed in my mind's eye. It occurred to me that Violet could have been an actress—she had the ability to make her audience see what she saw.

"They sailed away," she said again. Then she coughed, clearing away the apparition. "And I was left on the shore in this charade of a life."

I said nothing, reluctant to leave the spell of that marvelous vessel, plowing the waves, sailing into the unknown.

"You remind me of her," Violet said.

This brought me round. "Of Sarah Briggs?"

She nodded.

"Was she tall?"

"No." She scrutinized me for the point of comparison. "You don't look like her; it's something in your manner."

"The way I talk?"

"Perhaps it's only that you don't entirely approve of me."

"I don't disapprove of you," I lied.

"Of course you do," she said. "How could you not? I'm a nonentity. I do nothing. I create nothing. I'm a parasite feeding on the blood of fools who haven't the sense to swat me."

"That's going too far," I objected.

"No. It's true. It's the truth. I know what I am, though I'm not exactly sure how I got to be what I am." This conundrum held her attention and she furrowed her brow, her eyes settling on the package in my hands. "But something is changing in me; I can feel it. I have the sense that even I may have my little moment of courage."

"I hope you will," I said.

"Do you?" she replied. "The idea terrifies me."

The White Crow

S.S. Campania, 1894

I shall not see thee. Dare I say
  No spirit ever brake the band
  That stays him from the native land
Where first he walk'd when claspt in clay?

No visual shade of some one lost,
  But he, the Spirit himself, may come
  Where all the nerve of sense is numb;
Spirit to Spirit, Ghost to Ghost.

Tennyson, "In Memoriam"

Mrs. Millicent Atlas of Brooklyn had come to Spiritualism by way of the suffragist movement, and though she had no doubts about the continuity of life, her chief interest was the struggle for justice on this side of the veil. William, her husband, had made his fortune in the shipping industry. He and her four exuberant daughters all supported her in every cause. Their home, a spacious brownstone set well back from the muddy street behind an iron fence, was a continual hubbub of visitors, meals, and heated conversations. One didn't visit the Atlas residence; one was enfolded into it. For Violet Petra, who had spent so much of her time with the desperately bereaved, the atmosphere was unnerving and fraught with peril. She wasn't sure what to expect or what was expected, and so, during her brief visit, she stayed in the cluttered, chintz-festooned guest room as much as she politely could. The sound of talking, laughter, singing, guests or daughters trooping up and down the stairs in groups, shouts from room to room, the clatter of dishes in the dining room, where it seemed some version of a meal was continually under way, all rose up to Violet, tempting her. *Join us,* the voices seemed to say. *This is life; this is joy. Let us meet and talk and strive. Let us change the world.*

Mrs. Atlas, a stately matron with a large nose, close-set brown eyes, and black hair cut short and curled in the Titus style, had the efficient manner of an aristocrat turned politician, which, indeed, she was. She knew who Violet was, why she had come, and where she was going, but she showed no interest in any of this, beyond commending the Society for Psychical Research for debunking "that dreadful Blavatsky woman." Surely Mrs. Atlas knew Miss Petra was crossing the ocean to court the same fate as the disgraced Russian. "Do you know," Mrs. Atlas continued, "she had actually hired an assistant to push spirit messages on slips of paper through a crack in the ceiling?" Violet acquiesced in her hostess's condemnation of such fraudulent practices.

"And then poor Margaret Fox," Mrs. Atlas concluded. "Such a confusing spectacle."

"Indeed," Violet concurred.

Mr. Atlas, a small, stout, explosive personage, with bulging eyes, tumid lips, and moist hands that he rubbed together when waiting for the opportunity to make a point, was most interested in Miss Petra's ship, the *Campania,* which he declared to be as fine a vessel as one could hope for a crossing, with all manner of luxury and captained by one of the ablest men on the seas. He would escort his guest on her departure, and if Captain Hains was aboard, introduce her to him, thereby guaranteeing that she might want for nothing on her voyage. At lunch, the day before her departure, it was revealed that Violet's ticket was for the second class, which news caused a distinct cooling in the general excitement about her trip. Though no one said it, she understood that Captain Hains was unlikely to take a "special" interest in a passenger who would never promenade on the saloon deck and must dine by the bugle, and not, as was the new fashion, à la carte. "I understand all the accommodations are excellent," Mrs. Atlas assured her. "You'll have a comfortable crossing, and really, it's all the same food."

When the hour came for her departure, Mr. Atlas was engaged at his offices and it was Mrs. Atlas, unacquainted with the estimable Captain Hains, who delivered their guest to the pier. A house servant loaded Violet's luggage into the back of a phaeton drawn up to the gate. To Violet's surprise, her hostess, having pulled on a cloak and a pair of sturdy boots at the door, strode across the slush beyond the curb and leaped onto the bench, taking the reins into her gloved hands with practiced confidence. Violet followed, careful of her skirts, and climbed into the space beside her indomitable hostess. The enforced zeal and energy of Mrs. Atlas irritated her, but she knew what she was expected to say and she said it. "You drive your own carriage!"

Mrs. Atlas's dark eyes flashed combatively. "Don't ladies drive in Philadelphia?" she asked. However, she evidenced no interest in the answer to this question, tightening the reins and snapping her horse's head to attention.

It was a cold, damp morning with a sky as close and smoke-stained as a tenement ceiling. The phaeton whirled along the narrow streets toward the waterfront and up the ramp to the bridge where the traffic was heavy but brisk. Mrs. Atlas occupied herself with her driving, and Violet was left to look out over the river, which was dotted with ferries, barques, brigs, schooners, barges, and steamers, all meandering upstream and -down in an orchestrated dance choreographed by some unseen, all-knowing god of wind, water, and commerce. It made her head ache to look at it. She had slept poorly—the Atlas home was teetotal—and her nerves were frayed and raw. As the phaeton cleared the bridge and steered toward the wharf, the traffic thickened, and finally ground to a halt. Violet gazed listlessly at the pressed confusion of cabs, private carriages, men in caps pushing all manner of barrows and carts, men in top hats, and ladies wrapped in fur descending from the vehicles, clots of ragged children and clusters of gibbering foreigners, sharp young men in uniforms pulling luggage down from cabs, horses stamping their hooves and tossing their heads, or standing patiently while their drivers shouted at one another. "There she is," Mrs. Atlas said, pointing over her right shoulder. "I'll try to get you as close as I can."

Violet turned to see what Mrs. Atlas pointed at, what everyone in this whirlpool of shouting, maddening humanity packed between a row of dreary warehouses and a behemoth was pushing toward. Indeed, there she was, her great black hulk topped by two gleaming white decks and towering above that, as tall as a lighthouse and raked at an angle that made them look already windswept, two great red smokestacks.

Scattered passengers and a few sailors were already aboard, leaning on the rail of the upper deck, breathing the better air above the mob. The steepest gangway was dotted with passengers, who were being admitted a few at a time. Another, lower ramp was manned by the sharp young men, passing in luggage from the carts. Mrs. Atlas maneuvered the horse a few steps closer and turned the phaeton to face the ship. She hailed one of the uniformed porters, who leaped a cordoned area piled with luggage and rushed to the carriage, pulling Violet's bags from the back. Having accomplished this task, he came to the phaeton door and stood staring expectantly at the two ladies within. "He'll need to see your ticket, my dear," Mrs. Atlas said pleasantly. Violet handed down the ticket, which the porter examined momentarily, then returned to the luggage, slapped a white label on each piece, and wrote a few numbers across it with a thick crayon. "I wish I could get closer," Mrs. Atlas assured Violet. "Can you make your way through this awful mob?" The porter turned back, holding out his hand to Violet with his cheerful, noncommittal expression. She cast the most fleeting glance at Mrs. Atlas, who was clearly eager to take up her reins and trot back to the world of those who needed and adored her. "I'll be fine," Violet said, but as her foot reached the ground she stumbled, and the porter, with a mumbled "Steady there," caught her elbow to right her. "Thank you," she said, but he had already turned away to whistle at a lad with a barrow.

"Bon voyage, Miss Petra," Mrs. Atlas called out cheerfully. She clucked to her horse and the phaeton's big wheels creaked against the wharf as it pulled away.

"I'll be fine," Violet said again, but no one heard her.

The journey through the crowded pier to the door of stateroom 144 on the second deck of the S.S. *Campania* took more than an hour, during which, Violet assured herself, she rubbed shoulders with every station of society. When she had turned the key, pushed open the heavy metal door, and stepped inside, she viewed the interior with a palpable sense of relief. Though the ceiling was necessarily low and the cabin small, everything in it was pristine, tasteful, and designed to take advantage of the limited space. Bouquets of violets were stenciled in a pattern above a creamy yellow wainscot that matched the two built-in drawers and the cabinet beneath the commode. Every modern convenience was available: electric lights, a sink with two faucets, adequate ventilation, and a water closet. A pillow and a clean towel were laid out on the neatly made bunk. Another bunk attached to the wall above had been folded up and latched in place, as the management knew Miss Petra was traveling alone. Her luggage—how had they achieved it?—was already there, stacked on the long sofa that occupied one end of the room. There was no window, save a small curtained square that opened into the corridor—it was an interior cabin—but a view was provided by a painting of a pastoral scene, complete with two cows grazing in the background, full of light and serenity. This picture would be her daylight for the next week.

She sat down on the sofa next to her trunk, her hat box and the bulky travel bag containing a few books, writing tablets, fountain pens, and toilet articles. She leaned her arm upon the trunk and closed her eyes. She might, she thought, never leave this room. She wouldn't be required to, though of course she would have to eat.

But for that she had only to present herself three times a day, or four if she took tea, at the dining room where, surrounded by strangers, she might contrive to be virtually invisible. She dreaded the condescending looks, the polite smiles that would greet the announcement that she was a medium en route to be investigated by the Society for Psychical Research. She had spent most of her adult life among believers—this would be different. Occasional intrusions, scoffers at public sittings, skeptical relatives or curiosity seekers, and, of course, Phoebe Grant, had operated upon her not as threats but as diversions. But here, the materialists, the unbelievers, would be in the majority, and since the Fox sisters' recantation, they were sometimes bitter and vengeful.

There were upwards of fifteen hundred people on the ship, all settling into their respective places, the wealthy above her, out of reach, the poor below, and among them, at all levels, there were doubtless a few who might defend her, or even seek her out, but she wouldn't risk it. She was out of her element here, in more ways than one, and she had no desire to become an object of interest and possibly derision to her fellow voyagers.

She opened her eyes and busied herself with pulling the pins out of her hat, removing it from the nest of her hair. She would have to come up with a story. She was traveling for her health, to visit family abroad, to take up a position of some kind, a governess perhaps, or she was going out to be married and then follow her new husband to India or Africa. A rich uncle had passed on and she was an heiress to his grand estate. Or small estate—hence the second-class dining room. Why, why would a middle-aged American woman be traveling to England alone?

Considering the amount of human activity that must be going forth all over the ship, the stateroom was remarkably quiet. She could hear a distant shout, the sound of the opposite door opening and closing, muffled footsteps moving away, then nothing. Warm air drifted in through the ventilation system; she could hear a faint hum. She stood up, removed her coat, went to the basin, and turned on the tap, lowering her hands into the stream of cool water. She would need one credible story with not much elaboration, a straightforward mission. Best not to include a death. A visit to a relative, a sister, living where? London? No, too vast. Bath. Yes. She had never been to Bath but had read Jane Austen and so had some idea what the atmosphere was like. Her sister was a widow or a spinster, like herself, living in Bath and she was going out to visit her. They had not seen each other in many years. How many?

Twenty-two years.

No. Too long. Five years. Four.

The soap was of a good quality, lathering up thickly in her hands and leaving a faint fragrance of verbena as she rinsed it away. She raised her eyes to her reflection in the oval mirror affixed to the wall. Keep your chin up, she thought. Then she studied her face, which, she observed with conscious irony, was beginning to look unfamiliar. She gave her image a tentative smile. "Who do you think you are?" she said softly.

Outside the visitors were advised to repair to the wharf, the tugs drew alongside, and the lines were secured to haul the great steaming hulk out of the harbor. Violet could hear the deep thrumming horn announcing the imminent departure of the vessel. When she looked outside, the corridor was empty, the other passengers having made their way to the deck. She pulled her coat back on and hurried along the plush carpet to the staircase, compelled by a confusing combination of excitement, fear, and curiosity.

It was early evening and the lamps were glittering in the seedy establishments along the wharf, though there was enough light to make out the upturned faces of the gathered crowd, waving and calling out their farewells as the space between the dock and the ship's hull gradually widened and the prow veered steadily away from the harbor. Steamer chairs were strewn on the deck nearest the house, and a handrail separated the lounging from the promenading area nearer the sea, where her fellow passengers were gathered in groups, chatting, leaning over the rail, pointing out the various features of the ship to each other. The intermittent fire of champagne corks and the lilting strains of a violin on the upper deck suggested that a ship's departure was a joyful occasion, though, Violet thought, the crew must look on it as the commencement of responsibility and labor. The strip of dark water widened, but she had no sensation of motion; it was as if the dock was being pulled away from the ship. A mother and her teenage son, standing nearby, burst into laughter at some droll remark from the father. Violet smiled, turning to look at them, and catching, momentarily, the father's gratified eye. She looked back at the wharf, where the crowd had begun to thin.

She had no special consciousness of being alone. She had spent much of her life among strangers and was accustomed to fitting herself to the habits and whims of her various patrons. She had a public identity that shielded her from their occasional thoughtlessness and cruelty. She kept up with the world—it was important to do so and indeed she was interested in literature, music, painting, even science. Being informed and engaged deflected the disquietude people felt around her—her urbanity set them at ease. When she met a doctor or a lawyer, or a suffragette, she had no particular feelings about their professions, but she knew they were convinced of the necessity to take a stand about hers. And what a range of emotions the presence of Miss Petra provoked in those who doubted the continuity of life. A little distance had to be declared, a social desperation set in when she entered the room. It was as though she practiced some shameful art: black magic, voodoo, or poetry. She knew things she shouldn't know; she was not of this world. She had powers—she was to be envied; she was sensitive and suffered—she was to be pitied; she had visions, the dead talked to her—she was to be shunned.

When all she really was, she thought, as the night descended and the ship's lights futilely stabbed at the darkness, was weary. The investigators had worn her down to a bundle of quivering nerves.

They wanted her to tell them how she produced her effects, but it was like asking a composer to explain exactly how a sequence of musical notes appeared on the staff. Obviously he put them there. Did he hear them in his head? Well then, who put them *there?*

She had impressions, she told them. She went into a space, a very clear, still, close space and she concentrated and listened. The messages, whatever they were, didn't come to her; they came through her. Neither the living nor the dead had much interest in the medium.

She felt she had been created by the demands of others, by their insatiable appetite for something beyond ordinary life. They craved a world without death and they had spotted her, in their hunger, like wolves alert to any poor sheep that might stray from the fold and stand gazing ignorantly up at the stars.

"There she is," someone said, and Violet's thoughts were so turned inward that she assumed the remark referred to her. "Oh, look!" another passenger exclaimed. A murmur of approbation circulated along the deck. She looked up, following the eyes of her companions. It was Bartholdi's statue, holding high her torch to light the world to her shores. Again the illusion was that the statue, not the ship, was moving, that she was floating toward her captive audience eerily over the water, her mouth stern, her heavy-lidded eyes beneath the starry crown serious and sad. *Holding up a torch,* Violet thought. *Forever.* She sent the severe lady a sympathetic smile. The tugs let off a few cheerful hoots from their short stacks, saluting the symbol of liberty, as she, appearing to change her mind, slid silently away. On the saloon deck an orchestra struck up a march—what was it from? *Aïda?* What an odd choice to commence an ocean voyage.

A ship's officer holding a bugle appeared at the dining room door and latched it open. As the passengers alerted each other to his presence, he brought the instrument to his lips and blew three quick blasts, which collided out of tune with the strains of Aïda's Triumphal March pouring out from the gods above. Dinner was served.

As the passengers filed toward the dining room they could see the first-class passengers descending from above to their own superior accommodation, which the brochure promised had seating for four hundred and a crystal dome glittering above a room three decks high.

Violet had half a mind to skip dinner and spend the time leaning on the rail watching the outskirts of the city drift by. She'd heard one experienced passenger remark to another that it would be hours before they were on the open sea. But it was a cloudy, damp night and there were fewer and fewer lights from the shore. After a few minutes there was nothing to see and it seemed the best option to join her fellow passengers in the dining room. Meals, after all, were included in her ticket.

The room was long, the ceiling low, but it was brightly lit, with white-clothed tables flanked by lines of upholstered swivel chairs. One sat, evidently, anywhere. She stood back as families or clutches of friends commandeered blocks of seats. Her goal was to find a place near the end of a row, preferably next to a woman.

A toothy young lady, in company with a burly white-haired matriarch, whose black-satin-encased bulk put Violet in mind of the ship's prow, took two seats at a near table, leaving one empty at the end. Violet slipped past a trio of gentlemen, who were bemoaning the state of the economy, and dropped into the chair. A paper menu lay in front of her and, at some invisible signal, waiters appeared in a line, working their way up and down the lengths of the tables, bending low to hear the orders over the din of conversation. Violet scanned the menu—boiling and roasting appeared to be the preferred methods of cooking. On the back of the page was a wine list, blessedly inexpensive. The prices brought a smile to her lips. Her stomach felt too weak for heavy food, of which there was plenty on offer, steak and oyster pie, roast beef, roast stuffed pork, boiled beef tail. Spaghetti in cream appealed to her, and boiled potatoes, a white meal. She could feel her seatmate's eyes upon her, intent on opening a conversation. *Bath*, she reminded herself, *my sister. Her name is Laura. I'm a widow, going out to visit.* She raised her eyes to meet the candid scrutiny of the toothy lady—poor woman, it was an underbite that forced her lower lip to protrude so far her teeth were always visible. "Is this your first crossing?" this lady asked. Her accent told Violet she was on a return trip.

"It is," Violet admitted, then, nodding at her menu, added, "What do you recommend?"

Her name was Celia Durham and she recommended the boiled cod. She accepted Violet's story of the sister in Bath without question, eager to get to her own biography. She and her aunt Tilda, the satin-clad lady, were returning from a visit to her grandparents, who live in Maine. She was trained as an illustrator and was going to London to finish her studies at the Kensington Design Institute.

Violet gave herself over to the pleasure of not having to attend too closely to the conversation. She wanted nothing from this young woman but that she shield her from the scrutiny of other passengers, which Celia was clearly eager to do. After the food and the wine appeared, it was easier still. Celia knew a lot about ocean travel; she had been crossing once or twice a year since she was ten years old. She'd come over on this same ship the month before and it was the best crossing she'd ever experienced. The ladies' lounge was comfortable, and there was a good piano. She encouraged Violet to make an appointment with the steward for a bath. The tubs were divine and the hot and cold water came out of one spout, so you had no fear of being boiled or chilled.

Violet expressed surprise, interest, pleasure; she hardly had to say a word—it was perfect. It was a pity, Celia insisted, that Violet's first crossing was so late in the year, because the weather could be very rough and it was often too wet and cold to walk out on the deck. A summer crossing was delightful and one could walk as much aboard ship as one might in town.

At some point Aunt Tilda distracted Celia with a question, and Violet was left to her spaghetti. She was on her second glass of wine; the familiar, welcome lassitude set in, and she felt positively cheerful. She looked about the room at her fellow diners, catching snatches of their conversation. Two young men, clean-shaven and foppish—one had a checked silk scarf tied around his throat—were collapsed in laughter at some shared witticism. When the hilarity threatened to subside, one barked out a further inducement to the other and they were off again. Violet smiled, it was impossible not to, until her eyes fell on a hirsute, bespectacled gentleman a few seats down who was clearly not amused. As he lifted his fork, on which he had speared a wad of pork, dripping with juices, he glowered at the joyful young men. Then he stuffed the meat into the shocking red, wet hole in the black bramble of his beard, which opened and closed like a trap baited with the pinkish-gray flesh of his tongue. She clamped her stomach muscles tight over a surge of nausea. A waiter leaned over her shoulder, lowering a plate of potatoes.

At the conclusion of the meal, Violet declined Celia's invitation to join her in the ladies' lounge by pleading fatigue. She made her way along the deck, glancing out at the sparkling lights of the tugs, like strings of fallen stars leading the way to the open sea. Various passengers strolled up and down in twos and threes. A gentleman with white whiskers doffed his hat on passing, as if she were meeting him in the street. The sea was of secondary interest to these voyagers, but Violet found she could think of little else. She could feel it out there, pressing and pushing at the ship, vast and changeable and cruel.

In her cabin she sat on the sofa, opened her travel bag, and took out her writing book, thinking she might work on a poem she'd begun at the hotel, and her copy of *The White Company*, which she was finding heavy going. Then she paused, looking down at the spine of a slim volume bound in dark brown cloth, tucked in between the folds of her mauve dressing gown and the tortoiseshell lid of her dressing case. Tenderly, as if it were fragile, she drew it out and held it in her open palm, resting her hand on her lap. The title engraved in gilt on the spine and again on the front board was *A Pageant and Other Poems*, by Christina Rossetti. She opened the cover and turned the blank page to the title page, inscribed in a clear, bold hand: *For Violet, my muse, my love, from your Ned.*

She touched her fingertips lightly to the handwriting.

How long ago, that brief, ecstatic time.

He was home from college for the school break. Bertha had been in a fever of anticipation for a week. Violet, who had an artistic sensibility, had been entrusted with the flower arrangements, and she was carrying a vase of daffodils into the dining room when he arrived. He passed swiftly from the door to his mother's embrace, but his eyes met Violet's over her shoulder in an éclat of recognition that he would later describe as "souls colliding on eyebeams." She continued to the dining room, where she could hear him, calming his mother as he climbed the stairs to his room. In the afternoon, at the family gathering, she was introduced to him—"My dear friend Miss Petra, my son Ned Bakersmith"—and he took her hand, but they hardly spoke. For three days, though she heard him on the stairs or going out the door or conferring with his father in his study, she didn't see him. He was a busy, popular, handsome, and wealthy young man about town. Once he completed his law studies at Harvard College, he was destined for great things.

On the fourth day of his visit, Violet sat alone, as she often did in the afternoons, reading in the library. She heard footsteps approaching from the hall. She was seated in a high-backed chair with her back to the door, so he didn't see her as he strode purposefully into the room, directly to the glass case containing the Bakersmiths' modest collection of poetry. He opened the case and raised his hand to the very shelf from which Violet had taken the volume she had in her hands. His fingers paddled the empty space, as if to conjure what wasn't there.

Violet placed the ribbon of her open book into the spine and snapped the cover shut, making a soft rap that sounded largely in the quiet room, startling the youthful poetry enthusiast, who wheeled about, his widened eyes taking in the unexpected challenge: a woman reading a book. "Miss Petra!" he exclaimed. "I didn't know you were there."

"I'm sorry," she said. "I couldn't think of a way to let you know without alarming you."

"Please," he said. "There's no need to apologize." His face softened and a gentle interest drew his brows together. He took her in,
puzzled, intrigued, and she looked back, amused, imperious.

"I believe this must be the volume you're looking for," she said,
turning the book so that he might read the cover.

"Yes. The Tennyson." Wonder slackened his jaw. "That's amaz-
ing, don't you agree? That I should come at this moment in search
of the very book you've chosen from all these . . ." He gestured at the
cases lining the walls.

The truth, Violet thought, was that the Bakersmiths' library
was not so very extensive, and as Mr. Bakersmith's passion was mar-
itime law and his wife had been known to express her conviction
that no one ever need look beyond the complete works of Dickens
for moral edification and entertainment, the range was not wide,
but Violet felt no desire to contradict this attractive, evidently sensitive young man. "It suggests your tastes are old-fashioned," she said.
"I thought young men preferred Mr. Meredith these days."

"I'm not so young as all that," he replied. "Nor do I prefer cyni-
cism to passion."

Not yet, thought Violet, liking him for his combativeness.
"'Modern Love' is stringent," she agreed.

"What are you reading? Is it 'Maud'?"

She opened the book to the ribbon, allowing the pages to fall
open before him. "It's 'In Memoriam.'"

He touched his hand to his breast and recited, "*I sometimes hold
it half a sin to put in words the grief I feel.*"

"I never tire of it," Violet said. "Such a patient, determined grap-
pling with a great loss; grief stricken but without self-pity. I think
that's rare."

"It is," he agreed. "The first time I read it, I wept. I felt it was my
friend who had died." He bent over her, easing the book from her
hands. "May I?" he said.

"Of course."

"I love these lines . . ." He turned the pages back, searching
for what he knew was there. As he scrutinized the neatly printed

verses, Violet gazed up at his face. She noted that what made him handsome was not the regularity of his features, though these were fine enough—a wide smooth brow shaded by thick brown curls, thickly lashed dark eyes, a sharp bony blade of nose, a shapely mouth and solid jaw—but the animation with which he occupied them. His gaze was intense; his nose visibly breathed, his lips, when he alighted upon the exigent verse, pressed together as his brows lifted. He straightened his spine and bowed his head over the book in preparation for reading. Violet drew back, expecting some stentorian blast, but his voice, like the verse he had chosen, was soft, almost a whisper. "Here it is," he said. *"Calm on the seas, and silver sleep, /And waves that sway themselves in rest, /And dead calm in that noble Breast, /Which heaves but with the heaving deep."*

"Yes," Violet said. "His dear friend's body returning in the hold of the ship."

And so it began.

Ned wasn't as young as Violet had thought, but there was still a decade between them. For a time their attraction to each other passed as an innocent shared enthusiasm. Ned was still out every evening, as tantalizingly eligible as a rich young man could be, but in the afternoons he invariably sought Violet's company. He had spent two years on the Continent, perfecting his French and German, and he introduced her to the great poets of these languages by seeking out English translations, which he borrowed from a lending library that specialized in such titles. Violet had school French and so they pored together over the poems of Musset, Mallarmé, Baudelaire, Rimbaud. Ned read the French aloud in his soft, husky voice while she followed the English translations, many of which, they agreed, were inadequate. They discussed the perils of translation and one day he showed her his own effort at this most exacting science—a short poem by Mallarmé titled "Brise Marine." *The flesh is sad, alas, and I've read all the books.*

She suspected that he wrote poetry himself, and of course it wasn't long before he confided that he did. To be a poet was the great longing of his soul, but not one he dared to reveal to his parents, or even to most of his friends, especially his lady friends, who were mostly interested in the latest fashions and thought the poetry of Mrs. Wheeler Wilcox the height of artistic sentiment. Together they scoffed at the pedestrian sensibilities of the average reader. They viewed the ordinary world from a distance.

Violet was wise enough to keep her own ambitions along these lines to herself; indeed, she had no desire to expose her efforts to the critical eye of her cultivated friend. But it wasn't long before he arrived at the library with an envelope containing a sheaf of carefully printed pages and asked her if she would be willing to "pass judgment, showing no mercy," on his poor verses. She agreed, taking the pages away to read in her room while he was dining at the home of yet another fashionable heiress.

It was an unseasonably warm, wet, windy night, and she opened her window for the fresh air, loosened her corset, and propped herself upon her pillows so that she could hold the pages close to the lamp.

Ned's poems were imitative and competent, neither good nor bad. The subject matter was sometimes frustration and/or loneliness, sometimes rage against the hypocrisy of society, which, thought Violet wryly, must be difficult for a young man of means to endure. There were three pretty sonnets on dawn, noon, and sunset, which she thought the best of the lot; she would marvel at his strengths as a nature poet. Two poems, one titled "Affinity," and the other "His Muse," were dedicated "to VP." "Affinity" described their first meeting. *That book was flown. He found to his surprise, true poetry in those lambent, knowing eyes.*

As she allowed this sheet to slip through her fingers and join the others scattered on the counterpane, she saw the future as clearly as if she'd just lived through it. It ended badly; it could not do otherwise. It was preordained, requiring no exercise of psychic powers to discern. How long would it be before Bertha Bakersmith realized that her son was smitten with the treacherous clairvoyant she

sheltered under her own roof? A title—"The Fury of Bertha"—
ran across her mind and made her smile. She gathered the pages
together and replaced them in the envelope.

So be it, she thought. Ned might never be more than a middling
poet, but she wouldn't be the one to tell him. And indeed it wouldn't
be difficult to encourage him. He wasn't vain; he was charming, perhaps too earnest, but his passion for poetry was sincere and he had
introduced her to great poets she wouldn't have found without him.
Most wonderful was his complete lack of interest in her psychic
powers. He knew she was occasionally closed up with his mother
for some kind of consultation that included conversations with his
dead sister, but he was as indifferent to this as if he'd been told they
were occupied in sewing a quilt. She realized, with a shiver that
should have been a warning to her, that she was never bored in his
company.

Violet rose up on one elbow, passed the envelope to the nightstand, and fell back upon the pillows, resting her fingertips against
her eyelids. *Those lambent, knowing eyes,* she thought. A smile lifted
the corners of her mouth. "So be it," she said to the empty room.

The first touch, his hand brushing hers, the first glancing kiss,
his lips upon her cheek on parting. The first outing together, a chilly
spring day, a long ramble near the river, stopping for tea at a charming teahouse. The first tender embrace, stolen behind a column in
the picture gallery; the first passionate fumbling on the sofa in the
library. The declarations: of affection; of devotion, commitment,
determination; of love. Their passion had a deadline; Ned would
be returning to Boston in a few short weeks. They contrived not to
talk about this. One day he brought her the volume of Miss Rossetti's poems—he'd found it at a bookstall and thought it an excellent
edition. She opened it, read the incautious inscription. "I'll treasure
this," she said.

Violet kept her head, allowing herself to be adored. It was an
agreeable secret, because, of course, it must be kept a secret. On

the occasional evenings when Ned dined at home, they addressed each other over the roast lamb with a distant politeness that was as shiny and impenetrable as steel armor. Ned really was a talented actor, Violet observed. The next day in the library, they choked with laughter over their performance.

They went out separately, meeting at appointed places so as not to be seen arriving and going out together. Ned complained that they were never alone. He wanted to find a place where they could meet without fear of apprehension.

Violet recognized this wish as what it was, a scandalous proposition, and it surprised her that Ned, who, in spite of his contempt for bourgeois respectability, was a conventional young man, would suggest it. More alarming was her realization that, should he actually come up with a plan, she would not refuse him. This revelation came to her late one evening after a particularly torrid session in the library from which they had both emerged—he to dress for an evening entertainment, she for a quiet dinner with his mother—shaken to their depths. She sat at her dressing table, languidly brushing out her hair, feeling again the pressure of his mouth against her lips, her neck, his fingers fumbling with the buttons of her bodice, her own palm resting on the warm flesh of his neck, the sensation of heat, of swelling in her lips and her breasts. She gazed at her own reflection, her hair loose, her eyes dreamy, the dressing gown loose over her shoulders. He should see me like this, she thought. Tears welled up. She laid the brush down and took up her handkerchief. "Don't be a fool," she chided her reflection, dabbing at the too ready tears. But then she thought, *Heaven help me; I love him.*

It was a week before his return to college. He said he didn't want to go back, that he hated Boston, the college, and, most of all, the law. Yet he was miserable in his father's house and bored by the endless social obligations, the rounds of dinners, dances, the banality of the conversations, the overheated, overconfident mothers plying their daughters like trade goods. It was inconceivable that he should spend his life yoked to one of these petty, indolent creatures with the endless tedium of the law as his only diversion.

They were walking along the river, bundled up in their coats, their heads beneath their hats inclined toward each other. Patches of crocus and snowdrops sparkled on the bank, the sun was bright, but the air was bitterly cold. Like the lovers, all nature was betwixt and between. Ned, holding her arm in his, pulled her in close, stopping her, so that they stood face to face. "I think we must run away," he said. "We can go to New Jersey and be married by a judge there. Will you come?"

She laughed. "What an odd proposal," she said.

"Is it? Oh. Of course it is. Violet, will you marry me? I can't live without you; you know that. Shall I go down on my knee?"

"I think the ground is wet."

"I don't care," he said, dropping to one knee, pressing her gloved hand to his lips. "Say, yes," he said. "Say you'll be my wife."

She felt a sharp constriction in her chest and she thought, in a panic, That's my heart breaking. "Oh, get up, get up," she cried. "Come to your senses."

He rose, grasped her arm, and pulled her along the path without speaking. They walked quickly, huddled against the cold. "So you won't even consider it?" he asked, in a voice cold with injury.

"My dear," she said. "You know nothing about me. I have no money. I have no family. I'm too old for you. Your father would disown you."

This brought him up short, and he turned to her, holding her about the waist, his lips pressed against her cheek. "But you love me," he insisted. "You can't say you don't love me."

She raised her mouth to his. "No," she said. "I can't say that."

They had drawn back into the shelter of a cherry tree laden with fragrant blooms. The drive to the teahouse was just beyond, and as their lips met, a cab pulled up and at a command from its passenger came to a halt. The driver leaped from his box, yanked open the door, and extended his hand to the large lady within, who was wrapped in furs from her neck to her pudgy ankles. She ignored his hand, glaring past him at the appalling sight of a man and a woman brazenly embracing beneath a tree. As she struggled for breath, the gentleman, if such he could be called, raised his head, glancing toward the cab. To her horror she recognized him—it was her nephew Ned Bakersmith. In the next moment he released the woman he held in his arms and steered her toward the river, but as they made their way to the path, the woman cast a fearful glance over her shoulder.

And fearful she should be, thought Ned's aunt Lydia. Bertha would be apoplectic when she learned her son was disgracing himself in broad daylight with that too clever little clairvoyant friend of hers, Miss Violet Petra. And she would receive this unpleasant information before the afternoon was out. Aunt Lydia waved away the driver, who stood with outstretched hand, still as a statue. "Go back up at once, sir," she said impatiently. "I've changed my mind."

The fury of Bertha Bakersmith turned out to be a much colder, more calculated, and implacable force than Violet had reckoned upon. There were no scenes. At breakfast Ned was closed up with his father in the office. Over a plate piled with scrambled eggs and smoked trout, Bertha announced that she was planning an evening at-home at which she would present Violet to a select circle of the family's friends. "So many have expressed interest in your abilities, I've begun to feel selfish for keeping you to myself," she said pleasantly.

At dinner—the gentlemen dined in town—Bertha expressed her annoyance that her son had been called back urgently to his college, as his course of study appeared to be under some sort of review. "I don't understand it myself," she confessed. "He'll miss the dance at the Pendergasts', which is a shame, as Irene is so fond of him."

In the afternoon Bertha insisted that Violet accompany her on a shopping expedition. "I want your advice about my gown for the at-home," she said. "Mrs. Green tells me she has a few very fine Paris creations. Perhaps we'll find something wonderful for you to wear as well."

At supper it was revealed that Ned had departed for Boston,

and that his father would follow him on the morrow. When Mr. Bakersmith joined them a little later, his wife regaled him with the successes of the day's shopping. She had not been able to choose between two gowns that were equally stunning on Violet, so she had ordered them both. And the shoes this year were so thinly soled, she'd purchased two pairs for Violet and three for herself, as they would surely wear out before summer.

The next day was occupied in completing the guest list and writing the invitations. It was Violet's practice to assist with the mail, and so she found herself inviting Bertha's friends to a gathering to meet herself. As she addressed the envelopes, her patroness gave her a brief account of each guest. "Poor Dr. Macabee's father died just a month ago, he was a surgeon in the war. Quite the tyrant, actually. He didn't make Henry's life any easier. Dora Winter, such a lovely woman. Her daughter is expecting a baby this month and Dora is anxious because she's miscarried twice before." Later, as Bertha fished the money for the postage from her bag, she remarked, "You're looking pale, my dear. I hope you are perfectly well." Their eyes met and Violet had the sensation that she was being scrutinized by a tigress, one who was in no hurry for her next meal, though she had identified it.

Surely Ned would write. Surely he wouldn't allow himself to be silenced by his parents. It was as if they'd closed him up in a vault.

For five days Violet dithered between wild hope and despair. Each night she persuaded herself that a happy, ordinary life with a loving husband, perhaps even children, was within her grasp. She considered a trip to Boston, a surprise knock at his door, his delight when he opened it to find her there, laughing at her own daring. His silence, she told herself, was meaningful rather than meaningless, and he was searching for what he called "a way" for them to reunite. She pictured herself at the judge's pretty little house in New Jersey, taking her vows in the new dress Bertha had provided.

But each morning she woke with the certainty that there had never been the slightest chance of such an outcome, and the proof was that Ned had fled the city without a word. Yet her nightly fantasies, which persuaded her that he might write, combined with her morning clear-headedness, which suggested that Bertha would intercept such a letter if it came, resulted in a fierce determination to be at the door each morning before the mail arrived.

When the letter was finally handed in, buried in the usual stack of expensive envelopes addressed to Bertha, Violet carried it with trembling fingers and swiftly beating heart up the stairs to her bedroom, where she sat down at her writing table. For several moments she held the envelope before her, reading her own name as if there might be some doubt that it was actually written there, so much had she longed to see it. She took up the ivory knife from the tray, carefully slit the flap, and drew out the folded page within.

The letter was not long. It began and ended with the words "forgive me." He had been in a pitched battle with his father for days; there was never anything like it; he had resisted with all his strength, but to no avail. She would perhaps be relieved to learn that he had wrestled from his stern progenitor the concession that he would henceforth change his course of study from law to theology. He had behaved shamefully, this he confessed. The only honor he could claim for himself, the one he would forever cherish, was that a woman of her magnificence had deigned to care for him.

Violet read the cowardly missive several times. The first two readings merely stunned her. She felt the blow physically, as if someone had slapped the back of her head with something dull and heavy, like a book. She folded the page, got up, and briefly paced the room. Then she sat down and read it three more times, searching for any evidence, however flimsy, that its author had given her feelings a moment's serious consideration. But she could find nothing. It was, in fact, a model of unqualified duplicity. She rose again, this time to leave the room.

Stealthily she descended the stairs. In the kitchen, where the cook was already rolling out pie shells, she begged a cup of tea and carried it back to her room. As she sipped the restorative liquid, she read the letter three more times, committing it to memory. She noted that her lover's defiance was a flexible instrument. Having been deflected from an inappropriate marriage, it had evidently fixed on throwing off the tyranny of law studies. She doubted that theology would prove a liberating alternative, though it would have the virtue of vexing his father.

After all, Violet thought, Ned Bakersmith was a good and dutiful boy; there was nothing remarkable about him. His parents could be justly proud.

When high hopes and great expectations are dashed, the effects may well be a reinvigoration of the will, but if a skeptical view of future prospects is confirmed, the result is more often an enduring loss of vitality. As Violet sat drinking her tea, she realized that in spite of everything she knew about the world and her place in it, she had truly longed to be proven wrong. But she had been right. All the energy drained from her body; it was as if she had opened a vein. She was too weary for tears. She finished her tea, setting the cup and saucer aside. Then she refolded the letter, replaced it in its envelope, and tore it into four pieces.

The rest was mercifully brief. The day before the at-home, she came down to tea to find Bertha in languid conversation with a young woman of regal beauty, all golden curls and rose-petal skin, who inspected and dismissed Violet in one swift stroke of her avaricious dark eyes. "Here's my friend, Miss Petra," said Bertha. "Let me introduce you to Miss Irene Pendergast."

Violet took a step closer, but as Miss Pendergast's neatly folded hands didn't move, she merely nodded her head in acknowledgment.

Bertha's eyes bathed the blond princess in an oleaginous beam of maternal solicitude. "It's not official, " she continued, "but Irene will soon be Mrs. Bakersmith. We'll be announcing the engagement when Ned comes down at the end of the term."

After an excruciating hour during which Miss Pendergast's mental vista was revealed to be neither as wide nor as deep as her teacup, Violet escaped on some fabricated errand. She walked where they had walked, through the park and along the river, her mind ablaze with unfocused and unmanageable rage. It was a blustery, wet, inhospitable afternoon, and when she came to the little bluff that looked over the swiftly moving river, where a forest of schooner masts bobbed at anchor, she had half a mind to jump in. Why not? she thought. Why ever not? She pressed out farther, allowing the toes of her boots to extend over the stone ledge. The void yawned before her and she could sense the pull it would exert if she simply took one more step. She felt Ned's hands about her waist, his lips at the nape of her neck. She let herself sink into him. The heel of her left boot snagged in a fissure of the stone and she came down on her hands, twisting her ankle cruelly. For a moment she was still, half expecting some passerby to come to her rescue, mortified by that prospect. But no one came, no one saw her. She sat up, gazing at her boots. The ankle throbbed. She doubted she could bear much weight upon it. Gradually she rose, brushing the dirt from her coat, readjusting her hat, putting her weight on the good ankle, and easing the bad one alongside. She took a step, whimpering as a stab of pain shot across her instep. Carefully, slowly, she hobbled back toward the park gate, where she flagged a cab and with the aid of the driver collapsed upon the seat.

At the house, when she finally got the boot off, the ankle was revealed, swollen and bruised. Bertha, in consultation with the cook, packed it in ice, which brought the swelling down. The next day, miserable and feverish, she played her part in the drawing room, confounding the credulous. Afterward Jeremiah Babin waited half an hour to make her acquaintance.

And that, Violet thought, as she sat in her stateroom on the S.S. *Campania*, fondling the slim volume of poetry—the sole memento of her lost love—was the nearly comic end of it. She turned to the table of contents. Here was the poem "Echo," which Ned had read so feelingly. *Come to me in the silence of the night, / Come in the speaking silence of a dream.* She turned to her own favorite and read it out to the empty cabin. *What would I give for a heart of flesh to warm me through, / Instead of this heart of stone ice-cold whatever I do! / Hard and cold and small, of all hearts the worst of all.* She nodded, comforted by these lines. They made her feel less lonely. Then she closed the book and slipped it back into her bag.

She was conscious of the ship engine's dull throb; how it must roar and fume at the stokers somewhere down in the dark hull, and how they must feel they were fueling the furnaces of hell. Yet in her narrow stateroom the air was cool, and as she stood at the basin unfastening her bodice, she had no sensation that this room was one of many, stacked chock-a-block in all directions—a small town's worth of residents sealed in an iron-and-steel canister pushing through the bay to the open sea. It wasn't really so bad, she thought, lowering her face close to the tap to splash the cool water onto her cheeks. No one knew anything about her; she was just another passenger, traveling to Bath to meet her sister. She patted her face with the towel, changed into her cotton gown, hung up her dress, and sat down on the bunk, fluffing up the pillow. When she lay with her ear against the pillow, she could hear the engines more clearly. If she turned flat on her back, she could feel the sway of the ship. It would probably get worse, she advised herself, but she was too tired to think about that. There was no going back now.

She awoke in darkness to the sound of voices. Her first thought was that passengers had gathered in the corridor, and the next was that she was on a ship and it was sinking. But the voices were not raised or excited; they were just talking. She sat up, swinging her legs over the edge of the mattress. There were all manner of voices; men, women, children, some deep, others high-pitched, halting, low, all talking, though strangely she didn't have the sense that they were talking to each other. She crossed the carpet to the curtained window, pulled back the cloth, and peered into the section of the corridor visible through the square of glass. Electric bulbs in copper rosettes studded the long passage, casting dim blobs of pink light upon the carpet. No one was directly outside her room. She unlatched the heavy door and pulled it open a few inches, then wide enough to see the length of the hall—no one was there. The voices were louder, but not clearer. She couldn't make out a word. Were they coming from the gentlemen's smoking room, or the dining room? She closed the door and went back to the bed, switching on the light over the sofa on the way and glancing at the clock. It was two fifteen.

Where were these talking people? What were they saying? It sounded like a crowd at a sporting event, before the game began. Was it coming from the upper deck? Were passengers gathered there and their voices funneled through the ventilation system to her room?

There was nothing to be done about it but to try to ignore them and sleep. But when she rested her head on the pillow, the voices grew louder, as if they came from the pillow itself. She sat up, keeping still, listening. Though she couldn't detach a word from the general racket, she determined that more than one language was being spoken. Several in fact.

It must be coming through the floor. It was doubtless the steerage mob, sleepless, restless, as she was now. Would they talk all night?

She slipped from the bed, dropping to her hands and knees and pressing one ear to the carpet. It wasn't coming from there. She stood, then sat on the sofa and took up *The White Company*, but she read only a few sentences before the mumbling voices distracted her.

It must be coming from the deck. She stood up, paced back and forth the few steps between the sofa and the bed, pressing her palms over her ears, which muffled the sound. So the voices weren't coming from inside her head: that was a relief. Perhaps it had something to do with the electricity in the cabin. She pressed her ear against the wall nearest the sink, then nearer the door. It wasn't coming from the wall.

It must be the steerage. They were closed up down there with no light but a row of portholes. They had their own section of the deck where they washed their dishes, so they probably went up in shifts, like the sailors, some sleeping while others were awake. That must be it. She should just ignore it. They were only talking, not fighting or shouting or even singing.

She returned to the bed, lay flat on her back, and closed her eyes. What were they saying? Her eyes flew open. She tried counting, got to a thousand, and started backward. Suppose this racket, this talking, went on for the entire trip? Eventually she slept a few hours. When she woke the voices were still talking. It was six a.m., two hours to breakfast.

She pressed one palm over her forehead, the other over her chest, breathing deeply, trying to calm the rising panic in her brain and heart. Her eyes rested on the bucolic scene in the painting over the sofa, a summer's day, the cows in the distance, the green world, all serene. England, she thought. Will I have to stay there? Will I die there? Would that be preferable to going through this again?

She washed at the sink, not examining her pallid reflection in the mirror. She would dress, go out on the deck, and inquire into the source of the infernal noise. She laid her dress out on the bed and sat on the sofa in her chemise, pulling on her black stockings. The air in the stateroom was stuffy with a faint odor of fried fish. At least on the deck the air would be fresh.

When she opened her door and stepped into the corridor, the voices didn't rise in volume, which meant they weren't being piped into her stateroom through the ventilation system. At the end of the hall she could see the backs of two ladies ascending the stairs to the deck. She followed them, feeling an eagerness to be under the sky, to have the company of her fellow passengers, who must surely know something she didn't about the incessant clamor of human voices. At the top of the steps, a steward, waiting to descend, smiled down upon her, but he didn't speak. He moved aside as she reached the open door and stepped out into the lively atmosphere on the deck. The voices swelled excitedly, expectantly, like a swarm of hornets disturbed by an intruder in their nest.

On the inner deck the passengers, bundled in blankets and shawls like hospital patients, reclined in deck chairs, dozing or reading books. Outside the rail they promenaded, arm in arm, two or three abreast. Here and there small groups gathered for intense conversations. There were a few children, eyeing each other hopefully from behind their mothers' skirts. Beyond them all, dazzling and undulating, neatly framed by the ship rail and the floor of the upper deck and occupying the recommended two-thirds of the composition, was the sea.

Violet leaned for support on a nearby column, resting her hand on the cold metal of the rail. A passing steward stopped to inquire if madam would like to make an appointment for a bath. "Not just yet," she said, relieved to hear her own voice so calm, so normal. "I haven't planned the day."

"Certainly, madam," he said, touching his hat in some version of a salute and passing on. Violet peered past him, along the deck, where everyone appeared cheerful, animated, absorbed by reading and conversations. Their voices rose and fell; she could hear them in the ordinary way. The other voices, which dominated the airwaves, as an orchestra might drown out a string quartet, did not, evidently, distract them from their pleasant pursuits.

How was it possible? Violet thought. She pushed past the handrail, dodging a young couple so deep in conversation they didn't notice her, and crossed the promenade deck to the outer rail. A gentleman in a felt cap and Norfolk jacket, leaning, as was the fashion, with his elbows propped behind him on the balustrade, the better to watch the passing parade, nodded approvingly at her as she found an open space nearby.

She gripped the rail and faced, at long last, the vast, churning expanse of the open sea. Her heart contracted as the voices rose, howling now, insistent and unintelligible, furious and terrible. She stood very still, breathing in slowly, allowing the roar to wash over her, recognizing the futility of resisting the cruel irony of her fate. The voices came from the sea. They had been waiting for her there. No one could hear them but her.

By the time she got back to her stateroom, Violet's dress was soaked with a cold sweat. She shrugged off her coat, rushed to the WC, and vomited twice, then staggered to the basin to cup cool water into her mouth. Over the static of the voices she heard the bugle call to breakfast. The thought of food, and especially of fried fish—the sickening odor still wafting into her room left no doubt that fish was on the menu—made her stomach shudder. She collapsed on the sofa, falling over on her side. A numbing lethargy invaded her. Groaning, she sat up, unbuttoned and pulled off her shoes, unfastened her corset, and fell back among the cushions, where, attended by the timbreless drone of the voices, she lay in a fitful sleep for the rest of her first day at sea.

She woke in the night to the murmuring voices, punctuated by the repeated booming blasts of the foghorn. It was a dolorous sound, a long moan with a sharp *m* sound at the end, as if some wounded giant, struggling for breath, pressed his lips together after each painful exhalation. She recognized it from her youth on Buzzards Bay, where the fog socked in the coast like cotton batting and you couldn't see your own feet. Had she been dreaming of that place, that sparkling little town where most of the men were sea captains and every house had some exotic article, a lacquer table from Japan, a tin lamp from Peru, linens from Brittany or Italy, a tea service from Britain, wooden sabots from Holland, a crystal vase from France? She remembered one cold winter afternoon, coming back home from school in a fog so thick she had to feel her way, one hand caressing the familiar fences and walls as she went along, smiling to herself at the unhelpful blaring of the lighthouse horn at Ned's point. When she got to the garden gate, she ran smack into her sister, who was coming out to find her.

She sat up, moved by this vivid recollection to a sense of wellbeing, which stayed with her for some moments, filling her senses like the scent of a fragrant flower carried on a current of nostalgia from the past.

A sharp rap at her stateroom window startled her so that she leaped to her feet, uncertain which way to turn. She stood stiffly, while the voices grumbled and the foghorn wailed, unable to move. Gradually who and where she was came clear to her, and her brain busily manufactured sensible explanations for the knock on the window—it was the steward, come to warn her about the fog, or perhaps he was still anxious for her to bathe, or it could be that the sway of the vessel, which she noted was much increased, had thrown some passerby off balance and caused an outflung hand to meet her window pane. She crossed to the curtain and pulled it aside, peering out in time to see a woman turning away from her door.

There was something familiar about the curve of the woman's jaw, the slope of her shoulder, which was all Violet could see, something that confused her. She patted her hair and glanced back moodily at her shoes lying on the carpet. Then she unlatched the lock, yanked the heavy door open, and stepped into the corridor. The woman moved briskly down the passage. As she approached the stairs to the deck, she pulled up the hood of her old-fashioned woolen cloak. Violet paused, one hand still on the door handle, as the lock clicked into place and she realized she'd left her key in the pocket of her coat. She would have to find a steward to get back in.

"Did you knock for me?" she called out to the woman, who paused on the stairs without looking back. Violet hurried after her, conscious of her stocking feet padding along the carpet. When she reached the stairs, the woman pushed the door open and stepped out ahead of her onto the deck.

Violet followed, bracing herself for cold air and wet feet, the raised volume of the murmuring voices, but she was unprepared for the curtain of white that hid everything—including the woman—from sight. The foghorn's melancholy moan wasn't so much louder as more penetrating; it seemed to go through to her bones. She put her hands out before her and took two steps, careful to put one foot in front of the other. That was all it took to leave the visible world behind. "Are you there?" she called out, for surely the woman must be close by. But there was no answer. A few more steps and her fingers found the inner rail, which she clutched, bringing her body in to press against it and standing with her feet apart, for the ship was rolling in a rhythm that felt calibrated to the blasts of the horn.

There might be other passengers on the deck, she thought, perhaps a sailor or two, and indeed she had the sense that there were others near, though shrouded in fog. "Is anyone there?" she said, but softly this time, as if there might be, unbeknownst to her, a comrade standing an arm's length away.

She heard a sound, separate from the others, a sharp crack of metal against wood, such as a chain might make dropped on a plank floor. She stepped toward it, one hand lightly resting on the rail, straining her eyes to see into the fog, and she made out something, a darker patch, just ahead. She let go of the rail, took a few more steps, feeling the empty air before her and reeling as she failed to adjust for the sway of the deck beneath her feet. The woman was there, she could see her dark shape bending over, standing up, bending down again. She stepped up on the crossbar, her hips even with the balustrade and her torso leaning out over the water. She was going to jump.

"No," Violet shouted, rushing toward her, but the deck was slick and she slid, landing on her hands and knees. As she lifted her head she realized that the voices were stilled, that the blare of the foghorn sounded distant, as if a bell jar had come down and sealed the space around her in a cone of deepest silence.

She rose to her knees. The woman standing high above the water looked back at her, but she couldn't make out her face inside the hood. Then she spoke in a calm, clear voice, a voice that Violet knew so well, that she had yearned to hear for so long it sliced into her consciousness like a double-edged blade, one side joy, the other terror. "Dearest," the voice said. "Come home now."

And she was gone. Violet struggled to her feet and hurled herself at the rail, scrambling up the crossbar and leaning out over the water as far as she could, batting the fog with her hands as if she could remove it. "Sallie," she cried, "Sallie." The sea grumbled and the foghorn complained. She thought she saw something moving just ahead, and she pushed up on her toes, leaning out farther into the frigid air. Her feet slipped, losing purchase of the wet rail. She reached down to grasp the wooden balustrade, but as she bent from her waist, the deck tilted and her hand missed its mark. Now gravity was against her and she fought it with all her strength, wrenching her back up, flailing her arms, but her efforts only served to pull her heels free of the rail. A reflex of self-preservation made her tuck her chin into her chest and fold her arms over her head, as if she feared a blow from behind. Soundlessly her skirts slipped over the wood and soundlessly her body arched out into the white mist, plummeting down, down, to the fathomless and waiting sea far below.

From: PERSONAL RECOLLECTIONS:
MY LIFE IN JOURNALISM
BY PHOEBE GRANT, EDITED BY LUCY DIAL

A PROMISE KEPT

Violet was right: Arthur Briggs hadn't strayed far from his hometown and it didn't require the genius of a great detective to track him down. My inquiry to the postal official at Marion drew a quick reply, directing me to an address in Uxbridge, the home of a Rev. William Cobb, who was, my correspondent informed me, the uncle of Arthur Briggs and most likely to know his current address. My letter to Rev. Cobb was answered by his wife, who explained that Arthur Briggs was employed at the First National Bank of New Bedford and could be reached in care of that institution.

I was familiar with New Bedford, that cacophonous city built on whale oil, as I'd spent some weeks there a year earlier covering the trial of Miss Elizabeth Borden, who was accused of murdering her parents with an ax. By the time the famous trial was over, the journalists' pool filled half the courtroom and greatly augmented the income of a nearby café, which provided us with sandwiches at all hours. I was among the few who thought Miss Borden probably did the deed, but the prosecutor was reckless, at one point tossing the skulls of the dead parents on the evidence table, which caused

Miss Borden to swoon for upward of twenty minutes. The defense was patient, pointing out again and again that hearsay wasn't evidence. In the end, the judge practically instructed the jury to find the lady innocent, which they promptly did.

In the course of that trial, I had struck up a friendship with the "other" lady journalist, Miss Lucy Dial, who was reporting for the *Boston Herald*, and as I had an invitation to visit her over Thanksgiving and a few days off at the end of the month, I accordingly wrote to Arthur Briggs, describing myself as a friend of a friend of his mother's, and stating my mission, the delivery of a memento that had belonged to his mother and therefore now rightly belonged to him. I concluded citing my availability to deliver it to him at some time between November 24 and the last day of the month.

Arthur Briggs responded almost at once, a cordial though slightly stiff response, thanking me for my note and informing me that he took a noon meal every working day at a restaurant near his bank and suggesting that this would be "as good a place as any" for the meeting I proposed.

And so, on a blustery day in late November, I found myself looking through the plate-glass window of Darcy's Café in downtown New Bedford. It was an unpretentious room with no more than a dozen tables, perhaps half of which were occupied by businessmen in twos or threes, eating and talking cheerfully. Two gentlemen were dining alone, and as one was white-haired and crusty, I knew the other, who had chosen a table near the back of the room, where he was dreamily perusing the menu, must be Arthur Briggs. As I opened the door and stepped into the warm, moist, fishy atmosphere, he looked up, met my eyes, and lifted his chin and eyebrows at once, signaling his expectation of my arrival. I made my way through the tables, pulling off my gloves and loosening my coat. The other diners cast quick glances as I passed, the only woman in a male domain and not, their brief surveys informed them, a particularly interesting specimen.

Arthur stood up, a faint smile playing about his lips as he put out his hand to mine and we exchanged a brief, lifeless handshake.

"Miss Grant," he said. "Thank you for coming." He pulled out a chair and I sank upon it, setting my briefcase to one side of the table. Arthur frankly stared at my battered old case; most men do. It sets me apart from my sex and, combined with my plain attire and above-average height, makes them check off a few boxes in their catalog of female possibilities. "Have you dined?" he asked politely.

"I haven't," I said. "I just got off the train from Boston. If you don't mind, I'll join you." He signaled to a waiter, who instantly brought a paper menu and a glass of water, pointing out that the fried haddock was the special. "I'll have that, then," I said.

Arthur, exchanging an approving nod with the waiter, doubtless because my indifference to the menu saved them having to watch me read it, said, "I will too."

When the waiter was gone, Arthur studied his hands, which were loosely folded on the table. I applied myself to the water glass. I had sensed at once that he suffered from extreme shyness—his encounters with my eyes had thus far been of the briefest duration— and I took him to be screwing up his courage. He was a remarkably plain-looking young man—I knew him to be not yet thirty—neatly dressed in a gray frock coat like the bank clerk he was, with thin brown hair cut square across his forehead, mild brown eyes with long feminine lashes, and a small, thin-lipped mouth. He was clean-shaven, which was unusual. "I wonder," he said, "that your friend would keep . . . whatever it is you've brought me for so many years."

"It is odd," I agreed.

"And why return it now?"

"She has gone abroad and she feared she might not return. She didn't know your address, so she asked me to find you."

"Your friend," he said, with the faint smile I began to understand was his manner of expressing incredulity.

"Her name is Violet Petra. She was a school chum of your mother's."

"That's a peculiar name. I think I'd remember it if I'd ever heard it."

"It is odd," I agreed. "Frankly, I suspect it's not her real name."

"I see," he said. Our waiter appeared and set two plates piled with fish and potatoes before us.

"This is a generous portion," I observed.

To my surprise, Arthur essayed a humorous remark. "Bankers have big appetites," he said. "Money makes them hungry."

I glanced about the room at the busy forks and knives of our fellow diners. "I see that," I said.

He cut off a bit of potato with his fork and swallowed it, hardly moving his lips. "When I read your letter, " he said, "I couldn't help thinking that in those Sherlock Holmes stories when someone says he's acting on behalf of a friend, it usually turns out he's acting for himself."

I cut into my fish, which yielded promisingly. "You mean you think I've had the book for twenty years and don't want to be held responsible for keeping it from you?"

"Is that what it is?" he said. "A book?"

"That's what Violet said it was. I haven't seen it." Our eyes coalesced upon my briefcase. "Shall I give it to you now?" I asked.

"Let's finish our meal," he said. "The table is too crowded."

"Do you know the name of any close friends of your mother's?" I asked.

He chewed reflectively, his quiet eyes resting on the middle distance. When he had swallowed, he said, "I went to live with my uncle in Uxbridge when I was eight. I remember my grandparents' house in Marion, but I don't recall much about the town. I'm sure my mother had many friends, especially in the singing society, but I never heard their names."

"And how long have you been in New Bedford?"

"About seven years. My father's mother was ill. She passed away five years ago now. I had the bank job by then, so I stayed on."

"It's an interesting town," I said. "I spent some weeks here last year, for the Borden trial."

He grimaced. "That awful business. Why were you here for that?"

"I'm a journalist," I said. "I was covering the trial for my paper in Philadelphia."

This considerable tipping of my hand was designed to provoke a range of emotions in my dining companion. The first, I anticipated, was a deepening of what I took to be an habitual suspicion of anyone connected with the business of making information public. Then there was the combination of horror and interest kindled in most quiet gentlemen by the very idea of a woman in the thick of things, jostling with tough-talking male reporters for access to thieves, murderers, swindlers, and politicians, filling her notebook with the details of anything that qualified as scandalous, sordid, and newsworthy. He'd probably been thinking I was an old maid librarian or someone's crackpot aunt who carried her knitting around in a briefcase, and lo, I was a female with a nose for news.

We addressed our plates for a few minutes as I allowed him to work through the conflict I represented to his sensibilities—I never tire of watching men struggle to fathom what I am. In the end, after another mouthful of fish had been thoroughly masticated, he laid his fork down on the plate and said, "A journalist."

Was that a glimmer of respect I detected?

"Don't be anxious," I said. "I'm on vacation."

"Truly?" he said. "You're not out to solve the mystery of the *Mary Celeste?*"

"I assure you," I said.

The waiter approached to clear our plates away. "Coffee and pie goes with the special," he informed me.

"Is there a choice of pie?" I asked.

"Apple, custard, lemon crème."

"Take the apple," said Arthur, looking knowledgeable and pleased with himself.

"The apple," I said.

The waiter stacked our plates on one hand and sailed away to the kitchen. I reached for my briefcase, unfastened the latches, and took out the package. As I handed it to its owner, I said, "You know,

it's an odd thing, but Conan Doyle's name keeps popping up in connection to your family."

"He wrote a scurrilous story about the ship," Arthur said. "Do
you know about that?"

"I do," I said. "He was also partly responsible for Miss Petra's
decision to go abroad, and hence to send you this book."

He turned the package over, set it between us, and pulled at the
string. "Well, what book is it?" he said petulantly. "Not one of his.
My mother was gone before his time." The string came loose and he
stuffed it into his waistcoat pocket. Then he folded the brown paper
back carefully, revealing a green cloth book embossed with a small
gilt pineapple. He lifted the board cover, turned over the marbled
flyleaf, and read the handwritten inscription on the following page:

THIS BOOK FOR MY DAUGHTER SARAH,
WITH LOVE FROM HER FATHER.
MAY 12, 1860

He turned to the next page, which was entirely covered in a neat
cursive hand. The ink had faded to brown. He read the first few
sentences to himself. Before he closed the book, I made out the first
four words—*My sister has dreams.*

"It's my mother's diary," he said, resting his palm gently across
the cloth cover. "From before I was born."

I said nothing, thinking of how he must feel, how I would feel,
if a total stranger brought me a diary written by my mother in her
youth. "Did you know of its existence?" I asked after a few moments.

"I did not," he said.

"Are you certain it's hers?"

"I have a few letters still. It's her handwriting."

The waiter arrived with our coffee and pie. Arthur rewrapped
the book and set it carefully aside. When he raised his dark eyes to
mine, his gaze was gentle and diffident. "I don't know how to thank
you, Miss Grant," he said. "You've brought me my mother's voice."

For a few months I was on the lookout for a letter from Violet, though I had no reason to think she would write. Her correspondence had generally been in the form of a summons. I assumed she had arrived in London and had submitted to the tests of the investigating gentlemen. After that, well, I didn't like to think about what might happen after that. I hoped she had found a better way of life. Several years passed, busy ones for me, and though Violet was sometimes in my thoughts, I couldn't let her know, as she hadn't left me an address.

When the letter from the Boston law firm of Clarence, Fogg, & Little arrived on my desk, I had no premonition that it might have anything to do with Violet Petra. The Boston postmark puzzled me. My friendship with Lucy Dial, which had so flourished that we were in more or less constant touch with each other, was my only real connection to that city. Lucy and I had our eye on a little house on Cape Cod, which we were in hopes of purchasing together with the intention of renting it out and eventually retiring, or at least summering there together in future, and my first thought was that it must have something to do with this venture. Had the owners come down enough on their price to bring the sale into our range? Eagerly, I took up my letter knife, slit the envelope open, and unfolded the single page inside.

Mr. Albert Little wrote to inform me that he represented the estate of Violet Petra, who had been missing for more than five years. All efforts by his office to contact her had been to no avail, and she was last known to have boarded a steamer to Britain in November 1894. In the intervening years she had made no effort to contact the firm or to withdraw funds from the account in her name. It was assumed that she had passed away, possibly at sea.

The law required that, as her heir, I be notified and that I contact Mr. Little's office as soon as possible. In order for his firm to follow Miss Petra's wishes and execute her will as she intended, it would be necessary to petition the court to declare Miss Petra legally dead. Mr. Little looked forward to assisting me in the matter and hoped to hear from me at my earliest convenience.

I folded the letter and closed my eyes, overcome by a surge of sadness and shock too powerful for tears. She was gone; she had been gone, year after year, and I hadn't known it. It hadn't occurred to me, when I left the hotel that gloomy day in November, that I would never see Violet again. I recalled her bitterness and anxiety, as well as her wry acceptance of her complex fate. Her caustic remark—"Even I may have my little moment of courage"—came back to me. Had she? I wondered. Or had she simply despaired?

Sadder still was the news that she had named me as her heir. To have lived, as she had, in the constant company of strangers, without family, with no dearer friend than I was—really little more than an acquaintance—struck me as terrible. But perhaps I was simply the poorest person she knew.

It was a consolation to me that we had parted that afternoon in the hotel lounge on such good terms. She had been gratified to discover that my good will toward her could survive the revelation that she was not what she pretended to be. Perhaps what we both learned that afternoon in Philadelphia was that Violet Petra was a great deal better than she pretended to be. That much, at least, is all I want the indifferent world to know about her now.

The Giant Rat of Sumatra

Hindhead and London, 1898

*"Matilda Briggs was not the name of a young woman, Watson," said
Holmes in a reminiscent voice. "It was a ship associated with the giant
rat of Sumatra, a story for which the world is not yet prepared."*

ARTHUR CONAN DOYLE, "THE ADVENTURE OF THE SUSSEX VAMPIRE"

The new study was lined with windows, which gave out over the
gardens to a stretch of heath and from thence to the valley all the way
to the Downs. The walls were richly paneled and hung with curious watercolor paintings of fairies parading in gardens, of enormous
birds talking to people smaller than they were, of an angel, wings
spread, hands folded, hovering over a field, of strange pale horses,
skeletal men, and helpless women, their skirts streaming behind
them, cascading like a waterfall from the rooftop of a tall, gloomy
building. On one wall a few harpoons were displayed together; a
stuffed falcon brooded on a bookcase; a bear skull had a corner of
the mantelpiece to itself. The desk was massive and dark; the carpets
thick and Belgian. It was a study befitting, at long last, what Conan
Doyle had so precipitously become, an author of wealth and reputa-

tion. For the past three years he had traveled abroad, living in hotels and, on his return, in rented lodgings, and during that time he was constantly wrangling with architects, deranged neighbors, builders, lawyers, tradesmen of every stripe; and there were problems with the electricity, the heraldic arms in the great stained-glass window of the entry, siting the stables, procuring the furnishings. He had hired a coachman and bought a landau and two horses, paying extra to have the family crest displayed on the carriage and the harness. Bills poured in, for laying the cellar, sinking the well, erecting the engine house for the electricity and the cottage on the grounds, for other outbuildings, landscaping, paving; it was an avalanche requiring constant attention to details, and the burden of it all fell entirely on him, as his poor wife was, had been, would be, very ill.

And now, at last, he was in residence, and so was she, plying her needle patiently in the room above his study. They both had the south view. He sat at his desk, in his comfortable flannel suit. The electric lamp cast a steady light on the page before him. He was composing a letter to his mother, asking her for the third time to come to his new house for Christmas. His pen scratched, making an audible whisper in the quiet April afternoon. *Did I tell you that Sidney Paget is coming down to paint my picture for this year's academy?*

His mind wandered; the pen stalled. What would he wear for his portrait? Would Paget insist on formal wear, or could he be taken in his flannels? Outside his window a croaking band of ravens marched into view, keeping a loose formation like soldiers on maneuvers. Raucous creatures with eyes as shiny as the black stone of Mecca, big as cats and just as fearless. He never saw them without thinking how grand it would be to discover a white one among them, and he never had that thought without the image of the unfortunate Miss Petra popping up like a disturbing jack-in-the-box in his mind's eye.

His white crow.

He didn't feel responsible for what had happened; how could he? He had hardly known the woman, though she had mightily impressed him. Myers had made the arrangements in concert with

Dr. Bishop in Philadelphia. Doyle had gone off on his tour, confident that he had put her in the hands of professional, qualified investigators who would have been, he still believed, awed by her powers. On his return from America, he was in London only a day before heading off to Davos to join his invalid wife, his children, and his sister. It was a year before they settled in yet another rented house near the site of his future mansion, and a few months after that before he communicated with his friends at the SPR. Miss Petra, Myers informed him, had not arrived. There was some question as to whether she had gotten on the ship at all, as her hosts in Brooklyn admitted they'd left her on the dock. But her luggage was aboard and scattered about the stateroom; one steward said he might have seen her. The Cunard authorities were understandably reluctant to admit that one of their passengers had gone overboard without anyone noticing, and Myers himself was of the opinion that, as he didn't know what she looked like, she might well have milked the society for her transatlantic fare and simply disappeared into the crowd on the dock. She evidently had no family—no one was looking for her. Cunard held her luggage for someone to claim, but after a year they disposed of it. As Doyle rehearsed this defensive explanation, one detail refused, as it always did, to jibe with Myers's theory. If she had wanted to fleece the SPR for her passage, why would she have left her luggage in the stateroom?

He'd asked this at once, and Myers had replied impatiently, "Why, to make us all think she'd gone overboard so we wouldn't seek her out. She wanted to disappear."

It wasn't a foregone conclusion, but he found it hard to credit the confident little woman he'd met with such relentless cunning. It was equally difficult to imagine her willfully going over the rail of a ship. She had betrayed no signs of depression or even agitation. She had, in fact, struck him as unusually composed.

Perhaps Myers was right, and his white crow had always meant to fly away.

At some signal they alone apprehended, the belligerent congregation outside his window burst into the air and swooped off toward the town in a squawking black swarm. Doyle returned his attention to his letter, scribbling a few last lines about his brother's shoulder injury. If she wouldn't come to see his house, perhaps the temptation of Innes in a sling would bring her round. Or did she really prefer spending Christmas in her cottage on Bryan Waller's estate, fussing over his Christmas pudding until it was just as he liked it?

He didn't write this last bit. Instead he signed himself *devotedly*, folded the page, and slipped it into the envelope, which he had already addressed. This he placed atop another, larger envelope, in which was secreted a square card bearing a message that began, *My own darling girl.* She would be in London in three days, and so, incidentally, would he. The dreamy thoughts that ensued were interrupted by a timid knock at the study door. Irritation sounded firmly in his command, "Come in."

It was Vanderhoek, his little Dutch page, as he liked to call him, begging, as always, his pardon, but there was a lady calling and she'd sent in her card.

"A lady?" he said. He wasn't expecting a visit from a lady. The young man handed over the card, stepping back at once in his eagerness to appear unassuming. "What manner of lady is she?" Doyle asked, turning over the card, on which the name *Matilda Briggs* was printed in square black letters.

"A tall lady," replied the servant. "Most elegant in her dress and refined in her manner. But I believe she is a foreigner."

"But?" said Doyle.

"She has an accent, sir. I don't identify it."

"Could it be German or Austrian?"

"I think I could tell that, sir. I believe she is not a German."

Doyle dropped the card negligently upon his blotter. "The name means nothing to me," he said. "Did she state her business?"

"She said she had information on a matter she believed to be of interest to you, sir."

Doyle chuckled. "Elegant in her dress?" he repeated.

"Yes, sir."

"Well," he said, "show her in. I like to keep up with the fashions."

The Dutchman went out and Doyle busied himself in taking up a few books stacked on a table between the fireplace chairs and stowing them on the mantel. Then he returned to his desk, drew out a sheet of paper from the drawer, took up his pen, and wrote the words "a foreign lady calls." He could hear the familiar, always encouraging sound of skirts rustling against the parquet in the hall, coming steadily closer, but he kept his eyes on his page, starting a doodle of a horse, until Vanderhoek announced, "Miss Briggs to see you, sir," at which point he laid the pen down with just the finest shade of reluctance, and, narrowing his eyes, looked up at the shimmering form hesitating in the doorway.

Now *this* is elegance, he thought. Miss Briggs was a column of heliotrope, silver, and gold, from the gleaming crown of ash-gold hair fastened in a love knot with a silver comb to the tips of her embroidered kid boots peeking out from beneath a full gored skirt of deep purple silk with a sheen to it that called to mind the surface of a mirror. Her pouched bodice, high-necked and long-waisted, was of heliotrope satin with a complex of tucks, each tacked into place with a running stitch of deep orange, a pattern repeated in the folds of the tight muslin sleeves from elbow to wrist, and at the inset of the gigot bulge at the shoulder, which was not so full as some he had seen. Doyle was not a fan of the gored skirt, it so often resembled a bell, but this one fit like wax over the hips, cascaded in folds to a full base, and gathered at the back to give the illusion of the now unfashionable bustle—how he missed the bustle. Furtively he noted the details of this costume—he would give a full account of it to his sister Lottie—but he stood up at the same time, coming out from behind his desk with a pleasant surprised smile, such as he didn't doubt this lady was accustomed to seeing. Her face was lovely, though not English. Her complexion was fair, her eyes deep set, hawkish, dark, almost black, her chin was a little heavy and her nose rather sharp. Her full, lightly rouged lips looked designed to bestow fond kisses. French, he thought from the look of her, and now he was eager to hear her accent. He had only a moment of anticipation, for as he took her hand she said, "Dr. Doyle. I so appreciate your willingness to see me, as I'm sure you have many demands upon your time."

Not French. "Not so many," he said. "And, in fact, I was just thinking of having a break for tea. Will you join me?" He indicated the chairs before the empty grate. She nodded agreeably, gliding past him, and perched like a fluttering dove on the indicated cushion, her long back stretched forward into the room. "With pleasure," she said. She placed a silvery beaded bag he hadn't noticed on the table next her.

"You do me honor," he said, stepping into the hall to signal the hovering Vanderhoek and send him off in search of tea.

Miss Briggs didn't move, though her eyes followed him as he closed the door and crossed the carpet to take the seat opposite her.

"Now," he said. "I'm curious to hear the reason for your visit, Miss Briggs." He noted two details as she replied. First, she lowered her eyes when he said her name, second, that she had a scar on her forehead, descending from the hairline, an old wound that had undoubtedly required stitches.

"I'm by way of a messenger," she replied. When she hit the double *ss* she turned it into *sh*, which gave a shushing sound to the word. Not Italian, certainly. "I've come at the behest of a friend who must remain nameless. She is in possession of an object she believes will be of interest to you."

"I see," said Doyle. "What sort of object is it?"

"I believe it's a book."

"But you don't have it with you."

"No," she admitted. "My friend wouldn't entrust it to me. She wants to put it in your hands herself."

"Is it extremely valuable?"

"You may think so."

There was a tap at the door. "Here's our tea," said Doyle, rising to let in Mrs. Corrie, who bustled about, taking in the pretty visitor with surreptitious glances and giving Doyle a curt nod as she went out. He returned to his chair, smiling to himself. The servants were working out wonderfully well. He'd hired them all in London and hadn't regretted for a moment the expense of bringing them down to Hindhead. They were city-bred and knew what was what. He resumed his seat and poured out tea. There were oat biscuits on the tray and marmalade, his favorite, put up by his sister Dodo from the shipment of Seville oranges he'd sent his mother. "Does your friend think I would be interested in purchasing the volume? Sugar?"

She accepted the cup, holding it out for one lump of sugar. "I believe she means to give it to you. She has a great respect for your work."

Doyle sat back in his chair, stirring his cup, looking thoughtful. He was thinking about several things at once: the revelation, when Miss Briggs moved her legs to cross them at the ankles, that her petticoat was of mauve silk shot with gold, the impenetrability of her accent, the clearly spurious "friend" for whom she pretended to be acting, the likelihood that Matilda Briggs was not her real name. "I really must ask you," he said. "I hope you won't take it amiss, but you speak with a charming accent that I fail to identify, and I flatter myself that I'm good at that sort of thing, so I'm wondering where you might have learned your English."

She smiled, revealing strong white teeth packed in so tightly that the canines were twisted. "I'm from the island of Madeira."

"Of course," he said. "Portuguese is your native tongue."

She nodded but made no comment.

"I have a fond memory of Funchal Bay," he said. "I was a surgeon on an old steamer bound for Africa. We'd had a week of heavy weather, so the harbor lights—this was years ago, and I was very young—were a welcome sight, as you can imagine. I remember the pretty town; the hills rising behind it, and over all there stretched a lunar rainbow—quite a magical phenomenon I had never seen before. Nor have I since. Have you ever seen a lunar rainbow, Miss Briggs?"

"No," she said indifferently. "I grew up in Santana, in the north."

So much for reminiscence, he thought, and natural wonders. "Is it your first visit to our shores?" he asked.

"Oh no," she replied. "I've been here often. I have family connections in Sussex and a few friends in London."

"You are staying with your friend, then. The one who has the book."

"I always stay at Morley's when I'm in London," she said.

"Yes, it's the best," he agreed. "When we go down as a family, we always stay there. It's comfortable and unpretentious."

"Yes," she said.

He was conscious that his interest in his attractive guest had faded. She was too immobile, too monosyllabic, and he hadn't much interest in her mission, which evidently involved his going to some unknown woman's house to receive the last thing he needed in the world—another book. He wished he could simply tell her to go away now, but rudeness to ladies was not in his character.

"Will you have a biscuit?" he asked, purposefully leaving the next conversational gambit to her.

"No, thank you," she said. She sipped her tea, her dark eyes flashing over the cup rim momentarily, and he thought, Is it possible that she's as bored as I am? She set the cup down and slid her beaded bag into her lap. "I won't take up any more of your time," she said. "My friend asked me to deliver this message to you." She snapped open the bag and extracted a folded envelope. "I believe it contains information about the book. You may decide for yourself if you wish to pursue it. She will make no further attempt to contact you, you may be assured."

He raised himself from the chair, reached out to take the envelope, sank back down, then came up again, this time to his feet, as she stood before him, slipping the chain of the bag over her wrist. "It was so kind of you to invite me to tea," she said. "Truly, I expected to be turned away at the door, and I've left the cab waiting. But now I can tell my friend I've had tea with Dr. Arthur Conan Doyle and put her message into his hands. She will be immensely gratified."

He made for the door, as she evidently expected to pass through it, and pulled it open before her. Relief and gloom vied for dominance as he followed her into the hall. He felt like a rejected suitor in his own home. "Let me see you out," he said. As they passed the billiard room, he thought to say, "Here is the billiard room," because he was fond of pointing out the delights of his house to visitors, but as she didn't so much as glance at the open doorway, he decided against it. In a moment they were upon the gravel drive, where the cab was indeed waiting, the driver napping in his box in the afternoon sun. Doyle was alongside Miss Briggs now and hastened ahead to open the carriage door and hand her in. "I apologize for interrupting you again," she said. "My friend isn't able to go out, and she was so certain her book would interest you, I couldn't refuse her. I gather it has some bearing on a long unsolved mystery."

He felt a chill about the heart. "Did she write the book?" he asked.

Miss Briggs laughed. "Oh no. I don't think she could write a book. She's nearly blind." She slipped her hand into his and lifted her boot to the step. "It was such a pleasure to meet you here at your beautiful home."

At last, a remark he could entertain. "You are most welcome," he said. Then, as she settled herself in the interior of the cab, he closed the door and spoke sternly to the driver, who was rubbing his eyes with his fists. "Look sharp," he said. "This lady is going to Morley's Hotel."

When he got back to his study, he found he had the folded envelope in his coat pocket. "An unsolved mystery," he muttered, tearing open the flap impatiently. It occurred to him that Miss Briggs had not once mentioned Sherlock Holmes—a point decidedly in her favor. He drew out the folded page and flapped it open. It took scarcely a moment to read it. He carried it to his desk and laid it open on the blotter, staring down upon it with a knitted brow. In the center was a simple line drawing of a fish, with a hook and line stretching up from the protruding lip. Neatly printed in the fish's body were the initials *A.C.D.* At the bottom of the page, two words writ large in red ink with a calligraphic pen comprised the message: *MARY CELESTE.*

"Not that again," he said softly.

At supper he failed to mention his unexpected visitor. His wife, having slept in the afternoon and finished a bit of needlework, felt well enough to join the family at the table, and she drew the children out about the events of their day, so the subject of his didn't arise. He had slipped the cryptic message into his desk and out of his mind, reproving himself for having wasted time better spent on his new novel. This was the best, the most original, work of his life, and he was already anxious about its critical reception. It concerned a man who is tempted by an old liaison to betray a gentle, loving wife of many years—a domestic drama—and as such, utterly new terrain. He only wanted the children to stop chattering and his wife to ascend to her aerie so that he could get back to it.

In the next few days Miss Briggs and her heliotrope imposition crossed his mind lightly, and with it the name of the ship, and with that the recollection of his own connection to the *Mary Celeste*. It was fifteen years ago that he'd written the story in Southsea, hoping to bring in a little money. He'd placed a few stories, one in *Bow Bells* and a few in *All the Year Round*, making two pounds here, five there, then he'd written a ghost story based on his Artic adventure, "The Captain of the Polestar," and sold it to *Temple Bar* for . . . ten pounds, was it? So he thought to try another spooky tale. The public, he knew, demanded a strong plot, adventures at sea went well, also ghosts and mysteries of all kinds. Why not put them all together? A ghost ship. The *Mary Celeste*. A survivor's tale. Through the shifting mists of his imagination, the image of the ship hove into view, a few of her sails torn away, but otherwise in perfect trim, coming into the wind, then falling away, at the mercy of the currents and the wind, and no one aboard. When the trial at Gibraltar was in the news, there wasn't a schoolboy in Britain who hadn't asked himself the unanswerable question: Why did the crew leave the ship?

He'd meant no harm. He was desperate for money; it was that simple. He could easily have gotten a loan from his rich uncle, but it came with strings attached to the pope and he was through with that. The Jesuits had driven the love of Christ right out of his soul and he wouldn't pretend to be a believer, no matter what it cost, no matter how his mother protested. The family had withdrawn their support—well, let them, he told her.

Writing that story had filled a few pleasant days when there was nothing to eat but potatoes and no patients ringing his bell. The bell that never rang—he could have spun a mystery out of that. He sat at his table recalling his African adventure, Captain Wallace and the Negro American consul—Garner? Garnett?—a civilized and erudite gentleman who evidently harbored a resentment so profound against his native country that he had dragged his dying body across the sea to die in Africa. Doyle had taken up his pen to sketch out his impressions, to set out upon a tale. What he hadn't done was any research.

He wasn't thinking that the captain of the *Mary Celeste* might have a family who wouldn't be pleased to see their lost loved ones treated to summary execution. All he had wanted was to entertain the public and especially to attract the attention of James Payn at the *Cornhill*, and he'd been successful beyond his dreams. Payn had paid twenty-nine guineas for that story. He could still feel the relief, like cool water washing over his shoulders, when he'd opened the check. Twenty-nine guineas! It was half a year's rent.

That story had changed his life, but as his name wasn't on it, no one knew it for some time. For a brief period he followed the flutter of reviews and opinions, the little fuss about what it was, a true account or a fantasy, the joy when all the London papers reported the telegram from the proctor at the salvage trial in Gibraltar, who was evidently still hot on the trail of the mystery. *Solly Flood*, the item ran, *Her Majesty's advocate-general at Gibraltar, telegraphs that the statement of J. Habakuk Jephson is nothing less than a fabrication.*

The success of Jephson's "Statement" didn't make it easier to sell the next story—James Payn turned down the subsequent three submissions—but it made it easier to write it. A door he had been knocking upon for years had flown open before him, and he was ready and eager to pass through.

Miss Matilda Briggs called on a Saturday, a fine April day when spring beckoned to summer with its spritely allure, but by Monday, when Doyle went up to London to make arrangements for a jaunt to the Continent, the wind was wet and the air chill. He dropped his bags at the Reform Club, ran out to his banker, and returned in time for supper with his comical friend James Barrie, who always had enough hilarious theater gossip to get them through to cigars. When they had crossed the mosaic floor beneath the darkening crystal dome and stepped into Pall Mall, they found the rain had stopped and a thin fog settled in. They went out for a stroll regardless, pausing at Trafalgar to enjoy the glow of the lamps, the cab lanterns like oversized fireflies, the eerie faces of the horses materializing from the white vapor and disappearing into it again. Barrie went on to the Strand and Doyle turned back, thinking he would have a look at the papers before retiring, and there he was, at the very door of Morley's Hotel. Out of the dull fog in his own brain, Miss Briggs and her cryptic message emerged, as ghostly as the horses' heads. The porter held the heavy hotel door open before him. Uncertain of his own intentions, but with the ticklish and pleasing sensation of following a lead, he turned in to the familiar lobby and approached the desk.

A few guests, lounging about in the deep couches and chairs scattered across the wide expanse of carpet, cast languid glances as he passed. He heard one woman say to another, "That's Conan Doyle." His spine stiffened, he lifted his chin and dropped his shoulders, his stride widened; he was invigorated by the consciousness of who he was. Unfortunately the clerk at the desk, a dull young man, didn't recognize him, forcing him to make his inquiry as if he were a person of no consequence. "Would you mind telling me," he said, as the fellow presented a simulation of attention, "if you have a Miss Matilda Briggs staying with you."

"I'll see," said the clerk, pulling the register in close and bending over it so that his large nose nearly touched the page. High myopia, Doyle thought. Best not trust him in the kitchen with a knife. He inspected the clerk's index finger, moving down the list of names, and there was the proof; two thin white scars, and an unhealed cut on the thumb, a nasty slice still red and slightly open. "We've no Matilda Briggs," said the young man, not looking up. "We have a Miss Sophia Briggs, but she checked out this morning."

This was odd, thought Doyle. Why would she change her first name and not her last if she hoped to escape detection? Now the clerk looked up from the book, making his face a bland mask of subservience. "Is there anything else I can do for you, sir?"

Meaning, thought Doyle, *Would you please be gone, you daft old dog, snooping around after a woman who has slipped out on you, as you deserve.*

"No," he said. "No, thank you for your trouble." As he was turning away, a voice from the far end of the counter called out, "Dr. Doyle, sir," and he followed it to find Jeffrey, the desk manager, who knew him, who knew his poor wife and the children and even his mother, and who never failed to ask him when the public might expect a new "masterpiece" from his pen. This reliable and efficient Jeffrey approached, cheerful and expansive, his bald pate gleaming in the diffuse light of the electric lamps, the wide white expanse of his immaculate shirtfront bulging with the pride he took in his station. "I've been on the lookout for you, sir," he said, pausing in his passage behind the counter to pull an envelope from a box beneath the wall of keys. "The lady said she thought you'd be in sometime today, and I was to give you this message." He swept the bemused clerk aside with a wave of one hand, brandishing the envelope with the other. "And here you are," he concluded.

Doyle reached out to receive the envelope, which he tucked into his frock coat pocket without looking at it. "Thank you, Jeffrey," was all he needed to say.

"Very welcome, sir. Happy to be of service. Family all well, sir, I hope?"

"Very well," he said.

"And we'll soon be seeing a new masterpiece fresh from your pen, I hope, sir."

"Not too soon," he replied, because Jeffrey amused him. "I'm working in a new vein."

"Not a Sherlock Holmes vein then, sir."

"I fear the great detective has few of those left in him," he replied.

Jeffrey's eyelids fluttered, taking in the pun, savoring it. "Have you bled the fellow dry, sir? I surely hope not."

Doyle chuckled. "Not completely," he said. "But he is somewhat anemic and I fear may require a transfusion of fresh blood."

"Well, if it can be done, sir," Jeffrey said, "you are the doctor to do it."

"I'm hoping it won't come to that," replied Doyle. "For the time being I'm recommending citrate and bed rest."

"Bed rest is never amiss, sir," agreed Jeffrey heartily, "as I'm constantly reminding the wife."

Remarkable, thought Doyle, how skillfully this manager had brought the conversation to a convenient and agreeable close. "Very right," he said, and with a brief exchange of thanks and best wishes to the family, he was on his way out the door. As he sailed across the carpet, nodding to the doorman, who flung the portal open before him, he could feel the pointed edge of the envelope protruding from the shallow inner pocket of his coat, pricking irritatingly against his sternum.

The actors will come regardless of danger to encourage and applaud sixty-five giant rats of Sumatra dancing in the road.

For the fifth time Doyle read this sentence; the entirety of the enigmatic message left for him by the exasperating Miss Briggs. He turned to the envelope—hotel stationery, *Doctor Arthur Conan Doyle* printed neatly across the front—noting for the fourth time that the address was written in different ink and by a different hand than that of the single sentence on the page inside. So Miss Briggs wasn't working alone; she and her accomplice were having him on. What he found more disturbing than the message was Miss Briggs's evident confidence that he would appear at the hotel to claim it. How could she be so well informed of his whereabouts? He had entered the hotel on a whim because he happened to be in the neighborhood. Her visit to his home had not been—she must know—a great success; she had failed to charm him. He had, in fact, found her wanting on nearly every score, apart from beauty, and even in that she was too icy and humorless to kindle any spark beyond the natural interest aroused by her figure, her face, and her style. The card she'd delivered for the friend—and clearly now there was a friend—wasn't provocative enough to move a busy man to more than a few moments of recollection. The fish, the name of a ship, his initials. It was nonsense, and this message was more nonsense. They thought he was a fish and they could make him bite.

"They've been reading too many detective stories," he said, folding the page and stuffing it back into the envelope.

He resolved to give it no more thought and stretched out on his bed, his brain abuzz with travel plans. In a few days he would be in Rome. His brother-in-law had written to say Wells was there, and a dinner planned—it would be a gathering of authors and the talk would doubtless be of politics and war. Wells had fantastical ideas, some of which were as practical as the umbrella. But the Naval Office ignored him, possibly at their peril.

In the morning he breakfasted alone at the club, feeling, as he buttered his scone, the absence of James Payn in the world. He was gone to his reward only a few weeks previously, and this was Doyle's first occasion to be in London without a visit to Maida Vale. He mused upon their long association, which had begun all those years ago when he was a struggling young doctor, churning out stories by gaslight, laid low for days on end by the microbe that had climbed aboard his body in Africa and the neuralgia that made light unbearable. His thoughts drifted again to that first acceptance. The *Cornhill*, it was the gold standard. He sliced his sausage in three neat pieces and his mind sailed upon the *Marie Celeste* back to the message he'd left in his room. Giant rats of Sumatra. Were there giant rats in Sumatra?

After his breakfast he had an hour before the travel agent's office opened, so he returned to his room. There was time to get a note off to her, to tell her of his plan for their meeting, to tell her of his longing for a meeting every minute of his day. On the desk the envelope—it was clearly some sort of silly female prank—caught his attention, and he read the queer message once again.

> *The actors will come regardless of danger to encourage and applaud sixty-five giant rats of Sumatra dancing in the road.*

It was a code, he thought. Of course, that was obvious. He tried the first letters of every word—*t a w c r o d t e a a s f g r o s d i t r*. He shuffled a few letters, got *Crows eat fast* with some letters left over. Not much to be made of that.

He read it backward; nothing there. Clearly it wasn't mirror writing.

He pushed it away. Nonsense.

Was it every other word? *Actors come of to . . .* No.

And then he saw it. It was as clear as a windowpane—every fourth word.

Come to sixty-five Sumatra road.

Why not? That was the question that got him to Sumatra Road that afternoon. He had cleared up his travel business, dined with his agent, and his afternoon was his own. As always, before a meeting with her, he was restless. Their reunion—public, as required, brief, as necessary—was scheduled for the following morning; he would meet her train and escort her to her sister's house near Regent's

Park. They would have twenty minutes in the cab, half an hour if there was, as he prayed there would be, traffic.

So rather than wander the streets or drowse about at the club jabbering with any gentleman who happened to be at loose ends, why not take a pleasant drive to West Hampstead, where, the club porter assured him, the housing market was being cornered by such a lot of Jews and bohemian types a workingman might wonder what country he was in?

The fog had cleared off, the sky, a flat gray sheet with a smudge of yellow in the west, promised nothing, and the air was freshened by a westerly breeze. He could walk across the park and find a cab at Lancaster Gate. He was curious about the area, the bohemians and the Jews, about the promised book, and he wanted to demonstrate to Miss Briggs that he had cracked with dispatch her childish code. Some paltry species of honor had come into play, and it spurred him on.

One knew, without trying to, that the great thrumming metropolis was spreading, that grand country estates had been swallowed up by building associations, that the appetite of the working classes for a neat housefront and a walled yard had no limits, and that tradesmen and clerks of all sorts now schooled themselves in the finer points of freeholds and leases, but as his cab turned in to the third long rank of redbrick terraced houses, their identical bowed windows like drooping eyes looking out at the hip-high stucco walls punctuated by identical iron gates, he grasped for the first time the magnitude of the development. He saw no signs of Jews or bohemians; in fact few humans of any condition were about on the bleak, treeless pavement. Everything was fresh, even the geraniums in the upper-story window boxes looked brighter than the ones in town, and there was something dulling and cruel about all this newness. Behind the neat, narrow housefronts the residents were packed in tight, though not as they were in the stinking, overcrowded slums of Shoreditch or Cheapside, where poverty made the rules and the street was often safer than the wretched domicile. Here they were packed in decorously, like shiny little fish lined up in tins, and they were packed in willingly, because the point of all this clean brick and glass was that they were not poor, starving little fish anymore, and living in this place proved it.

The horses' hooves clopped briskly on the long expanse of Dennington Park Road, and then slowed as the cab turned onto Sumatra Road, the last street before the rail tracks. In fact, as they made the turn, Doyle could see that the wee yards of these smaller, taller houses backed right up to the tracks. The tracks, he thought, which carried the trains, which moved the men who lived in the houses that Dennington built.

Number 65 Sumatra Road was distinguished from its neighbors by a Mediterranean panache. The small front plot was abloom with geraniums. Fragrant rosemary bushes pruned into pyramids defined the four corners, a hedge of lavender lined the walk, a lush bougainvillea overpowered a trellis fastened to the wall, and two enormous pots of exotic striped cannas occupied pride of place on either side of the door, which was painted an unusual sea-foam blue. Doyle alighted from the cab and asked the driver to wait, as his visit would be a brief one. He didn't want to get trapped in this monumental maze of brick with no easy way out. As he strode up the walk, he noticed the curtain at the window of number 64 dropping back into place. Neighbor-watching. There must be a lot of that, he thought.

He rang the bell. There was no sound from within. The absurdity of his mission touched him, but he brushed it away. It was a lark. He could set a crime in this place; no telling how much professional and personal disgruntlement festered behind the endless succession of smartly painted doors. As he waited, a tomato-red door two fronts down opened and the rear end of a pram issued from within. Then he heard a bolt turning in the blue door and looked round to see it open.

The small woman who stood before him didn't look at him, or anything else for that matter, as her eyes, clouded with cataracts, had the unsettling milky appearance that sometimes frightens children. "Here you are, Dr. Doyle," she said cheerfully. "I thought I might find you at my door this afternoon." She stepped aside, holding the doorknob with one hand and a walking stick in the other. "You are most welcome," she continued. "Do come in."

"If you knew I was coming," he said jovially, passing her in the narrow entry hall, "you know more about my plans than I do, as I only resolved to pay you a visit an hour ago."

She closed the door, plunging the hall into gloom. "I know gentlemen don't generally credit the ladies with much capacity for deductive reasoning," she said. "But it's my opinion that we are rather good at it than not. Especially where gentlemen's motives are concerned." She turned to him, extending her frail, bony hand, which he took in his own, careful not to crush it. "I am Mrs. Blatchford," she said.

He observed her closely, from the old-fashioned bonnet fastened over her wispy mouse-gray hair to her plain Mother Hubbard and clean white apron to the black stockings and practical brogans peeking out beneath the skirt. She was, he guessed, in her sixties, fair complexion, not excessively wrinkled, something Welsh about the downturn at the outer corners of her eyes and the weakness of her chin. She was thin, her spine straight, her movements confident, in spite of her blindness, and sprightly in her manner.

She was a little character, he thought, tucked away behind her bougainvillea-festooned blue door. This was going to be entertaining. Curious old ladies were one of his strong suits.

"I'm afraid I must ask you to follow me to the kitchen," she said, as he released her hand. "I have our tea laid out, but I can't manage the tray."

"With pleasure," he said.

Moving quickly, as she was familiar with the territory and doubtless careful that all objects stayed in their places, she led him past the staircase and the parlor door. Doyle set himself to noticing everything, the Chinese silk carpet runner—he'd rarely seen a finer one, very delicate in its colors and smooth in its weave—the embossed wallpaper largely hidden by all manner of pictures:

Japanese prints, maps, prints of sailing ships, framed photographs of harbors—he recognized Liverpool and another he took to be Gibraltar—a very good painting of Vesuvius, seen from Naples, and another of Mt. Fuji, with its neat snow-capped peak. A lacquer chest against the wall, hand-painted with chrysanthemums in the Japanese style, sported a bowl in the shape of bundled leaves, hand-painted with chrysanthemums in the English style. A mahogany salver with a few envelopes and cards scattered upon it suggested that, in spite of her blindness, Mrs. Blatchford kept up with her correspondence.

There was more light in the kitchen and a view of the back garden, which was as exuberant as the front. Honeysuckle swarmed over the wall and a shady corner was thick with blue-green hosta, clumps of wild ginger, and pots of begonias, shiny as porcelain. Mrs. Blatchford skillfully poured the boiling kettle into the pot and spooned in the tea—she accomplished this by keeping one fingertip near the rim of the opening. Sensing his interest she said, "I can see shapes."

"I wondered," he said.

"For example, I can see your shape and it is a large one. Shall we proceed to the parlor?"

He took up the tray and followed her back through the hall to the room where the large front window, curtained in old lace, admitted the afternoon light. "Your garden is paradisiacal," he said. "And very unusual. I wonder how you keep it—"

"With my poor eyesight," she finished for him. "My husband, Captain Blatchford, planned it, and he brought back many of the bulbs and seeds from his travels. When he passed away two years ago, my niece took over what work there is to do. I've been in this house five years and the plants are well established. They don't need much care, though I do bring in the cannas if it freezes."

Doyle set the tray on a beaten-brass table of a Moorish design and took his seat in the plain Queen Anne chair facing his hostess. Here, too, the walls were crowded with pictures of all sorts. In a tall wrought-iron cage near the window, two canary birds twittered, hopping in their incessant, febrile way from bar to bar. From the large oil painting over the mantel, a serious gentleman with long whiskers and heavy-lidded eyes gazed past the viewer, contemplating the horizon, or perhaps a distant sail.

"That's my husband," said Mrs. Blatchford. How did she know he was looking at the painting?

"Yes, I thought so," he said. "And Miss Briggs is your niece?" He poured out the tea and handed her a cup.

Mrs. Blatchford lifted the cup from the saucer and held it between her palms. "Matilda Briggs is not her real name," she said, evidently amused by this fact.

"No. I didn't think so," he said.

"We were surprised you didn't recognize it."

"Is there some reason I should?"

Carefully his hostess tilted the cup to her lips, making a sucking sound as she sipped the steaming liquid. She lowered it with a soft chuckle. "Sophia Matilda Briggs was the child who disappeared from the *Mary Celeste*," she said.

"I didn't know that," Doyle said. "I only know what I read in the papers. I was really just a boy when it happened."

"Yes, we realized that. We thought—even my husband thought—that you changed all the names and didn't mention that the child was a girl because you wanted to disguise the facts. It didn't occur to us that you simply didn't know the facts."

Was she trying to offend him? She looked so cheerful and sly. She was positively chortling over her teacup.

"It was a fantastic tale," he said. "I never intended it to be anything more than that."

"It was the only story of yours my husband didn't care for," she said, "and that was for reasons that will soon be obvious. Apart from that one, he was a great admirer of your work. He read everything you wrote, that is, while he was alive. He enjoyed the Holmes stories, but he really admired your historical novels, and he even said you were better at the sea than anyone, except perhaps Stevenson. Do you know what story was one of his favorites?" She turned her face toward him, blinking her sightless eyes. "I think it will surprise you."

Mollified by this praise from the dead captain, Doyle gazed up at the portrait of his fan. Was that merriment he detected in those far-seeing eyes? "Perhaps one of the Brigadier Gerard stories?" he ventured.

"It was 'De Profundis,'" Mrs. Blatchford announced joyfully.

Now it was his turn to chuckle. "That grisly little tale?" he said.

"'The shark is a surface feeder and is plentiful in those parts,'" she quoted. "George thought 'De Profundis' a perfect gem of a story."

"Well, I'm gratified to hear it," Doyle replied. "Though it wasn't a tale that cost a great effort." A silence fell as they both sipped their tea. Somewhere a clock was ticking; one of the canaries let out a high-pitched trill. They always sounded so mad with joy, those birds, Doyle thought.

"Well," said Mrs. Blatchford, setting her cup back on the tray. "Now that you've followed our trail and cracked our code, I'm sure you'd like to know why you're here."

"The code did briefly stymie me," he admitted.

"Until you recognized it as a variant of the message in 'The Gloria Scott.'"

"Was that it? I knew I'd used something like it somewhere."

"Which, most interestingly, is another tale of mutiny at sea," she reminded him.

"Yes. I'd forgotten. You have been thorough."

"Since George passed on and my sight declined, I've tried to keep my mind alert, and I have a great deal of time."

"And your niece . . ."

"Her name is Annie Blatchford. She is the daughter of Captain James Blatchford, my husband's brother. He married a Portuguese lady whose family lived in Madeira, and as they had no children, they adopted a little girl from an orphanage there, so Annie is not related to me by blood. James died nearly ten years ago now. His ship—it was the *Theodore*—was lost with all hands in a hurricane near Mauritius. Then Annie's mother died two years ago now of pneumonia. Annie was just seventeen. We were both alone in the world, so I invited her to come to me. She's been an enormous help and comfort to me. I don't know what I should do without her."

"And she lives with you here?" Doyle asked.

"Yes. She's very much the modern woman. She wasn't here six weeks before she found a position at the telephone exchange. She takes the train in every day and comes home in time for supper. We've had good fun with our scheme to entice the great detective to our little hideaway in West Hampstead."

Doyle flinched at the conflation of his person with his creation, but Mrs. Blatchford's story interested him, so he let it pass. He found it hard to picture the immobile and chilly Miss Briggs having good fun at anything.

"Annie's a great reader as well," she continued. "She reads to me before bed. She adores Mrs. Gaskell and Mrs. Braddon. She writes stories herself and sends them round to the journals. Very pretty things they are."

Doyle poured out more tea as his interest flagged like a sail entering the doldrums. So that was it. Miss Briggs fancied herself a writer. "Mrs. Braddon is very good at plots, isn't she?" he said.

"I find her work a bit overwrought and sensational," replied Mrs. Blatchford. "Just between us."

Doyle made no response, gazing hopelessly at the canaries. How was he to get to the cab without one of the niece's stories in his pocket?

"George," his hostess continued, changing tack, and then, "my husband," as if there might be some doubt as to her relationship to the captain. "George liked to fancy that Annie might actually be Sophia Briggs. She was three when they took her from the orphanage and that was a year after the ship turned up derelict. So she's the right age. But there's no evidence for such a claim. The nuns didn't know where she was born, or they wouldn't say."

Doyle was only half-listening, consumed now by his desire to get back to the club, but his brain picked up a discrepancy that puzzled it and he asked without thinking, "How did your husband come to know the child's name?"

"Ah," said Mrs. Blatchford brightly, holding up one index finger to call attention to her point. "That's the question, isn't it? That's the very detail you need to know to understand why you're here in this room."

Doyle smiled, giving in a little to the engaging manner of his hostess. "And what is the answer to this vital question?" he asked gamely.

"George Blatchford," she said, "was the captain who took command of the *Mary Celeste* in Gibraltar. He sailed her to Genoa, unloaded the cargo there, and then sailed her back to Boston."

Doyle looked up at the portrait. "Really?" he said. "I've always wondered what happened to the ship after the salvage hearing."

"She sat on the wharf in Gibraltar for three solid months while that hearing went on and on. Near the end, George was retained by the owner, a Mr. Winchester. It took him three weeks to raise a crew because the sailors were all shy of the ship. All he could get was Basques. She was a bad-luck ship."

"And did George have bad luck with her?"

"Not a bit of it. He said she was tight as a drum and a fair sailer. Not much speed to be gotten from her. He had an easy crossing, brought her into Boston without a hitch, and then to New York, where word had got out and a crowd turned up to have a look at her."

"And he left her there?"

"That's right. The owner paid him off and George caught a steamer back as he couldn't find another ship, and he was eager to get home."

"I see," said Doyle. But then he didn't see and he said so. "But that still doesn't explain why he knew the name of the missing child."

"No," she agreed. "There's still that little missing piece to the puzzle, isn't there?" Her expression was as smug as a cat before a dish of cream.

"Which you are about to supply," Doyle concluded.

"If you will please open the top drawer of the chest under George's portrait, you will find a package with your name on it."

He did as she directed, crossing to the chest and opening the drawer, which contained only a small brown paper package tied up with a thin black ribbon, his name in its entirety printed across the front in red ink. He picked it up, divining by the heft of it that it was a book with hard covers, not, praise heaven, a manuscript of loose typed pages. He returned to his seat before the lady to await her full explanation.

"As you've determined, it's a book," she said when he was seated. "Before he died, George asked me to deliver it to you. 'And don't just put it in the mails,' he said. 'If it goes in the mails some factotum will find it first and consign it to oblivion. You must put it in his hands and give him my fond regards as you do.'"

Doyle studied the bold lettering of his name. "And now you've accomplished your husband's mission. And very cleverly, I might add."

"I'm flattered to hear *you* think so." She raised her cloudy eyes to the portrait, as if to bask in her husband's approbation. "Oh, I do believe George would be proud of me."

"Do you know how he came by the book?"

"I do," she said. "And George wanted you to know it as well. He found it under the mattress of the captain's bed on the *Mary Celeste*."

"Good heavens," said Doyle. "Shouldn't he have turned it over to the authorities?"

"I suppose he should have. But he didn't."

"Does it bear on the fate of the crew?"

"Really, sir. I think that will be for you to say."

One of the canaries warbled gleefully and his companion joined in. Doyle gripped the package, conscious of a visceral reluctance to open it before the blind eyes of Mrs. Blatchford and the dead eyes of her seagoing husband, who sent, from beyond the grave, his fond regards. As if she sensed his diffidence, Mrs. Blatchford neatly closed the interview.

"Now, if you'll excuse me, Dr. Doyle," she said. "As you've observed, I've done my duty. It has left me very tired." And indeed her little frame sagged in the chair. "And I believe your cab is waiting."

"Of course," he said, leaping to his feet. "Shall I take the tray back for you?"

"No, thank you," she said. "You are so very kind. Annie will be home soon and she'll take care of it."

"Is there anything else I can do for you?"

"No," she said. "I'll just have a little rest here in my chair. If you don't mind, I'll ask you to see yourself out."

He stood before her feeling enormous and useless, a distinctly unusual sensation. He had been eager to leave, but now he was uncertain how to "see himself out" gracefully. Even the package in his hand felt tentative; it was a slim volume, whatever it was, and his fingers gripped it tightly to keep it from slipping away. He offered his hostess a quick awkward bow. "It has been a pleasure to meet you, Mrs. Blatchford."

She roused herself, extending her hand, which he gently caressed in his own. "I'm honored by your visit," she said. "And so would my husband be, if he were here."

"Please give my regards to your niece."

"I certainly will," she said.

He turned toward the hall, pausing in the doorway to ask a final question. "Does this book contain the solution to the mystery of the *Mary Celeste*?" he asked.

She smiled, nodding her head contentedly. It was the question she'd been waiting for. "Let's just say it deepens it," she said.

As the cab pulled away from the curb, he heard the bleat of the train whistle, and by the time the horse had turned onto Dennington Park Road, staggered clutches of pedestrians appeared, plodding along the pavement from a narrow lane that must have been a shortcut to the station. He imagined that Miss Briggs might be among them and pressed his back against the seat, averting his face from the window, for the thought of seeing her—waving to her from the window—had no appeal to him. He remained rigid and aloof as the cab wove through the blocks of increasingly large and respectable houses. "A fool's errand," he thought, sliding the package onto the seat beside him. He would have a look at it when he was in his room at the club.

On arrival at this safe haven, he found two messages waiting for him: one from Bennett inviting him to come round for supper, and another from her, a brief billet-doux, expressing her joyful anticipation of their meeting on the morrow. Amid lively fantasies, some charming, others perhaps grave, but with honorable conclusions, he climbed the carpeted marble steps to his room, where his bed was made up, the linen clean, the curtains drawn, and a pitcher of water waiting on the corner table next to a decanter of claret. He dropped the book on the desk, opened the curtains to let in the cool, damp, not particularly fresh air, poured out a glass from the decanter, and sat down to his task. As the breeze lifted the curtain liner and the sound of a distant piano drifted into the room, he had a moment of deep satisfaction with his lot. He adored his family, his house, his position, but it was also a delight to be alone, in his room in the great city, as free of cares as a bachelor, and with the promise of a romantic encounter with one—a most beautiful, talented, adoring, and patiently devoted one—whose chaste kisses would leave him both exhilarated and sick with love.

He took up the package and loosened the ribbon, which came free at once. The paper sprang open, and there was the book, a black cloth cover, with a red ribbon marker and gilt edging across the top—a plain, masculine-looking journal, such as he occasionally used himself. There were pale stains marking a rectangle neatly centered on the cover, as if a label had been pasted there and fallen away. A purplish smudge near the lower outside edge looked, upon examination, more like jam than blood. He opened the cover to the marbled end pages, which were lightly foxed with age. It did appear to be an old book.

But, he thought, anyone could buy such a book for a few pence at a street market, and if it looked as if it had been lying in a store-room for years, that was because it probably had.

He turned the page and read the designation, written in brown ink in a round feminine hand.

The Log of the Mary Celeste.

As if a fierce skirmish were imminent, a battery of defenses rushed into place. The peculiar Miss Briggs, who wrote pretty sto-ries, the elaborate device to get him to the outskirts of town, the complex explanation of the provenance of the book, the presuppo-sition that he must take an interest because a seafaring man who admired him thought he must. Was it possible that the book he had before him was an original document, squirreled away for twenty-six years by a captain who had failed in his duty to deliver it to the proper authorities?

Or was it simply another hoax, the desperate ploy of a poor, ambitious young writer, just as he had been, who schemed, just as he had schemed, to captivate the fickle attention of the public by tying a painter to the taffrail of a famous mystery ship?

He turned the page and read:

Pier 50, East River, New York
November 1, 1872

The Log of the Mary Celeste

PIER 50, EAST RIVER, NEW YORK
NOVEMBER 1, 1872

*B*enjamin laughed when he saw the title I had pasted on the cover of this book. "Will you be needing the sextant," he asked, "or are you set on dead reckoning?"

"No," I replied. "I leave all that to you. This is the log of the little world belowdecks, where the sun never shines and no reckoning is of use."

He looked up at the skylight, eight panes of pale gray interrupted by the slash of the boom. "Surely some light will filter into your principality."

I followed his eyes. "It is to be hoped," I agreed.

In fact, my principality, as he called it, is spacious compared to some quarters we've shared, especially on the *Arthur*, where we couldn't both stand together in the space outside the berth and B. had to duck to pass into the wardroom. The previous owner of the *Mary Celeste* had her refitted from stem to stern. As he planned to take his wife and young son aboard, he expanded the captain's quarters, which are raised above the deck. We have not only the skylight, but windows on three sides, through which we will have a fine view of sailors' legs. She's not a grand ship, but as B. observes, neat, in good trim, and her hull is fresh-clad. The Lord willing we will have a safe and speedy passage, though all agree November is not the best month for an Atlantic crossing.

It was fair when Sophy and I made the trip down on the steamer. She's a good traveler, though she wants to climb over everything and everyone in sight. As the crew is not yet aboard, we spent this morning in a fine explore of the ship, which delighted her, as she was allowed to run up and down the decks and peer into every closet and cubby in the forecastle. It's pleasant to stroll on the deck amidst the forest of masts in the harbor, a little town made of ships all coming, going, or, like us, waiting. In the afternoon B. helped me get my sewing machine and the melodeon set up so we will at least have some songs and I won't die of boredom.

NOVEMBER 2

B. is off to the registry office this morning. Sophy's teeth kept her (and us) awake half the night, but now she is napping peacefully. I had hopes of some shopping and visiting here, as the loading progresses and B. is less occupied with paperwork, but alas there is horse disease in the city and the horse cars aren't running. One can hire a carriage but the price is prohibitive, so it looks as though Sophy and I shall be thoroughly familiar with our quarters well before we sail.

As the present is without event, I'm thinking of the past, and especially of my dear father, who passed away two months ago today, and also of B.'s father, Captain Nathan, who, having weathered a lifetime of perilous voyages at sea, departed this life in his own parlor, struck by a lightning bolt that came through the window. On past voyages we wrote letters to these progenitors, but now we are without them and the world feels smaller, and duller.

They were both proud, occasionally thunderous men, willing and eager to cast the pearls of their wisdom widely. They were solid friends and enjoyed each other's company until the war came and they fell out for its duration. Captain Nathan thought all wars were a waste of daylight and energy, as well as human lives, and recommended that the government could save the nation untold grief if they would simply purchase all the slaves and set them free. My father advocated a complex blend of Old Testament justice and New Testament mercy. This "quarrel of the patriarchs," as Olie called it, was resolved once the slaves were freed and the union reunited. One summer morning Father vowed he would no longer live in enmity with his brother-in-law. He marched over to Rose Cottage and knocked boldly on the door. Captain Nathan, who was standing on the piazza—which he calls the "quarterdeck"—saw him there. He came down, threw the door open, glowered at Father for a moment, and said commandingly, "Walk in, sir." And that was that.

NOVEMBER 3

*T*his afternoon our officers came aboard to settle in and be introduced to one another, and, most important, to the captain's wife and daughter.

Mr. Albert Richardson, our chief mate, arrived first, followed by a rough-looking boy he'd enlisted to haul his sea chest to his quarters. Fortunately for him he is a man of small stature, as his berth is tight. He sailed with B. on the *Sea Foam* some years ago and proved a reliable officer, so B. was pleased to get him. I found him pleasant enough, respectful of B., very neat in his dress, even foppish. He was wearing a blue satin waistcoat embroidered with little green fish, which Sophy was mad to touch. Her enthusiasm clearly made Mr. R. anxious, though he tried mightily not to let on, as it wouldn't do to slap away the sticky fingers of the captain's daughter on first meeting. Poor Sophy has a head cold and is not at her most winning.

Mr. Richardson is recently married and very keen to mention "Fanny, my dear wife," every other sentence. His father-in-law, the great Winchester, owns us all, and it's doubtless through dear Fanny's influence that her dapper bridegroom has got his post. Later, when I expressed my amusement at Mr. R.'s prudish manner and fancy attire, B. said, "He'll loosen up, once we sail."

He has an absurd, pencil-thin mustache, like a theater villain, and his hair pomade, generously applied, smells of lard.

Mr. Edward Head, our steward, came aboard next, followed closely by Mr. Andrew Gilling, our second mate, neither of whom could be accused of personal vanity.

Mr. Head is not taller than Mr. R., but has three times his girth, a rotundity of a man with wispy light hair and sparkling light eyes in a fleshy, florid face. His manner is respectful but not obsequious, frank, and open. He blinks rather more than seems necessary to refresh the eyes. Mr. Gilling is sallow and chinless, with flat, lifeless eyes and a mass of springy, mouse-colored hair that put me in mind of the Spanish moss we saw in the trees in New Orleans, which the citizens there use to stuff mattresses. Once this comparison came to me, I couldn't look at him without conjuring silly names like Mate Mattress-Head, or Mr. Bedding, or Mate Mossy Top. He might wonder why I smile when I look at him, or perhaps he won't, as he appears perfectly vacant, without interests or humor. B. has heard of him that he lacks ambition and will never rise above his present rank, which suits him, as he is at ease neither with the common sailors nor with the officers, but the sea has been his life and he wants no other.

Mr. Richardson will share space with us here in the stern. Mr. Gilling has a decent little room in the forecastle and Mr. Head has a berth of his own in the galley, where the stove will keep him warm while we are not.

Tomorrow the crew arrives—four Germans!

NOVEMBER 4

This morning B. was in the registry office again, signing the articles of agreement. In the afternoon our crew came on, four young German men, as like each other as painted wooden dolls; fresh complexions, mops of flaxen hair, bright blue eyes, and strong jaws. They stamp people out from molds in Europe, or so it seems to me. They are settling themselves in the forecastle as I write. They understand no English but officers' orders. So I don't envy Mr. Head, who will have to feed them and rouse them in shifts from their dreams of German girls and German beer and German songs to hot coffee and the call of duty. Oompah, Oompah, Oompah-pah.

The weather is ugly, rain and a chill wind, so we are stuck below. Sophy's cold is better and she is eating well. She occupies herself with her doll and her blocks and in looking at the album, naming the absent. She asks for Arthur now and then, always with a note of anticipation in her voice, as if she expects him to come in at the door. The way she says his name sounds like "Otter."

Otter must be missing her as well—he is fond of his little sister, who is as full of energy and joy as he is lacking in both. My poor, shy, serious boy. He wanted to come with us badly, and his father would have taken him, but he's doing too poorly in school to miss a few months and, saddest of all reasons, there's just no place to put him aboard ship. So he will stay with his grandmother at Rose Cottage, where there is perhaps too much room. B. insisted on paying his mother for her grandson's board. I've no doubt she'll soon have him doing chores, as Mother Briggs is great on chores, and perhaps that will give him an appetite and he'll put on weight. He wept when we left and promised to write to me at least once a week. His grandmother will see that he does that too.

We haven't left the harbor and already I am hoping for letters.

NOVEMBER 5

*O*ur voyage begins by not beginning. We set out this morning in a freshening breeze, but it turned blustery, with such a strong head wind that B. determined we would only be beat about, so we anchored here, scarcely a mile from the city. Sophy is playing with her toys and talking to herself; she is a cheerful companion, and B. is writing a letter to his mother. I have written to Arthur and to my spendthrift brother William, who is squandering his small inheritance in Philadelphia, though it does sound as if he's finally found a position at a firm there. We had words after Father died and I attempted to give him some useful advice about handling his finances. He has never much confided in me, but now he is distant, though he did write a sweet note when I sent him a few mementos of our mother, especially a little "eye" box Father left, which Mother had made for him when they were courting. It is a black lacquer box, about the size of a pillbox, containing a perfect painted likeness of our mother's left eye. I might have given it to Hannah, as she was fascinated by it as a child, but I know Father would have wanted William to have it, and also Mother's eye might prove too disturbing a subject of contemplation to a nature as fantastical as my sister's. I am thinking of her much, and never with an easy heart. After Father's death, she was set on going off to Boston. She had an invitation from one of those awful Spiritualist ladies, who have so much money that they buy themselves young women to use in peddling their vicious religion—which is filling the madhouses, Father believed, and so I told Hannah. I talked her into waiting until we return from this trip, and I begged her to come and live with us then. She agreed to wait, but I fear as soon as we sail she will be in touch with what I suppose must be her preferred companions, both the living and the dead.

When B. and I were on our wedding trip, she ran off—she was barely fifteen. Father, through his contacts, found her within a week—she was staying in a judge's house, of all things, in upstate New York. Father got on a train, went over there, and brought her home. She had lied to the judge, saying she had no family. Father said, "You may want no family, but you have a family, and one that loves you dearly and prays that you will come to your senses and return our love and trust." She stayed home then, but not because she'd come to her senses. She just knew our father would find her and bring her back.

This afternoon when I stepped out onto the poop for a breath of rather too fresh air, I thought I must have lost my wits, for I heard a pretty tune drifting toward me from the forecastle. I thought it must be a flute. When I mentioned it to Mr. Head, he said, yes, it was. One of the Germans had packed his flute in his sea chest and was practicing a few airs. It seems the fellow is bookish as well and has a stack of books in his chest. He plans to make a shelf for them at the end of his bunk.

Mr. Head brought us some nice apples baked with honey and a walnut inside. He makes an excellent hash, which Sophy adores.

B. says he believes we will get outside tomorrow.

NOVEMBER 6

*A*nother day spent lolling about at anchor, while the wind and rain have evidently agreed to blow us back to the city to find if we have any mail. It makes me groggy not to walk about, but it makes Sophy more energetic, and she has one fixed idea, which is to get out of our cabin and explore the ship. After dinner I thought to let her wear herself out running the length of the companionway and climbing up and down the steps to the hatch, which she can do handily now. As I opened the door, she shot out past me, and as Mr. Richardson was lying in his bunk with the door open, she burst in upon him, crowing at her own cleverness.

I followed, calling after her, but of course she didn't answer. When I looked in, Mr. R. was sitting up, having laid his book aside, and Sophy was attempting to crawl up on the chair at his desk. He was smiling at her, somewhat bemusedly, and when I apologized for her intrusion, he said, "Not at all. She's a welcome visitor," which I thought a nice bit of politesse. I went in and picked her up, rather hoping she wouldn't make a fuss about being carried away. "Shall we go and play on the steps?" I said. She knows the word "steps" and nodded in the vigorous way she has, reaching her arms out toward the door, so I set her down and out she ran.

"She's easily distracted," observed Mr. R., and I said something to the effect that this was true. I, too, was distracted, because I was looking about the cabin, taking in various bits of information. There was a letter addressed to Fanny Richardson on the desk. He'd laid the book with its spine turned away so I couldn't read the title, he had a hole in one of his socks, but most interestingly, as I turned to follow my wayward child, I noticed a round clock screwed to the wall—the oddity of it was that it had no hands and was hanging upside down.

I looked out the door to find Sophy up the steps and trying to shove the hatch open, so I bolted out, waving gaily to Mr. R., who lifted a few fingers from his knee in reply.

Why would anyone hang a clock upside down, even one with no hands? Was it some sort of joke?

NOVEMBER 7

At last we have set sail. The Sandy Hook pilot came on early this morning. I scratched off a quick letter to Mother B. and another to Arthur, just to say we were finally off, and the pilot took them when he left us. I should have written to Hannah, but hadn't time. Mother B. will tell her we are outside. We have a steady breeze and are plowing along nicely. Only two thousand miles to go! B. is in fine spirits, as he always is at the commencement of a voyage, and I noted at dinner that even Mr. Gilling had a bit of color spanked into his cheeks by the fresh air above deck.

The usual duties of the captain's wife at the beginning of a trip include a thorough scrubbing of the cabin, but that won't be necessary as this one is as clean as a whistle. I bless the previous owner, who outfitted our quarters with his own family in mind, sparing no expense. The carpet is thick, the windows are tight, the skylight is large and lets in a nice slab of sunlight—Sophy never wearies of looking up at it. The bed is wide enough for us all, and the settee deep enough for a nap.

B. and I are all in all to each other at sea, crammed in a small space with little privacy. It suits us, for if ever two were one, we are one. We grew up almost as brother and sister; in fact, until I was three Benjamin's family lived in our house. He held me in his arms when I was a baby. Much that I loved as a child, B. taught me to love, the woods at the back of the cemetery, the walk to the old wharf, the picnics to Ram Island. He was my earliest confidant, and I was conscious that he looked out for me and was always willing to talk with me and calm my babyish fears. When we were older, we were separated. Captain Nathan built Rose Cottage, and B. went to sea when he was twelve. I remember how empty my world was without him, how poorly everyone, save possibly Olie, who loved him as I did, compared to him.

The world intervened, the sea kept us apart, and when we met again, we were shy of each other. He brought me presents from his travels—he brought everyone presents—a silver thimble, the one I still use, a sandalwood tray, a cashmere shawl, a red leather box— for my treasures, he said—a roll of fine French lace to trim my collars. When he was at home, I found excuses to go to Rose Cottage, and many an evening B. strolled over to the parsonage with some message from his mother, which, Father observed, was seldom news to him. Yet, beyond the familial, I wasn't sure of his affection. He liked to tease me, but never cruelly, and he grew so handsome, so much a man, while I was still a girl, that I was awed by him. When he was twenty, his brother Nathan died at sea and four years later his sister Maria was lost at sea, along with her husband, and then a year after that their little son Natie left this world in his sleep. So B. had that sadness and loss sobering him just as he came of age.

Then, how did it happen? He was at sea. He sent me a drawing; I wrote a foolish poem. When he came home from that trip, my heart was in my throat and his, God bless him, was frankly on his sleeve. How well I remember that first kiss at the garden gate. I raised up on my toes to receive it. I felt his arm about my waist and I shivered. I thought, he loves me; he has always loved me.

Once he told Arthur, "I fell in love with Mother when she was born."

We were innocents in love, ready to be tested by the world. I had no mother to tell me what to expect on my wedding night, and I certainly had no wish to consult Benjamin's, though my poor father—his face crimson with embarrassment—recommended I might. I trusted Benjamin to show me the way. And he did, and so amusingly. How vividly I recall that night.

We faced each other in the bridal chamber, next to the bed neatly made by his mother, covered by the quilt Hannah and I spent the summer finishing. The embroidered pillowcases were Hannah's wedding present. The long-sleeved cotton gown folded at the foot of the bed was of Mother Briggs's manufacture.

Benjamin fixed me with his penetrating eyes, carefully unfastening his necktie. "Thus saith the Lord," he said sententiously. "Remove the diadem and take off the crown." His expression made me giggle. I pulled the pins from my veil and let it slide to the floor.

"God loveth a cheerful giver," he said, solemnly removing his shirt.

"Does he?" I said, unfastening the buttons of my bodice.

He pulled off his belt and began removing his trousers with one hand, holding the other before him with the index finger pointing up, in just the way Father does on the pulpit. "Let thine eyes look right on, and let thine eyelids look straight before thee."

This bent me over with laughter. "Have you been scouring the Good Book in preparation for this night?" I asked, setting to work on my skirt buttons. When I looked up he was in his woolens.

"Look not every man on his own things, but every man also on the things of others."

I dropped my dress to my ankles and stood up in my chemise and crinoline, struggling to keep a straight face.

"Stand therefore, having your loins girt about with truth, and having on the breastplate of righteousness." He pulled his woolen shirt briskly over his head.

"So will I stand," I said, feeling confident, even saucy. I unlaced the ties on the crinoline and stepped out of it, smiling up at him. Then I unfastened the hooks down the front of my corset and pulled it away.

My husband put his hands on my shoulders, gently pushing

down the straps of my chemise, leaning over to whisper close to my ear, "Let love be without dissimulation." And then he lifted me up, laid me upon the quilt, and climbed in beside me. "At last, Sallie," he said, turning to me. "Wedded bliss."

How many brides, I wonder now, pass their wedding nights convulsed in laughter.

NOVEMBER 8

*S*ophy and I like to walk around the skylight on the house deck, or run around in her case. I could wish the rail were less appealing to those with climbing instincts. I have to watch her every second. If she could, she'd be up in the rigging with the Germans. The wind is brisk and B. says we're running along nicely at eight knots. I know nothing about the daily business of sailing, though there are some captain's wives who make quite a point of fiddling with the sextant, taking positions, or offering their views on the trimming of sails. In Havre we met a lady whose husband encouraged her to plot the course, and at Messina we encountered a portly British dame who insisted on pulling lines. My interests do not that way lie, and B. allows that he finds such carrying on repugnant. I can keep pretty busy with looking after Sophy, supervising the pantry, sewing, and playing songs.

Mr. Head is an excellent young man, and I discovered yesterday, when the main cabin and hatches were all open, that he has a fine voice. He sings as he crosses the deck with our dinner. His song was one of Olie's favorites, "Beware," and so it made me think of him and wonder where he is—perhaps just behind that last wave aft of us for all we know. We had planned to meet in New York, but his ship was delayed. We kept a lookout for him when we were stuck near Staten Island, but to no avail. We are to meet in Messina, God willing, and have a fine meal at one of the restaurants in that sunny port. It's a lovely town. We had Arthur with us when last we put in there, and

I recall his hooting with joy at a lady carrying a basket of fish on her head. He thought it was a hat!

In the afternoon I played on the melodeon and Sophy sat next to me on the bench, trying to make her doll pick out a tune. She understands a great many more words than she can say and has started to put two or three together, to her own delight. At supper she reached out for the potato bowl as it was going the rounds and announced "pass 'tatoes."

Here is B., coming in from his watch, looking mischievous, I must say.

NOVEMBER 9

*T*he sea was rough today and all were occupied with trying to get the best of the capricious wind. Lots of pitching bow to stern, which makes Sophy fall when she wants to run. At first she wailed and I tried to comfort her, but after a while she started bending her knees, attempting to roll with the ship, and seemed to think it funny when she landed on her bottom.

We had to put the rack on the table for dinner, to keep the dishes from sliding away, which interested her greatly. Mr. Richardson opined that the Germans do well enough, but he thinks one of them is hard of hearing, as he turns one ear toward anyone who speaks to him. Mr. R. tried speaking softly to his back and got no response. So, having scientifically tested his theory, he feels willing to advance it—the man has poor hearing. Mr. Gilling, who was with us, as B. had the watch, said he believed the fellow was lazy and didn't want to take orders, so pretended not to hear them. They had all four aloft trimming sails and Mr. R. said he thought they pitched in well and worked together smoothly. Two are brothers, traveling the world together with one sea chest between them.

And so forth. Mr. R. and Mr. G., I note, are not fond of each other, and contradiction is something of a sport with them. When I related this conversation to B., he said Mr. G. is a bit of a hard driver and likes to give orders in confusing bundles, so that the sailor is uncertain which task is to be done first.

Life at sea. Men watching each other for signs of weakness. I believe Mr. G. is of the type who must resist those set above him and dominate all below. Mr. R. is more sanguine, and like many a sailor preoccupied with orderliness.

And my darling husband, the captain of my heart, takes it all in and chuckles with me under the bedclothes. "Did you see how many dumplings Gilling ate?" he said. "I had to spear one quick to save for Sophy."

Last night we lay awake in stitches of laughter because Sophy was snoring to beat the band. "God help us," said B. "She sounds just like my father."

NOVEMBER 10

A blustery day, though we did get some sun and I took Sophy up to have the benefit of fresh air. I dislike just about everything at sea, but one does dress more comfortably. I wear a short wash dress and an apron with a big pocket, and an old sun hat I use at home for the garden, and wooden pattens over my slippers. At night I wear a silk wrapper, which B. calls an "unwrapper" as it is easy of access. It's pleasant not having a skirt dragging the floor and easier to keep clean.

On our house deck we are mostly private unless the sailors are in the mainmast rigging. I can look down on the helmsman and see forward as far as the forecastle house, which is all above deck, so it blocks the view beyond. The boom is enormous and squeaks like a bat. Sophy is content to go round and round the skylight and so it is exercise just to keep up with her. It was chilly and I'd not put on my cloak, so I came down feeling headachy, but she was exhilarated and it took several songs and a patient going over of the album, while she pointed out "Otter," and "Grama," and "Ha-han," until she started rubbing her eyes and agreed to be put down for a nap.

As I was repairing a hole in B.'s stocking, there was a tap at the cabin door. When I opened it, there was Mr. Head, with a steaming pot of tea. "I saw you come in and thought you might be chilled," he said. I took the pot gratefully while he dug in his pocket and brought out a toy he'd made for Sophy. It was an owl fashioned from a walnut shell with tiny chicken feathers stuck on and wire feet. "She'll love this," I said. "She knows how to say the sound owls make. You are so artistic." This sent him away beaming. So I put the owl on the bookshelf and sat down at the table with my pot of tea and this book to chronicle yet another dull day at sea for the captain's wife.

NOVEMBER 13

For three days I haven't been able to hold a pen to the page. Our ship has been so pitched and batted and rolled about, and so much water washed over her decks and down every opening, including into our cabin, bursting in with such force it lifted the sewing machine and deposited it on the settee where Sophy and I sat clutching each other while I said our prayers. Before we could heave-to, one of the Germans, going aloft to shorten sail, was swept by a wave hard into the deckhouse, and from thence out to the rail, where he was nearly washed overboard, but Mr. Gilling got hold of him until the deck rolled the other way and they were both knocked back into the house. In the tumult the German's arm was broken between the wrist and elbow, a bad break; the bone came through the skin. Mr. Gilling got him to the main cabin and we put him on the table, as there was water standing knee deep on the floor. B. set the arm—it took nearly an hour and the German was in agony throughout and probably swore fierce oaths—I'll never know—but he trusted B. and when I gave him some coffee laced with laudanum from the medicine chest he drank it down and said *"Danke"* between gasps of pain, handing back the cup with his good hand.

After the arm was set, Mr. Head came in to help Mr. Gilling get the injured man back to his berth. Poor fellow, he was pale as a ghost, even his ruddy lips lost their color. And now we will be short-handed, as he won't be able to go aloft or even take the helm until he's up and about. I learned his name, he is Mr. Lorenzen, and now I can tell him apart from the others, though I doubt I'll see much of him. B. said he's the best sailor of the four, which is a pity.

Once we had the proper heading there was nothing to do but hold on to something solidly attached to the ship and wait. I got Sophy in the bed with me and B. brought a board to fasten across the opening and there we lay, gazing up at the skylight, which appeared to be under the sea.

NOVEMBER 14

At last we are in calmer waters, though there's still a strong headwind making things difficult on deck. When I woke this morning, I was nauseated and had to rush to the water closet. This seemed odd, as the ship is running along without much pitching about and I haven't eaten anything unusual, but then it dawned on me that it is two months since last I employed a grandy rag. I packed a store thinking I was only late, but, after another bout of retching, I did the calculation, putting one and one together to equal three. When I came out, B. was on the settee with Sophy on his lap—she likes to cuddle with him when she wakes up if he's near—crooning, "I see a ship a-sailing."

I stood in the doorway smiling at them; they are so sweet together. B. finished the verse—"and the captain says quack, quack." Sophy quacked along with him; she knows that song well and waits for the ending with rising excitement. Her father looked up at me and said, "Mother, are you well?"

"I'll be fine," I said. "But you might ask Sophy if she'd like a little sister, or would she prefer another brother."

Sophy caught the word "brother" and said "Otter." B. set her down on the carpet, which was still wet from the flood and crunchy with salt, and came to me, passing his arm round my waist. "Sweetheart," he said. "Is it true?"

"I think so," I said.

Then he looked anxious. I lost a babe three years ago, early on, but there was no trouble with Sophy, so I feel confident this time. "I'm fine," I said.

"When will it be, do you think?"

"May or June. I can't be very far along."

Sophy picked up one of her blocks and brought it to us, holding it up high, wanting to know the sound for the letter. "It's a G," I said. "Gh, gh. Good. Good girl." She followed my lips, as she does, and made a very respectable *g* sound.

"Won't she be a fine big sister?" her papa said.

Later, after his watch, B. came in looking thoughtful. "I've made up my mind," he said. "We should have enough saved after this trip for me to stay home until this new baby is safe among us. With the interest I've got in this ship, I'll have a little coming in, and if I can find a good investment, I won't let it slip away this time. With any luck this will be my last voyage."

Well, this is good news, of course, and I breathed a sigh of relief, but my poor darling has made this vow before and been forced by circumstances to break it. He and Olie were set to take over Mr. Hardy's store, but they hesitated when it came down to it and the chance eluded them. Olie is of the same mind. They are both sick of going to sea and want to be home. Olie bought the land abutting his father's house last year and before he left, he built a wall around it. Hopefully, between them, they can make a go of some shore concern and we can raise a passel of glorious landlubbers and do our sailing on a ferry.

At supper Mr. Head reported that Mr. Lorenzen has a fever

and is delirious. B. went forward and dosed him with laudanum for the pain and bathed his forehead with vinegar. B. said the other Mr. Lorenzen stood by, murmuring to his brother in German, trying to comfort him. B. was reminded of Olie and the time when they shipped together—Olie was just a boy—and B. felt he was growing a third eye that kept a lookout for his brother. Then we both wished we'd not missed Olie in New York before we sailed, and we said a prayer that we find him, hale and hearty, in Messina.

NOVEMBER 15

*H*ave I mentioned that I dislike going to sea? And here is the reason: if it isn't one thing, it's another. Today it is fog, all day, socked in over us like—well—like a sock! A heavy, sodden, white woolen sock. It even smells a little like sheep. And as we can't see a thing and as the sea is wide and plied by ships, we must ring a bell constantly and hang out lamps, and creep along with every sailor squinting into the mist and every officer taking a turn at the scope to see if he can detect a sail in time to get out of its way. They are rotating the sick German's watch and B. did two in a row, because he said he wouldn't sleep anyway, and came in tired to death, but of course, he still couldn't sleep. I took Sophy up to have a look and she said, "Clouds." "Fog," I said, and she gave a nod, though she didn't try to say it. Gloom is universal, as it is common knowledge that these fog banks on the Atlantic presage a storm.

Mr. Head and I got together in the pantry and decided to cheer everyone up with a plum dessert, as I've got two dozen jars put up and we may as well eat them. He only knows duff, but I suggested something more elegant, since there are only nine of us plus Sophy, so I amused myself in mixing up a cake in the cabin and Mr. Head came later to take it off to his oven. It came out well, with the plums all knit into the top in a pattern, and B. smiled to see it for the first time today. Mr. Head said the Germans wolfed it down. Mr. Lorenzen is still suffering, but B. said his fever is down. It is revealed that he has brought thirteen books on board, two of which B. recognized as navigation texts. Well, he will have plenty of time for reading, though I doubt he'll navigate much beyond the galley for the near future.

After supper Sophy wanted singing, so I played and sang the old tunes I know she likes, and B. joined in on the ones he knows. I always end with "There Is a Happy Land," which is soporific, and also a favorite of Olie's. It made me think of home and of Arthur, who is, God willing, asleep in his bed. He's afraid of the dark. It gets dark so early now, and he has to go out to do the evening chores. I used to go with him to get the milk, but I doubt Mother B. will indulge his childish anxiety. She'll advise him to pray.

NOVEMBER 16

*H*ere's a conundrum. I sit in the dying light though it's not yet noon. All I can hear is pounding hammers.

B. came in, looking serious and stern, to tell me that the men will be battening the windows, as we are already shipping seas over the bow, and the barometrical instruments, including the one B. has in his head, prognosticate rough weather ahead. There. They have fit the canvas over the first one and hammered the boards into the frame.

"Must we?" I wanted to say, but of course, I know we must. Sophy is sitting among her blocks gazing up curiously. "Legs," she shouted when the two sailors arrived, hauling their lumber, for that was all she could see of them. B. says we'll have the skylight, so we won't be in utter darkness—though of course we will be, once whatever is coming for us comes for us.

Because this sea is dark, though sometimes it sparkles gaily, and it is often angry.

And we are nothing to it.

This morning before it got so choppy, the fog lifted and I took Sophy up. B., coming off his watch, escorted us for a stroll along the deck. He keeps the same rule his father did—no sailor may stand between the captain and the wind—so it's amusing to watch the Germans, who have somehow been informed of this rule, which, being Germans, they embrace wholeheartedly, being careful to stay on the lee side of the "old man." B. says of our ship that she is only a fair sailer. He would like to open the hatches to ventilate the cargo, which is volatile, but now is not the time.

We are barreling along before a west wind, very choppy sea now. Our ship's bow thwacks the waves as she rams through them. Now they have the canvas on the second window and are hammering away. I can hear their voices, but, of course, don't understand what they are saying.

We'll have to light the paraffin lamps at dinner. B. is in a confab with Mr. Richardson in the main cabin. They are anxious because, with Mr. Lorenzen down, we are shorthanded.

And now I must lay down my pen, as Sophy is weepy and the dimly lit cabin in which I am sitting has commenced to roll.

NOVEMBER 18

*H*ow can I write these words? Benjamin. My life. My love.

NOVEMBER 21

I'll try to write what I can. But why should I? I hardly know who I am. I haven't eaten, washed, left this room for three days, except that first night when I opened the cabin door and found Mr. Head on the settee. I was angry. What are you doing here? I cried, and he sat up looking flustered. He explained that Mr. Richardson had the watch and he didn't want Sophy and me to be left alone in the stern in case we might need something.

What could I possibly need? I said and closed the door. But the look on his face let me know they are afraid of me.

My poor Sophy. I frightened her as well, and she was terrified enough by the storm. The roar of the wind, the ship nearly vertical climbing each wave bow up, and then, the sea pouring over the deck, stern up, descending. We huddled in the bed together and I held her close to my heart singing the lullabies she likes, but her eyes were wild with terror and she sobbed until she fell asleep from exhaustion.

Benjamin said, Mr. Gilling is lashed to the helm.

And he was pulling on his boots to take the watch. He'd hardly slept at all.

And I said. What did I say?

Did I say, Be careful?

It didn't matter. He couldn't hear for the noise. We were sliding down a wave; the cabin floor was uphill.

He fell to his knees before he got to the door, then staggered to his feet and went out. He looked like a walking tent in his waterproofs.

I had Sophy tucked in the curve of my legs and I clung to the footboard as the bed rose up, pushing us steadily down, and then went down, driving us back up, like sands in an hourglass being turned over and over forever.

I heard the hatch open and close. No, what I heard was the bellow of the storm grow louder and then less. And I thought, He has gone out. I felt sick to my stomach and my head ached, but there was nothing to do but hold on.

I heard a shout. I couldn't make it out. Mr. Richardson's voice, his cabin door flung open, his rapid footsteps and again the hatch opening, the roar of the wind, and then the shout again, this time from him, and I heard it. I understood it. He had shouted—Man Overboard.

What did I do? My first thought was that it must be Mr. Gilling, because it couldn't be Benjamin. But then I knew it must be. I leaped from the bed and fell headlong on the floor. Sophy plummeted out behind me and let out a wail. I gathered her in my arms and staggered through the cabin into the companionway, up the steps to the hatch. I struggled to open it.

The men were shouting. Where the sky should have been was a white cliff made of water, dark, yet strangely bright. From somewhere Mr. Richardson appeared, blocking me. Sophy was howling; his face was livid. "Go back down," he shouted, "for God's sake."

"Who is it?" I said.

The stern dropped away and a great sea shipped over the bow, so that we both clung to the hatch rail while water surged over the deck and down the hatch around my legs.

"It's the captain," he shouted. "Please go back."

"No!" I screamed. "Where is he? Let me out." I tried to push past him but as the ship pitched, my feet went out from under me. I lost my grip on the rail and landed on my back in a foot of water with Sophy clinging to my neck. Mr. Richardson leaped down and lifted us up, counseling me as he helped me to my feet. "We're trying to find him, Mrs. Sarah. You can help us best by staying below. I'll come to you as soon as I can." Then he rushed up the steps, closing the hatch behind him, and I found myself standing in water to my knees, clutching my terrified, wailing daughter in my arms.

I carried her back to the cabin. "We have to pray," I said to her. "We have to pray so hard for Papa." I remember saying that.

And I did pray. But God wasn't listening.

NOVEMBER 22

I have lived now four days in this cruel world without my beloved. He is gone, without a word of farewell, without a grave, swallowed by the sea. I can't realize it.

Last night I saw him in a dream, walking ahead of me. I woke, reached out for him. Sophy turned toward me in her sleep and said, "Papa." And I thought, *He's here.*

She keeps looking for him, not fearfully—she doesn't understand that he's gone—just expectantly, whenever one of the men passes outside the door or overhead on the deck.

It's a nightmare from which I can't awaken.

But wake I must. I must cast a line and hold on to life. I have my darling's darling, the sweetest child I've ever known, and his poor, anxious son, waiting at home, bearing up as best he can, and this unknown, unborn child, whose mother is a widow.

I don't think I have the strength to bear this test. I can't say, as Mother Briggs never stops saying, God's will be done. His will *will* be done.

Is this His will?

Mr. Head is saving his own soul by his great kindness to me. That first day, when I was simply raving—I have no idea what I said or did—he came and took Sophy away to the galley and looked after her, even put her down for a nap in his own berth. She came toddling back in the evening holding his hand. Now she calls him Ed-ded. That night he slept on the settee in the cabin again, insisting that when Mr. Richardson was on deck, he didn't think it right that Sophy and I should be alone in the stern. He brought me food I couldn't touch. He took it away without comment.

The storm went on for twenty-five hours: we ran before it. Running away from my beloved, leaving him behind. Mr. Richardson came to me as he promised, within an hour. Sophy and I were flat on the carpet, as it was the only location that couldn't toss us down. I was praying; I actually had some mad hope that they would pull Benjamin out of the sea, though I'd seen that high white wedge of water, and I knew the only boat we had was lashed across the hatch, impossible to launch in such a fury, and even if they had tried, it would have been more men lost, for there could be no rowing about in the towering mountains of water bearing down on this little ship. Mr. Richardson looked like he'd been beaten near to death; he was pouring off water, his face was ashen. The floor pitched up and swatted him down onto the floor with us. When he got to his knees I saw tears streaming from his eyes. "Mrs. Sarah," he said. "We couldn't save him. He was gone so fast. The wave picked him up off the poop; it took him straight up. He was high above us. Then he was gone."

I felt a hard fist of pain gathering in my gut. Sophy was screaming, clinging to my waist. "Leave me," I managed to say. I have no clear memory of what happened next. Presumably he went out and left me howling on the floor.

This afternoon, as I lay on the settee trying to feel anything but dead, there was a knock at the door. Sophy was on the floor trying to teach her doll to talk. She looked up and said, "Papa." Tears leaked from my eyes. I turned my face toward the cushion and croaked, "Come in."

It was Mr. Head. He had a brown Betty in a covered pan warm from the oven. I knew what it was because the mouth-watering smell of apples and cinnamon preceded him into the cabin. Sophy got to her feet and rushed to him, saying "Ed-ded, Ed-ded," joyfully. I turned to face him. He was bending over Sophy, patting her head and saying "Apples, Miss Sophy. I brought you a nice apple pudding."

"Are you married, Mr. Head?" I asked through my tears.

He looked up, startled, I think, by both my haggard appearance and my evident lucidity.

"Just these six months, ma'am."

"Ah," I said. "Just six months."

"I'll leave this here," he said, lowering the dish to the table. Sophy immediately began climbing onto the chair. I pulled myself up and shoved my feet into the pattens on the floor. Mr. Head's eyes followed me, full of hope and as kind as a mother's. He will make a dear father to his children, with his gentleness and his cooking. He just wants to see me eat something, I thought, and he won't rest until I do. I patted my hair down, it felt moist and flat like a mouse's nest, and wiped my eyes with my fingertips. "It smells delicious," I said. "Sophy, say thank you to Mr. Head." She looked from his face to mine and said "Anka."

So, to please them both, I got to my feet and joined my daughter at the table, where we took up our spoons and ate brown Betty from a pan.

*H*ow can I bear it? I'm trying to bear it. I've washed my face and changed my dress. I've eaten apple pudding. I've answered Sophy's questions about the album and her blocks. I've sounded out the letters *P* and *K. K. K.* Kitty. But I won't go out of this cabin. I won't go and look at the sea, which is calm now, a light wind moving us along at a good clip. Through the skylight I can see a patch of blue sky. It's warmer than it's been since we left New York. Sophy slept all night without a blanket. I don't sleep but in snatches. When I do, I seem to hear Benjamin coming into the cabin, or I feel him standing by the bed, or I wake because I hear him calling my name.

They are busily running the ship around me. I am the cold, dead heart of it, which the sea has killed, and no one but Mr. Head cares whether I come back to life or not. Well, in truth, they are so short-handed every man must be on double watches and taking orders from Mr. Gilling, who passes them on from Captain Richardson. I hear Mr. R. going in and out of his cabin. He's taking his meals in the galley with the others, I presume so as not to disturb me here.

It's still dark as a dungeon, as the crew hasn't had time to uncover the windows, though once the sun rises, the skylight sheds a block of white light down the center of the room. Mr. Head opened the skylights yesterday so we are aired out. This morning he looked in and offered to take Sophy up for a walk. She is full of energy and I am a worn-out thing who prefers the gloom, so I agreed. Then he tried to get me to come as well. "It's a bright, clear day, ma'am," he said. "It would do you good to walk about. Mr. Richardson is on deck and he charged me to encourage you to come up."

I was helping Sophy with her shoes. It all feels so automatic, this life. "No, thank you," I said. "I have some letters to write. And I'd best do it while the desk isn't pitching about and there's enough light to see the page."

"Of course," he said.

Will everyone look at me with this indulgent pity now?

As soon as her laces were tied, Sophy ran to him, her Ed-ded.

How easily her affections are transferred, lucky darling. It burdens me that she'll grow to be a woman with no memory of her father. It's unbearable, actually. He loved her so.

I did have it in my head to begin a letter to Olie, but all I do is write in this book. I am of two minds about what to do. The obvious choice is to cable Mother Briggs from Gibraltar, book a passage on whatever ship I can find, and head for home. But part of me wants to go on to Messina and meet Olie, as we planned—in our tragic innocence, I see that now—and sail back with him on the *Julia A. Hallock*. Or Sophy and I could wait at Gibraltar for Olie to pass through on his ship. Finally, I might simply stay on this ship for the duration. This last, I confess, has little appeal to me. Am I to sew and play our melodeon and interest myself in the rivalry between Captain Richardson and Mr. Gilling, which is in abeyance now, but how long will that last, as the days drag by and every one reminds me that five, six, ten, twenty days ago, I woke in the night to find my darling at my side? I hate this ship.

I will ask Mother Briggs—how does one compose a telegram to tell a mother her son is lost at sea?—I will ask her not to tell Arthur. I will write a letter to him—but how to tell him? He is such a serious child; it's as if he knew there was a dark cloud upon his future. And he adores his father. I remember Benjamin's expression, just exactly, the delight, the hesitancy, the pride, the sheer wonder, when he first held his red-faced baby son in his arms. He'd seen, he said, many babies, but none like this one.

How bright the sun is on my page.

I'm not going up there to stand on the deck and look out as far as I can see at the lightly dancing, sparkling waves, or feel the warm breeze rustling my hair, or gaze up into the blinding white of the sails, or receive kind condolences from Captain Richardson as he strides the deck of his first command. What madness. What vanity of men, to sail about in fragile wooden boxes tricked out with sails, putting their lives, their fortunes, their families at the mercy of this ravenous, murderous, heartless beast of a sea. No. I'm not going up until I can put my feet on land. The sea is my enemy, and it has defeated me.

NOVEMBER 24

*L*ast night I dreamed Benjamin and I were running, holding hands and running in a field. It was a bright day, windy, with an October sun, low and confusing. I stumbled and fell. Benjamin let slip my hand, running ahead, not looking back. I called out, but still he didn't turn. Why won't he wait for me? I thought, and then I woke up in the dark. Sophy was breathing softly, her damp little hand resting on my shoulder. I could hear the dull *thwack-thwack* of the bow, slapping steadily into the waves. I said into the darkness, "Wait for me."

Later, at breakfast, Mr. Richardson—Captain Richardson— knocked and asked permission to sit with us. "Of course," I said. "Come in. There's coffee in the pot."

"I don't want to disturb you, Mrs. Sarah," he said. "But I thought I should speak with you."

I felt calm in his presence, but the memory of my dream—it was so vivid—had left me disinterested and bereft of feeling. At once he told me something I didn't know—where in this world we are. We are south of the Azores, he says; St. Mary's is six miles distant. We are off course, but Captain Richardson will take advantage of the calm seas and relative shelter of the islands to open our hatches. The one over the hold, which has the boat lashed across it, will be opened in the morning. The crew will remove the battens from our windows then too, if I so wish it.

"How is Mr. Lorenzen?" I asked.

He looked pleased at this question. It showed I was capable of normal human discourse. "Much improved," he said. "Up and about with his arm in a sling. It will be weeks before it's healed enough to bear any weight, but he's on the mend."

If only, I thought, it was my husband on the mend and Mr. Lorenzen in the sea. This thought vexed me, as if I'd spoken it, though it wasn't exactly shame I felt at having had it. "I'm pleased to hear it," I said.

He sat, fidgeting a bit with his watch. Sophy was spooning in her porridge. She starts a bowl and works at it steadily until it's empty, like an old woman.

He said a few more things, I don't remember what. He would wire Mr. Winchester on arrival in Gibraltar. To tell him my husband is gone, I thought. Of course. To ask for further orders. "Why are sailors so eager for orders?" I asked Benjamin once. "How else will they know what to do?" he replied.

At last Mr. Richardson left us, asking again about the battened windows as he went out.

"I don't care," I said. My indifference displeased him, but I was indifferent to that too.

NOVEMBER 25

I will never speak of this.

Last night I couldn't sleep. The moon was bright and the cabin warm, so when I put Sophy down for the night, I opened the door between the bedroom and the main cabin. I paced about, talking to myself, trying to calm myself, but what I felt was rising panic. For an hour or so I dozed on the settee, waking to hear Mr. Richardson come in from his watch. I dozed again. When I woke, Sophy was standing in the doorway between the cabins, wide-eyed and with the determined look her father had when he knew exactly what he wanted, and would brook no obstacle. "Can't you sleep, darling?" I said.

Her answer stopped my heart. "Papa," she said. She ran across the carpet to the door and struggled to reach the latch. "Papa," she said again.

I went to her, kneeled beside her. "He's not here, love," I said.

"Come back to bed. Mother will come with you." But she was having none of my promises. She slapped the door with the flat of her hand, her voice rising and insistent. "Papa, Papa," she said.

"Do you want to go up on the deck?" I asked, to which she nodded her head forcefully and added, "Papa."

It was strange and it gave me a chill, but I thought I'd best give in and take her up to see for herself that her dear papa was not at the helm. If I refused, neither of us would sleep anytime soon. "All right," I said. "I'll take you. But you must hold my hand. Will you hold my hand while we go up?"

Again she nodded, thrusting her hand out to take mine. She's such a reasonable child. I opened the door and she pulled me along the companionway, and up the stairs to the open hatch. Together we stepped out into the wondrous dome of stars in which the full moon, suspended like a porcelain disk, drew a slender skein of white across the softly rustling blue-black meadow of the sea.

Oh you trickster, I thought, addressing the ocean. You cruel goddess, addressing the moon. Calling me out of my sorrow to break my heart with beauty. Sophy too was moved to awe by the serenity of the night. "See the moon," I said, to make it only a word, to make it expressible. She raised her face as if to bathe in the magical light and said softly "Moon."

Together, hand in hand, we stepped to the rail and stood looking out to sea. There was no clear horizon. The sky, a deep blue-green, blended into a darker hue of the same color. Nothing was black in this world of tender light, of undulating waves stirring up flashes of phosphorescence. Above us a few full sails pulled us smoothly through the placid water. I glanced to the stern and made out the figure of Mr. Gilling at the helm, holding the wheel steady. Near the mainmast one of the Germans was sitting with his back to the house working over a mass of rope. The only sound was the continual whoosh of water rushing back from the prow.

I had witnessed such a night at sea only once before, long ago, on the *Arthur*, when we sailed along the East Coast, bound for New

Orleans. We had come into the Gulf Stream and the air, though not sultry, was warm. Benjamin came below after his watch was done and leaned over me in the bed, whispering, "Sallie, are you awake?"

"Yes," I said. "I can't sleep."

"I know why," he said. "Come up with me." I got out of bed and went to put on my pattens, but he said, "You can come out in your bare feet. No one cares." And I did. He took my hand and we went up together and it was like this, a moon, bright and heatless, like a sun made of chalk, a sea put to sleep by its own repetitive tides, moist air that caressed and opened the pores so that my whole body seemed to breathe through my skin. We stood at the rail and Benjamin said, "This is heaven, don't you think, Sallie?"

And I said, "It may be like this." I didn't know it then, but I was pregnant with Arthur. When we found out, Benjamin said it was thanks to that ship bunk, which was hardly big enough for two. Whenever we woke with our limbs in a tangle, he stroked my back, or my hair, or whatever part of me was close to his hand and said, "How I love these close quarters."

This came back to me, standing with Sophy, last night. She pulled my hand and said, "Cumup," which meant she wanted me to hold her. I came to myself and bent over her, lifting her onto my hip. She rested one arm on my shoulder, turned toward the sea, pointed to the middle distance, and said, "Papa."

Tears burst from my eyes, my mouth went dry, and I struggled for breath. "Oh don't," I sobbed. "Please don't." She looked at me, touched my cheek with her fingertips, turned back to the sea and pointed again, but this time she didn't speak. My knees were rubbery and I had the sense that I must fall, but also that something was holding me up. Sophy closed her hand in a fist and rubbed it into her eye. Then she turned to me, nestling her face against my shoulder, wrapping both arms loosely around my neck. "You're ready for sleep, now," I said softly.

I couldn't turn away. A combination of fear and fascination kept me there. The sensation that something was holding me up mutated into the conviction that someone was standing behind me.

I bent my head over Sophy, pressing a kiss into her temple, then I fixed my gaze on the moon, conscious that I was afraid to look at the water. I felt an intake of breath at my ear. I knew what it was, who it was. The warm breath whispered; it was his voice. "Sallie."

"Don't go," I said, while the tears coursed down my face. "Stay with me." But even as I spoke, I knew he was gone.

Somehow I got back to the cabin and laid Sophy in the bed; she was already asleep. Though I felt feverish, I was shivering and weak. I wrapped myself in my cloak on the settee and sat there, in a state between terror and ecstasy, until the translucent moonlight was driven out by the more substantial light of dawn.

This was no dream.

I know that, now, in the cold light of day. He was with me. He called Sophy in her sleep because he couldn't reach me; I wouldn't listen. He wanted me to stand with him in that otherworldly calm, that bliss that must be what calls sailors to the sea, the marvelous hush of the waves beneath the confounding silence of the stars, which he once told me was heaven. He wanted to remind me, as if I needed reminding, of our happiness, of our indissoluble bond. He only had to say my name to let me know; to let me go. It was so like him.

There, I hear the bells. Mr. Richardson will be going on deck, Mr. Head rattling his pots and pans in the galley. The Germans are rousing themselves from their slumbers, but for the one on deck, who will go down to rest. Sophy is awake; I hear her talking to herself.

I never believed that such things as I now know are possible were possible. I thought it a species of madness to believe so, but though my heart is broken, I know I'm not mad. I didn't imagine my husband's voice.

And I'm certainly not mad enough ever to speak of this night to a living soul. But how I will hold to it, my love. How it will sustain me, whatever comes.

There is such a strong odor of alcohol in this cabin. It must be coming from the hatch. Mr. Gilling has come down into the companionway to talk to Mr. Richardson. They are arguing about something, Mr. Gilling's voice is raised. One of the men is shouting on deck. Evidently something is amiss. Here comes my Sophy, dragging her doll, drowsy and sweet. When she passes Mr. Head's owl, she points at it and says, "Whoo-whoo."

Acknowledgments

Many friends and colleagues came to my aid as I navigated the course of this novel, and it is with pleasure that I take this opportunity to thank them.

Professor Christopher Pyle, Allen Meese, and Captain Walter Rybka all answered my questions about seagoing matters with a good will. Professor Pyle was particularly helpful and generous with clear and detailed comments. Whatever errors in sailing lore and terminology persist in this text are attributable to me; all accuracy is thanks to these three seagoing advisers.

My research assistant, Diana Gurske, spent a long, hot summer locating nineteenth-century records and newspapers, scrolling through mountains of microfiche and providing me with annotated printouts. Her help was invaluable, as was her good humor and comradeship throughout the process.

I am indebted to Mt. Holyoke College and to the John Simon Guggenheim Memorial Foundation for making it possible to take leave from teaching to finish this novel.

Thanks to the Phillips Library in Salem and especially to Pete Smith of the Marion Historical Society, who provided me with a copy of Oliver

Cobb's memoir, *Rose Cottage*, a window into the daily lives of the Briggs family.

Joyce and Bob Abel, former Lake Pleasant residents, brought to my attention the summer camp meetings of the Spiritualists there and gave me a copy of *Spirit and Spa*, Louise Shattuck's memoir of that world, for which assistance I remain truly grateful.

Thanks to Anthony Gerzina and Gretchen Gerzina, who provided on-the-ground reconnaissance in London during my search for the giant rat of Sumatra.

My fellow writers and friends, Ann Jones, Sabina Murray, Mary Morris, and Dara Wier, deserve thanks for their interest and willingness to talk about the mystery ship. Christopher Benfey, who looks under many of the same rocks I regularly lift, is a constant source of information, inspiration, and encouragement.

At the Friedrich agency, Molly Shulman gave this novel an early and thoughtful reading, and Lucy Carson, in a long phone conversation from the sickbed, patiently talked me to the right conclusion. Molly Friedrich, my agent, tireless in the pursuit of my interests, has been ever ready with sage advice, support, and wonderful humor. I am heartily indebted to this team.

Thanks also to Ronit Feldman and Dan Meyer at Random House, who read an early draft and offered thoughtful and helpful suggestions.

It is my privilege once again to express my deepest gratitude to my publisher and friend, Nan A. Talese.

W&N
blog and newsletter

For literary discussion, author insight,
book news, exclusive content,
recipes and giveaways, visit the
Weidenfeld & Nicolson blog and
sign up for the newsletter at:

www.wnblog.co.uk

For breaking news, reviews and exclusive competitions
Follow us 🐦 @wnbooks
Find us 📘 facebook.com/WNfiction